OXFORD WORL

JEROME K. JEROME

Three Men in a Boat
Three Men on the Bummel

Edited with an Introduction and Notes by
GEOFFREY HARVEY

OXFORD
UNIVERSITY PRESS

OXFORD
UNIVERSITY PRESS

Great Clarendon Street, Oxford OX2 6DP

Oxford University Press is a department of the University of Oxford.
It furthers the University's objective of excellence in research, scholarship,
and education by publishing worldwide in

Oxford New York

Athens Auckland Bangkok Bogotá Buenos Aires Calcutta
Cape Town Chennai Dar es Salaam Delhi Florence Hong Kong Istanbul
Karachi Kuala Lumpur Madrid Melbourne Mexico City Mumbai
Nairobi Paris São Paulo Shanghai Singapore Taipei Tokyo Toronto Warsaw

with associated companies in Berlin Ibadan

Oxford is a registered trade mark of Oxford University Press
in the UK and in certain other countries

Published in the United States
by Oxford University Press Inc., New York

Editorial matter © Geoffrey Harvey 1998

The moral rights of the author have been asserted
Database right Oxford University Press (maker)

First published as an Oxford World's Classics paperback 1998
Reissued 2008

British Library Cataloguing in Publication Data

Data available

Library of Congress Cataloging in Publication Data
Jerome, Jerome K. (Jerome Klapka), 1859–1927.
[Three men in a boat]
Three men in a boat; Three men on the bummel / Jerome K. Jerome;
edited with an introduction and notes by Geoffrey Harvey.
(Oxford world's classics)
Includes bibliographical references.
1. Young men—Travel—England—Thames River—Fiction. 2. Boats and boating—
England—Thames River—Fiction. 3. Thames River (England)—Fiction. 4. Dogs—
Fiction. 5. Black Forest (Germany)—Description and travel—Fiction. 6. Humorous
stories, English. I. Harvey, Geoffery, 1943– . II. Jerome, Jerome, K. (Jerome
Klapka), 1859–1927. Three men on the bummel. III. Title. IV. Title: Three men on the
bummel. V. Series: Oxford world's classics (Oxford University Press)

CONTENTS

INTRODUCTION

Jerome K. Jerome is known today principally for his huge best-seller *Three Men in a Boat*, which achieved immediate popularity on its appearance in 1889, and was promptly pirated by unscrupulous American publishers. It quickly made his name, not only in England and America, but throughout Europe, and has been filmed three times, in 1920, 1933, and 1956. Also a great success was its comic sequel, *Three Men on the Bummel*, about a cycle tour through the Black Forest region of Germany. However, although Jerome became a celebrity, to the contemporary reading public his was a somewhat enigmatic literary personality. There was his unsettling propensity to frequent switches of mood, from the farcical, as in *Three Men in a Boat*, to the sombre, in novels such as *Paul Kelver*, and from the light-hearted to the sentimental and back again, even within a single book. There was also his dual role of novelist and editor. For a while he was one of the foremost editors of the day, producing simultaneously the popular though very different periodicals *The Idler* and *To-day*. And he was also a successful playwright, the author of such diverse stage hits as *Miss Hobbs*, a play about the 'new woman' which drew on Shakespeare's *The Taming of the Shrew*, and *The Passing of the Third Floor Back*, an allegorical morality play which was frequently revived. Jerome's literary versatility was not always recognized, and in his autobiography he records wryly his response to a woman who was encouraging him to write a play:

I told her I had written nine: that six of them had been produced, that three of them had been successful both in England and America, that one of them was still running at the Comedy Theatre and approaching its two hundredth night. Her eyebrows went up in amazement.[1]

Jerome Klapka Jerome (his second name was in honour of a Hungarian general, George Klapka, who was staying with the Jeromes at the time of his birth) was born in 1859 in Walsall, where his father, a Nonconformist preacher and unsuccessful farmer, had

---

[1] Jerome K. Jerome, *My Life and Times* (London: John Murray, 1926; reprinted 1983), 100.

invested in a small coal pit, which came into production only after he had sold it. Jerome was brought up in relative deprivation in the East End of London, where his father's wholesale ironmongery business also failed to prosper; following his death Jerome began work at the age of 14 as a railway clerk at Euston Station, in order to support his mother and sister. However, from these unpromising beginnings, by middle age he was not only an established writer, who had achieved literary fame as a 'new humorist'; he was also financially secure, with a substantial house on the hills at Wallingford, close to his beloved Thames.

The years of Jerome's maturity coincided with the exciting period of cultural change around the turn of the century, and through his role as an editor he enjoyed the esteem and friendship of many of the rising literary men of the day, including H. G. Wells, George Bernard Shaw, J. M. Barrie, H. Rider Haggard, George Moore, George Gissing, Sir Arthur Conan Doyle, and Rudyard Kipling; while he was a welcome visitor to Thomas Hardy's Dorset home, Max Gate. Jerome also counted among his circle several famous people in the world of theatre, such as Sir Henry Irving, Marie Tempest, for whom he wrote a number of plays, and Sarah Bernhardt. He was acquainted with German royalty, knew important political figures such as Lloyd George and Ramsay MacDonald, and enjoyed the distinction of being invited to meet President Theodore Roosevelt during his first lecture tour of America.

Jerome's father died when he was 12, and his mother three years later. As an escape from loneliness and depression, following the subsequent marriage of his sister, and as a release from the tedium of his job, Jerome abandoned the station office for the stage. He spent three years touring with theatre companies, accumulating a wealth of experience, which he recorded in a volume of humorous sketches, *On the Stage—and Off*. (He notes, with some pride, that he played every part in *Hamlet* except Ophelia.) This period of his life proved useful later, in the writing not only of plays but of prose fiction, for many of the scenes in *Three Men in a Boat* and *Three Men on the Bummel* possess dramatic rhythm, reveal an ear for dialogue, and display a superb sense of comic timing. Although Jerome gave up acting, he never lost his passion for the theatre and, with a group of fellow first-nighters, he organized regular meetings to discuss the plays they had seen, later formalized as the 'Playgoers Club', which in due course launched its own periodical, *The Playgoer*.

Tired of provincial touring, Jerome returned to London with thirty shillings in his pocket. For a while he slept rough, selling his clothes to buy food, and to pay the ninepence a night required for a place in the doss-house, when the weather was bad. He was rescued from this by a chance meeting with a boyhood friend, who introduced him to journalism, and he soon found himself working as a penny-a-liner, reporting police court proceedings and coroners' inquests. It was in this competitive trade, he reveals, that he learned the craft of humour, in order to influence sub-editors in favour of his 'flimsy', in preference to other contributors' more soberly written reports. Then followed brief spells teaching in a school in Clapham, and working for a firm of commission agents, until he gained more regular employment as a solicitor's clerk, and began seriously to consider a legal career. However, during the whole of this period, Jerome the writer had also been at work, in what time he could find, producing stories, plays, and essays. In fact Jerome had decided firmly on authorship at the age of 10, and the confirmation of this choice of a literary life came about in a strange fashion, through a chance encounter with Charles Dickens, in Victoria Park, in Hackney. While admitting the possibility of a remarkable resemblance between the man in the park and photographs of the novelist, Jerome remained convinced of his identity, and later recorded their fascinating conversation in his autobiographical novel *Paul Kelver*.

Although by 1891, with the publication of *Three Men in a Boat* behind him, Jerome was fully engaged in writing, he took up the opportunity of a second career as an editor when Robert Barr chose him, in preference to Rudyard Kipling, to coedit *The Idler*, a sixpenny monthly illustrated magazine, to which he also contributed a series of essays. However, he had always nursed an ambition to edit his own periodical, and later he founded a more broadly-based weekly paper, *To-day*, a combination of magazine and journal, which included entertainment, reviews, news, and political comment. It soon carved out for itself a niche in the crowded periodical market, attracting contributors of the quality of Conan Doyle, Kipling, Gissing, and Hardy, and was highly successful until Jerome relinquished the editorship, after a costly libel action, five years later.

Jerome used *To-day* as the mouthpiece for his own opinions. His early political instinct was radical socialist, and his hatred of poverty and oppression expressed itself in several ways. When he was a young man he fell into the company of revolutionaries, both those who lived in Soho and those he met in Brighton at the home of Prince Kropotkin, the leading Russian anarchist, who had settled in England in 1886. Later, together with his friends Wells and Shaw, he joined the Fabian Society. Although he gradually became more of a liberal, he remained a man of firm convictions. And his political courage was considerable. On a lecture tour of America he once braved a sullenly hostile white audience, after a reading in Chattanooga, to speak out against the lynching of negroes in the South. During the war he questioned publicly the morality of the British propaganda campaign against the Germans, an action which brought upon him the wrath of the press, and distanced him from his friends Wells and Kipling. This serious side of Jerome comes through in one of his best works, *Paul Kelver*, which has overtones of Christian allegory, and also in the closing chapters of his autobiography, where he records his sense of shame at making no contribution to the war. He tells how, having been turned down for service on the grounds of age, he was finally accepted as a volunteer ambulance driver for the French Army in 1916, the same year that his fellow-writer John Galsworthy (also rejected by the War Office) went to work in a hospital for convalescent French soldiers. Jerome goes on to describe his experience of the front line, and closes with a reflective examination of the grounds of his religious faith.

Three Men in a Boat

The dual aspect of Jerome's personality—humorist and liberal humanitarian—which is graphically revealed in his own life and writing, enabled him to perceive a similar division within Mark Twain, when they met in London. But it is predominantly Jerome the humorist that the reader encounters in *Three Men in a Boat*, the writing of which saved him from the solicitor's office. The moving spirit behind the venture was his supportive wife, Georgina Stanley, the half-Irish daughter of a Spanish army officer. She persuaded him to pursue a literary career, and the result was *Three Men in a Boat*, written in a state of exhilaration in their top-floor flat in Chelsea Gardens, into which they had moved shortly after their honeymoon.

Three Men in a Boat was begun as a serious travel book, but it refused to conform to its author's intentions. This is Jerome's account of its genesis:

I did not intend to write a funny book, at first. I did not know I was a humorist. I never have been sure about it. In the Middle Ages, I should probably have gone about preaching and got myself burnt or hanged. There was to be 'humorous relief'; but the book was to have been 'The Story of the Thames', its scenery and history. Somehow it would not come. I was just back from my honeymoon, and had the feeling that all the world's troubles were over. About the 'humorous relief' I had no difficulty. I decided to write the 'humorous relief' first—get it off my chest, so to speak. After which, in sober frame of mind, I could tackle the scenery and history. I never got there. It seemed to be all 'humorous relief'. By grim determination I succeeded, before the end, in writing a dozen or so slabs of history and working them in, one to each chapter, and F. W. Robinson, who was publishing the book serially, in *Home Chimes*, promptly slung them out, the most of them. From the beginning he had objected to the title and had insisted upon my thinking of another. And half-way through I hit upon *Three Men in a Boat*, because nothing else seemed right.[2]

In spite of this, the Thames remains very much the book's centre. Jerome loved the river. His closest friends were enthusiastic boating men, with whom he had spent many weekends rowing at Richmond. And when they made their trip up the river to Oxford in 1889, according to Jerome, he simply recorded what happened. Thus the memorable characters of the fiction are drawn directly from life. George is George Wingrave, the best man at Jerome's wedding, who in due course became a bank manager. He had been a fellow lodger, and had shared a room with Jerome in Tavistock Place, which they found convenient for the British Museum. Harris is Carl Hentschel, whom Jerome had met at a theatrical first-night in London. He was a photographer, who later built up his father's business of photo-etching into a thriving concern. However, the dog Montmorency, Jerome admits, was pure invention, developed out of that area of inner consciousness which, he asserts, in all Englishmen contains an element of dog.

Three Men in a Boat retains enough of its original intention to offer a brilliant snapshot of a brief period of English social history—the

---

[2] Jerome K. Jerome, *My Life and Times*, 82.

Thames Valley in the late 1880s. Two profound changes in the life of
the Thames had taken place by this time, both the result of the
coming of the railways in the 1840s. In the early years of the century,
the river had been a very important commercial waterway, connect-
ing London with other areas of England, such as Bristol through the
junction with the Kennet and Avon canal at Reading, and it carried a
considerable volume of barge traffic. But by the 1880s competition
from the railways had virtually driven barges from the river.

   This process of economic change is reflected in contemporary
fiction. Anthony Trollope records the danger that commercial traffic
represented to other boats in the earlier years of the century, in *The
Three Clerks* (1857), when Henry Norman's wherry is struck by a
ponderous barge competing for water under Hampton Court Bridge.
However, by the time George Eliot came to write *Daniel Deronda*
(1876), in which she describes Daniel's rowing on the Thames
between Richmond (later the favourite haunt of Jerome and his
friends) and Kew, barges had been replaced by pleasure boats, so that
in her novel the passing of a great barge under Kew Bridge is of
particular interest to the people on the tow-path. As R. R. Bolland
records, in addition to the palatial houseboats which were towed up
and down the river from regatta to regatta, and the new luxury steam
launches (250 in 1888), there was a huge number of skiffs and punts
in use on the river. Indeed by 1889 there were 12,000 small pleasure
craft registered by the Thames Conservancy.[3]

   The reason for the rapidly growing popularity of the Thames
during the 1880s was the fact that the railways offered cheap
excursion tickets to stations along the river. From Waterloo people
could reach Teddington, Kingston, Hampton Court, and Windsor,
while the Great Western Railway brought Henley within the scope of
a day trip. It is recorded that on one Sunday evening at the end of
June 1888, 950 people caught the last train from Henley to London.[4]
Jerome notes in his autobiography that he and George Wingrave and
Carl Hentschel used to have the river between Richmond and Staines
almost to themselves on Sundays, but that year by year it grew
more crowded, and so their starting-point became Maidenhead. So it
did for thousands of other Londoners. The Thames rapidly became

   [3] R. R. Bolland, *Victorians on the Thames* (Tunbridge Wells: Parapress, 1974; reprinted 1994), 13, 73–9, 104.
   [4] Ibid. 13.

London's new playground, a venue for picnics, carnivals, and regattas. It attracted the wealthy, with their steam launches and houseboats, and also the clerks and shop assistants, with their wives and girlfriends in hired skiffs and punts. For the fashionable world, the Thames was the place to be seen. A new river society came into being, which by 1892 even had a periodical, *The Thames Times and Fashionable River Gazette*, devoted to it. Society took over the regatta at Henley, and it drew increasingly large crowds. According to the *Lock to Lock Times*, in 1888, on the second day of the regatta 6,768 people travelled there from London by train.[5] Henley Royal Regatta became comparable with Royal Ascot, and the newspapers gave more space to the presence of the titled and the wealthy than to the results of the racing. Jerome, in *My Life and Times*, is not entirely accurate, therefore, in blaming the later patronage of the king for transforming the whole ethos of the regatta, but his comment does point up the extraordinary changes that had taken place over a comparatively short period:

It was King Edward who spoilt Henley Regatta. His coming turned it into a society function, and brought down the swell mob. Before that, it had been a happy, gay affair, simple and quiet. People came in craft of all sorts, and took an interest in the racing. One could count the people on the tow-path: old blues, the townsfolk, with the farmers and their families from round about.[6]

The contemporary popularity of *Three Men in a Boat* depended to some extent on its presentation of a world with which many of its readers would be familiar and which for others had the interest of dealing with a contemporary craze, or registered the stirrings of social change. The success of *Three Men in a Boat* as a best-seller was also made possible by the transformation of the publishing industry, in response to the new mass readership that the 1870 Education Act had produced. It was a new, dynamic market for literature, and its demand for shorter books effectively killed the ample, highly priced three-volume novel, which had been the staple of the circulating libraries throughout the Victorian period. Jerome was very alert to these changing market forces, and in his negotiations with his publisher, J. W. Arrowsmith, over *Three Men in a Boat* he was

[5] Quoted ibid.   [6] *My Life and Times*, 181.

concerned to find the right niche for it. He did not want it to appear as one of Arrowsmith's one-shilling volumes of ephemeral fiction that happened to be the temporary 'rage', but to come out in their increasingly popular three-and-sixpenny series, to whose readers Jerome felt that he was better known. And this was what he and Arrowsmith finally agreed. Jerome's judgement proved to be sound, for this series was soon to include work by such promising writers as Conan Doyle and Anthony Hope.

The market also demanded variety. Among the different new forms that were spawned at this period, blurring the distinction between high and popular fiction, was the regional novel. Stories of the river had always been popular, and in Victorian fiction the Thames afforded a mechanism for bridging the abysses of class, sex, and race. In Trollope's *The Three Clerks* and Eliot's *Daniel Deronda* these are overcome by the heroes' actions in rescuing their future wives from drowning in the river. However, more specifically, Patrick Parrinder has identified the later emergence of a particular form, the Thames Valley 'romance'.[7] Indeed, two years after the appearance of *Three Men in a Boat* William Morris published his Utopian romance *News from Nowhere*, which also describes a journey up the Thames from London to beyond Oxford. These romances of the river not only treat the Thames Valley as an ideal landscape, but, as Patrick Parrinder points out, do so in ways that suggest that they are also anti-railway. Jerome notes in *Three Men in a Boat* how the proximity of the railway at Tilehurst spoils the beauty of the river upstream from Reading. Moreover, the tiresome railway journeys of Harris and J. to Kingston, and of George to Weybridge at the start of their river jaunt, find an echo in Morris's details of his narrator's trip by the underground railway to Hammersmith, at the beginning of *News from Nowhere*. By contrast, the landscape of the river valley, the hinterland of the great metropolis and its burgeoning suburbs, is a symbol of a pre-urban, and pre-railway world.

In keeping with the river's general symbolic role, there are moments in *Three Men in a Boat* when it is briefly taken to represent the journey of life, as in Jerome's cheerful injunction to the reader to travel lightly:

[7] Patrick Parrinder, 'From Mary Shelley to *The War of the Worlds*: The Thames Valley Catastrophe', in David Seed (ed.), *Anticipations* (Liverpool: Liverpool University Press, 1995), 58–74.

Throw the lumber over, man! Let your boat of life be light, packed with only what you need—a homely home and simple pleasures, one or two friends, worth the name, someone to love and someone to love you, a cat, a dog, and a pipe or two, enough to eat and enough to wear, and a little more than enough to drink; for thirst is a dangerous thing. (p. 22)

But for the most part Jerome exploits the metaphor of the journey for sustained comic effect, through the opportunity that it affords for an extended parody of the epic voyage. This element is prepared for early in the story, when he details the travellers' extravagant accumulation of provisions for their journey; and it is sharpened when, waiting with their baggage for a cab to take them to the railway station, Harris and J. attract the unwelcome attention of the local errand boys, led by the youth who is employed by their greengrocer, Biggs:

'They ain't a-going to starve, are they?' said the gentleman from the boot-shop.

'Ah! you'd want to take a thing or two with *you*,' retorted 'The Blue Posts', 'if you was a-going to cross the Atlantic in a small boat.'

'They ain't a-going to cross the Atlantic,' struck in Biggs's boy; 'they're a-going to find Stanley.' (pp. 39–40)

The crescendo of sarcasm and ironic hyperbole, culminating in the comic absurdity of the suggestion that they are replicating Stanley's heroic expedition into the heart of Africa in search of Dr Livingstone, the supreme quest of the Victorian era, places their paddling up the homely Thames Valley in a sharply satirical perspective. Far from raw adventure, feats of daring, and the ritual tests of the traditional quest narrative, the trials and obstacles that Jerome's heroes endure involve duckings in the river, encounters with monster steam launches, and a drunken battle with swans. The achievement of their quest is not privileged knowledge, or some kind of illumination, but the complacent, muted Elysium of a couple of pleasant days in Oxford, where Montmorency, in his own private doggy heaven, gets into twenty-five fights. And the great expedition ends in comic bathos as the three heroes, feasting on a cold veal pie in a damp boat in the evening rain, fortified by some toddy, seek to cheer themselves by singing 'Two Lovely Black Eyes' to the accompaniment of George's banjo, only to succumb to sentiment and break down in tears. This signals their rapid retreat by train to the civilized comfort of London: to the Alhambra music-hall, followed by a decent restaurant.

Jerome's conduct of his story in *Three Men in a Boat* is reminiscent, in some respects, of Laurence Sterne's *A Sentimental Journey*. Sterne utilizes every incident of his travels to luxuriate in the exercise of an exquisite sensibility, which he calls into question by simultaneous ironic undercutting; Jerome, a superb raconteur, also adopts patterns of seemingly inconsequential anecdote, in order to engage in the firm, comic debunking of sentiment. Jerome's treatment of incidents always involves the abrupt deflation of excessive feeling by the intrusion of physical reality. The glorious, romantic dawn in which George, Harris, and J. anticipate revelling in an early swim brings instead a chilly, windy morning, and a most unpleasant plunge into a very cold river; and their day-dreaming, when sailing, about crossing a mystic lake like knights in an old legend is similarly brought to a sudden end by their collision with a punt containing three old fishermen. Even love is undermined by an anecdote about an infatuated young couple's failure to realize that the boat containing auntie that they are towing has been replaced by that of George and his friends, who have gleefully attached themselves to the empty tow-line for a free pull up to Marlow.

Structurally, Jerome's simple tale of a journey up the Thames is complicated by his breaking off to record historical events, by his excursions into the by-paths of memory, and, principally, by anecdotes: stories embedded in the main narrative that occasionally belong to another genre and are written in a different style but which develop out of a foregoing digression, by an association of ideas. J.'s sentimental meditation on the maternal nature of night leads naturally into a medieval legend, beginning with the formulaic 'Once upon a time', which turns out to be a religious allegory, and then the following chapter returns the reader to the comic holiday world of a cold morning on the Victorian river. These narrative meanderings recall George's own anecdote about his experience of the maze at Hampton Court, where after forays down various paths, followed by a procession of hopeful escapees, he kept finding himself at the point from which he started. If the river operates as the dominant metaphor in Jerome's tale, the maze is also a prominent one, as the reader is returned from frequent digressions—shot through with comic observations, exaggerations, embarrassments, and reversals—to the narrator's current situation in a boat on the Thames.

Although *Three Men in a Boat* is composed of humorous anecdote and farce, it also includes a strong element of travelogue. Jerome slides easily into this mode, extolling the beauty of Clifton Hampden, and advising the reader to put up at the 'Barley Mow', 'the quaintest, most old-world inn up the river' (p. 149). In addition, because the novel set out to be seriously historical, it retains a framework of historical reference. Characteristically, Jerome tends to pick out the stories of the river which have the greatest human interest—the ghost of Lady Hoby, who murdered her little boy at Bisham Abbey; the Hell-Fire Club at Medmenham, where groups of aristocratic young men engaged in satanic rituals; or Tennyson's quiet wedding to Emily at the little church in Shiplake. And he works hard at dramatizing the signing of Magna Charta at Runnymede. But sometimes he simply cannot resist the book's basic comic impulse, and the narrative breaks away into the absurd. Jerome's transposition of Tudor courtship into the modern idiom, in his treatment of the pursuit of Anne Boleyn by Henry VIII, is a piece of historical fantasy which culminates in a general comic flight from the royal presence—from the embarrassment of continually coming across 'that wretched couple, kissing under the Abbey walls' (p. 95).

In his Preface to *Three Men in a Boat*, Jerome claims that 'for hopeless and incurable veracity, nothing yet discovered can surpass it'. One interesting aspect of Jerome's veracity is his close observation of various aspects of contemporary river life. He reflects the concern, recorded in a number of river journals, about the growing predilection among river users for being towed upstream, especially on windy days, by unskilled loiterers on the banks, which led to crowding, dangerous incidents, and even the occasional fatality. Jerome also testifies in passing to the abundance of fish in the Thames. And he notices the social gradations among the river's fishermen: the distinction between the gentlemen anglers, assisted by a professional, who moor their boats in midstream, oblivious to the steam launches, and the local anglers who are strung along the muddy banks.

The subjects of Jerome's observation include river fashions. Like the Victorian seaside, the Thames had become an area of recreation that afforded great opportunities for display. He notes the women's elegant dresses—fashion-plate young ladies, he calls them—and the men's river uniform of blazers and caps, in terms that are echoed in the periodicals devoted to Thames social life. George's purchase of a particularly flamboyant blazer for his boating trip is a response to the dictates of river fashion. So, too, is his decision to bring a banjo with him, even though he is unable to play it. These were widely popular, and magazine illustrations of the day include pictures of young ladies sitting languidly on the river bank, strumming banjos as a means of attracting the amorous attention of boating men. Another river ritual was the taking of photographs. In the locks the jams of river traffic were turned to commercial advantage by speculative photographers, who took pictures of the little flotilla of boats as the water rose. And one such episode provides Jerome with the opportunity for farce, as George, Harris, and J. strive unsteadily to pose for the camera, while their boat, jostling among the others, becomes dangerously entangled with the structure of the lock.

Running counter to Jerome's gypsy spirit, and his evident irritation with the crowdedness of the river, is his nostalgic, Utopian feeling for a shared landscape. This ideal comes into sharp conflict with the Victorian property culture, symbolized for Jerome by the enclosure of the river's banks. He is especially angered by those landowners who stretch chains across tributary streams, and erect notices forbidding trespass. In other respects, as a pleasure-ground, of course the Thames was very much a shared landscape, where the social classes came into close contact, and although Jerome refers, in the slang of the time, to their having left both 'Arry and Lord Fitznoodle behind at Henley, it is clear that he had no time for snobbery. Encountering 'a party of provincial 'Arrys and 'Arriets, out for a moonlight sail' (p. 75), and engaged in rendering a popular song, to the accompaniment of a badly played accordion, he hails them in the spirit of river fellowship. It is the opposite end of the social scale that comes in for Jerome's censure. Maidenhead is described as 'too snobby to be pleasant. It is the haunt of the river swell and his overdressed female companion. It is the town of showy hotels, patronised chiefly by dudes and ballet girls' (p. 101).

Like all rowing men, he regards these swells and their steam-launches as the enemy. Here Jerome's humour functions as a safety-valve, as his murderous rage at their arrogant, imperious whistles is deflected into whimsical fantasy: 'I never see a steam launch but I feel

I should like to lure it to a lonely part of the river, and there, in the
silence and the solitude, strangle it' (p. 110). In this continuous class
warfare between the little boats and the monsters of the river, two
alternative strategies are employed, the physical and the psycho-
logical: that of remaining defiantly in midstream, deaf to the frantic
whistling until the launch is brought to a halt; or, more subtly, in
dealing with the aristocratic type of steam launch, 'to mistake them
for a beanfeast, and ask them if they were Messrs Cubit's lot or the
Bermondsey Good Templars, and could they lend us a saucepan'
(p. 111).

While *Three Men in a Boat* was hugely successful, its new vein of
humour was identified by critics as consisting essentially of collo-
quialisms, slang, and vulgarity. It was, as Jerome puts it,

damned by the critics. One might have imagined—to read some of
them—that the British Empire was in danger. One Church dignitary went
about the country denouncing me. *Punch* was especially indignant, scent-
ing an insidious attempt to introduce 'new humour' into comic literature.
For years, 'New Humorist' was shouted after me wherever I wrote. Why in
England, of all countries in the world, humour, even in new clothes, should
be mistaken for a stranger to be greeted with brickbats, bewildered me.[8]

Jerome's humour, which creates the atmosphere of holiday from
reality, the rationale for the boating trip, is genial. It is directed both
at human foibles, including his own, and at the recurrent, ironic
experience of things continually turning out differently from the
expected. It involves a number of well-tried comic routines: the
substitute victim joke, when the shirt in the river, which George
finds so amusing when he thinks it is J.'s, turns out to be his own; or
the running joke about the trespassing notices along the river banks,
which builds to a climax of comic rage; or the self-mocking reversal of
attitude when, being towed grandly behind his friend's steam launch,
J. betrays his own irritation at the small boats that impede his
grand progress. However, an important aspect of Jerome's humour is
its function of release, a mode of response to frustration with
reality—what Jerome calls 'the natural cussedness of things in
general' (p. 111). This ranges from impotent rage at the impenetrable
stupidity of bureaucracies, institutions, and systems, such as the

---

[8] *My Life and Times*, 87.

London and South-Western Railway, which manages to lose a train at Waterloo, so that George and J. have to bribe a driver with half-a-crown to take the Exeter mail train to Kingston for them instead, to playing mind-games with a kettle in order to get it to boil. Many of their encounters with the 'natural cussedness of things' (p. 84) involve an element of clowning, for the main source of frustration is the sheer intransigent physicality of things, such as the boat hoops, and the tow-ropes that seem to have a life of their own, and the tin of pineapple chunks that cannot be opened, and is finally flung into the river in comic despair.

The newness of Jerome's humour was perhaps somewhat exaggerated by contemporary critics. The episode, told to George by his father, about his experience of two men sleeping in the same bed and fighting in the dark for sole possession of it, is part of a long comic tradition. But the important element that Jerome contributes to the 'new' humour is absurdism. What Jerome does in the incident of the bed is pile whimsy on top of farce. The coincidence of precisely the same thing having happened to Harris's father suggests a comic inevitability about the current relationship between their sons, and about the farcical adventures that befall them. It emphasizes their living in a comically malevolent universe. Jerome's comedy depends on presenting the reader with a skewed view of the world. Occasionally this extends into the surreal, as in his inversion of the metaphor of the river of life. The Thames becomes a literal conveyor of death, when the corpses of the dog and the woman come floating past the friends' boat. These are unsettling, not simply because the dog is described as if it were contentedly alive, while the woman is made the subject of an essay in social morality, but because of the abrupt inconsequentiality with which the story returns to the normal (to their concern about contracting typhoid, and J.'s extolling the delights of Goring and Streatley). However, in the process the reality to which the reader has been returned has been significantly modified.

Three Men on the Bummel

Three Men on the Bummel is also based on an actual trip by Jerome, George, and Harris ten years later, and was published shortly after its completion in 1900. A 'Bummel' (German for a ramble) is amplified by Jerome in the book's final paragraph: 'A "Bummel" . . . I should describe as a journey, long or short, without an end; the only thing regulating it being the necessity of getting back within a given time to the point from which one started' (p. 324). In America it was published under the title *Three Men on Wheels*.

Like boating in the 1880s, in the following decade cycling became a very fashionable pastime, though more widely practised. Jerome's autobiography records, as a matter of personal interest, that his nephew was the first man in London to ride the new 'safety' bicycle, which superseded the 'spider', with its very large front wheel. The coming of this machine made cycling universally popular, although there arose a controversy over whether ladies should ride bicycles, for, before the invention of the dropped bar, daring lady cyclists had to wear knickerbockers. However, like boating on the river, cycling was a craze that soon involved both sexes and all social classes, as Jerome points out in his vivid, comic sketch of their collective participation and occasional collisions:

Bicycling became the rage. In Battersea Park, any morning between eleven and one, all the best blood in England could be seen, solemnly peddling up and down the half-mile drive that runs between the river and the refreshment kiosk. But these were the experts—the finished article. In shady by-paths, elderly countesses, perspiring peers, still at the wobbly stage, battled bravely with the laws of equilibrium; occasionally defeated, they would fling their arms round the necks of hefty young hooligans who were reaping a rich harvest as cycling instructors: 'Proficiency guaranteed in twelve lessons'. Cabinet Ministers, daughters of a hundred Earls might be recognised by the initiated, seated on the gravel, smiling feebly and rubbing their heads. Into quiet roads and side-streets, one ventured at the peril of one's limbs. All the world seemed to be learning bicycling.[9]

Before the narrative proper gets under way, Jerome digresses characteristically on the subject of cycling mania, particularly the preoccupation with overhauling machines at every opportunity. His keen sense of incongruity also extends to the gulf between the ideal and the real in cycling: between the glamorous, cigarette-smoking women and the courting couples (the 'Edwins' and 'Angelinas') portrayed on the early poster advertisements for magical new bicycles, such as the 'Camberwell Company's Jointless Eureka', in which

[9] *My Life and Times*, 68.

the machines glide effortlessly along of their own volition; and the reality, which as middle-aged men they endured in Germany, of puffing laboriously on older machines up the hills of the Black Forest.

There are more digressions at the beginning of *Three Men on the Bummel* than in *Three Men in a Boat*, and they have to do with the way cycling crystallizes different attitudes to domesticity and adventure. The wanderlust of the intrepid cyclists is implicitly contrasted with J.'s earlier experience of Captain Goyles, whose love of home comforts was such that he declined to take J. and Ethelbertha on a yachting trip, claiming that he could not leave port whatever point of the compass the wind was blowing from. The story of Harris's cycling trip in Holland, where after an interlude of marital discord he inadvertently managed to lose his wife from the rear seat of their tandem, illustrates the degree of his obsession. By contrast there is the comic tale of Uncle Podger's stifling suburban routine which precedes his daily sprint to the railway station. But the most extensive digression begins with a story, recounted in dialect, about the manipulative courtship of a young girl by her prudent Scots lover, who uses confession as a means of achieving perpetual freedom from domestic responsibility. This is then adroitly turned by Jerome into a self-parodying reminiscence of his early days as a journalist, dispensing advice to his readership, and leads in turn, by the familiar process of association of ideas, to an explanation of why the present book will contain 'no description of towns, no historical reminiscences, no architecture, no morals' (p. 218). All of which are of course included.

The success of both *Three Men in a Boat* and *Three Men on the Bummel* depends to a considerable extent on Jerome's securing an intimate relationship with the reader, grounded in familiar experience. In *Three Men in a Boat* he achieves this by involving the reader in the hypochondria of the three friends, and their feeling that they are very much in need of a holiday. The same technique is employed in the introductory section of *Three Men on the Bummel*, which also takes as its starting-point the need for a change. Now in their forties and married, Harris and J. are desperate for a taste of adventure, and they persuade George, whose bachelor status and freedom they secretly envy, to accompany them on a cycling tour. Jerome, who after his marriage maintained his close male friendships, particularly with George Wingrave, and continued to hold evenings of conversation and smoking, seeks to elicit the reader's provisional endorsement of a thoroughly Edwardian middle-class, male-centred view of the world. However, his story also contains within it elements of self-mockery and comic deflation.

Jerome's description of the family routine they are seeking to escape, the negotiations with their wives, and the ensuing digressions, take up almost one third of the story. There is the comic hubris of Harris and J. parading their marital authority before George, when their immediate problem is how to broach the subject of the holiday, and secure their wives' consent without forfeiting their dignity. The joke is that, quite independently, Ethelbertha and Mrs Harris have decided on their own need for a change. The comedy of expectations reversed is developed when, unlike the Scots suitor of Jerome's digression, the manipulator is manipulated. J. not only discovers Ethelbertha's desire for freedom, but perceives in her hyperbolic reference to him as the 'glory of the sun' (p. 178)—a comic echo of his previously imagined conversation with her—a strategic pandering to his male ego. This transposition of fantasy into ironic fact produces the comically disturbing revelation that domestic authority resides with the women. Ethelbertha gets her holiday in Folkestone, while Harris's wife trades his absence for a fashionable bathroom and a new kitchen stove.

In order to create the social basis for his comedy of escape in *Three Men on the Bummel*, Jerome includes a greater degree of personal detail about the three characters' lives. The emphasis falls on J.'s literary preoccupations, and substantial house complete with a paddock, where he practises his golf shots, on Harris's extensive and demanding family, and on George's comfortable routine at the bank. Finding security and responsibility increasingly irksome, the three plot their great adventure. What this amounts to is a muted rebellion against Edwardian middle-class life: the claustrophobic nature of the family, the dull routines of suburban existence, the tyranny of the morning train, and the rigidity of the class system. One of the functions of the Jeromian anecdote is to encapsulate related concerns such as these, and they are vividly summarized in J.'s story about Uncle Podger's highly ritualized morning leave-taking at the family home in Ealing, and his dash for the 9.13 train to Moorgate Street, running the daily gauntlet of the working-classes' comic scorn, about which he writes indignantly but vainly to the local newspaper. It is a significant anecdote, because Jerome uses it as a point of contrast with his experience in Germany. He is clearly impressed by the collectivist ethos of its society, by the way that everyone rides the city tramcars, ladies in evening dress sitting beside porters with their baskets. Jerome finds this strange but attractive. And he amplifies his observation in the final chapter with the incisive comment that, outside the landed aristocracy, class distinction is less entrenched as an organizing principle of German society: 'In Germany there is not, at all events as yet, sufficient distinction between the classes to make the struggle for position the life and death affair it is in England' (p. 319).

Jerome loved Germany. His first visit was to see the Oberammergau Passion Play, in the days when visitors shared the homes and food of the rural peasants, a trip he records in *The Diary of a Pilgrimage*. Later he and his wife spent two years in Dresden, where he enjoyed the hospitality of the Saxons and made many friends, including the Crown Princess Louise, who frequently chose him as her skating partner. Here he also received a message from King Albert, letting him know how much he enjoyed *Three Men on the Bummel*. Indeed, the text was adopted in Germany as a school reading book. In return Jerome found much to admire: the German education system, the Germans' proficiency with languages, and their kindness to animals. Writing in 1926, he asserts: 'Knowing Germany well, it would amuse me, if it did not so much disgust me, to hear the Germans spoken of as brutal and ferocious. As a matter of fact, they are the kindest and homeliest of people.'[10]

While there are passages in *Three Men in a Boat* where Jerome responds quite powerfully to the scenery of the river itself, in *Three Men on the Bummel* his interest is very much in the customs and character of the German people. He makes clear his altered focus in an extended comment, expressing the view that only the conscientious or weak-minded readers would attend to passages of description, in these days of the steam-engine and the camera, when personal experience and photography have superseded the need for prose. Readers who want fully developed stories rather than observation and anecdote are enjoined to 'cook the dish for yourself' (p. 219).

[10] *My Life and Times*, 156

An organizing comic principle of *Three Men on the Bummel* is the contrast between the instinctive decorum of the German people and the anarchic nature of the three itinerant Englishmen. There is the comic irony that the country in which they are cycling, which they had imagined to be ruggedly romantic, is in truth a model of sobriety and order. Here bird-boxes are built to keep gardens free from litter, and mountain torrents are made into well-regulated streams because 'in Germany there is no nonsense talked about untrammelled nature. In Germany nature has got to behave herself, and not set a bad example to the children' (p. 239). There is a further comic irony in the way that, when they taste the heady freedom of being abroad, the respectable middle-aged, middle-class Londoners descend to the level of children. George and J. have to keep a tight rein on Harris, who discovers an eye for German ladies, while Harris and J. find it necessary to concoct an elaborate and positively surreal plot, which involves creating the illusion of an endlessly self-replicating statue, in order to cure George of his addiction to German beer. The anarchic traits in Harris and George are illustrated as each inhabits his own story, embedded in the larger narrative, when they do their own individual 'bummeling'. Here Jerome invokes his familiar comic reversal of perspective, and includes an element of visual clowning. When Harris finds himself inside a speeding Dresden tram, colliding with the other passengers as it weaves its way around the city, it is Harris who finds the situation hilarious, while the faces of his fellow passengers register sober concern. And in his parallel independent escapade, George causes comic confusion when, in purchasing a cushion for his aunt, he ventures rashly into the German language and mistakenly solicits a kiss from the shop girl for twenty marks.

Jerome finds the stern decorum of German social life admirable, but only up to a point. At one level the oppressively regimented social order is a source of amusement: the absurdity of the law forbidding the shooting of crossbows in the streets; the multiple notices regulating people's progress through the public parks; and the baffling complexities of the regulations governing German transport. However, Jerome deplores the practice of duelling among university students, which is symptomatic of the general ethos of militarism he detects in German society. But what most alarms his liberal instinct is the tyranny of the State, which, although socialist, he regards as despotic. This, he observes, is apparent in the Germans' unnatural

respect for authority figures, such as policemen, and it results, he
argues, in a lack of individualism, responsibility, and initiative.
Jerome lays this at the door of their education system, which
inculcates above all a sense of duty: 'The German idea of it would
appear to be: "blind obedience to everything in buttons" . . . the
antithesis of the Anglo-Saxon scheme' (p. 318). And as if to demon-
strate the truth of this perception, Jerome's Englishmen abroad, with
their romantic individualism, their instinctive preference for
muddle, their contempt for authority, and their schoolboy irrespon-
sibility, continually fall foul of the law—walking on forbidden paths,
hitching an illegal ride on a train, and inadvertently stealing a bicycle.

As the narrator of *Three Men in a Boat* and *Three Men on the
Bummel*, Jerome creates for himself a genial comic persona, that of an
observer and raconteur, who is also excellent company. Jerome's
generous comedy combines the traditional and the modern. Although its subjects are the universal ones of bureaucracy, pomposity,
and moral stupidity, wherever he finds them, these are balanced by
his absurdist impulse to present a skewed view of the world, best seen
in some of his anecdotes and digressions. And these are artfully
deployed within a deceptively casual narrative form. Simultaneously
conservative and anarchic, involved and detached, Jerome's humour
maintains a sense of comic equipoise. And the basis of its essential
sanity is the ironic perspective of time—Jerome's guide, phil-
osopher, friend, and jester—'good master TIME' to whom *Three
Men on the Bummel* is dedicated, and which also controls his perception of the comically malevolent world of *Three Men in a Boat*.

NOTE ON THE TEXT

This text is based on the first edition of *Three Men in a Boat*, published by J. W. Arrowsmith of Bristol in 1889, and the first edition of *Three Men on the Bummel*, also published by Arrowsmith in 1900.

SELECT BIBLIOGRAPHY

Place of publication is London unless otherwise stated.

Jerome's autobiography, *My Life and Times* (John Murray, 1926; reprinted 1983), was followed shortly after his death by Alfred Moss's somewhat reverential biography, *Jerome K. Jerome* (Selwyn & Blount, 1928). Reminiscences of Jerome may be found in Sir Arthur Conan Doyle, *Memories and Adventures* (Hodder & Stoughton, 1924); Coulson Kernahan, *Celebrities* (Hutchinson, 1923); and Francis Gribble, *Seen in Passing* (Ernest Benn, 1929). Olaf E. Bossom's *Slang and Cant in Jerome K. Jerome's Works* (Cambridge: Heffer, 1911) reveals a contemporary preoccupation with Jerome's language. A useful reference work is Robert G. Logan's *Jerome K. Jerome: A Concise Bibliography* (Walsall Libraries, 1971). Ruth Marie Faurot published a general critical study, *Jerome K. Jerome*, in 1974 (New York: Twayne); and Joseph Connolly's *Jerome K. Jerome: A Critical Biography* was published by Orbis in 1982. A notable discussion of Jerome as a humorist in *Three Men in a Boat* is V. S. Pritchett's review, 'The Tin-openers', in *The New Statesman and Nation* (15 June 1957), 783–4. Of more general interest are Patrick Parrinder's essay, 'From Mary Shelley to *The War of the Worlds*: The Thames Valley Catastrophe', in David Seed (ed.), *Anticipations* (Liverpool: Liverpool University Press, 1995), 58–74; and R. R. Bolland, *Victorians on the Thames* (Tunbridge Wells: Parapress, 1974, reprinted 1994).

A CHRONOLOGY OF JEROME K. JEROME

1859 Born 2 May, Walsall, the fourth child of Jerome Clapp Jerome, Nonconformist preacher, former farmer, and owner of a small coal-mine, and his wife, Marguerite (née Jones), the daughter of a Swansea solicitor.

1862 The family moves to Poplar in London, where Jerome's father had opened a wholesale ironmongery business.

1869 Attends the Philological School in Lisson Grove.

1871 On the death of his father, the family moves to Finchley.

1873 Commences work as a railway clerk at Euston Station.

1874 Following the death of his mother, joins a theatrical touring company.

1877 Begins a series of jobs: actor, teacher, secretary, penny-a-line journalist, and solicitor's clerk.

1885 With George Wingrave moves into a room in Tavistock Place. Contributes essays to the new journal *Home Chimes*. *On the Stage—and Off*, humorous sketches (published Field & Tuer).

1886 Contributes essays to *The Playgoer*. Essays that had appeared in *Home Chimes* published as *The Idle Thoughts of an Idle Fellow* (Field & Tuer). *Barbara* opens at the Globe Theatre (published Lacy).

1888 Marriage with Georgina Henrietta Stanley, the daughter of a Spaniard, Lieutenant George Nesza, following her divorce, at St Luke's Church, Chelsea. *Sunset*, adapted from Tennyson's 'The Two Sisters', opens at the Comedy Theatre (published Fitzgerald). *Fennel*, adapted from François Coppée's *Le Luthier de Crémone*, opens at the Novelty Theatre (published French). *Woodbarrow Farm* opens at the Comedy Theatre (published French).

1889 *Stage-Land*, satire on the theatre (published Chatto & Windus). *Three Men in a Boat*, novel, published in *Home Chimes*, and in book form by Arrowsmith.

1890 Produces two plays, *New Lamps for Old*, and *Ruth*. Visits Germany for the Oberammergau Passion Play.

1891 *The Diary of a Pilgrimage (and Six Essays)* (published Arrowsmith). *Told After Supper*, ghost stories (published Leadenhall Press).

1892   Appointed coeditor of a new monthly magazine, *The Idler*, founded by Robert Barr, to which he also contributes.

1893   *Novel Notes*, essays that appeared in *The Idler* (published Leadenhall Press). Founds and edits *To-day*, a weekly illustrated paper.

1894   Moves to Alpha Place, St John's Wood. *John Ingerfield and Other Stories* (published McClure). Edits and contributes to *My First Book*, a collection of essays (published Chatto & Windus).

1895   Lecture tour of the country. *The Prude's Progress* (with Eden Philpotts) opens at the Comedy Theatre (published Chatto & Windus). *The Rise of Dick Halward* opens at the Garrick Theatre.

1897   Birth of daughter, Rowena. *Sketches in Lavender, Blue and Green* (published Longman). Contributes an essay, 'Women and Wheels', to *The Humours of Cycling* (published Chatto & Windus, 1905).

1898   *The Second Thoughts of an Idle Fellow*, essays (published Hurst & Blackett). Gives up editorship of *To-day* following a financially crippling libel suit.

1899   The Jerome family moves to Wallingford. *Miss Hobbs* opens at the Lyceum, New York, later transferring to the Duke of York's Theatre, London (published French, 1902).

1900   Cycling tour with George Wingrave and Carl Hentschel through Germany. Takes his family to live for two years in Dresden. *Three Men on the Bummel*, novel (published Arrowsmith).

1901   *The Observations of Henry*, stories (published Arrowsmith).

1902   On return from Germany, purchases Gould's Grove, Wallingford. *Paul Kelver*, autobiographical novel (published Hutchinson). *Tea Table Talk* (published Hutchinson).

1904   Visits Brussels during the winter with his wife and daughter. *Tommy and Co.*, novel (published Hutchinson). *American Wives and Others*, essays (published Stokes).

1905   *Idle Ideas in 1905*, selection of essays from *American Wives and Others*, with altered titles (published Hurst & Blackett).

1907   *The Passing of the Third Floor Back*, stories (published Hurst & Blackett).

1908   Lecture tour of America. Invited to meet President Theodore Roosevelt. *The Angel and the Author—and Others*, essays (published Hurst & Blackett). *The Passing of the Third Floor Back* (the play) opens at the St James's Theatre (published Hurst & Blackett, 1910).

1909 Spends winter skiing with wife in Switzerland. *They and I*, novel (published Hutchinson). *Fanny and the Servant Problem* opens at the Aldwych Theatre (published Lacy).

1911 *The Master of Mrs Chilvers* opens at the Royalty Theatre (published T. Fisher Unwin).

1913 *Esther Castways* opens at the Prince of Wales' Theatre. The cast includes Marie Tempest and Rowena Jerome. *Robina in Search of a Husband* opens at the Vaudeville Theatre (published Lacy).

1914 *The Great Gamble* opens at the Haymarket Theatre.

1916 Visits America on behalf of the British Government. Interviews President Woodrow Wilson. To France as volunteer member of the French Army Ambulance Unit. *Malvina of Brittany*, novella and stories (published Cassell).

1917 Returns to England. Moves from Gould's Grove to the smaller, nearby Monk's Place. *Cook* opens at the Kingsway Theatre, published under its original title, *The Celebrity* (Hodder & Stoughton, 1926).

1919 *All Roads Lead to Calvary*, novel (published Hutchinson).

1923 *Anthony John*, novel (published Cassell). *A Miscellany of Sense and Nonsense* (published Arrowsmith).

1924 Having recently moved back to London, settles in Belsize Park for his health, accompanied by his wife and daughter.

1926 *My Life and Times*, autobiography (published Hodder & Stoughton).

1927 (17 February) Made Freeman of the Borough of Walsall. (14 June) Dies while on holiday in Devon. *The Soul of Nicholas Snyders* opens at the Everyman Theatre.

THREE MEN IN A BOAT

(TO SAY NOTHING OF THE DOG)

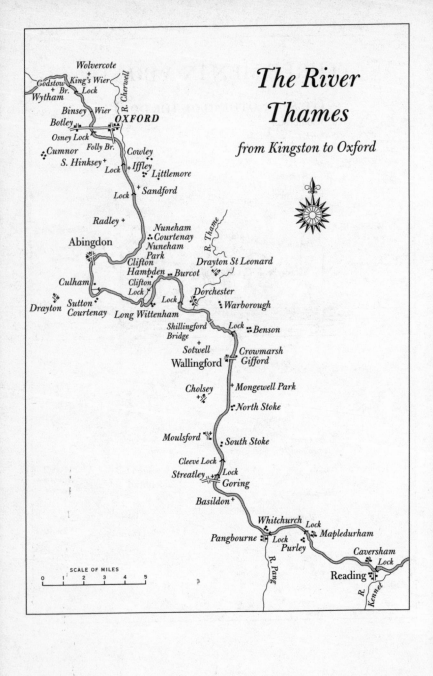

The River Thames

from Kingston to Oxford

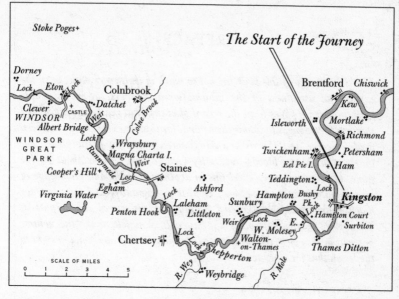

Stoke Poges+

Dorney
Lock *Eton* Lock **Colnbrook**
Clewer *Datchet*
WINDSOR + CASTLE
Albert Bridge
Lock
WINDSOR
GREAT
PARK
Cooper's Hill +
Virginia Water
Egham
Penton Hook
Chertsey
Lock

Wraysbury
Magna Charta I.
Weir
Staines
Lock
Ashford
Laleham
Littleton
Weir
Lock
Lock
Shepperton

R. *Wey* *Weybridge*

Brentford *Chiswick*
Kew
Isleworth *Mortlake*
Richmond
Twickenham *Petersham*
Eel Pie I. + *Ham*
Teddington
Lock **Kingston**
Hampton Bushy
Pk.
Sunbury Lock *Hampton Court* *Surbiton*
Lock E.
W. Molesey
Walton-on-Thames *Thames Ditton*

R. *Mole*

The Start of the Journey

SCALE OF MILES
0 1 2 3 4 5

Colne Brook
Runnymede

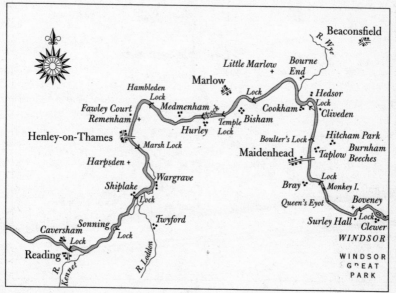

R. *Wye* **Beaconsfield**

Little Marlow *Bourne End*
Marlow *Hedsor*
Hambleden Lock Lock Lock
Fawley Court *Medmenham* *Cookham* *Cliveden*
Remenham + Lock *Bisham*
Hurley Temple Lock *Boulter's Lock* *Hitcham Park*
Henley-on-Thames *Marsh Lock* **Maidenhead** *Taplow* *Burnham Beeches*
Harpsden + *Wargrave* *Bray* Lock
Shiplake Lock *Monkey I.*
Lock *Twyford* *Queen's Eyot* *Boveney*
Sonning *Surley Hall* Lock
Caversham Lock *Clewer*
Lock **WINDSOR**
Reading
R. *Kennet* R. *Loddon* **WINDSOR**
GREAT
PARK

PREFACE

The chief beauty of this book lies not so much in its literary style, or in the extent and usefulness of the information it conveys, as in its simple truthfulness. Its pages form the record of events that really happened. All that has been done is to colour them; and, for this, no extra charge has been made. George and Harris and Montmorency are not poetic ideals, but things of flesh and blood—especially George, who weighs about twelve stone. Other works may excel this in depth of thought and knowledge of human nature: other books may rival it in originality and size; but, for hopeless and incurable veracity, nothing yet discovered can surpass it. This, more than all its other charms, will, it is felt, make the volume precious in the eye of the earnest reader; and will lend additional weight to the lesson that the story teaches.

LONDON, *August*, 1889.

CHAPTER I

Three Invalids—Sufferings of George and Harris—A victim to one hundred and seven fatal maladies—Useful prescriptions—Cure for liver complaint in children—We agree that we are overworked, and need rest—A week on the rolling deep?—George suggests the River—Montmorency lodges an objection—Original motion carried by majority of three to one.

THERE were four of us—George, and William Samuel Harris, and myself, and Montmorency. We were sitting in my room, smoking, and talking about how bad we were—bad from a medical point of view I mean, of course.

We were all feeling seedy, and we were getting quite nervous about it. Harris said he felt such extraordinary fits of giddiness come over him at times, that he hardly knew what he was doing; and then George said that *he* had fits of giddiness too, and hardly knew what *he* was doing. With me, it was my liver that was out of order. I knew it was my liver that was out of order, because I had just been reading a patent liver-pill circular, in which were detailed the various symptoms by which a man could tell when his liver was out of order. I had them all.

It is a most extraordinary thing, but I never read a patent medicine advertisement without being impelled to the conclusion that I am suffering from the particular disease therein dealt with in its most virulent form. The diagnosis seems in every case to correspond exactly with all the sensations that I have ever felt.

I remember going to the British Museum one day to read up the treatment for some slight ailment of which I had a touch—hay fever, I fancy it was. I got down the book, and read all I came to read; and then, in an unthinking moment, I idly turned the leaves, and began to indolently study diseases, generally. I forget which was the first distemper I plunged into—some fearful, devastating scourge, I know—and, before I had glanced half down the list of 'premonitory symptoms,' it was borne in upon me that I had fairly got it.

I sat for awhile, frozen with horror; and then, in the listlessness of despair, I again turned over the pages. I came to typhoid fever—read the symptoms—discovered that I had typhoid fever, must have had it for months without knowing it—wondered what else I had got; turned up St Vitus's Dance—found, as I expected, that I had that too,—began to get interested in my case, and determined to sift it to the bottom, and so started alphabetically—read up ague, and learnt that I was sickening for it, and that the acute stage would commence in about another fortnight. Bright's disease, I was relieved to find, I had only in a modified form, and, so far as that was concerned, I might live for years. Cholera I had, with severe complications; and diphtheria I seemed to have been born with. I plodded conscientiously through the twenty-six letters, and the only malady I could conclude I had not got was housemaid's knee.

I felt rather hurt about this at first; it seemed somehow to be a sort of slight. Why hadn't I got housemaid's knee? Why this invidious reservation? After a while, however, less grasping feelings prevailed. I reflected that I had every other known malady in the pharmacology, and I grew less selfish, and determined to do without housemaid's knee. Gout, in its most malignant stage, it would appear, had seized me without my being aware of it; and zymosis I had evidently been suffering with from boyhood. There were no more diseases after zymosis, so I concluded there was nothing else the matter with me.

I sat and pondered. I thought what an interesting case I must be from a medical point of view, what an acquisition I should be to a class! Students would have no need to 'walk the hospitals,' if they had me. I was a hospital in myself. All they need do would be to walk round me, and, after that, take their diploma.

Then I wondered how long I had to live. I tried to examine myself. I felt my pulse. I could not at first feel any pulse at all. Then, all of a sudden, it seemed to start off. I pulled out my watch and timed it. I made it a hundred and forty-seven to the minute. I tried to feel my heart. I could not feel my heart. It had stopped beating. I have since been induced to come to the opinion that it must have been there all the time, and must have been beating, but I cannot account for it. I patted myself all over my front, from what I call my waist up to my head, and I went a bit round each side, and a little way up the back. But I could not feel or hear anything. I tried to look at my tongue. I stuck it out as far as ever it would go, and I shut one eye, and tried to examine it with the other. I could only see the tip, and the only thing that I could gain from that was to feel more certain than before that I had scarlet fever.

I had walked into that reading-room a happy, healthy man. I crawled out a decrepit wreck.

I went to my medical man. He is an old chum of mine, and feels my pulse, and looks at my tongue, and talks about the weather, all for nothing, when I fancy I'm ill; so I thought I would do him a good turn by going to him now. 'What a doctor wants,' I said, 'is practice. He shall have me. He will get more practice out of me than out of seventeen hundred of your ordinary, commonplace patients, with only one or two diseases each.' So I went straight up and saw him, and he said:

'Well, what's the matter with you?'

I said:

'I will not take up your time, dear boy, with telling you what is the matter with me. Life is brief, and you might pass away before I had finished. But I will tell you what is *not* the matter with me. I have not got housemaid's knee. Why I have not got housemaid's knee, I cannot tell you; but the fact remains that I have not got it. Everything else, however, I *have* got .'

And I told him how I came to discover it all.

Then he opened me and looked down me, and clutched hold of my wrist, and then he hit me over the chest when I wasn't expecting it—a cowardly thing to do; I call it—and immediately afterwards butted me with the side of his head. After that, he sat down and wrote out a prescription, and folded it up and gave it me, and I put it in my pocket and went out.

I did not open it. I took it to the nearest chemist's, and handed it in. The man read it, and then handed it back.

He said he didn't keep it.

I said:

'You are a chemist?'

He said:

'I am a chemist. If I was a co-operative stores and family hotel combined, I might be able to oblige you. Being only a chemist hampers me.'

I read the prescription. It ran:

> '1 lb. beefsteak, with
> 1 pt. bitter beer
> every 6 hours.
> 1 ten-mile walk every morning.
> 1 bed at 11 sharp every night.

And don't stuff up your head with things you don't understand.'

I followed the directions, with the happy result—speaking for myself—that my life was preserved, and is still going on.

In the present instance, going back to the liver-pill circular, I had the symptoms, beyond all mistake, the chief among them being 'a general disinclination to work of any kind.'

What I suffer in that way no tongue can tell. From my earliest infancy I have been a martyr to it. As a boy, the disease hardly left me for a day. They did not know, then, that it was my liver. Medical science was in a far less advanced state than now, and they used to put it down to laziness.

'Why, you skulking little devil, you,' they would say, 'get up and do something for your living, can't you?'—not knowing, of course, that I was ill.

And they didn't give me pills; they gave me clumps on the side of the head. And, strange as it may appear, those clumps on the head often cured me—for the time being. I have known one clump on the head have more effect upon my liver, and make me feel more anxious to go straight away then and there, and do what was wanted to be done, without further loss of time, than a whole box of pills does now.

You know, it often is so—those simple, old-fashioned remedies are sometimes more efficacious than all the dispensary stuff.

We sat there for half-an-hour, describing to each other our maladies. I explained to George and William Harris how I felt when I got up in the morning, and William Harris told us how he felt when he went to bed; and George stood on the hearth-rug, and gave us a clever and powerful piece of acting, illustrative of how he felt in the night.

George *fancies* he is ill; but there's never anything really the matter with him, you know.

At this point, Mrs Poppets knocked at the door to know if we were ready for supper. We smiled sadly at one another, and said we supposed we had better try to swallow a bit. Harris said a little something in one's stomach often kept the disease in check; and Mrs Poppets brought the tray in, and we drew up to the table, and toyed with a little steak and onions, and some rhubarb tart.

I must have been very weak at the time; because I know, after the first half-hour or so, I seemed to take no interest whatever in my food—an unusual thing for me—and I didn't want any cheese.

This duty done, we refilled our glasses, lit our pipes, and resumed the discussion upon our state of health. What it was that was actually the matter with us, we none of us could be sure of; but the unanimous opinion was that it—whatever it was—had been brought on by overwork.

'What we want is rest,' said Harris.

'Rest and a complete change,' said George. 'The overstrain upon our brains has produced a general depression throughout the system. Change of scene, and absence of the necessity for thought, will restore the mental equilibrium.'

George has a cousin, who is usually described in the charge-sheet as a medical student, so that he naturally has a somewhat family-physicianary way of putting things.

I agreed with George, and suggested that we should seek out some retired and old-world spot, far from the madding crowd, and dream away a sunny week among its drowsy lanes—some half-forgotten nook, hidden away by the fairies, out of reach of the noisy world—some quaint-perched eyrie on the cliffs of Time, from whence the surging waves of the nineteenth century would sound far-off and faint.

Harris said he thought it would be humpy.* He said he knew the sort of place I meant; where everybody went to bed at eight o'clock, and you couldn't get a *Referee** for love or money, and had to walk ten miles to get your baccy.

'No,' said Harris, 'if you want rest and change, you can't beat a sea trip.'

I objected to the sea trip strongly. A sea trip does you good when you are going to have a couple of months of it, but, for a week, it is wicked.

You start on Monday with the idea implanted in your bosom that you are going to enjoy yourself. You wave an airy adieu to the boys on shore, light your biggest pipe, and swagger about the deck as if you were Captain Cook, Sir Francis Drake, and Christopher Columbus all rolled into one. On Tuesday, you wish you hadn't come. On Wednesday, Thursday, and Friday, you wish you were dead. On Saturday, you are able to swallow a little beef tea, and to sit up on deck, and answer with a wan, sweet smile when kind-hearted people ask you how you feel now. On Sunday, you begin to walk about again, and take solid food. And on Monday morning, as, with your bag and umbrella in your hand, you stand by the gunwale, waiting to step ashore, you begin to thoroughly like it.

I remember my brother-in-law going for a short sea trip once, for the benefit of his health. He took a return berth from London to Liverpool; and when he got to Liverpool, the only thing he was anxious about was to sell that return ticket.

It was offered round the town at a tremendous reduction, so I am told; and was eventually sold for eighteenpence to a bilious-looking youth who had just been advised by his medical men to go to the sea-side, and take exercise.

'Sea-side!' said my brother-in-law, pressing the ticket affection-ately into his hand; 'why, you'll have enough to last you a lifetime; and as for exercise! why, you'll get more exercise, sitting down on that ship, than you would turning somersaults on dry land.'

He himself—my brother-in-law—came back by train. He said the North-Western Railway was healthy enough for him.

Another fellow I knew went for a week's voyage round the coast, and, before they started, the steward came to him to ask whether he would pay for each meal as he had it, or arrange beforehand for the whole series.

The steward recommended the latter course, as it would come so much cheaper. He said they would do him for the whole week at two pounds five. He said for breakfast there would be fish, followed by a grill. Lunch was at one, and consisted of four courses. Dinner at six—soup, fish, entrée, joint, poultry, salad, sweets, cheese, and dessert. And a light meat supper at ten.

My friend thought he would close on the two-pound-five job (he is a hearty eater), and did so.

Lunch came just as they were off Sheerness. He didn't feel so hungry as he thought he should, and so contented himself with a bit of boiled beef, and some strawberries and cream. He pondered a good deal during the afternoon, and at one time it seemed to him that he had been eating nothing but boiled beef for weeks, and at other times it seemed that he must have been living on strawberries and cream for years.

Neither the beef nor the strawberries and cream seemed happy, either—seemed discontented like.

At six, they came and told him dinner was ready. The announce-ment aroused no enthusiasm within him, but he felt that there was some of that two-pound-five to be worked off, and he held on to ropes and things and went down. A pleasant odour of onions and hot ham, mingled with fried fish and greens, greeted him at the bottom of the ladder; and then the steward came up with an oily smile, and said:

'What can I get you, sir?'

'Get me out of this,' was the feeble reply.

And they ran him up quick, and propped him up, over to leeward, and left him.

For the next four days he lived a simple and blameless life on thin captain's biscuits (I mean that the biscuits were thin, not the captain) and soda-water; but, towards Saturday, he got uppish, and went in for weak tea and dry toast, and on Monday he was gorging himself on chicken broth. He left the ship on Tuesday, and as it steamed away from the landing-stage he gazed after it regretfully.

'There she goes,' he said, 'there she goes, with two pounds' worth of food on board that belongs to me, and that I haven't had.'

He said that if they had given him another day he thought he could have put it straight.

So I set my face against the sea trip. Not, as I explained, upon my own account. I was never queer. But I was afraid for George. George said he should be all right, and would rather like it, but he would advise Harris and me not to think of it, as he felt sure we should both be ill. Harris said that, to himself, it was always a mystery how people managed to get sick at sea—said he thought people must do it on purpose, from affectation—said he had often wished to be, but had never been able.

Then he told us anecdotes of how he had gone across the Channel when it was so rough that the passengers had to be tied into their berths, and he and the captain were the only two living souls on board who were not ill. Sometimes it was he and the second mate who were not ill; but it was generally he and one other man. If not he and another man, then it was he by himself.

It is a curious fact, but nobody ever is sea-sick—on land. At sea, you come across plenty of people very bad indeed, whole boat-loads of them; and I never met a man yet, on land, who had ever known at all what it was to be sea-sick. Where the thousands upon thousands of bad sailors that swarm in every ship hide themselves when they are on land is a mystery.

If most men were like a fellow I saw on the Yarmouth boat one day, I could account for the seeming enigma easily enough. It was just off Southend Pier, I recollect, and he was leaning out through one of the port-holes in a very dangerous position. I went up to him to try and save him.

'Hi! come further in,' I said, shaking him by the shoulder. 'You'll be overboard.'

'Oh my! I wish I was,' was the only answer I could get; and there I had to leave him.

Three weeks afterwards, I met him in the coffee-room of a Bath hotel, talking about his voyages, and explaining, with enthusiasm, how he loved the sea.

'Good sailor!' he replied in answer to a mild young man's envious query; 'well, I did feel a little queer *once*, I confess. It was off Cape Horn. The vessel was wrecked the next morning.'

I said:

'Weren't you a little shaky by Southend Pier one day, and wanted to be thrown overboard?'

'Southend Pier!' he replied, with a puzzled expression.

'Yes; going down to Yarmouth, last Friday three weeks.'

'Oh, ah—yes,' he answered, brightening up; 'I remember now. I did have a headache that afternoon. It was the pickles, you know. They were the most disgraceful pickles I ever tasted in a respectable boat. Did *you* have any?'

For myself, I have discovered an excellent preventive against sea-sickness, in balancing myself. You stand in the centre of the deck, and, as the ship heaves and pitches, you move your body about, so as to keep it always straight. When the front of the ship rises, you lean forward, till the deck almost touches your nose; and when its back end gets up, you lean backwards. This is all very well for an hour or two; but you can't balance yourself for a week.

George said:

'Let's go up the river.'

He said we should have fresh air, exercise and quiet; the constant change of scene would occupy our minds (including what there was of Harris's); and the hard work would give us a good appetite, and make us sleep well.

Harris said he didn't think George ought to do anything that would have a tendency to make him sleepier than he always was, as it might be dangerous. He said he didn't very well understand how George was going to sleep any more than he did now, seeing that there were only twenty-four hours in each day, summer and winter alike; but thought that if he *did* sleep any more, he might just as well be dead, and so save his board and lodging.

Harris said, however, that the river would suit him to a 'T.' I don't know what a 'T' is (except a sixpenny one, which includes bread-and-butter and cake *ad lib.*, and is cheap at the price, if you haven't had any dinner). It seems to suit everybody, however, which is greatly to its credit.

It suited me to a 'T' too, and Harris and I both said it was a good idea of George's; and we said it in a tone that seemed to somehow imply that we were surprised that George should have come out so sensible.

The only one who was not struck with the suggestion was Montmorency. He never did care for the river, did Montmorency.

'It's all very well for you fellows,' he says; 'you like it, but *I* don't. There's nothing for me to do. Scenery is not in my line, and I don't smoke. If I see a rat, you won't stop; and if I go to sleep, you get fooling about with the boat, and slop me overboard. If you ask me, I call the whole thing bally foolishness.'

We were three to one, however, and the motion was carried.

CHAPTER II

Plans discussed—Pleasures of 'camping-out,' on fine nights—Ditto, wet nights—Compromise decided on—Montmorency, first impressions of—Fears lest he is too good for this world, fears subsequently dismissed as groundless—Meeting adjourns.

WE pulled out the maps, and discussed plans.

We arranged to start on the following Saturday from Kingston. Harris and I would go down in the morning, and take the boat up to Chertsey, and George, who would not be able to get away from the City till the afternoon (George goes to sleep at a bank from ten to four each day, except Saturdays, when they wake him up and put him outside at two), would meet us there.

Should we 'camp out' or sleep at inns?

George and I were for camping out. We said it would be so wild and free, so patriarchal like.

Slowly the golden memory of the dead sun fades from the hearts of the cold, sad clouds. Silent, like sorrowing children, the birds have ceased their song, and only the moorhen's plaintive cry and the harsh croak of the corncrake stirs the awed hush around the couch of waters, where the dying day breathes out her last.

From the dim woods on either bank, Night's ghostly army, the grey shadows, creep out with noiseless tread to chase away the lingering rearguard of the light, and pass, with noiseless, unseen feet, above the waving river-grass, and through the sighing rushes; and Night, upon her sombre throne, folds her black wings above the darkening world, and, from her phantom palace, lit by the pale stars, reigns in stillness.

Then we run our little boat into some quiet nook, and the tent is pitched, and the frugal supper cooked and eaten. Then the big pipes are filled and lighted, and the pleasant chat goes round in musical undertone; while, in the pauses of our talk, the river, playing round the boat, prattles strange old tales and secrets, sings low the old child's song that it has sung so many thousand years—will sing so many thousand years to come, before its voice grows harsh and old—a song that we, who have learnt to love its changing face, who have so often nestled on its yielding bosom, think, somehow, we understand, though we could not tell you in mere words the story that we listen to.

And we sit there, by its margin, while the moon, who loves it too, stoops down to kiss it with a sister's kiss, and throws her silver arms around it clingingly; and we watch it as it flows, ever singing, ever whispering, out to meet its king, the sea—till our voices die away in silence, and the pipes go out—till we, common-place, everyday young men enough, feel strangely full of thoughts, half sad, half sweet, and do not care or want to speak—till we laugh, and, rising, knock the ashes from our burnt-out pipes, and say 'Good-night,' and, lulled by the lapping water and the rustling trees, we fall asleep beneath the great, still stars, and dream that the world is young again—young and sweet as she used to be ere the centuries of fret and care had furrowed her fair face, ere her children's sins and follies had made old her loving heart—sweet as she was in those bygone days when, a new-made mother, she nursed us, her children, upon her own deep breast—ere the wiles of painted civilization had lured us away from her fond arms, and the poisoned sneers of artificiality had made us ashamed of the simple life we led with her, and the simple, stately home where mankind was born so many thousands years ago.

Harris said:

'How about when it rained?'

You can never rouse Harris. There is no poetry about Harris—no wild yearning for the unattainable. Harris never 'weeps, he knows not why.' If Harris's eyes fill with tears, you can bet it is because Harris has been eating raw onions, or has put too much Worcester over his chop.

If you were to stand at night by the sea-shore with Harris, and say:

'Hark! do you not hear? Is it but the mermaids singing deep below the waving waters; or sad spirits, chanting dirges for white corpses, held by seaweed?' Harris would take you by the arm, and say:

'I know what it is, old man; you've got a chill. Now, you come along with me. I know a place round the corner here, where you can get a drop of the finest Scotch whisky you ever tasted—put you right in less than no time.'

Harris always does know a place round the corner where you can get something brilliant in the drinking line. I believe that if you met Harris up in Paradise (supposing such a thing likely), he would immediately greet you with:

'So glad you've come, old fellow; I've found a nice place round the corner here, where you can get some really first-class nectar.'

In the present instance, however, as regarded the camping out, his practical view of the matter came as a very timely hint. Camping out in rainy weather is not pleasant.

It is evening. You are wet through, and there is a good two inches of water in the boat, and all the things are damp. You find a place on the banks that is not quite so puddly as other places you have seen, and you land and lug out the tent, and two of you proceed to fix it.

It is soaked and heavy, and it flops about, and tumbles down on you, and clings round your head and makes you mad. The rain is pouring steadily down all the time. It is difficult enough to fix a tent in dry weather: in wet, the task becomes herculean. Instead of helping you, it seems to you that the other man is simply playing the fool. Just as you get your side beautifully fixed, he gives it a hoist from his end, and spoils it all.

'Here! what are you up to?' you call out.

'What are *you* up to?' he retorts; 'leggo, can't you?'

'Don't pull it; you've got it all wrong, you stupid ass!' you shout.

'No, I haven't,' he yells back; 'let go your side!'

'I tell you you've got it all wrong!' you roar, wishing that you could get at him; and you give your ropes a lug that pulls all his pegs out.

'Ah, the bally idiot!' you hear him mutter to himself; and then comes a savage haul, and away goes your side. You lay down the mallet and start to go round and tell him what you think about the whole business, and, at the same time, he starts round in the same direction to come and explain his views to you. And you follow each other round and round, swearing at one another, until the tent tumbles down in a heap, and leaves you looking at each other across its ruins, then you both indignantly exclaim, in the same breath:

'There you are! what did I tell you?'

Meanwhile the third man, who has been baling out the boat, and who has spilled the water down his sleeve, and has been cursing away to himself steadily for the last ten minutes, wants to know what the thundering blazes you're playing at, and why the blarmed tent isn't up yet.

At last, somehow or other, it does get up, and you land the things. It is hopeless attempting to make a wood fire, so you light the methylated spirit stove, and crowd round that.

Rainwater is the chief article of diet at supper. The bread is two-thirds rainwater, the beefsteak-pie is exceedingly rich in it, and the jam, and the butter, and the salt, and the coffee have all combined with it to make soup.

After supper, you find your tobacco is damp, and you cannot smoke. Luckily you have a bottle of the stuff that cheers and inebriates, if taken in proper quantity, and this restores to you sufficient interest in life to induce you to go to bed.

There you dream that an elephant has suddenly sat down on your chest, and that the volcano has exploded and thrown you down to the bottom of the sea—the elephant still sleeping peacefully on your bosom. You wake up and grasp the idea that something terrible really has happened. Your first impression is that the end of the world has come; and then you think that this cannot be, and that it is thieves and murderers, or else fire, and this opinion you express in the usual method. No help comes, however, and all you know is that thousands of people are kicking you, and you are being smothered.

Somebody else seems in trouble, too. You can hear his faint cries coming from underneath your bed. Determining, at all events, to sell your life dearly, you struggle frantically, hitting out right and left with arms and legs, and yelling lustily the while, and at last something gives way, and you find your head in the fresh air. Two feet off, you dimly observe a half-dressed ruffian, waiting to kill you, and you are preparing for a life-and-death struggle with him, when it begins to dawn upon you that it's Jim.

'Oh, it's you, is it?' he says, recognising you at the same moment.

'Yes,' you answer, rubbing your eyes; 'what's happened?'

'Bally tent's blown down, I think,' he says. 'Where's Bill?'

Then you both raise up your voices and shout for 'Bill!' and the ground beneath you heaves and rocks, and the muffled voice that you heard before replies from out the ruin:

'Get off my head, can't you?'

And Bill struggles out, a muddy, trampled wreck, and in an unnecessarily aggressive mood—he being under the evident belief that the whole thing has been done on purpose.

In the morning you are all three speechless, owing to having caught severe colds in the night; you also feel very quarrelsome, and you swear at each other in hoarse whispers during the whole of breakfast time.

We therefore decided that we would sleep out on fine nights; and hotel it, and inn it, and pub. it, like respectable folks, when it was wet, or when we felt inclined for a change.

Montmorency hailed this compromise with much approval. He does not revel in romantic solitude. Give him something noisy; and if a trifle low, so much the jollier. To look at Montmorency you would imagine that he was an angel sent upon the earth, for some reason withheld from mankind, in the shape of a small fox-terrier. There is a sort of Oh-what-a-wicked-world-this-is-and-how-I-wish-I-could-do-something-to-make-it-better-and-nobler expression about Montmorency that has been known to bring the tears into the eyes of pious old ladies and gentlemen.

When first he came to live at my expense, I never thought I should be able to get him to stop long. I used to sit down and look at him, as he sat on the rug and looked up at me, and think: 'Oh, that dog will never live. He will be snatched up to the bright skies in a chariot, that is what will happen to him.'

But, when I had paid for about a dozen chickens that he had killed; and had dragged him, growling and kicking, by the scruff of his neck, out of a hundred and fourteen street fights; and had had a dead cat brought round for my inspection by an irate female, who called me a murderer; and had been summoned by the man next door but one for having a ferocious dog at large, that had kept him pinned up in his own tool-shed, afraid to venture his nose outside the door for over two hours on a cold night; and had learned that the gardener, unknown to myself, had won thirty shillings by backing him to kill rats against time, then I began to think that maybe they'd let him remain on earth for a bit longer, after all.

To hang about a stable, and collect a gang of the most disreputable dogs to be found in the town, and lead them out to march round the slums to fight other disreputable dogs, is Montmorency's idea of 'life;' and so, as I before observed, he gave to the suggestion of inns, and pubs., and hotels his most emphatic approbation.

Having thus settled the sleeping arrangements to the satisfaction of all four of us, the only thing left to discuss was what we should take with us; and this we had begun to argue, when Harris said he'd had enough oratory for one night, and proposed that we should go out and have a smile, saying that he had found a place, round by the square, where you could really get a drop of Irish worth drinking.

George said he felt thirsty (I never knew George when he didn't); and, as I had a presentiment that a little whisky, warm, with a slice of lemon, would do my complaint good, the debate was, by common assent, adjourned to the following night; and the assembly put on its hats and went out.

CHAPTER III

Arrangements settled—Harris's method of doing work—How the elderly, family-man puts up a picture—George makes a sensible remark —Delights of early morning bathing—Provisions for getting upset.

So, on the following evening, we again assembled, to discuss and arrange our plans. Harris said:

'Now, the first thing to settle is what to take with us. Now, you get a bit of paper and write down, J., and you get the grocery catalogue, George, and somebody give me a bit of pencil, and then I'll make out a list.'

That's Harris all over—so ready to take the burden of everything himself, and put it on the backs of other people.

He always reminds me of my poor Uncle Podger. You never saw such a commotion up and down a house, in all your life, as when my Uncle Podger undertook to do a job. A picture would have come home from the frame-maker's, and be standing in the dining-room, waiting to be put up; and Aunt Podger would ask what was to be done with it, and Uncle Podger would say:

'Oh, you leave that to *me*. Don't you, any of you, worry yourselves about that. *I'll* do all that.'

And then he would take off his coat, and begin. He would send the girl out for sixpen'orth of nails, and then one of the boys after her to tell her what size to get; and, from that, he would gradually work down, and start the whole house.

'Now you go and get me my hammer, Will,' he would shout; 'and you bring me the rule, Tom; and I shall want the step-ladder, and I had better have a kitchen-chair, too; and, Jim! you run round to Mr Goggles, and tell him, "Pa's kind regards, and hopes his leg's better; and will he lend him his spirit-level?" And don't you go, Maria, because I shall want somebody to hold me the light; and when the girl comes back, she must go out again for a bit of picture-cord; and Tom!—where's Tom?—Tom, you come here; I shall want you to hand me up the picture.'

And then he would lift up the picture, and drop it, and it would come out of the frame, and he would try to save the glass, and cut himself; and then he would spring round the room, looking for his handkerchief. He could not find his handkerchief, because it was in the pocket of the coat he had taken off, and he did not know where he had put the coat, and all the house had to leave off looking for his tools, and start looking for his coat; while he would dance round and hinder them.

'Doesn't anybody in the whole house know where my coat is? I never came across such a set in all my life—upon my word I didn't. Six of you!—and you can't find a coat that I put down not five minutes ago! Well, of all the——'

Then he'd get up, and find that he had been sitting on it, and would call out:

'Oh, you can give it up! I've found it myself now. Might just as well ask the cat to find anything as expect you people to find it.'

And, when half an hour had been spent in tying up his finger, and a new glass had been got, and the tools, and the ladder, and the chair, and the candle had been brought, he would have another go, the whole family, including the girl and the charwoman, standing round in a semi-circle, ready to help. Two people would have to hold the chair, and a third would help him up on it, and hold him there, and a fourth would hand him a nail, and a fifth would pass him up the hammer, and he would take hold of the nail, and drop it.

'There!' he would say, in an injured tone, 'now the nail's gone.'

And we would all have to go down on our knees and grovel for it, while he would stand on the chair, and grunt, and want to know if he was to be kept there all evening.

The nail would be found at last, but by that time he would have lost the hammer.

'Where's the hammer? What did I do with the hammer? Great heavens! Seven of you, gaping round there, and you don't know what I did with the hammer!'

We would find the hammer for him, and then he would have lost sight of the mark he had made on the wall, where the nail was to go in, and each of us had to get up on the chair, beside him, and see if we could find it; and we would each discover it in a different place, and he would call us all fools, one after another, and tell us to get down. And he would take the rule, and re-measure, and find that he wanted half thirty-one and three-eighths inches from the corner, and would try to do it in his head, and go mad.

And we would all try to do it in our heads, and all arrive at different results, and sneer at one another. And in the general row, the original number would be forgotten, and Uncle Podger would have to measure it again.

He would use a bit of string this time, and at the critical moment, when the old fool was leaning over the chair at an angle of forty-five, and trying to reach a point three inches beyond what was possible for him to reach, the string would slip, and down he would slide on to the piano, a really fine musical effect being produced by the suddenness with which his head and body struck all the notes at the same time.

And Aunt Maria would say that she would not allow the children to stand round and hear such language.

At last, Uncle Podger would get the spot fixed again, and put the point of the nail on it with his left hand, and take the hammer in his right hand. And, with the first blow, he would smash his thumb, and drop the hammer, with a yell, on somebody's toes.

Aunt Maria would mildly observe that, next time Uncle Podger was going to hammer a nail into the wall, she hoped he'd let her know in time, so that she could make arrangements to go and spend a week with her mother while it was being done.

'Oh! you women, you make such a fuss over everything,' Uncle Podger would reply, picking himself up. 'Why, I *like* doing a little job of this sort.'

And then he would have another try, and, at the second blow, the nail would go clean through the plaster, and half the hammer after it, and Uncle Podger be precipitated against the wall with force nearly sufficient to flatten his nose.

Then we had to find the rule and the string again, and a new hole was made; and, about midnight, the picture would be up—very crooked and insecure, the wall for yards round looking as if it had been smoothed down with a rake, and everybody dead beat and wretched—except Uncle Podger.

'There you are,' he would say, stepping heavily off the chair on to the charwoman's corns, and surveying the mess he had made with evident pride. 'Why, some people would have had a man in to do a little thing like that!'

Harris will be just that sort of man when he grows up, I know, and I told him so. I said I could not permit him to take so much labour upon himself. I said:

'No; *you* get the paper, and the pencil, and the catalogue, and George write down, and I'll do the work.'

The first list we made out had to be discarded. It was clear that the upper reaches of the Thames would not allow of the navigation of a boat sufficiently large to take the things we had set down as indispensable; so we tore the list up, and looked at one another!

George said:

'You know we are on a wrong track altogether. We must not think of the things we could do with, but only of the things that we can't do without.'

George comes out really quite sensible at times. You'd be surprised. I call that downright wisdom, not merely as regards the present case, but with reference to our trip up the river of life, generally. How many people, on that voyage, load up the boat till it is ever in danger of swamping with a store of foolish things which they think essential to the pleasure and comfort of the trip, but which are really only useless lumber.

How they pile the poor little craft mast-high with fine clothes and big houses; with useless servants, and a host of swell friends that do not care twopence for them, and that they do not care three ha'pence for; with expensive entertainments that nobody enjoys, with formalities and fashions, with pretence and ostentation, and with—oh, heaviest, maddest lumber of all!—the dread of what will my neighbour think, with luxuries that only cloy, with pleasures that bore, with empty show that, like the criminal's iron crown of yore, makes to bleed and swoon the aching head that wears it!

It is lumber, man—all lumber! Throw it overboard. It makes the boat so heavy to pull, you nearly faint at the oars. It makes it so cumbersome and dangerous to manage, you never know a moment's freedom from anxiety and care, never gain a moment's rest for dreamy laziness—no time to watch the windy shadows skimming lightly o'er the shallows, or the glittering sunbeams flitting in and out among the ripples, or the great trees by the margin looking down at their own image, or the woods all green and golden, or the lilies white and yellow, or the sombre-waving rushes, or the sedges, or the orchis, or the blue forget-me-nots.

Throw the lumber over, man! Let your boat of life be light, packed with only what you need—a homely home and simple pleasures, one or two friends, worth the name, someone to love and someone to love you, a cat, a dog, and a pipe or two, enough to eat and enough to wear, and a little more than enough to drink; for thirst is a dangerous thing.

You will find the boat easier to pull then, and it will not be so liable to upset, and it will not matter so much if it does upset; good, plain merchandise will stand water. You will have time to think as well as to work. Time to drink in life's sunshine—time to listen to the Æolian music that the wind of God draws from the human heart-strings around us—time to——

I beg your pardon, really. I quite forgot.

Well, we left the list to George, and he began it.

'We won't take a tent,' suggested George; 'we will have a boat with a cover. It is ever so much simpler, and more comfortable.'

It seemed a good thought, and we adopted it. I do not know whether you have ever seen the thing I mean. You fix iron hoops up over the boat, and stretch a huge canvas over them, and fasten it down all round, from stem to stern, and it converts the boat into a sort of little house, and it is beautifully cosy, though a trifle stuffy; but there, everything has its drawbacks, as the man said when his mother-in-law died, and they came down upon him for the funeral expenses.

George said that in that case we must take a rug each, a lamp, some soap, a brush and comb (between us), a toothbrush (each), a basin, some tooth-powder, some shaving tackle (sounds like a French exercise, doesn't it?), and a couple of big towels for bathing. I notice that people always make gigantic arrangements for bathing when they are going anywhere near the water, but that they don't bathe much when they are there.

It is the same when you go to the sea-side. I always determine —when thinking over the matter in London—that I'll get up early every morning, and go and have a dip before breakfast, and I religiously pack up a pair of drawers and a bath towel. I always get red bathing drawers. I rather fancy myself in red drawers. They suit my complexion so. But when I get to the sea I don't feel somehow that I want that early morning bathe nearly so much as I did when I was in town.

On the contrary, I feel more that I want to stop in bed till the last moment, and then come down and have my breakfast. Once or twice virtue has triumphed, and I have got out at six and half-dressed myself, and have taken my drawers and towel, and stumbled dismally off. But I haven't enjoyed it. They seem to keep a specially cutting east wind, waiting for me, when I go to bathe in the early morning; and they pick out all the three-cornered stones, and put them on the top, and they sharpen up the rocks and cover the points over with a bit of sand so that I can't see them, and they take the sea and put it two miles out, so that I have to huddle myself up in my arms and hop, shivering, through six inches of water. And when I do get to the sea, it is rough and quite insulting.

One huge wave catches me up and chucks me in a sitting posture, as hard as ever it can, down on to a rock which has been put there for me. And, before I've said 'Oh! Ugh!' and found out what has gone, the wave comes back and carries me out to mid-ocean. I begin to strike out frantically for the shore, and wonder if I shall ever see home and friends again, and wish I'd been kinder to my little sister when a boy (when *I* was a boy, I mean). Just when I have given up all hope, a wave retires and leaves me sprawling like a star-fish on the sand, and I get up and look back and find that I've been swimming for my life in two feet of water. I hop back and dress, and crawl home, where I have to pretend I liked it.

In the present instance, we all talked as if we were going to have a long swim every morning. George said it was so pleasant to wake up in the boat in the fresh morning, and plunge into the limpid river. Harris said there was nothing like a swim before breakfast to give you an appetite. He said it always gave him an appetite. George said that if it was going to make Harris eat more than Harris ordinarily ate, then he should protest against Harris having a bath at all.

He said there would be quite enough hard work in towing sufficient food for Harris up against stream, as it was.

I urged upon George, however, how much pleasanter it would be to have Harris clean and fresh about the boat, even if we did have to take a few more hundredweight of provisions; and he got to see it in my light, and withdrew his opposition to Harris's bath.

Agreed, finally, that we should take *three* bath towels, so as not to keep each other waiting.

For clothes, George said two suits of flannel would be sufficient, as we could wash them ourselves, in the river, when they got dirty. We asked him if he had ever tried washing flannels in the river, and he replied: 'No, not exactly himself like; but he knew some fellows who had, and it was easy enough'; and Harris and I were weak enough to fancy he knew what he was talking about, and that three respectable young men, without position or influence, and with no experience in washing, could really clean their own shirts and trousers in the river Thames with a bit of soap.

We were to learn in the days to come, when it was too late, that George was a miserable impostor, who could evidently have known nothing whatever about the matter. If you had seen these clothes after—but, as the shilling shockers* say, we anticipate.

George impressed upon us to take a change of under-things and plenty of socks, in case we got upset and wanted a change; also plenty of handkerchiefs, as they would do to wipe things, and a pair of leather boots as well as our boating shoes, as we should want them if we got upset.

CHAPTER IV

The food question—Objections to paraffin oil as an atmosphere—Advantages of cheese as a travelling companion—A married woman deserts her home—Further provision for getting upset—I pack—Cussedness of tooth-brushes—George and Harris pack—Awful behaviour of Montmorency—We retire to rest.

THEN we discussed the food question.

George said:

'Begin with breakfast.' (George is so practical.) 'Now for breakfast we shall want a frying-pan'—(Harris said it was indigestible; but we merely urged him not to be an ass, and George went on)—'a tea-pot and a kettle, and a methylated spirit stove.'

'No oil,' said George, with a significant look; and Harris and I agreed.

We had taken up an oil-stove once, but 'never again.' It had been like living in an oil-shop that week. It oozed. I never saw such a thing as paraffin oil is to ooze. We kept it in the nose of the boat, and, from there, it oozed down to the rudder, impregnating the whole boat and everything in it on its way, and it oozed over the river, and saturated the scenery and spoilt the atmosphere. Sometimes a westerly oily wind blew, and at other times an easterly oily wind, and sometimes it blew a northerly oily wind, and maybe a southerly oily wind; but whether it came from the Arctic snows, or was raised in the waste of the desert sands, it came alike to us laden with the fragrance of paraffin oil.

And that oil oozed up and ruined the sunset; and as for the moonbeams, they positively reeked of paraffin.

We tried to get away from it at Marlow. We left the boat by the bridge, and took a walk through the town to escape it, but it followed us. The whole town was full of oil. We passed through the church-yard, and it seemed as if the people had been buried in oil. The High Street stunk of oil; we wondered how people could live in it. And we walked miles upon miles out Birmingham way; but it was no use, the country was steeped in oil.

At the end of that trip we met together at midnight in a lonely field, under a blasted oak, and took an awful oath (we had been swearing for a whole week about the thing in an ordinary, middle-class way, but this was a swell affair)—an awful oath never to take paraffin oil with us in a boat again—except, of course, in case of sickness.

Therefore, in the present instance, we confined ourselves to methylated spirit. Even that is bad enough. You get methylated pie and methylated cake. But methylated spirit is more wholesome when taken into the system in large quantities than paraffin oil.

For other breakfast things, George suggested eggs and bacon, which were easy to cook, cold meat, tea, bread and butter, and jam. For lunch, he said, he could have biscuits, cold meat, bread and butter, and jam—but *no cheese*. Cheese, like oil, makes too much of itself. It wants the whole boat to itself. It goes through the hamper, and gives a cheesy flavour to everything else there. You can't tell whether you are eating apple-pie or German sausage, or strawberries and cream. It all seems cheese. There is too much odour about cheese.

I remember a friend of mine, buying a couple of cheeses at Liverpool. Splendid cheeses they were, ripe and mellow, and with a two hundred horse-power scent about them that might have been warranted to carry three miles, and knock a man over at two hundred yards. I was in Liverpool at the time, and my friend said that if I didn't mind he would get me to take them back with me to London, as he should not be coming up for a day or two himself, and he did not think the cheeses ought to be kept much longer.

'Oh, with pleasure, dear boy,' I replied, 'with pleasure.'

I called for the cheeses, and took them away in a cab. It was a ramshackle affair, dragged along by a knock-kneed, broken-winded somnambulist, which his owner, in a moment of enthusiasm, during conversation, referred to as a horse. I put the cheeses on the top, and we started off at a shamble that would have done credit to the swiftest steam-roller ever built, and all went merry as a funeral bell, until we turned the corner. There, the wind carried a whiff from the cheeses full on to our steed. It woke him up, and, with a snort of terror, he dashed off at three miles an hour. The wind still blew in his direction, and before we reached the end of the street he was laying himself out at the rate of nearly four miles an hour, leaving the cripples and stout old ladies simply nowhere.

It took two porters as well as the driver to hold him in at the station; and I do not think they would have done it, even then, had not one of the men had the presence of mind to put a handkerchief over his nose, and to light a bit of brown paper.

I took my ticket, and marched proudly up the platform, with my cheeses, the people falling back respectfully on either side. The train was crowded, and I had to get into a carriage where there were already seven other people. One crusty old gentleman objected, but I got in, notwithstanding; and, putting my cheeses upon the rack, squeezed down with a pleasant smile, and said it was a warm day. A few moments passed, and then the old gentleman began to fidget.

'Very close in here,' he said.

'Quite oppressive,' said the man next to him.

And then they both began sniffing, and, at the third sniff, they caught it right on the chest, and rose up without another word and went out. And then a stout lady got up, and said it was disgraceful that a respectable married woman should be harried about in this way, and gathered up a bag and eight parcels and went. The remaining four passengers sat on for a while, until a solemn-looking man in the corner, who, from his dress and general appearance, seemed to belong to the undertaker class, said it put him in mind of dead baby; and the other three passengers tried to get out of the door at the same time, and hurt themselves.

I smiled at the black gentleman, and said I thought we were going to have the carriage to ourselves; and he laughed pleasantly, and said that some people made such a fuss over a little thing. But even he grew strangely depressed after we had started, and so, when we reached Crewe, I asked him to come and have a drink. He accepted, and we forced our way into the buffet, where we yelled, and stamped, and waved our umbrellas for a quarter of an hour; and then a young lady came, and asked us if we wanted anything.

'What's yours?' I said, turning to my friend.

'I'll have half-a-crown's worth of brandy, neat, if you please, miss,' he responded.

And he went off quietly after he had drunk it and got into another carriage, which I thought mean.

From Crewe I had the compartment to myself, though the train was crowded. As we drew up at the different stations, the people, seeing my empty carriage, would rush for it. 'Here y' are, Maria; come along, plenty of room.' 'All right, Tom; we'll get in here,' they would shout. And they would run along, carrying heavy bags, and fight round the door to get in first. And one would open the door and mount the steps, and stagger back into the arms of the man behind him; and they would all come and have a sniff, and then droop off and squeeze into other carriages, or pay the difference and go first.

From Euston, I took the cheeses down to my friend's house. When his wife came into the room she smelt round for an instant. Then she said:

'What is it? Tell me the worst.'

I said:

'It's cheeses. Tom bought them in Liverpool, and asked me to bring them up with me.'

And I added that I hoped she understood that it had nothing to do with me; and she said that she was sure of that, but that she would speak to Tom about it when he came back.

My friend was detained in Liverpool longer than he expected; and, three days later, as he hadn't returned home, his wife called on me. She said:

'What did Tom say about those cheeses?'

I replied that he had directed they were to be kept in a moist place, and that nobody was to touch them.

She said:

'Nobody's likely to touch them. Had he smelt them?'

I thought he had, and added that he seemed greatly attached to them.

'You think he would be upset,' she queried, 'if I gave a man a sovereign to take them away and bury them?'

I answered that I thought he would never smile again.

An idea struck her. She said:

'Do you mind keeping them for him? Let me send them round to you.'

'Madam,' I replied, 'for myself I like the smell of cheese, and the journey the other day with them from Liverpool I shall ever look back upon as a happy ending to a pleasant holiday. But, in this world, we must consider others. The lady under whose roof I have the honour of residing is a widow, and, for all I know, possibly an orphan too. She has a strong, I may say an eloquent, objection to being what she terms "put upon." The presence of your husband's cheeses in her house she would, I instinctively feel, regard as a "put upon"; and it shall never be said that I put upon the widow and the orphan.'

'Very well, then,' said my friend's wife, rising, 'all I have to say is, that I shall take the children and go to an hotel until those cheeses are eaten. I decline to live any longer in the same house with them.'

She kept her word, leaving the place in charge of the charwoman, who, when asked if she could stand the smell, replied, 'What smell?' and who, when taken close to the cheeses and told to sniff hard, said she could detect a faint odour of melons. It was argued from this that little injury could result to the woman from the atmosphere, and she was left.

The hotel bill came to fifteen guineas;* and my friend, after reckoning everything up, found that the cheeses had cost him eight-and-sixpence* a pound. He said he dearly loved a bit of cheese, but it was beyond his means; so he determined to get rid of them. He threw them into the canal; but had to fish them out again, as the bargemen complained. They said it made them feel quite faint. And, after that, he took them one dark night and left them in the parish mortuary. But the coroner discovered them, and made a fearful fuss.

He said it was a plot to deprive him of his living by waking up the corpses.

My friend got rid of them, at last, by taking them down to a seaside town, and burying them on the beach. It gained the place quite a reputation. Visitors said they had never noticed before how strong the air was, and weak-chested and consumptive people used to throng there for years afterwards.

Fond as I am of cheese, therefore, I hold that George was right in declining to take any.

'We shan't want any tea,' said George (Harris's face fell at this); 'but we'll have a good round, square, slap-up meal at seven—dinner, tea, and supper combined.'

Harris grew more cheerful. George suggested meat and fruit pies, cold meat, tomatoes, fruit, and green stuff. For drink, we took some wonderful sticky concoction of Harris's, which you mixed with water and called lemonade, plenty of tea, and a bottle of whisky, in case, as George said, we got upset.

It seemed to me that George harped too much on the getting-upset idea. It seemed to me the wrong spirit to go about the trip in.

But I'm glad we took the whisky.

We didn't take beer or wine. They are a mistake up the river. They make you feel sleepy and heavy. A glass in the evening when you are doing a mouch round the town and looking at the girls is all right enough; but don't drink when the sun is blazing down on your head, and you've got hard work to do.

We made a list of the things to be taken, and a pretty lengthy one it was, before we parted that evening. The next day, which was Friday, we got them all together, and met in the evening to pack. We got a big Gladstone* for the clothes, and a couple of hampers for the victuals and the cooking utensils. We moved the table up against the window, piled everything in a heap in the middle of the floor, and sat round and looked at it.

I said I'd pack.

I rather pride myself on my packing. Packing is one of those many things that I feel I know more about than any other person living. (It surprises me myself, sometimes, how many of these subjects there are.) I impressed the fact upon George and Harris, and told them that they had better leave the whole matter entirely to me. They fell into the suggestion with a readiness that had something uncanny about it. George put on a pipe and spread himself over the easy-chair, and Harris cocked his legs on the table and lit a cigar.

This was hardly what I intended. What I had meant, of course, was, that I should boss the job, and that Harris and George should potter about under my directions, I pushing them aside every now and then with, 'Oh, you——!' 'Here, let me do it.' 'There you are, simple enough!'—really teaching them, as you might say. Their taking it in the way they did irritated me. There is nothing does irritate me more than seeing other people sitting about doing nothing when I'm working.

I lived with a man once who used to make me mad that way. He would loll on the sofa and watch me doing things by the hour together, following me round the room with his eyes, wherever I went. He said it did him real good to look on at me, messing about. He said it made him feel that life was not an idle dream to be gaped and yawned through, but a noble task, full of duty and stern work. He said he often wondered now how he could have gone on before he met me, never having anybody to look at while they worked.

Now, I'm not like that. I can't sit still and see another man slaving and working. I want to get up and superintend, and walk round with my hands in my pockets, and tell him what to do. It is my energetic nature. I can't help it.

However, I did not say anything, but started the packing. It seemed a longer job than I had thought it was going to be; but I got the bag finished at last, and I sat on it and strapped it.

'Ain't you going to put the boots in?' said Harris.

And I looked round, and found I had forgotten them. That's just like Harris. He couldn't have said a word until I'd got the bag shut and strapped, of course. And George laughed—one of those irritating, senseless, chuckle-headed, crack-jawed laughs of his. They do make me so wild.

I opened the bag and packed the boots in; and then, just as I was going to close it, a horrible idea occurred to me. Had I packed my tooth-brush? I don't know how it is, but I never do know whether I've packed my tooth-brush.

My tooth-brush is a thing that haunts me when I'm travelling, and makes my life a misery. I dream that I haven't packed it, and wake up in a cold perspiration, and get out of bed and hunt for it. And, in the morning, I pack it before I have used it, and have to unpack again to get it, and it is always the last thing I turn out of the bag; and then I repack and forget it, and have to rush upstairs for it at the last moment and carry it to the railway station, wrapped up in my pocket-handkerchief.

Of course I had to turn every mortal thing out now, and, of course, I could not find it. I rummaged the things up into much the same state that they must have been before the world was created, and when chaos reigned. Of course, I found George's and Harris's eighteen times over, but I couldn't find my own. I put the things back one by one, and held everything up and shook it. Then I found it inside a boot. I repacked once more.

When I had finished, George asked if the soap was in. I said I didn't care a hang whether the soap was in or whether it wasn't; and I slammed the bag to and strapped it, and found that I had packed my tobacco-pouch in it, and had to re-open it. It got shut up finally at 10.5 p.m., and then there remained the hampers to do. Harris said that we should be wanting to start in less than twelve hours' time, and thought that he and George had better do the rest; and I agreed and sat down, and they had a go.

They began in a light-hearted spirit, evidently intending to show me how to do it. I made no comment; I only waited. When George is hanged, Harris will be the worst packer in this world; and I looked at the piles of plates and cups, and kettles, and bottles and jars, and pies, and stoves, and cakes, and tomatoes, &c., and felt that the thing would soon become exciting.

It did. They started with breaking a cup. That was the first thing they did. They did that just to show you what they *could* do, and to get you interested.

Then Harris packed the strawberry jam on top of a tomato and squashed it, and they had to pick out the tomato with a teaspoon.

And then it was George's turn, and he trod on the butter. I didn't say anything, but I came over and sat on the edge of the table and watched them. It irritated them more than anything I could have said. I felt that. It made them nervous and excited, and they stepped on things, and put things behind them, and then couldn't find them when they wanted them; and they packed the pies at the bottom, and put heavy things on top, and smashed the pies in.

They upset salt over everything, and as for the butter! I never saw two men do more with one-and-twopence worth of butter in my whole life than they did. After George had got it off his slipper, they tried to put it in the kettle. It wouldn't go in, and what *was* in wouldn't come out. They did scrape it out at last, and put it down on a chair, and Harris sat on it, and it stuck to him, and they went looking for it all over the room.

'I'll take my oath I put it down on that chair,' said George, staring at the empty seat.

'I saw you do it myself, not a minute ago,' said Harris.

Then they started round the room again looking for it; and then they met again in the centre, and stared at one another.

'Most extraordinary thing I ever heard of,' said George.

'So mysterious!' said Harris.

Then George got round at the back of Harris and saw it.

'Why, here it is all the time,' he exclaimed, indignantly.

'Where?' cried Harris, spinning round.

'Stand still, can't you!' roared George, flying after him.

And they got it off, and packed it in the teapot.

Montmorency was in it all, of course. Montmorency's ambition in life, is to get in the way and be sworn at. If he can squirm in anywhere where he particularly is not wanted, and be a perfect nuisance, and make people mad, and have things thrown at his head, then he feels his day has not been wasted.

To get somebody to stumble over him, and curse him steadily for an hour, is his highest aim and object; and, when he has succeeded in accomplishing this, his conceit becomes quite unbearable.

He came and sat down on things, just when they were wanted to be packed; and he laboured under the fixed belief that, whenever Harris or George reached out their hand for anything, it was his cold, damp nose that they wanted. He put his leg into the jam, and he worried the teaspoons, and he pretended that the lemons were rats, and got into the hamper and killed three of them before Harris could land him with the frying-pan.

Harris said I encouraged him. I didn't encourage him. A dog like that don't want any encouragement. It's the natural, original sin that is born in him that makes him do things like that.

The packing was done at 12.50; and Harris sat on the big hamper, and said he hoped nothing would be found broken. George said that if anything was broken it *was* broken, which reflection seemed to comfort him. He also said he was ready for bed. We were all ready for bed. Harris was to sleep with us that night, and we went upstairs.

We tossed for beds, and Harris had to sleep with me. He said:

'Do you prefer the inside or the outside, J.?'

I said I generally preferred to sleep *inside* a bed.

Harris said it was old.

George said:

'What time shall I wake you fellows?'

Harris said:

'Seven.'

I said:

'No—six,' because I wanted to write some letters.

Harris and I had a bit of a row over it, but at last split the difference, and said half-past six.

'Wake us at 6.30, George,' we said.

George made no answer, and we found, on going over, that he

had been asleep for some time; so we placed the bath where he could tumble into it on getting out in the morning, and went to bed ourselves.

CHAPTER V

Mrs P. arouses us—George, the sluggard—The 'weather forecast' swindle—Our luggage—Depravity of the small boy—The people gather round us—We drive off in great style, and arrive at Waterloo—Innocence of South Western Officials concerning such worldly things as trains—We are afloat, afloat in an open boat.

IT was Mrs Poppets that woke me up next morning.

She said:

'Do you know that it's nearly nine o'clock, sir?'

'Nine o'what?' I cried, starting up. 'Nine o'clock,' she replied, through the keyhole. 'I thought you was a-oversleeping yourselves.'

I woke Harris, and told him. He said:

'I thought you wantd to get up at six?'

'So I did,' I answered; 'why didn't you wake me?'

'How could I wake you, when you didn't wake me?' he retorted. 'Now we shan't get on the water till after twelve. I wonder you take the trouble to get up at all.'

'Um,' I replied, 'lucky for you that I do. If I hadn't woke you, you'd have lain there for the whole fortnight.'

We snarled at one another in this strain for the next few minutes, when we were interrupted by a defiant snore from George. It reminded us, for the first time since our being called, of his existence. There he lay—the man who had wanted to know what time he should wake us—on his back, with his mouth wide open, and his knees stuck up.

I don't know why it should be, I am sure; but the sight of another man asleep in bed when I am up, maddens me. It seems to me so shocking to see the precious hours of a man's life—the priceless moments that will never come back to him again—being wasted in mere brutish sleep.

There was George, throwing away in hideous sloth the inestimable gift of time; his valuable life, every second of which he would have to account for hereafter, passing away from him, unused. He might have been up stuffing himself with eggs and bacon, irritating the dog, or flirting with the slavey,* instead of sprawling there, sunk in soul-clogging oblivion.

It was a terrible thought. Harris and I appeared to be struck by it at the same instant. We determined to save him, and, in this noble resolve, our own dispute was forgotten. We flew across and slung the clothes off him, and Harris landed him one with a slipper, and I shouted in his ear, and he awoke.

'Wasermarrer?' he observed, sitting up.

'Get up, you fat-headed chunk!' roared Harris. 'It's quarter to ten.'

'What!' he shrieked, jumping out of bed into the bath; '——Who the thunder put this thing here?'

We told him he must have been a fool not to see the bath.

We finished dressing, and, when it came to the extras, we remembered that we had packed the tooth-brushes and the brush and comb (that tooth-brush of mine will be the death of me, I know), and we had to go downstairs, and fish them out of the bag. And when we had done that George wanted the shaving tackle. We told him that he would have to go without shaving that morning, as we weren't going to unpack that bag again for him, nor for anyone like him.

He said:

'Don't be absurd. How can I go into the City like this?'

It was certainly rather rough on the City, but what cared we for human suffering? As Harris said, in his common, vulgar way, the City would have to lump it.

We went downstairs to breakfast. Montmorency had invited two other dogs to come and see him off, and they were whiling away the time by fighting on the doorstep. We calmed them with an umbrella, and sat down to chops and cold beef.

Harris said:

'The great thing is to make a good breakfast,' and he started with a couple of chops, saying that he would take these while they were hot, as the beef could wait.

George got hold of the paper, and read us out the boating fatalities, and the weather forecast, which latter prophesied 'rain, cold, wet to fine' (whatever more than usually ghastly thing in weather that may be), 'occasional local thunderstorms, east wind, with general depression over the Midland Counties (London and Channel). Bar. falling.'

I do think that, of all the silly, irritating tomfoolishness by which we are plagued, this 'weather-forecast' fraud is about the most aggravating. It 'forecasts' precisely what happened yesterday or the day before, and precisely the opposite of what is going to happen to-day.

I remember a holiday of mine being completely ruined one late autumn by our paying attention to the weather report of the local newspaper. 'Heavy showers, with thunderstorms, may be expected to-day,' it would say on Monday, and so we would give up our picnic, and stop indoors all day, waiting for the rain. And people would pass the house, going off in wagonettes and coaches as jolly and merry as could be, the sun shining out, and not a cloud to be seen.

'Ah!' we said, as we stood looking out at them through the window, 'won't they come home soaked!'

And we chuckled to think how wet they were going to get, and came back and stirred the fire, and got our books, and arranged our specimens of seaweed and cockle shells. By twelve o'clock, with the sun pouring into the room, the heat became quite oppressive, and we wondered when those heavy showers and occasional thunderstorms were going to begin.

'Ah! they'll come in the afternoon, you'll find,' we said to each other. 'Oh, *won't* those people get wet. What a lark!'

At one o'clock, the landlady would come in to ask if we weren't going out, as it seemed such a lovely day.

'No, no,' we replied, with a knowing chuckle, 'not we. *We* don't mean to get wet—no, no.'

And when the afternoon was nearly gone, and still there was no sign of rain, we tried to cheer ourselves up with the idea that it would come down all at once, just as the people had started for home, and were out of the reach of any shelter, and that they would thus get more drenched than ever. But not a drop ever fell, and it finished a grand day, and a lovely night after it.

The next morning we would read that it was going to be a 'warm, fine to set-fair day; much heat;' and we would dress ourselves in flimsy things, and go out, and, half-an-hour after we had started, it would commence to rain hard, and a bitterly cold wind would spring up, and both would keep on steadily for the whole day, and we would come home with colds and rheumatism all over us, and go to bed.

The weather is a thing that is beyond me altogether. I never can understand it. The barometer is useless: it is as misleading as the newspaper forecast.

There was one hanging up in a hotel at Oxford at which I was staying last spring, and, when I got there, it was pointing to 'set fair.' It was simply pouring with rain outside, and had been all day; and I couldn't quite make matters out. I tapped the barometer, and it jumped up and pointed to 'very dry.' The Boots* stopped as he was passing, and said he expected it meant to-morrow. I fancied that maybe it was thinking of the week before last, but Boots said, No, he thought not.

I tapped it again the next morning, and it went up still higher, and the rain came down faster than ever. On Wednesday I went and hit it again, and the pointer went round towards 'set fair,' 'very dry,' and 'much heat,' until it was stopped by the peg, and couldn't go any further. It tried its best, but the instrument was built so that it couldn't prophesy fine weather any harder than it did without breaking itself. It evidently wanted to go on, and prognosticate drought, and water famine, and sunstroke, and simooms, and such things, but the peg prevented it, and it had to be content with pointing to the mere commonplace 'very dry.'

Meanwhile, the rain came down in a steady torrent, and the lower part of the town was under water, owing to the river having overflowed.

Boots said it was evident that we were going to have a prolonged spell of grand weather *some time*, and read out a poem which was printed over the top of the oracle, about

> 'Long foretold, long last;
> Short notice, soon past.'

The fine weather never came that summer. I expect that machine must have been referring to the following spring.

Then there are those new style of barometers, the long straight ones. I never can make head or tail of those. There is one side for 10 a.m. yesterday, and one side for 10 a.m. to-day; but you can't always get there as early as ten, you know. It rises or falls for rain and fine, with much or less wind, and one end is 'Nly' and the other 'Ely' (what's Ely got to do with it?), and if you tap it, it doesn't tell you anything. And you've got to correct it to sea-level, and reduce it to Fahrenheit, and even then I don't know the answer.

But who wants to be foretold the weather? It is bad enough when it comes, without our having the misery of knowing about it before-hand. The prophet we like is the old man who, on the particularly gloomy-looking morning of some day when we particularly want it to be fine, looks round the horizon with a particularly knowing eye, and says:

'Oh no, sir, I think it will clear up all right. It will break all right enough, sir.'

'Ah, he knows,' we say, as we wish him good-morning, and start off; 'wonderful how these old fellows can tell!'

And we feel an affection for that man which is not at all lessened by the circumstances of its *not* clearing up, but continuing to rain steadily all day.

'Ah, well,' we feel, 'he did his best.'

For the man that prophesies us bad weather, on the contrary, we entertain only bitter and revengeful thoughts.

'Going to clear up, d'ye think?' we shout, cheerily, as we pass.

'Well, no, sir; I'm afraid it's settled down for the day,' he replies, shaking his head.

'Stupid old fool!' we mutter, 'what's *he* know about it?' And, if his portent proves correct, we come back feeling still more angry against him, and with a vague notion that, somehow or other, he has had something to do with it.

It was too bright and sunny on this especial morning for George's blood-curdling readings about 'Bar. falling,' 'atmospheric disturbance, passing in an oblique line over Southern Europe,' and 'pressure increasing,' to very much upset us: and so, finding that he could not make us wretched, and was only wasting his time, he sneaked the cigarette that I had carefully rolled up for myself, and went.

Then Harris and I, having finished up the few things left on the table, carted out our luggage on to the doorstep, and waited for a cab.

There seemed a good deal of luggage, when we put it all together. There was the Gladstone and the small hand-bag, and the two hampers, and a large roll of rugs, and some four or five overcoats and macintoshes, and a few umbrellas, and then there was a melon by itself in a bag, because it was too bulky to go in anywhere, and a couple of pounds of grapes in another bag, and a Japanese paper umbrella, and a frying pan, which, being too long to pack, we had wrapped round with brown paper.

It did look a lot, and Harris and I began to feel rather ashamed of it, though why we should be, I can't see. No cab came by, but the street boys did, and got interested in the show, apparently, and stopped.

Biggs's boy was the first to come round. Biggs is our greengrocer, and his chief talent lies in securing the services of the most abandoned and unprincipled errand-boys that civilisation has as yet produced. If anything more than usually villainous in the boy-line crops up in our neighbourhood, we know that it is Biggs's latest. I was told that, at the time of the Great Coram Street murder,* it was promptly concluded by our street that Biggs's boy (for that period) was at the bottom of it, and had he not been able, in reply to the severe cross-examination to which he was subjected by No. 19, when he called there for orders the morning after the crime (assisted by No. 21, who happened to be on the step at the time), to prove a complete *alibi*, it would have gone hard with him. I didn't know Biggs's boy at that time, but, from what I have seen of them since, I should not have attached much importance to that *alibi* myself.

Biggs's boy, as I have said, came round the corner. He was evidently in a great hurry when he first dawned upon the vision, but, on catching sight of Harris and me, and Montmorency, and the things, he eased up and stared. Harris and I frowned at him. This might have wounded a more sensitive nature, but Biggs's boys are not, as a rule, touchy. He came to a dead stop, a yard from our step, and, leaning up against the railings, and selecting a straw to chew, fixed us with his eye. He evidently meant to see this thing out.

In another moment, the grocer's boy passed on the opposite side of the street. Biggs's boy hailed him:

'Hi! ground floor o' 42's a-moving.'

The grocer's boy came across, and took up a position on the other side of the step. Then the young gentleman from the boot-shop stopped, and joined Biggs's boy; while the empty-can superintendent from 'The Blue Posts' took up an independent position on the curb.

'They ain't a-going to starve, are they?' said the gentleman from the boot-shop.

'Ah! you'd want to take a thing or two with *you*,' retorted 'The Blue Posts', 'if you was a-going to cross the Atlantic in a small boat.'

'They ain't a-going to cross the Atlantic,' struck in Biggs's boy; 'they're a-going to find Stanley.'*

By this time, quite a small crowd had collected, and people were asking each other what was the matter. One party (the young and giddy portion of the crowd) held that it was a wedding, and pointed out Harris as the bridegroom; while the elder and more thoughtful among the populace inclined to the idea that it was a funeral, and that I was probably the corpse's brother.

At last, an empty cab turned up (it is a street where, as a rule, and when they are not wanted, empty cabs pass at the rate of three a minute, and hang about, and get in your way), and packing ourselves and our belongings into it, and shooting out a couple of Montmorency's friends, who had evidently sworn never to forsake him, we drove away amidst the cheers of the crowd, Biggs's boy shying a carrot after us for luck.

We got to Waterloo at eleven, and asked where the eleven-five started from. Of course nobody knew; nobody at Waterloo ever does know where a train is going to start from, or where a train when it does start is going to, or anything about it. The porter who took our things thought it would go from number two platform, while another porter, with whom he discussed the question, had heard a rumour that it would go from number one. The station-master, on the other hand, was convinced it would start from the local.

To put an end to the matter, we went upstairs, and asked the traffic superintendent, and he told us that he had just met a man, who said he had seen it at number three platform. We went to number three platform, but the authorities there said that they rather thought that train was the Southampton express, or else the Windsor loop. But they were sure it wasn't the Kingston train, though why they were sure it wasn't they couldn't say.

Then our porter said he thought that must be it on the high-level platform; said he thought he knew the train. So we went to the high-level platform, and saw the engine-driver, and asked him if he was going to Kingston. He said he couldn't say for certain of course, but that he rather thought he was. Anyhow, if he wasn't the 11.5 for Kingston, he said he was pretty confident he was the 9.32 for Virginia Water, or the 10 a.m. express for the Isle of Wight, or somewhere in that direction, and we should all know when we got there. We slipped half-a-crown into his hand, and begged him to be the 11.5 for Kingston.

'Nobody will ever know, on this line,' we said, 'what you are, or where you're going. You know the way, you slip off quietly and go to Kingston.'

'Well, I don't know, gents,' replied the noble fellow, 'but I suppose *some* train's got to go to Kingston; and I'll do it. Gimme the half-crown.'

Thus we got to Kingston by the London and South-Western Railway.

We learnt, afterwards, that the train we had come by was really the Exeter mail, and that they had spent hours at Waterloo, looking for it, and nobody knew what had become of it.

Our boat was waiting for us at Kingston just below the bridge, and to it we wended our way, and round it we stored our luggage, and into it we stepped.

'Are you all right, sir?' said the man.

'Right it is,' we answered; and with Harris at the sculls and I at the tiller-lines, and Montmorency, unhappy and deeply suspicious, in the prow, out we shot on to the waters which, for a fortnight, were to be our home.

CHAPTER VI

Kingston—Instructive remarks on early English history—Instructive observations on carved oak and life in general—Sad case of Stivvings, junior—Musings on antiquity—I forget that I am steering—Interesting result—Hampton Court Maze—Harris as a guide.

IT was a glorious morning, late spring or early summer, as you care to take it, when the dainty sheen of grass and leaf is blushing to a deeper green; and the year seems like a fair young maid, trembling with strange, wakening pulses on the brink of womanhood.

The quaint back streets of Kingston, where they came down to the water's edge, looked quite picturesque in the flashing sunlight, the glinting river with its drifting barges, the wooded towpath, the trim-kept villas on the other side, Harris, in a red and orange blazer, grunting away at the sculls, the distant glimpses of the grey old palace of the Tudors, all made a sunny picture, so bright but calm, so full of life, and yet so peaceful, that, early in the day though it was, I felt myself being dreamily lulled off into a musing fit.

I mused on Kingston, or 'Kyningestun,' as it was once called in the days when Saxon 'kinges' were crowned there. Great Cæsar crossed the river there, and the Roman legions camped upon its sloping uplands. Cæsar, like, in later years, Elizabeth, seems to have stopped everywhere: only he was more respectable than good Queen Bess; he didn't put up at the public-houses.

She was nuts on public-houses, was England's Virgin Queen. There's scarcely a pub. of any attractions within ten miles of London that she does not seem to have looked in at, or stopped at, or slept at, some time or other. I wonder now, supposing Harris, say, turned over a new leaf, and became a great and good man, and got to be Prime Minister, and died, if they would put up signs over the public-houses that he had patronised: 'Harris had a glass of bitter in this house;' 'Harris had two of Scotch cold here in the summer of '88;' 'Harris was chucked from here in December, 1886.'

No, there would be too many of them! It would be the houses that he had never entered that would become famous. 'Only house in South London that Harris never had a drink in!' The people would flock to it to see what could have been the matter with it.

How poor weak-minded King Edwy must have hated Kyningestun! The coronation feast had been too much for him. Maybe boar's head stuffed with sugar-plums did not agree with him (it wouldn't with me, I know), and he had had enough of sack and mead; so he slipped from the noisy revel to steal a quiet moonlight hour with his beloved Elgiva.

Perhaps, from the casement, standing hand-in-hand, they were watching the calm moonlight on the river, while from the distant halls the boisterous revelry floated in broken bursts of faint-heard din and tumult.

Then brutal Odo and St Dunstan force their rude way into the quiet room, and hurl coarse insults at the sweet-faced Queen, and drag poor Edwy back to the loud clamour of the drunken brawl.

Years later, to the crash of battle-music, Saxon kings and Saxon revelry were buried side by side, and Kingston's greatness passed away for a time, to rise once more when Hampton Court became the palace of the Tudors and the Stuarts, and the royal barges strained at their moorings on the river's bank, and bright-cloaked gallants swaggered down the water-steps to cry: 'What Ferry, ho! Gadzooks, gramercy.'

Many of the old houses, round about, speak very plainly of those days when Kingston was a royal borough, and nobles and courtiers lived there, near their King, and the long road to the palace gates was gay all day with clanking steel and prancing palfreys, and rustling silks and velvets, and fair faces. The large and spacious houses, with their oriel, latticed windows, their huge fireplaces, and their gabled roofs, breathe of the days of hose and doublet, of pearl-embroidered stomachers, and complicated oaths. They were upraised in the days 'when men knew how to build.' The hard red bricks have only grown more firmly set with time, and their oak stairs do not creak and grunt when you try to go down them quietly.

Speaking of oak staircases reminds me that there is a magnificent carved oak staircase in one of the houses in Kingston. It is a shop now, in the market-place, but it was evidently once the mansion of some great personage. A friend of mine, who lives at Kingston, went in there to buy a hat one day, and, in a thoughtless moment, put his hand in his pocket and paid for it then and there.

The shopman (he knows my friend) was naturally a little staggered at first; but, quickly recovering himself, and feeling that something ought to be done to encourage this sort of thing, asked our hero if he would like to see some fine old carved oak. My friend said he would, and the shopman, thereupon, took him through the shop, and up the staircase of the house. The balusters were a superb piece of workmanship, and the wall all the way up was oak-panelled, with carving that would have done credit to a palace.

From the stairs, they went into the drawing-room, which was a large, bright room, decorated with a somewhat startling though cheerful paper of a blue ground. There was nothing, however, remarkable about the apartment, and my friend wondered why he had been brought there. The proprietor went up to the paper, and tapped it. It gave forth a wooden sound.

'Oak,' he explained. 'All carved oak, right up to the ceiling, just the same as you saw on the staircase.'

'But, great Cæsar! man,' expostulated my friend; 'you don't mean to say you have covered over carved oak with blue wall-paper?'

'Yes,' was the reply: 'it was expensive work. Had to match-board it all over first, of course. But the room looks cheerful now. It was awful gloomy before.'

I can't say I altogether blame the man (which is doubtless a great relief to his mind). From his point of view, which would be that of the average householder, desiring to take life as lightly as possible, and not that of the old curiosity-shop maniac, there is reason on his side. Carved oak is very pleasant to look at, and to have a little of, but it is no doubt somewhat depressing to live in, for those whose fancy does not lie that way. It would be like living in a church.

No, what was sad in his case was that he, who didn't care for carved oak, should have his drawing-room panelled with it, while people who do care for it have to pay enormous prices to get it. It seems to be the rule of this world. Each person has what he doesn't want, and other people have what he does want.

Married men have wives, and don't seem to want them; and young single fellows cry out that they can't get them. Poor people who can hardly keep themselves have eight hearty children. Rich old couples, with no one to leave their money to, die childless.

Then there are girls with lovers. The girls that have lovers never want them. They say they would rather be without them, that they bother them, and why don't they go and make love to Miss Smith and Miss Brown, who are plain and elderly, and haven't got any lovers? They themselves don't want lovers. They never mean to marry.

It does not do to dwell on these things; it makes one so sad.

There was a boy at our school, we used to call him Sandford and Merton.* His real name was Stivvings. He was the most extraordinary lad I ever came across. I believe he really liked study. He used to get into awful rows for sitting up in bed and reading Greek; and as for French irregular verbs there was simply no keeping him away from them. He was full of weird and unnatural notions about being a credit to his parents and an honour to the school; and he yearned to win prizes, and grow up and be a clever man, and had all those sorts of weak-minded ideas. I never knew such a strange creature, yet harmless, mind you, as the babe unborn.

Well, that boy used to get ill about twice a week, so that he couldn't go to school. There never was such a boy to get ill as that Sandford and Merton. If there was any known disease going within ten miles of him, he had it, and had it badly. He would take bronchitis in the dog-days, and have hay-fever at Christmas. After a six weeks' period of drought, he would be stricken down with rheumatic fever; and he would go out in a November fog and come home with sunstroke.

They put him under laughing-gas one year, poor lad, and drew all his teeth, and gave him a false set, because he suffered so terribly with toothache; and then it turned to neuralgia and ear-ache. He was never without a cold, except once for nine weeks while he had scarlet fever; and he always had chilblains. During the great cholera scare of 1871, our neighbourhood was singularly free from it. There was only one reputed case in the whole parish: that case was young Stivvings.

He had to stop in bed when he was ill, and eat chicken and custards and hot-house grapes; and he would lie there and sob, because they wouldn't let him do Latin exercises, and took his German grammar away from him.

And we other boys, who would have sacrificed ten terms of our school-life for the sake of being ill for a day, and had no desire whatever to give our parents any excuse for being stuck-up about us, couldn't catch so much as a stiff neck. We fooled about in draughts, and it did us good, and freshened us up; and we took things to make us sick, and they made us fat, and gave us an appetite. Nothing we could think of seemed to make us ill until the holidays began. Then, on the breaking-up day, we caught colds, and whooping cough, and all kinds of disorders, which lasted till the term recommenced; when, in spite of everything we could manœuvre to the contrary, we would get suddenly well again, and be better than ever.

Such is life; and we are but as grass that is cut down, and put into the oven* and baked.

To go back to the carved-oak question, they must have had very fair notions of the artistic and the beautiful, our great-great-grandfathers. Why, all our art treasures of to-day are only the dug-up commonplace of three or four hundred years ago. I wonder if there is real intrinsic beauty in the old soup-plates, beer-mugs, and candle-snuffers that we prize so now, or if it is only the halo of age glowing around them that gives them their charms in our eyes. The 'old blue'* that we hang about our walls as ornaments were the common every-day household utensils of a few centuries ago; and the pink shepherds and the yellow shepherdesses that we hand round now for all our friends to gush over, and pretend they understand, were the unvalued mantel-ornaments that the mother of the eighteenth century would have given the baby to suck when he cried.

Will it be the same in the future? Will the prized treasures of to-day always be the cheap trifles of the day before? Will rows of our willow-pattern dinner-plates be ranged above the chimneypieces of the great in the years 2000 and odd? Will the white cups with the gold rim and the beautiful gold flower inside (species unknown), that our Sarah Janes* now break in sheer light-heartedness of spirit, be carefully mended, and stood upon a bracket, and dusted only by the lady of the house?

That china dog that ornaments the bedroom of my furnished lodgings. It is a white dog. Its eyes are blue. Its nose is a delicate red, with black spots. Its head is painfully erect, and its expression is amiability carried to the verge of imbecility. I do not admire it myself. Considered as a work of art, I may say it irritates me. Thoughtless friends jeer at it, and even my landlady herself has no admiration for it, and excuses its presence by the circumstance that her aunt gave it to her.

But in 200 years' time it is more than probable that that dog will be dug up from somewhere or other, minus its legs, and with its tail broken, and will be sold for old china, and put in a glass cabinet. And people will pass it round, and admire it. They will be struck by the wonderful depth of the colour on the nose, and speculate as to how beautiful the bit of the tail that is lost no doubt was.

We, in this age, do not see the beauty of that dog. We are too familiar with it. It is like the sunset and the stars: we are not awed by their loveliness because they are common to our eyes. So it is with that china dog. In 2288 people will gush over it. The making of such dogs will have become a lost art. Our descendants will wonder how we did it, and say how clever we were. We shall be referred to lovingly as 'those grand old artists that flourished in the nineteenth century, and produced those china dogs.'

The 'sampler' that the eldest daughter did at school will be spoken of as 'tapestry of the Victorian era,' and be almost priceless. The blue-and-white mugs of the present-day roadside inn will be hunted up, all cracked and chipped, and sold for their weight in gold, and rich people will use them for claret cups; and travellers from Japan will buy up all the 'Presents from Ramsgate,' and 'Souvenirs of Margate,' that may have escaped destruction, and take them back to Jedo as ancient English curios.

At this point Harris threw away the sculls, got up and left his seat, and sat on his back, and stuck his legs in the air. Montmorency howled, and turned a somersault, and the top hamper jumped up, and all the things came out.

I was somewhat surprised, but I did not lose my temper. I said, pleasantly enough:

'Hulloa! what's that for?'

'What's that for? Why——'

No, on second thoughts, I will not repeat what Harris said. I may have been to blame, I admit it; but nothing excuses violence of language and coarseness of expression, especially in a man who has been carefully brought up, as I know Harris has been. I was thinking of other things, and forgot, as any one might easily understand, that I was steering, and the consequence was that we had got mixed up a good deal with the tow-path. It was difficult to say, for the moment, which was us and which was the Middlesex bank of the river; but we found out after a while, and separated ourselves.

Harris, however, said he had done enough for a bit, and proposed that I should take a turn; so, as we were in, I got out and took the tow-line, and ran the boat on past Hampton Court. What a dear old wall that is that runs along by the river there! I never pass it without feeling better for the sight of it. Such a mellow, bright, sweet old wall; what a charming picture it would make, with the lichen creeping here, and the moss growing there, a shy young vine peeping over the top at this spot, to see what is going on upon the busy river, and the sober old ivy clustering a little farther down! There are fifty shades and tints and hues in every ten yards of that old wall. If I could only draw, and knew how to paint, I could make a lovely sketch of that old wall, I'm sure. I've often thought I should like to live at Hampton Court. It looks so peaceful and so quiet, and it is such a dear old place to ramble round in the early morning before many people are about.

But, there, I don't suppose I should really care for it when it came to actual practice. It would be so ghastly dull and depressing in the evening, when your lamp cast uncanny shadows on the panelled walls, and the echo of distant feet rang through the cold stone corridors, and now drew nearer, and now died away, and all was death-like silence, save the beating of one's own heart.

We are creatures of the sun, we men and women. We love light and life. That is why we crowd into the towns and cities, and the country grows more and more deserted every year. In the sunlight—in the daytime, when Nature is alive and busy all around us, we like the open hill-sides and the deep woods well enough: but in the night, when our Mother Earth has gone to sleep, and left us waking, oh! the world seems so lonesome, and we get frightened, like children in a silent house. Then we sit and sob, and long for the gas-lit streets, and the sound of human voices, and the answering throb of human life. We feel so helpless and so little in the great stillness, when the dark trees rustle in the night-wind. There are so many ghosts about, and their silent sighs make us feel so sad. Let us gather together in the great cities, and light huge bonfires of a million gas-jets, and shout and sing together and feel brave.

Harris asked me if I'd ever been in the maze at Hampton Court. He said he went in once to show somebody else the way. He had studied it up in a map, and it was so simple that it seemed foolish—hardly worth the twopence charged for admission. Harris said he thought that map must have been got up as a practical joke, because it wasn't a bit like the real thing, and only misleading. It was a country cousin that Harris took in. He said:

'We'll just go in here, so that you can say you've been, but it's very simple. It's absurd to call it a maze. You keep on taking the first turning to the right. We'll just walk round for ten minutes, and then go and get some lunch.'

They met some people soon after they had got inside, who said they had been there for three-quarters of an hour, and had had about enough of it. Harris told them they could follow him, if they liked; he was just going in, and then should turn round and come out again. They said it was very kind of him, and fell behind, and followed.

They picked up various other people who wanted to get it over, as they went along, until they had absorbed all the persons in the maze. People who had given up all hopes of ever getting either in or out, or of ever seeing their home and friends again, plucked up courage at the sight of Harris and his party, and joined the procession, blessing him. Harris said he should judge there must have been twenty people, following him, in all; and one woman with a baby, who had been there all the morning, insisted on taking his arm, for fear of losing him.

Harris kept on turning to the right, but it seemed a long way, and his cousin said he supposed it was a very big maze.

'Oh, one of the largest in Europe,' said Harris.

'Yes, it must be,' replied the cousin, 'because we've walked a good two miles already.'

Harris began to think it rather strange himself, but he held on until, at last, they passed the half of a penny bun on the ground that

Harris's cousin swore he had noticed there seven minutes ago. Harris said: 'Oh, impossible!' but the woman with the baby said, 'Not at all,' as she herself had taken it from the child, and thrown it down there, just before she met Harris. She also added that she wished she never had met Harris, and expressed an opinion that he was an impostor. That made Harris mad, and he produced his map, and explained his theory.

'The map may be all right enough,' said one of the party, 'if you know whereabouts in it we are now.'

Harris didn't know, and suggested that the best thing to do would be to go back to the entrance, and begin again. For the beginning again part of it there was not much enthusiasm; but with regard to the advisability of going back to the entrance there was complete unanimity, and so they turned, and trailed after Harris again, in the opposite direction. About ten minutes more passed, and then they found themselves in the centre.

Harris thought at first of pretending that that was what he had been aiming at; but the crowd looked dangerous, and he decided to treat it as an accident.

Anyhow, they had got something to start from then. They did know where they were, and the map was once more consulted, and the thing seemed simpler than ever, and off they started for the third time.

And three minutes later they were back in the centre again.

After that, they simply couldn't get anywhere else. Whatever way they turned brought them back to the middle. It became so regular at length, that some of the people stopped there, and waited for the others to take a walk round, and come back to them. Harris drew out his map again, after a while, but the sight of it only infuriated the mob, and they told him to go and curl his hair with it. Harris said that he couldn't help feeling that, to a certain extent, he had become unpopular.

They all got crazy at last, and sang out for the keeper, and the man came and climbed up the ladder outside, and shouted out directions to them. But all their heads were, by this time, in such a confused whirl that they were incapable of grasping anything, and so the man told them to stop where they were, and he would come to them. They huddled together, and waited; and he climbed down, and came in.

He was a young keeper, as luck would have it, and new to the business; and when he got in, he couldn't find them, and he wandered about, trying to get to them, and then *he* got lost. They caught sight of him, every now and then, rushing about the other side of the hedge, and he would see them, and rush to get to them, and they would wait there for about five minutes, and then he would reappear again in exactly the same spot, and ask them where they had been.

They had to wait till one of the old keepers came back from his dinner before they got out.

Harris said he thought it was a very fine maze, so far as he was a judge; and we agreed that we would try to get George to go into it, on our way back.

CHAPTER VII

The river in its Sunday garb—Dress on the river—A chance for the men—Absence of taste in Harris—George's blazer—A day with the fashion-plate young lady—Mrs Thomas's tomb—The man who loves not graves and coffins and skulls—Harris mad—His views on George and Banks and lemonade—He performs tricks.

IT was while passing through Molesey lock that Harris told me about his maze experience. It took us some time to pass through, as we were the only boat, and it is a big lock. I don't think I ever remember to have seen Molesey lock, before, with only one boat in it. It is, I suppose, Boulter's not even excepted, the busiest lock on the river.

I have stood and watched it, sometimes, when you could not see any water at all, but only a brilliant tangle of bright blazers, and gay caps, and saucy hats, and many-coloured parasols, and silken rugs, and cloaks, and streaming ribbons, and dainty whites; when looking down into the lock from the quay, you might fancy it was a huge box into which flowers of every hue and shade had been thrown pell-mell, and lay piled up in a rainbow heap, that covered every corner.

On a fine Sunday it presents this appearance nearly all day long, while, up the stream, and down the stream, lie, waiting their turn, outside the gates, long lines of still more boats; and boats are drawing near and passing away, so that the sunny river, from the Palace up to Hampton Church, is dotted and decked with yellow, and blue, and orange, and white, and red, and pink. All the inhabitants of Hampton and Molesey dress themselves up in boating costume, and come and mouch round the lock with their dogs, and flirt, and smoke, and watch the boats; and, altogether, what with the caps and jackets of the men, the pretty coloured dresses of the women, the excited dogs, the moving boats, the white sails, the pleasant landscape, and the sparkling water, it is one of the gayest sights I know of near this dull old London town.

The river affords a good opportunity for dress. For once in a way, we men are able to show *our* taste in colours, and I think we come out very natty, if you ask me. I always like a little red in my things—red and black. You know my hair is a sort of golden brown, rather a pretty shade I've been told, and a dark red matches it beautifully; and then I always think a light-blue necktie goes so well with it, and a pair of those Russian-leather shoes and a red silk handkerchief round the waist—a handkerchief looks so much better than a belt.

Harris always keeps to shades or mixtures of orange or yellow, but I don't think he is at all wise in this. His complexion is too dark for yellows. Yellows don't suit him: there can be no question about it. I want him to take to blue as a background, with white or cream for relief; but, there! the less taste a person has in dress, the more obstinate he always seems to be. It is a great pity, because he will never be a success as it is, while there are one or two colours in which he might not really look so bad, with his hat on.

George has bought some new things for this trip, and I'm rather vexed about them. The blazer is loud. I should not like George to know that I thought so, but there really is no other word for it. He brought it home and showed it to us on Thursday evening. We asked him what colour he called it, and he said he didn't know. He didn't think there was a name for the colour. The man had told him it was an Oriental design. George put it on, and asked us what we thought of it. Harris said that, as an object to hang over a flower-bed in early spring to frighten the birds away, he should respect it; but that, considered as an article of dress for any human being, except a Margate nigger,* it made him ill. George got quite huffy; but, as Harris said, if he didn't want his opinion, why did he ask for it?

What troubles Harris and myself, with regard to it, is that we are afraid it will attract attention to the boat.

Girls, also, don't look half bad in a boat, if prettily dressed. Nothing is more fetching, to my thinking, than a tasteful boating costume. But a 'boating costume,' it would be as well if all ladies would understand, ought to be a costume that can be worn in a boat, and not merely under a glass-case. It utterly spoils an excursion if you have folk in the boat who are thinking all the time a good deal more of their dress than of the trip. It was my misfortune once to go for a water picnic with two ladies of this kind. We did have a lively time!

They were both beautifully got up—all lace and silky stuff, and flowers, and ribbons, and dainty shoes, and light gloves. But they were dressed for a photographic studio, not for a river picnic. They were the 'boating costumes' of a French fashion-plate. It was ridiculous, fooling about in them anywhere near real earth, air, and water.

The first thing was that they thought the boat was not clean. We dusted all the seats for them, and then assured them that it was, but they didn't believe us. One of them rubbed the cushion with the forefinger of her glove, and showed the result to the other, and they both sighed, and sat down, with the air of early Christian martyrs trying to make themselves comfortable up against the stake. You are liable to occasionally splash a little when sculling, and it appeared that a drop of water ruined those costumes. The mark never came out, and a stain was left on the dress for ever.

I was stroke. I did my best. I feathered some two feet high, and I paused at the end of each stroke to let the blades drip before returning them, and I picked out a smooth bit of water to drop them into again each time. (Bow said, after a while, that he did not feel himself a sufficiently accomplished oarsman to pull with me, but that he would sit still, if I would allow him, and study my stroke. He said it interested him.) But, notwithstanding all this, and try as I would, I could not help an occasional flicker of water from going over those dresses.

The girls did not complain, but they huddled up close together, and set their lips firm, and every time a drop touched them, they visibly shrank and shuddered. It was a noble sight to see them suffering thus in silence, but it unnerved me altogether. I am too sensitive. I got wild and fitful in my rowing, and splashed more and more, the harder I tried not to.

I gave it up at last; I said I'd row bow. Bow thought the arrangement would be better too, and we changed places. The ladies gave an involuntary sigh of relief when they saw me go, and quite brightened up for a moment. Poor girls! they had better have put up with me. The man they had got now was a jolly, light-hearted, thick-headed sort of a chap, with about as much sensitiveness in him as there might be in a Newfoundland puppy. You might look daggers at him for an hour and he would not notice it, and it would not trouble him if he did. He set a good, rollicking, dashing stroke that sent the spray playing all over the boat like a fountain, and made the whole crowd sit up straight in no time. When he spread more than a pint of water over one of those dresses, he would give a pleasant little laugh, and say:

'I beg your pardon, I'm sure;' and offer them his handkerchief to wipe it off with.

'Oh, it's of no consequence,' the poor girls would murmur in reply, and covertly draw rugs and coats over themselves, and try to protect themselves with their lace parasols.

At lunch they had a very bad time of it. People wanted them to sit on the grass, and the grass was dusty; and the tree-trunks, against which they were invited to lean, did not appear to have been brushed for weeks; so they spread their handkerchiefs on the ground and sat on those, bolt upright. Somebody, in walking about with a plate of beef-steak pie, tripped up over a root, and sent the pie flying. None of it went over them, fortunately, but the accident suggested a fresh danger to them, and agitated them; and, whenever anybody moved about, after that, with anything in his hand that could fall and make a mess, they watched that person with growing anxiety until he sat down again.

'Now then, you girls,' said our friend Bow to them, cheerily, after it was all over, 'come along, you've got to wash up!'

They didn't understand him at first. When they grasped the idea, they said they feared they did not know how to wash up.

'Oh, I'll soon show you,' he cried; 'it's rare fun! You lie down on your—I mean you lean over the bank, you know, and sloush the things about in the water.'

The elder sister said that she was afraid that they hadn't got on dresses suited to the work.

'Oh, they'll be all right,' said he light-heartedly; 'tuck 'em up.'

And he made them do it, too. He told them that that sort of thing was half the fun of a picnic. They said it was very interesting.

Now I come to think it over, was that young man as dense-headed as we thought? or was he—no, impossible! there was such a simple, child-like expression about him!

Harris wanted to get out at Hampton Church, to go and see Mrs Thomas's tomb.

'Who is Mrs Thomas?' I asked.

'How should I know?' replied Harris. 'She's a lady that's got a funny tomb, and I want to see it.'

I objected. I don't know whether it is that I am built wrong, but I never did seem to hanker after tombstones myself. I know that the proper thing to do, when you get to a village or town, is to rush off to the churchyard, and enjoy the graves; but it is a recreation that I always deny myself. I take no interest in creeping round dim and chilly churches behind wheezy old men, and reading epitaphs. Not even the sight of a bit of cracked brass let into a stone affords me what I call real happiness.

I shock respectable sextons by the imperturbability I am able to assume before exciting inscriptions, and by my lack of enthusiasm for the local family history, while my ill-concealed anxiety to get outside wounds their feelings.

One golden morning of a sunny day, I leant against the low stone wall that guarded a little village church, and I smoked, and drank in deep, calm gladness from the sweet, restful scene—the grey old church with its clustering ivy and its quaint carved wooden porch, the white lane winding down the hill between tall rows of elms, the thatched-roof cottages peeping above their trim-kept hedges, the silver river in the hollow, the wooded hills beyond!

It was a lovely landscape. It was idyllic, poetical, and it inspired me. I felt good and noble. I felt I didn't want to be sinful and wicked any more. I would come and live here, and never do any more wrong, and lead a blameless, beautiful life, and have silver hair when I got old, and all that sort of thing.

In that moment I forgave all my friends and relations for their wickedness and cussedness, and I blessed them. They did not know that I blessed them. They went their abandoned way all unconscious of what I, far away in that peaceful village, was doing for them; but I did it, and I wished that I could let them know that I had done it, because I wanted to make them happy. I was going on thinking away all these grand, tender thoughts, when my reverie was broken in upon by a shrill piping voice crying out:

'All right, sur, I'm a-coming, I'm a-coming. It's all right, sur; don't you be in a hurry.'

I looked up, and saw an old bald-headed man hobbling across the churchyard towards me, carrying a huge bunch of keys in his hand that shook and jingled at every step.

I motioned him away with silent dignity, but he still advanced, screeching out the while:

'I'm a-coming, sur, I'm a-coming. I'm a little lame. I ain't as spry as I used to be. This way, sur.'

'Go away, you miserable old man,' I said.

'I've come as soon as I could, sur,' he replied. 'My missis never see you till just this minute. You follow me, sur.'

'Go away,' I repeated; 'leave me before I get over the wall, and slay you.'

He seemed surprised.

'Don't you want to see the tombs?' he said.

'No,' I answered, 'I don't. I want to stop here, leaning up against this gritty old wall. Go away, and don't disturb me. I am chock full of beautiful and noble thoughts, and I want to stop like it, because it feels nice and good. Don't you come fooling about, making me mad, chivying away all my better feelings with this silly tombstone nonsense of yours. Go away, and get somebody to bury you cheap, and I'll pay half the expense.'

He was bewildered for a moment. He rubbed his eyes, and looked hard at me. I seemed human enough on the outside: he couldn't make it out.

He said:

'Yuise a stranger in these parts? You don't live here?'

'No,' I said, 'I don't. *You* wouldn't if *I* did.'

'Well then,' he said, 'you want to see the tombs—graves—folks been buried, you know—coffins!'

'You are an untruther,' I replied, getting roused; 'I do not want to see tombs—not your tombs. Why should I? We have graves of our own, our family has. Why my uncle Podger has a tomb in Kensal Green Cemetery, that is the pride of all that country-side; and my grandfather's vault at Bow is capable of accommodating eight visitors, while my great-aunt Susan has a brick grave in Finchley Churchyard, with a headstone with a coffee-pot sort of thing in bas-relief upon it, and a six-inch best white stone coping all the way round, that cost pounds. When I want graves, it is to those places that I go and revel. I do not want other folk's. When you yourself are buried, I will come and see yours. That is all I can do for you.'

He burst into tears. He said that one of the tombs had a bit of stone upon the top of it that had been said by some to be probably part of the remains of the figure of a man, and that another had some words, carved upon it, that nobody had ever been able to decipher.

I still remained obdurate, and, in broken-hearted tones, he said:

'Well, won't you come and see the memorial window?'

I would not even see that, so he fired his last shot. He drew near, and whispered hoarsely:

'I've got a couple of skulls down in the crypt,' he said; 'come and see those. Oh, do come and see the skulls! You are a young man out for a holiday, and you want to enjoy yourself. Come and see the skulls!'

Then I turned and fled, and as I sped I heard him calling to me:

'Oh, come and see the skulls; come back and see the skulls!'

Harris, however, revels in tombs, and graves, and epitaphs, and monumental inscriptions, and the thought of not seeing Mrs Thomas's grave made him crazy. He said he had looked forward to seeing Mrs Thomas's grave from the first moment that the trip was proposed—said he wouldn't have joined if it hadn't been for the idea of seeing Mrs Thomas's tomb.

I reminded him of George, and how we had to get the boat up to Shepperton by five o'clock to meet him, and then he went for George. Why was George to fool about all day, and leave us to lug this lumbering old top-heavy barge up and down the river by ourselves to meet him? Why couldn't George come and do some work? Why couldn't he have got the day off, and come down with us? Bank be blowed! What good was he at the bank?

'I never see him doing any work there,' continued Harris, 'whenever I go in. He sits behind a bit of glass all day, trying to look as if he was doing something. What's the good of a man behind a bit of glass? I have to work for my living. Why can't he work. What use is he there, and what's the good of their banks? They take your money, and then, when you draw a cheque, they send it back smeared all over with "No effects," "Refer to drawer." What's the good of that? That's the sort of trick they served me twice last week. I'm not going to stand it much longer. I shall withdraw my account. If he was here, we could go and see that tomb. I don't believe he's at the bank at all. He's larking about somewhere, that's what he's doing, leaving us to do all the work. I'm going to get out, and have a drink.'

I pointed out to him that we were miles away from a pub.; and then he went on about the river, and what was the good of the river, and was everyone who came on the river to die of thirst?

It is always best to let Harris have his head when he gets like this. Then he pumps himself out, and is quiet afterwards.

I reminded him that there was concentrated lemonade in the hamper, and a gallon-jar of water in the nose of the boat, and that the two only wanted mixing to make a cool and refreshing beverage.

Then he flew off about lemonade, and 'such-like Sunday-school slops,' as he termed them, ginger-beer, raspberry syrup, &c., &c. He said they all produced dyspepsia, and ruined body and soul alike, and were the cause of half the crime in England.

He said he must drink something, however, and climbed upon the seat, and leant over to get the bottle. It was right at the bottom of the hamper, and seemed difficult to find, and he had to lean over further and further, and, in trying to steer at the same time, from a topsy-turvy point of view, he pulled the wrong line, and sent the boat into the bank, and the shock upset him, and he dived down right into the hamper, and stood there on his head, holding on to the sides of the boat like grim death, his legs sticking up into the air. He dared not move for fear of going over, and had to stay there till I could get hold of his legs, and haul him back, and that made him madder than ever.

CHAPTER VIII

Blackmailing—The proper course to pursue—Selfish boorishness of river-side landowner—'Notice' boards—Unchristianlike feelings of Harris—How Harris sings a comic song—A high-class party—Shameful conduct of two abandoned young men—Some useless information—George buys a banjo.

WE stopped under the willows by Kempton Park, and lunched. It is a pretty little spot there: a pleasant grass plateau, running along by the water's edge, and overhung by willows. We had just commenced the third course—the bread and jam—when a gentleman in shirt-sleeves and a short pipe came along, and wanted to know if we knew that we were trespassing. We said we hadn't given the matter sufficient consideration as yet to enable us to arrive at a definite conclusion on that point, but that, if he assured us on his word as a gentleman that we *were* trespassing, we would, without further hesitation, believe it.

He gave us the required assurance, and we thanked him, but he still hung about, and seemed to be dissatisfied, so we asked him if there was anything further that we could do for him; and Harris, who is of a chummy disposition, offered him a bit of bread and jam.

I fancy he must have belonged to some society sworn to abstain from bread and jam; for he declined it quite gruffly, as if he were vexed at being tempted with it, and he added that it was his duty to turn us off.

Harris said that if it was a duty it ought to be done, and asked the man what was his idea with regard to the best means for accomplishing it. Harris is what you would call a well-made man of about number one size, and looks hard and bony, and the man measured him up and down, and said he would go and consult his master, and then come back and chuck us both into the river.

Of course, we never saw him any more, and, of course, all he really wanted was a shilling. There are a certain number of riverside roughs who make quite an income during the summer, by slouching about the banks and blackmailing weak-minded noodles in this way. They represent themselves as sent by the proprietor. The proper course to pursue is to offer your name and address, and leave the owner, if he really has anything to do with the matter, to summon you, and prove what damage you have done to his land by sitting down on a bit of it. But the majority of people are so intensely lazy and timid, that they prefer to encourage the imposition by giving in to it rather than put an end to it by the exertion of a little firmness.

Where it is really the owners that are to blame, they ought to be shown up. The selfishness of the riparian proprietor grows with every year. If these men had their way they would close the river Thames altogether. They actually do this along the minor tributary streams and in the backwaters. They drive posts into the bed of the stream, and draw chains across from bank to bank, and nail huge notice-boards on every tree. The sight of those notice-boards rouses every evil instinct in my nature. I feel I want to tear each one down, and hammer it over the head of the man who put it up, until I have killed him, and then I would bury him, and put the board up over the grave as a tombstone.

I mentioned these feelings of mine to Harris, and he said he had them worse than that. He said he not only felt he wanted to kill the man who caused the board to be put up, but that he should like to slaughter the whole of his family and all his friends and relations, and then burn down his house. This seemed to me to be going too far, and I said so to Harris; but he answered:

'Not a bit of it. Serve 'em all jolly well right, and I'd go and sing comic songs on the ruins.'

I was vexed to hear Harris go on in this bloodthirsty strain. We never ought to allow our instincts of justice to degenerate into mere vindictiveness. It was a long while before I could get Harris to take a more Christian view of the subject, but I succeeded at last, and he promised me that he would spare the friends and relations at all events, and would not sing comic songs on the ruins.

You have never heard Harris sing a comic song, or you would understand the service I had rendered to mankind. It is one of Harris's fixed ideas that he *can* sing a comic song; the fixed idea, on the contrary, among those of Harris's friends who have heard him try, is that he *can't*, and never will be able to, and that he ought not to be allowed to try.

When Harris is at a party, and is asked to sing, he replies: 'Well, I can only sing a *comic* song, you know;' and he says it in a tone that implies that his singing of *that*, however, is a thing that you ought to hear once, and then die.

'Oh, that *is* nice,' says the hostess. 'Do sing one, Mr Harris;' and Harris gets up, and makes for the piano, with the beaming cheeriness of a generous-minded man who is just about to give somebody something.

'Now, silence, please, everybody,' says the hostess, turning round; 'Mr Harris is going to sing a comic song!'

'Oh, how jolly!' they murmur; and they hurry in from the conservatory, and come up from the stairs, and go and fetch each other from all over the house, and crowd into the drawing-room, and sit round, all smirking in anticipation.

Then Harris begins.

Well, you don't look for much of a voice in a comic song. You don't expect correct phrasing or vocalization. You don't mind if a man does find out, when in the middle of a note, that he is too high, and comes down with a jerk. You don't bother about time. You don't mind a man being two bars in front of the accompaniment, and easing up in the middle of a line to argue it out with the pianist, and then starting the verse afresh. But you do expect the words.

You don't expect a man to never remember more than the first three lines of the first verse, and to keep on repeating these until it is time to begin the chorus. You don't expect a man to break off in the middle of a line, and snigger, and say, it's very funny, but he's blest if he can think of the rest of it, and then try and make it up for himself, and, afterwards, suddenly recollect it, when he has got to an entirely different part of the song, and break off, without a word of warning, to go back and let you have it then and there. You don't—well, I will just give you an idea of Harris's comic singing, and then you can judge of it for yourself.

HARRIS (*standing up in front of piano and addressing the expectant mob*): 'I'm afraid it's a very old thing, you know. I expect you all know it, you know. But it's the only thing I know. It's the Judge's song out of *Pinafore**—no, I don't mean *Pinafore*—I mean—you know what I mean—the other thing, you know. You must all join in the chorus, you know.'

[*Murmurs of delight and anxiety to join in the chorus. Brilliant performance of prelude to the Judge's song in 'Trial by Jury** *by nervous pianist. Moment arrives for Harris to join in. Harris takes no notice of it. Nervous pianist commences prelude over again, and Harris, commencing singing at the same time, dashes off the first two lines of the First Lord's song out of 'Pinafore.' Nervous pianist tries to push on with prelude, gives it up, and tries to follow Harris with accompaniment to Judge's song out of 'Trial by Jury,' finds that doesn't answer, and tries to recollect what he is doing, and where he is, feels his mind is giving way, and stops short.*]

HARRIS (*with kindly encouragement*): 'It's all right. You're doing it very well, indeed—go on.'

NERVOUS PIANIST: 'I'm afraid there's a mistake somewhere. What are you singing?'

HARRIS (*promptly*): 'Why the Judge's song out of *Trial by Jury*. Don't you know it?'

SOME FRIEND OF HARRIS'S (*from the back of the room*): 'No, you're

not, you chuckle-head, you're singing the Admiral's song from
Pinafore.'

[*Long argument between Harris and Harris's friend as to what Harris is
really singing. Friend finally suggests that it doesn't matter what
Harris is singing so long as Harris gets on and sings it, and Harris,
with an evident sense of injustice rankling inside him, requests pianist
to begin again. Pianist, thereupon, starts prelude to the Admiral's
song, and Harris, seizing what he considers to be a favourable
opening in the music, begins.*

HARRIS:

'"When I was young and called to the Bar."'

[*General roar of laughter, taken by Harris as a compliment. Pianist,
thinking of his wife and family, gives up the unequal contest and
retires; his place being taken by a stronger-nerved man.*

THE NEW PIANIST (*cheerily*): 'Now then, old man, you start off,
and I'll follow. We won't bother about any prelude.'

HARRIS: (*upon whom the explanation of matters has slowly
dawned—laughing*): 'By Jove! I beg your pardon. Of course—I've
been mixing up the two songs. It was Jenkins confused me, you know.
Now then.

[*Singing; his voice appearing to come from the cellar, and suggesting the
first low warnings of an approaching earthquake.*

'"When I was young I served a term
As office-boy to an attorney's firm."'

(*Aside to pianist*): 'It is too low, old man; we'll have that over again, if
you don't mind.'

[*Sings first two lines over again, in a high falsetto this time. Great
surprise on the part of the audience. Nervous old lady near the fire
begins to cry, and has to be led out.*

HARRIS (*continuing*):

'"I swept the windows and I swept the door,
And I——"'

No—no, I cleaned the windows of the big front door. And I polished
up the floor—no, dash it—I beg your pardon—funny thing, I can't
think of that line. And I—and I—Oh, well, we'll get on to the chorus,
and chance it (*sings*):

'"And I diddle-diddle-diddle-diddle-diddle-diddle-de,
    Till now I am the ruler of the Queen's navee."

Now then, chorus—it's the last two lines repeated, you know.'
GENERAL CHORUS:

'And he diddle-diddle-diddle-diddle-diddle-diddle-dēē'd,
    Till now he is the ruler of the Queen's navēē.'

And Harris never sees what an ass he is making of himself, and
how he is annoying a lot of people who never did him any harm. He
honestly imagines that he has given them a treat, and says he will sing
another comic song after supper.

Speaking of comic songs and parties, reminds me of a rather
curious incident at which I once assisted; which, as it throws much
light upon the inner mental working of human nature in general,
ought, I think, to be recorded in these pages.

We were a fashionable and highly cultured party. We had on our
best clothes, and we talked pretty, and were very happy—all except
two young fellows, students, just returned from Germany, commonplace young men, who seemed restless and uncomfortable, as if
they found the proceedings slow. The truth was, we were too clever
for them. Our brilliant but polished conversation, and our high-class
tastes, were beyond them. They were out of place, among us. They
never ought to have been there at all. Everybody agreed upon that,
later on.

We played *morceaux** from the old German masters. We discussed
philosophy and ethics. We flirted with graceful dignity. We were
even humorous—in a high-class way.

Somebody recited a French poem after supper, and we said it was
beautiful; and then a lady sang a sentimental ballad in Spanish, and it
made one or two of us weep—it was so pathetic.

And then those two young men got up, and asked us if we had ever
heard Herr Slossenn Boschen (who had just arrived, and was then
down in the supper-room) sing his great German comic song.

None of us had heard it, that we could remember.

The young men said it was the funniest song that had ever been
written, and that, if we liked, they would get Herr Slossenn Boschen,
whom they knew very well, to sing it. They said it was so funny that,
when Herr Slossenn Boschen had sung it once before the German
Emperor, he (the German Emperor) had had to be carried off to bed.

They said nobody could sing it like Herr Slossenn Boschen; he was so intensely serious all through it that you might fancy he was reciting a tragedy, and that, of course, made it all the funnier. They said he never once suggested by his tone or manner that he was singing anything funny—that would spoil it. It was his air of seriousness, almost of pathos, that made it so irresistibly amusing.

We said we yearned to hear it, that we wanted a good laugh; and they went downstairs, and fetched Herr Slossenn Boschen.

He appeared to be quite pleased to sing it, for he came up at once, and sat down to the piano without another word.

'Oh, it will amuse you. You will laugh,' whispered the two young men, as they passed through the room, and took up an unobtrusive position behind the Professor's back.

Herr Slossenn Boschen accompanied himself. The prelude did not suggest a comic song exactly. It was a weird, soulful air. It quite made one's flesh creep; but we murmured to one another that it was the German method, and prepared to enjoy it.

I don't understand German myself. I learned it at school, but forgot every word of it two years after I had left, and have felt much better ever since. Still, I did not want the people there to guess my ignorance; so I hit upon what I thought to be rather a good idea. I kept my eye on the two young students, and followed them. When they tittered, I tittered; when they roared, I roared; and I also threw in a little snigger all by myself now and then, as if I had seen a bit of humour that had escaped the others. I considered this particularly artful on my part.

I noticed, as the song progressed, that a good many other people seemed to have their eye fixed on the two young men, as well as myself. These other people also tittered when the young men tittered, and roared when the young men roared; and, as the two young men tittered and roared and exploded with laughter pretty continuously all through the song, it went exceedingly well.

And yet that German Professor did not seem happy. At first, when we began to laugh, the expression of his face was one of intense surprise; as if laughter were the very last thing he had expected to be greeted with. We thought this very funny: we said his earnest manner was half the humour. The slightest hint on his part that he knew how funny he was would have completely ruined it all. As we continued to laugh, his surprise gave way to an air of annoyance and indignation,

and he scowled fiercely round upon us all (except upon the two young
men who, being behind him, he could not see). That sent us into
convulsions. We told each other that it would be the death of us, this
thing. The words alone we said, were enough to send us into fits, but
added to his mock seriousness—oh, it was too much!

In the last verse, he surpassed himself. He glowered round upon us
with a look of such concentrated ferocity that, but for our being
forewarned as to the German method of comic singing, we should
have been nervous; and he threw such a wailing note of agony into the
weird music that, if we had not known it was a funny song, we might
have wept.

He finished amid a perfect shriek of laughter. We said it was the
funniest thing we had ever heard in all our lives. We said how strange
it was that, in the face of things like these, there should be a popular
notion that the Germans hadn't any sense of humour. And we asked
the Professor why he didn't translate the song into English, so that
the common people could understand it, and hear what a real comic
song was like.

Then Herr Slossenn Boschen got up, and went on awful. He swore
at us in German (which I should judge to be a singularly effective
language for that purpose), and he danced, and shook his fists, and
called us all the English he knew. He said he had never been so
insulted in all his life.

It appeared that the song was not a comic song at all. It was about a
young girl who lived in the Hartz Mountains, and who had given up
her life to save her lover's soul; and he died, and met her spirit in the
air; and then, in the last verse, he jilted her spirit, and went off with
another spirit—I'm not quite sure of the details, but it was something
very sad, I know. Herr Boschen said he had sung it once before the
German Emperor, and he (the German Emperor) had sobbed like a
little child. He (Herr Boschen) said it was generally acknowledged to
be one of the most tragic and pathetic songs in the German language.

It was a trying situation for us—very trying. There seemed to be
no answer. We looked around for the two young men who had done
this thing, but they had left the house in an unostentatious manner
immediately after the end of the song.

That was the end of that party. I never saw a party break up so
quietly, and with so little fuss. We never said good-night even to one
another. We came downstairs one at a time, walking softly, and

keeping the shady side. We asked the servant for our hats and coats in whispers, and opened the door for ourselves, and slipped out, and got round the corner quickly, avoiding each other as much as possible.

I have never taken much interest in German songs since then.

We reached Sunbury lock at half-past three. The river is sweetly pretty just there before you come to the gates, and the backwater is charming; but don't attempt to row up it.

I tried to do so once. I was sculling, and asked the fellows who were steering if they thought it could be done, and they said, oh, yes, they thought so, if I pulled hard. We were just under the little foot-bridge that crosses it between the two weirs, when they said this, and I bent down over the sculls, and set myself up, and pulled.

I pulled splendidly. I got well into a steady rhythmical swing. I put my arms, and my legs, and my back into it. I set myself a good, quick, dashing stroke, and worked in really grand style. My two friends said it was a pleasure to watch me. At the end of five minutes, I thought we ought to be pretty near the weir, and I looked up. We were under the bridge, in exactly the same spot that we were when I began, and there were those two idiots, injuring themselves by violent laughing. I had been grinding away like mad to keep that boat stuck still under that bridge. I let other people pull up backwaters against strong streams now.

We sculled up to Walton, a rather large place for a riverside town. As with all riverside places, only the tiniest corner of it comes down to the water, so that from the boat you might fancy it was a village of some half-dozen houses, all told. Windsor and Abingdon are the only towns between London and Oxford that you can really see anything of from the stream. All the others hide round corners, and merely peep at the river down one street: my thanks to them for being so considerate, and leaving the river-banks to woods and fields and water-works.

Even Reading, though it does its best to spoil and sully and make hideous as much of the river as it can reach, is good-natured enough to keep its ugly face a good deal out of sight.

Cæsar, of course, had a little place at Walton—a camp, or an entrenchment, or something of that sort. Cæsar was a regular up-river man. Also Queen Elizabeth, she was there, too. You can never get away from that woman, go where you will. Cromwell and Bradshaw* (not the guide man, but the King Charles's head man) likewise sojourned here. They must have been quite a pleasant little party, altogether.

There is an iron 'scold's bridle' in Walton Church. They used these things in ancient days for curbing women's tongues. They have given up the attempt now. I suppose iron was getting scarce, and nothing else would be strong enough.

There are also tombs of note in the church, and I was afraid I should never get Harris past them; but he didn't seem to think of them, and we went on. Above the bridge the river winds tremendously. This makes it look picturesque; but it irritates you from a towing or sculling point of view, and causes argument between the man who is pulling and the man who is steering.

You pass Oatlands Park on the right bank here. It is a famous old place. Henry VIII stole it from some one or the other, I forget whom now, and lived in it. There is a grotto in the park which you can see for a fee, and which is supposed to be very wonderful; but I cannot see much in it myself. The late Duchess of York, who lived at Oatlands, was very fond of dogs, and kept an immense number. She had a special graveyard made, in which to bury them when they died, and there they lie, about fifty of them, with a tombstone over each, and an epitaph inscribed thereon.

Well, I dare say they deserve it quite as much as the average Christian does.

At 'Corway Stakes'—the first bend above Walton Bridge—was fought a battle between Cæsar and Cassivelaunus. Cassivelaunus had prepared the river for Cæsar, by planting it full of stakes (and had, no doubt, put up a notice-board). But Cæsar crossed in spite of this. You couldn't choke Cæsar off that river. He is the sort of man we want round the backwaters now.

Halliford and Shepperton are both pretty little spots where they touch the river; but there is nothing remarkable about either of them. There is a tomb in Shepperton churchyard, however, with a poem on it, and I was nervous lest Harris should want to get out and fool round it. I saw him fix a longing eye on the landing-stage as we drew near it, so I managed, by an adroit movement, to jerk his cap into the water, and in the excitement of recovering that, and his indignation at my clumsiness, he forgot all above his beloved graves.

At Weybridge, the Wey (a pretty little stream, navigable for small boats up to Guildford, and one which I have always been making up my mind to explore, and never have), the Bourne, and the Basingstoke Canal all enter the Thames together. The lock is just opposite the town, and the first thing that we saw, when we came in view of it, was George's blazer on one of the lock gates, closer inspection showing that George was inside it.

Montmorency set up a furious barking, I shrieked, Harris roared; George waved his hat, and yelled back. The lock-keeper rushed out with a drag, under the impression that somebody had fallen into the lock, and appeared annoyed at finding that no one had.

George had rather a curious oilskin-covered parcel in his hand. It was round and flat at one end, with a long straight handle sticking out of it.

'What's that?' said Harris—'a frying-pan?'

'No,' said George, with a strange, wild look glittering in his eyes; 'they are all the rage this season; everybody has got them up the river. It's a banjo.'

'I never knew you played the banjo!' cried Harris and I, in one breath.

'Not exactly,' replied George: 'but it's very easy, they tell me; and I've got the instruction book!'

CHAPTER IX

George is introduced to work—Heathenish instincts of tow-lines—Ungrateful conduct of a double-sculling skiff—Towers and towed—A use discovered for lovers—Strange disappearance of an elderly lady—Much haste, less speed—Being towed by girls: exciting sensation—The missing lock or the haunted river—Music—Saved!

WE made George work, now we had got him. He did not want to work, of course; that goes without saying. He had had a hard time in the City, so he explained. Harris, who is callous in his nature, and not prone to pity, said:

'Ah! and now you are going to have a hard time on the river for a change; change is good for everyone. Out you get!'

He could not in conscience—not even George's conscience —object, though he did suggest that, perhaps, it would be better for him to stop in the boat, and get tea ready, while Harris and I towed, because getting tea was such a worrying work, and Harris and I looked tired. The only reply we made to this, however, was to pass him over the tow-line, and he took it, and stepped out.

There is something very strange and unaccountable about a tow-line. You roll it up with as much patience and care as you would take to fold up a new pair of trousers, and five minutes afterwards, when you pick it up, it is one ghastly, soul-revolting tangle.

I do not wish to be insulting, but I firmly believe that if you took an average tow-line, and stretched it out straight across the middle of a field, and then turned your back on it for thirty seconds, that, when you looked round again, you would find that it had got itself altogether in a heap in the middle of the field, and had twisted itself up, and tied itself into knots, and lost its two ends, and become all loops; and it would take you a good half-hour, sitting down there on the grass and swearing all the while, to disentangle it again.

That is my opinion of tow-lines in general. Of course, there may be honourable exceptions; I do not say that there are not. There may be tow-lines that are a credit to their profession—conscientious, respectable tow-lines—tow-lines that do not imagine they are crochet-work, and try to knit themselves up into antimacassars the instant they are left to themselves. I say there *may* be such tow-lines; I sincerely hope there are. But I have not met with them.

This tow-line I had taken in myself just before we had got to the lock. I would not let Harris touch it, because he is careless. I had looped it round slowly and cautiously, and tied it up in the middle, and folded it in two, and laid it down gently at the bottom of the boat. Harris had lifted it up scientifically, and had put it into George's hand. George had taken it firmly, and held it away from him, and had begun to unravel it as if he were taking the swaddling clothes off a new-born infant; and, before he had unwound a dozen yards, the thing was more like a badly-made door-mat than anything else.

It is always the same, and the same sort of thing always goes on in connection with it. The man on the bank, who is trying to disentangle it, thinks all the fault lies with the man who rolled it up; and when a man up the river thinks a thing, he says it.

'What have you been trying to do with it, make a fishing-net of it? You've made a nice mess you have; why couldn't you wind it up properly, you silly dummy?' he grunts from time to time as he struggles wildly with it, and lays it out flat on the tow-path, and runs round and round it, trying to find the end.

On the other hand, the man who wound it up thinks the whole cause of the muddle rests with the man who is trying to unwind it.

'It was all right when you took it!' he exclaims indignantly. 'Why don't you think what you are doing? You go about things in such a slap-dash style. You'd get a scaffolding pole entangled *you* would!'

And they feel so angry with one another that they would like to hang each other with the thing. Ten minutes go by, and the first man gives a yell and goes mad, and dances on the rope, and tries to pull it straight by seizing hold of the first piece that comes to his hand and hauling at it. Of course, this only gets it into a tighter tangle than ever. Then the second man climbs out of the boat and comes to help him, and they get in each other's way, and hinder one another. They both get hold of the same bit of line, and pull at it in opposite directions, and wonder where it is caught. It the end, they do get it clear, and then turn round and find that the boat has drifted off, and is making straight for the weir.

This really happened once to my own knowledge. It was up by Boveney, one rather windy morning. We were pulling down stream, and, as we came round the bend, we noticed a couple of men on the bank. They were looking at each other with as bewildered and helplessly miserable expression as I have ever witnessed on any human countenance before or since, and they held a long tow-line between them. It was clear that something had happened, so we eased up and asked them what was the matter.

'Why, our boat's gone off!' they replied in an indignant tone. 'We just got out to disentangle the tow-line, and when we looked round, it was gone!'

And they seemed hurt at what they evidently regarded as a mean and ungrateful act on the part of the boat.

We found the truant for them half a mile further down, held by some rushes, and we brought it back to them. I bet they did not give that boat another chance for a week.

I shall never forget the picture of those two men walking up and down the bank with a tow-line, looking for their boat.

One sees a good many funny incidents up the river in connection with towing. One of the most common is the sight of a couple of towers, walking briskly along, deep in an animated discussion, while

the man in the boat, a hundred yards behind them, is vainly shrieking
to them to stop, and making frantic signs of distress with a scull.
Something has gone wrong; the rudder has come off, or the boat-
hook has slipped overboard, or his hat has dropped into the water and
is floating rapidly down stream. He calls to them to stop, quite gently
and politely at first.

'Hi! stop a minute, will you?' he shouts cheerily. 'I've dropped my
hat overboard.'

Then: 'Hi! Tom—Dick! can't you hear?' not quite so affably this
time.

Then: 'Hi! Confound *you*, you dunder-headed idiots! Hi! stop! Oh
you——!'

After that he springs up, and dances about, and roars himself red
in the face, and curses everything he knows. And the small boys on
the bank stop and jeer at him, and pitch stones at him as he is pulled
along past them, at the rate of four miles an hour, and can't get out.

Much of this sort of trouble would be saved if those who are towing
would keep remembering that they *are* towing, and give a pretty
frequent look round to see how their man is getting on. It is best to let
one person tow. When two are doing it, they get chattering, and
forget, and the boat itself, offering, as it does, but little resistance, is
of no real service in reminding them of the fact.

As an example of how utterly oblivious a pair of towers can be to
their work, George told us, later on in the evening, when we were
discussing the subject after supper, of a very curious instance.

He and three other men, so he said, were sculling a very heavily
laden boat up from Maidenhead one evening, and a little above
Cookham lock they noticed a fellow and a girl, walking along the
tow-path, both deep in an apparently interesting and absorbing
conversation. They were carrying a boat-hook between them, and,
attached to the boat-hook was a tow-line, which trailed behind them,
its end in the water. No boat was near, no boat was in sight. There
must have been a boat attached to that tow-line at some time or other,
that was certain; but what had become of it, what ghastly fate had
overtaken it, and those who had been left in it, was buried in mystery.
Whatever the accident may have been, however, it had in no way
disturbed the young lady and gentleman, who were towing. They had
the boat-hook and they had the line, and that seemed to be all that
they thought necessary to their work.

George was about to call out and wake them up, but, at that moment, a bright idea flashed across him, and he didn't. He got the hitcher instead, and reached over, and drew in the end of the tow-line; and they made a loop in it, and put it over their mast, and then they tidied up the sculls, and went and sat down in the stern, and lit their pipes.

And that young man and young woman towed those four hulking chaps and a heavy boat up to Marlow.

George said he never saw so much thoughtful sadness concentrated into one glance before, as when, at the lock, that young couple grasped the idea that, for the last two miles, they had been towing the wrong boat. George fancied that, if it had not been for the restraining influence of the sweet woman at his side, the young man might have given way to violent language.

The maiden was the first to recover from her surprise, and, when she did, she clasped her hands, and said, wildly:

'Oh, Henry, then *where* is auntie?'

'Did they ever recover the old lady?' asked Harris.

George replied he did not know.

Another example of the dangerous want of sympathy between tower and towed was witnessed by George and myself once up near Walton. It was where the tow-path shelves gently down into the water, and we were camping on the opposite bank, noticing things in general. By-and-by a small boat came in sight, towed through the water at a tremendous pace by a powerful barge horse, on which sat a very small boy. Scattered about the boat, in dreamy and reposeful attitudes, lay five fellows, the man who was steering having a particularly restful appearance.

'I should like to see him pull the wrong line,' murmured George, as they passed. And at that precise moment the man did it, and the boat rushed up the bank with a noise like the ripping up of forty thousand linen sheets. Two men, a hamper, and three oars immediately left the boat on the larboard side, and reclined on the bank, and one and a half moments afterwards, two other men disembarked from the starboard, and sat down among boat-hooks and sails and carpet-bags and bottles. The last man went on twenty yards further, and then got out on his head.

This seemed to sort of lighten the boat, and it went on much easier, the small boy shouting at the top of his voice, and urging his steed into a gallop. The fellows sat up and stared at one another. It was some seconds before they realised what had happened to them, but, when they did, they began to shout lustily for the boy to stop. He, however, was too much occupied with the horse to hear them, and we watched them, flying after him, until the distance hid them from view.

I cannot say I was sorry at their mishap. Indeed, I only wish that all the young fools who have their boats towed in this fashion—and plenty do—could meet with similar misfortunes. Besides the risk they run themselves, they become a danger and an annoyance to every other boat they pass. Going at the pace they do, it is impossible for them to get out of anybody else's way, or for anybody else to get out of theirs. Their line gets hitched across your mast, and overturns you, or it catches somebody in the boat, and either throws them into the water, or cuts their face open. The best plan is to stand your ground, and be prepared to keep them off with the butt-end of a mast.

Of all experiences in connection with towing, the most exciting is being towed by girls. It is a sensation that nobody ought to miss. It takes three girls to tow always; two hold the rope, and the other one runs round and round, and giggles. They generally begin by getting themselves tied up. They get the line round their legs, and have to sit down on the path and undo each other, and then they twist it round their necks, and are nearly strangled. They fix it straight, however, at last, and start off at a run, pulling the boat along at quite a dangerous pace. At the end of a hundred yards they are naturally breathless, and suddenly stop, and all sit down on the grass and laugh, and your boat drifts out to mid-stream and turns round, before you know what has happened, or can get hold of a scull. Then they stand up, and are surprised.

'Oh, look!' they say; 'he's gone right out into the middle.'

They pull on pretty steadily for a bit, after this, and then it all at once occurs to one of them that she will pin up her frock, and they ease up for the purpose, and the boat runs aground.

You jump up, and push it off, and you shout to them not to stop.

'Yes. What's the matter?' they shout back.

'Don't stop,' you roar.

'Don't what?'

'Don't stop—go on—go on!'

'Go back, Emily, and see what it is they want,' says one; and Emily comes back, and asks what it is.

'What do you want?' she says; 'anything happened?'

'No,' you reply, 'it's all right; only go on, you know—don't stop.'

'Why not?'

'Why, we can't steer, if you keep stopping. You must keep some way on the boat.'

'Keep some what?'

'Some way—you must keep the boat moving.'

'Oh, all right, I'll tell 'em. Are we doing it all right?'

'Oh, yes, very nicely, indeed, only don't stop.'

'It doesn't seem difficult at all. I thought it was so hard.'

'Oh, no, it's simple enough. You want to keep on steady at it, that's all.'

'I see. Give me out my red shawl, it's under the cushion.'

You find the shawl, and hand it out, and by this time another one has come back and thinks she will have hers too, and they take Mary's on chance, and Mary does not want it, so they bring it back and have a pocket-comb instead. It is about twenty minutes before they get off again, and, at the next corner, they see a cow, and you have to leave the boat to chivy the cow out of their way.

There is never a dull moment in the boat while girls are towing it.

George got the line right after a while, and towed us steadily on to Penton Hook. There we discussed the important question of camping. We had decided to sleep on board that night, and we had either to lay up just about there, or go on past Staines. It seemed early to think about shutting up then, however, with the sun still in the heavens, and we settled to push straight on for Runnymede, three and a half miles further, a quiet wooded part of the river, and where there is good shelter.

We all wished, however, afterward that we had stopped at Penton Hook. Three or four miles up stream is a trifle, early in the morning, but it is a weary pull at the end of a long day. You take no interest in the scenery during these last few miles. You do not chat and laugh. Every half-mile you cover seems like two. You can hardly believe you are only where you are, and you are convinced that the map must be wrong; and, when you have trudged along for what seems to you at least ten miles, and still the lock is not in sight, you begin to seriously fear that somebody must have sneaked it, and run off with it.

I remember being terribly upset once up the river (in a figurative sense, I mean). I was out with a young lady—cousin on my mother's side—and we were pulling down to Goring. It was rather late, and we were anxious to get in—at least *she* was anxious to get in. It was half-past six when we reached Benson's lock, and the dusk was drawing on, and she began to get excited then. She said she must be in to supper. I said it was a thing I felt I wanted to be in at, too; and I drew out a map I had with me to see exactly how far it was. I saw it was just a mile and a half to the next lock—Wallingford—and five on from there to Cleeve.

'Oh, it's all right!' I said. 'We'll be through the next lock before seven, and then there is only one more;' and I settled down and pulled steadily away.

We passed the bridge, and soon after that I asked if she saw the lock. She said no, she did not see any lock; and I said, 'Oh!' and pulled on. Another five minutes went by, and then I asked her to look again.

'No,' she said; 'I can't see any signs of a lock.'

'You—you are sure you know a lock, when you do see one?' I asked hesitatingly, not wishing to offend her.

The question did offend her, however, and she suggested that I had better look for myself; so I laid down the sculls, and took a view. The river stretched out straight before us in the twilight for about a mile; not a ghost of a lock was to be seen.

'You don't think we have lost our way, do you?' asked my companion.

I did not see how that was possible; though, as I suggested, we might have somehow got into the weir stream, and be making for the falls.

This idea did not comfort her in the least, and she began to cry. She said we should both be drowned, and that it was a judgment on her for coming out with me.

It seemed an excessive punishment, I thought; but my cousin thought not, and hoped it would all soon be over.

I tried to reassure her, and to make light of the whole affair. I said that the fact evidently was that I was not rowng as fast as I fancied I was, but that we should reach the lock now; and I pulled on for another mile.

Then I began to get nervous myself. I looked again at the map. There was Wallingford lock, clearly marked, a mile and a half below

Benson's. It was a good, reliable map; and, besides, I recollected the lock myself. I had been through it twice. Where were we? What had happened to us? I began to think it must be all a dream, and that I was really asleep in bed, and should wake up in a minute, and be told it was past ten.

I asked my cousin if she thought it could be a dream, and she replied that she was just about to ask me the same question; and then we both wondered if we were both asleep, and if so, who was the real one that was dreaming, and who was the one that was only a dream; it got quite interesting.

I still went on pulling, however, and still no lock came in sight, and the river grew more and more gloomy and mysterious under the gathering shadows of night, and things seemed to be getting weird and uncanny. I thought of hobgoblins and banshees, and will-o'-the-wisps, and those wicked girls who sit up all night on rocks, and lure people into whirlpools and things; and I wished I had been a better man, and knew more hymns; and in the middle of these reflections I heard the blessed strains of 'He's got 'em on,' played, badly, on a concertina, and knew that we were saved.

I do not admire the tones of a concertina, as a rule; but, oh! how beautiful the music seemed to us both then—far, far more beautiful than the voice of Orpheus or the lute of Apollo, or anything of that sort could have sounded. Heavenly melody, in our then state of mind, would only have still further harrowed us. A soul-moving harmony, correctly performed, we should have taken as a spirit-warning, and have given up all hope. But about the strains of 'He's got 'em on,' jerked spasmodically, and with involuntary variations, out of a wheezy accordion, there was something singularly human and reassuring.

The sweet sounds drew nearer, and soon the boat from which they were worked lay alongside us.

It contained a party of provincial 'Arrys and 'Arriets, out for a moonlight sail. (There was not any moon, but that was not their fault.) I never saw more attractive, lovable people in all my life. I hailed them, and asked if they could tell me the way to Wallingford lock; and I explained that I had been looking for it for the last two hours.

'Wallingford lock!' they answered. 'Lor' love you, sir, that's been done away with for over a year. There ain't no Wallingford lock now, sir. You're close to Cleeve now. Blow me tight if 'ere ain't a gentleman been looking for Wallingford lock, Bill!'

I had never thought of that. I wanted to fall upon all their necks and bless them; but the stream was running too strong just there to allow of this, so I had to content myself with mere cold-sounding words of gratitude.

We thanked them over and over again, and we said it was a lovely night, and we wished them a pleasant trip, and, I think, I invited them all to come and spend a week with me, and my cousin said her mother would be so pleased to see them. And we sang the soldiers' chorus out of *Faust*,* and got home in time for supper, after all.

CHAPTER X

Our first night—Under canvas—An appeal for help—Contrariness of tea-kettles, how to overcome—Supper—How to feel virtuous—Wanted! a comfortably-appointed, well-drained desert island, neighbourhood of South Pacific Ocean preferred—Funny thing that happened to George's father—A restless night.

HARRIS and I began to think that Bell Weir lock must have been done away with after the same manner. George had towed us up to Staines, and we had taken the boat from there, and it seemed that we were dragging fifty tons after us, and were walking forty miles. It was half-past seven when we were through, and we all got in, and sculled up close to the left bank, looking out for a spot to haul up in.

We had originally intended to go on to Magna Charta Island, a sweetly pretty part of the river, where it winds through a soft, green valley, and to camp in one of the many picturesque inlets to be found round that tiny shore. But, somehow, we did not feel that we yearned for the picturesque nearly so much now as we had earlier in the day. A bit of water between a coal-barge and a gas-works would have quite satisfied us for that night. We did not want scenery. We wanted to have our supper and go to bed. However, we did pull up to the point—'Picnic Point,' it is called—and dropped into a very pleasant nook under a great elm-tree, to the spreading roots of which we fastened the boat.

Then we thought we were going to have supper (we had dispensed with tea, so as to save time), but George said no; that we had better get the canvas up first, before it got quite dark, and while we could see what we were doing. Then, he said, all our work would be done, and we could sit down to eat with an easy mind.

That canvas wanted more putting up than I think any of us had bargained for. It looked so simple in the abstract. You took five iron arches, like gigantic croquet hoops, and fitted them up over the boat, and then stretched the canvas over them, and fastened it down: it would take quite ten minutes, we thought.

That was an under-estimate.

We took up the hoops, and began to drop them into the sockets placed for them. You would not imagine this to be dangerous work; but, looking back now, the wonder to me is that any of us are alive to tell the tale. They were not hoops, they were demons. First they would not fit into their sockets at all, and we had to jump on them, and kick them, and hammer at them with the boat-hook; and, when they were in, it turned out that they were the wrong hoops for those particular sockets, and they had to come out again.

But they would not come out, until two of us had gone and struggled with them for five minutes, when they would jump up suddenly, and try and throw us into the water and drown us. They had hinges in the middle, and, when we were not looking, they nipped us with these hinges in delicate parts of the body; and, while we were wrestling with one side of the hoop, and endeavouring to persuade it to do its duty, the other side would come behind us in a cowardly manner, and hit us over the head.

We got them fixed at last, and then all that was to be done was to arrange the covering over them. George unrolled it, and fastened one end over the nose of the boat. Harris stood in the middle to take it from George and roll it on to me, and I kept by the stern to receive it. It was a long time coming down to me. George did his part all right, but it was new work to Harris, and he bungled it.

How he managed it I do not know, he could not explain himself; but by some mysterious process or other he succeeded, after ten minutes of superhuman effort, in getting himself completely rolled up in it. He was so firmly wrapped round and tucked in and folded over, that he could not get out. He, of course, made frantic struggles for freedom—the birthright of every Englishman,—and, in doing so (I learned this afterwards), knocked over George; and then George, swearing at Harris, began to struggle too, and got *himself* entangled and rolled up.

I knew nothing about this at the time. I did not understand the business at all myself. I had been told to stand where I was, and wait till the canvas came to me, and Montmorency and I stood there and waited, both as good as gold. We could see the canvas being violently jerked and tossed about, pretty considerably; but we supposed this was part of the method, and did not interfere.

We also heard much smothered language coming from underneath it, and we guessed that they were finding the job rather troublesome, and concluded that we would wait until things had got a little simpler before we joined in.

We waited some time, but matters seemed to get only more and more involved, until, at last, George's head came wriggling out over the side of the boat, and spoke up.

It said:

'Give us a hand here, can't you, you cuckoo; standing there like a stuffed mummy, when you see we are both being suffocated, you dummy!'

I never could withstand an appeal for help, so I went and undid them; not before it was time, either, for Harris was nearly black in the face.

It took us half an hour's hard labour, after that, before it was properly up, and then we cleared the decks, and got out supper. We put the kettle on to boil, up in the nose of the boat, and went down to the stern and pretended to take no notice of it, but set to work to get the other things out.

That is the only way to get a kettle to boil up the river. If it sees that you are waiting for it and are anxious, it will never even sing. You have to go away and begin your meal, as if you were not going to have any tea at all. You must not even look round at it. Then you will soon hear it sputtering away, mad to be made into tea.

It is a good plan, too, if you are in a great hurry, to talk very loudly to each other about how you don't need any tea, and are not going to have any. You get near the kettle, so that it can overhear you, and then you shout out, 'I don't want any tea; do you, George?' to which George shouts back, 'Oh, no, I don't like tea; we'll have lemonade instead—tea's so indigestible.' Upon which the kettle boils over, and puts the stove out.

We adopted this harmless bit of trickery, and the result was that, by the time everything else was ready, the tea was waiting. Then we lit the lantern, and squatted down to supper.

We wanted that supper.

For five-and-thirty minutes not a sound was heard throughout the length and breadth of that boat, save the clank of cutlery and crockery, and the steady grinding of four sets of molars. At the end of five-and-thirty minutes, Harris said, 'Ah!' and took his left leg out from under him and put his right one there instead.

Five minutes afterwards, George said, 'Ah!' too, and threw his plate out on the bank; and, three minutes later than that, Montmorency gave the first sign of contentment he had exhibited since we had started, and rolled over on his side, and spread his legs out; and then I said, 'Ah!' and bent my head back, and bumped it against one of the hoops, but I did not mind it. I did not even swear.

How good one feels when one is full—how satisfied with ourselves and with the world! People who have tried it, tell me that a clear conscience makes you very happy and contented; but a full stomach does the business quite as well, and is cheaper, and more easily obtained. One feels so forgiving and generous after a substantial and well-digested meal—so noble-minded, so kindly-hearted.

It is very strange, this domination of our intellect by our digestive organs. We cannot work, we cannot think, unless our stomach wills so. It dictates to us our emotions, our passions. After eggs and bacon, it says, 'Work!' After beefsteak and porter, it says, 'Sleep!' After a cup of tea (two spoonsful for each cup, and don't let it stand more than three minutes), it says to the brain, 'Now, rise, and show your strength. Be eloquent, and deep, and tender; see, with a clear eye, into Nature and into life; spread your white wings of quivering thought, and soar, a god-like spirit, over the whirling world beneath you, up through long lanes of flaming stars to the gates of eternity!'

After hot muffins, it says, 'Be dull and soulless, like a beast of the field—a brainless animal, with listless eye, unlit by any ray of fancy, or of hope, or fear, or love, or life.' And after brandy, taken in sufficient quantity, it says, 'Now, come, fool, grin and tumble, that your fellow-men may laugh—drivel in folly, and splutter in senseless sounds, and show what a helpless ninny is poor man whose wit and will are drowned, like kittens, side by side, in half an inch of alcohol.'

We are but the veriest, sorriest slaves of our stomach. Reach not after morality and righteousness, my friends; watch vigilantly your stomach, and diet it with care and judgment. Then virtue and contentment will come and reign within your heart, unsought by any effort of your own; and you will be a good citizen, a loving husband, and a tender father—a noble, pious man.

Before our supper Harris and George and I were quarrelsome and snappy and ill-tempered; after our supper, we sat and beamed on one another, and we beamed upon the dog, too. We loved each other, we loved everybody. Harris, in moving about, trod on George's corn. Had this happened before supper, George would have expressed wishes and desires concerning Harris's fate in this world and the next that would have made a thoughtful man shudder.

As it was, he said, 'Steady, old man; 'ware wheat.'

And Harris, instead of merely observing, in his most unpleasant tones, that a fellow could hardly help treading on some bit of George's foot, if he had to move about at all within ten yards of where George was sitting, suggesting that George never ought to come into an ordinary sized boat with feet that length, and advising him to hang them over the side, as he would have done before supper, now said: 'Oh, I'm so sorry, old chap; I hope I haven't hurt you.'

And George said: 'Not at all;' that it was his fault; and Harris said no, it was his.

It was quite pretty to hear them.

We lit our pipes, and sat, looking out on the quiet night, and talked.

George said why could not we be always like this—away from the world, with its sin and temptation, leading sober, peaceful lives, and doing good. I said it was the sort of thing I had often longed for myself; and we discussed the possibility of our going away, we four, to some handy, well-fitted desert island, and living there in the woods.

Harris said that the danger about desert islands, as far as he had heard, was that they were so damp; but George said no, not if properly drained.

And then we got on to drains, and that put George in mind of a very funny thing that happened to his father once. He said his father was travelling with another fellow through Wales, and, one night, they stopped at a little inn, where there were some other fellows, and they joined the other fellows, and spent the evening with them.

They had a very jolly evening, and sat up late, and, by the time they came to go to bed, they (this was when George's father was a very young man) were slightly jolly, too. They (George's father and George's father's friend) were to sleep in the same room, but in different beds. They took the candle, and went up. The candle lurched up against the wall when they got into the room, and went out, and they had to undress and grope into bed in the dark. This they did; but, instead of getting into separate beds, as they thought they were doing, they both climbed into the same one without knowing it—one getting in with his head at the top, and the other crawling in from the opposite side of the compass, and lying with his feet on the pillow.

There was silence for a moment, and then George's father said:

'Joe!'

'What's the matter, Tom?' replied Joe's voice from the other end of the bed.

'Why, there's a man in my bed,' said George's father; 'here's his feet on my pillow.'

'Well, it's an extraordinary thing, Tom,' answered the other; 'but I'm blest if there isn't a man in my bed, too!'

'What are you going to do?' asked George's father.

'Well, I'm going to chuck him out,' replied Joe.

'So am I,' said George's father, valiantly.

There was a brief struggle, followed by two heavy bumps on the floor, and then a rather doleful voice said:

'I say, Tom!'

'Yes!'

'How have you got on?'

'Well, to tell you the truth, my man's chucked *me* out.'

'So's mine! I say, I don't think much of this inn, do you?'

'What was the name of that inn?' said Harris.

'The Pig and Whistle,' said George. 'Why?'

'Ah, no, then it isn't the same,' replied Harris.

'What do you mean?' queried George.

'Why it's so curious,' murmured Harris, 'but precisely that very same thing happened to *my* father once at a country inn. I've often heard him tell the tale. I thought it might have been the same inn.'

We turned in at ten that night, and I thought I should sleep well, being tired; but I didn't. As a rule, I undress and put my head on the pillow, and then somebody bangs at the door, and says it is half-past eight: but, to-night, everything seemed against me; the novelty of it all, the hardness of the boat, the cramped position (I was lying with my feet under one seat, and my head on another), the sound of the lapping water round the boat, and the wind among the branches, kept me restless and disturbed.

I did get to sleep for a few hours, and then some part of the boat which seemed to have grown up in the night—for it certainly was not there when we started, and it had disappeared by the morning—kept digging into my spine. I slept through it for a while, dreaming that I had swallowed a sovereign, and that they were cutting a hole in my back with a gimlet, so as to try and get it out. I thought it very unkind of them, and I told them I would owe them the money, and they should have it at the end of the month. But they would not hear of that, and said it would be much better if they had it then, because otherwise the interest would accumulate so. I got quite cross with them after a bit, and told them what I thought of them, and then they gave the gimlet such an excruciating wrench that I woke up.

The boat seemed stuffy, and my head ached; so I thought I would step out into the cool night-air. I slipped on what clothes I could find about—some of my own, and some of George's and Harris's—and crept under the canvas on to the bank.

It was a glorious night. The moon had sunk, and left the quiet earth alone with the stars. It seemed as if, in the silence and the hush, while we her children slept, they were talking with her, their sister —conversing of mighty mysteries in voices too vast and deep for childish human ears to catch the sound.

They awe us, these strange stars, so cold, so clear. We are as children whose small feet have strayed into some dim-lit temple of the god they have been taught to worship but know not; and, standing where the echoing dome spans the long vista of the shadowy light, glance up, half hoping, half afraid to see some awful vision hovering there.

And yet it seems so full of comfort and of strength, the night. In its great presence, our small sorrows creep away, ashamed. The day has been so full of fret and care, and our hearts have been so full of evil and of bitter thoughts, and the world has seemed so hard and wrong to us. Then Night, like some great loving mother, gently lays her hand upon our fevered head, and turns our little tear-stained faces up to hers, and smiles, and, though she does not speak, we know what she would say, and lay our hot flushed cheek against her bosom, and the pain is gone.

Sometimes, our pain is very deep and real, and we stand before her very silent, because there is no language for our pain, only a moan. Night's heart is full of pity for us: she cannot ease our aching; she takes our hand in hers, and the little world grows very small and very far away beneath us, and, borne on her dark wings, we pass for a moment into a mightier Presence than her own, and in the wondrous light of that great Presence, all human life lies like a book before us, and we know that Pain and Sorrow are but the angels of God.

Only those who have worn the crown of suffering can look upon that wondrous light; and they, when they return, may not speak of it, or tell the mystery they know.

Once upon a time, through a strange country, there rode some goodly knights, and their path lay by a deep wood, where tangled briars grew very thick and strong, and tore the flesh of them that lost their way therein. And the leaves of the trees that grew in the wood were very dark and thick, so that no ray of light came through the branches to lighten the gloom and sadness.

And, as they passed by that dark wood, one knight of those that rode, missing his comrades, wandered far away, and returned to them no more; and they, sorely grieving, rode on without him, mourning him as one dead.

Now, when they reached the fair castle towards which they had been journeying, they stayed there many days, and made merry; and one night, as they sat in cheerful ease around the logs that burned in the great hall, and drank a loving measure, there came the comrade they had lost, and greeted them. His clothes were ragged, like a beggar's, and many sad wounds were on his sweet flesh, but upon his face there shone a great radiance of deep joy.

And they questioned him, asking him what had befallen him: and he told them how in the dark wood he had lost his way, and had wandered many days and nights, till, torn and bleeding, he had lain him down to die.

Then, when he was nigh unto death, lo! through the savage gloom there came to him a stately maiden, and took him by the hand and led him on through devious paths, unknown to any man, until upon the darkness of the wood there dawned a light such as the light of day was unto but as a little lamp unto the sun; and, in that wondrous light, our way-worn knight saw as in a dream a vision, and so glorious, so fair the vision seemed, that of his bleeding wounds he thought no more, but stood as one entranced, whose joy is deep as is the sea, whereof no man can tell the depth.

And the vision faded, and the knight, kneeling upon the ground, thanked the good saint who into that sad wood had strayed his steps, so he had seen the vision that lay there hid.

And the name of the dark forest was Sorrow; but of the vision that the good knight saw therein we may not speak nor tell.

CHAPTER XI

How George, once upon a time, got up early in the morning—George, Harris, and Montmorency do not like the look of the cold water—Heroism and determination on the part of J.—George and his shirt: story with a moral—Harris as cook—Historical retrospect, specially inserted for the use of schools.

I WOKE at six the next morning; and found George awake too. We both turned round, and tried to go to sleep again, but we could not. Had there been any particular reason why we should *not* have gone to sleep again, but have got up and dressed then and there, we should have dropped off while we were looking at our watches, and have slept till ten. As there was no earthly necessity for our getting up under another two hours at the very least, and our getting up at that time was an utter absurdity, it was only in keeping with the natural cussedness of things in general that we should both feel that lying down for five minutes more would be death to us.

George said that the same kind of thing, only worse, had happened to him some eighteen months ago, when he was lodging by himself in the house of a certain Mrs Gippings. He said his watch went wrong one evening, and stopped at a quarter-past eight. He did not know this at the time because, for some reason or other, he forgot to wind it up when he went to bed (an unusual occurrence with him), and hung it up over his pillow without ever looking at the thing.

It was in the winter when this happened, very near the shortest day, and a week of fog into the bargain, so the fact that it was still very dark when George woke in the morning was no guide to him as to the time. He reached up, and hauled down his watch. It was a quarter-past eight.

'Angels and ministers of grace defend us!'* exclaimed George; 'and here have I got to be in the City by nine. Why didn't somebody call me? Oh, this is a shame!' And he flung the watch down, and sprang out of bed, and had a cold bath, and washed himself, and dressed himself, and shaved himself in cold water because there was not time to wait for the hot and then rushed and had another look at the watch.

Whether the shaking it had received in being thrown on the bed had started it, or how it was, George could not say, but certain it was that from a quarter-past eight it had begun to go, and now pointed to twenty minutes to nine.

George snatched it up, and rushed downstairs. In the sitting-room, all was dark and silent: there was no fire, no breakfast. George said it was a wicked shame of Mrs G., and he made up his mind to tell her what he thought of her when he came home in the evening. Then he dashed on his greatcoat and hat, and, seizing his umbrella, made for the front door. The door was not even unbolted. George anathematized Mrs G. for a lazy old woman, and thought it was very strange that people could not get up at a decent, respectable time, unlocked and unbolted the door, and ran out.

He ran hard for a quarter of a mile, and at the end of that distance it began to be borne in upon him as a strange and curious thing that there were so few people about, and that there were no shops open. It was certainly a very dark and foggy morning, but still it seemed an unusual course to stop all business on that account. *He* had to go to business: why should other people stop in bed merely because it was dark and foggy!

At length he reached Holborn. Not a shutter was down! not a bus was about! There were three men in sight, one of whom was a policeman; a market-cart full of cabbages, and a dilapidated looking cab. George pulled out his watch and looked at it: it was five minutes to nine! He stood still and counted his pulse. He stooped down and felt his legs. Then, with his watch still in his hand, he went up to the policeman, and asked him if he knew what the time was.

'What's the time?' said the man, eyeing George up and down with evident suspicion; 'why, if you listen you will hear it strike.'

George listened, and a neighbouring clock immediately obliged.

'But it's only gone three!' said George in an injured tone, when it had finished.

'Well, and how many did you want it to go?' replied the constable.

'Why, nine,' said George, showing his watch.

'Do you know where you live?' said the guardian of public order, severely.

George thought, and gave the address.

'Oh! that's where it is, is it?' replied the man; 'well, you take my advice and go there quietly, and take that watch of yours with you; and don't let's have any more of it.'

And George went home again, musing as he walked along, and let himself in.

At first, when he got in, he determined to undress and go to bed again; but when he thought of the re-dressing and re-washing, and the having of another bath, he determined he would not, but would sit up and go to sleep in the easy-chair.

But he could not get to sleep: he never felt more wakeful in his life; so he lit the lamp and got out the chess-board, and played himself a game of chess. But even that did not enliven him: it seemed slow somehow; so he gave chess up and tried to read. He did not seem able to take any sort of interest in reading either, so he put on his coat again and went out for a walk.

It was horribly lonesome and dismal, and all the policemen he met regarded him with undisguised suspicion, and turned their lanterns on him and followed him about, and this had such an effect upon him at last that he began to feel as if he really had done something, and he got to slinking down the by-streets and hiding in dark doorways when he heard the regulation flip-flop approaching.

Of course, this conduct made the force only more distrustful of him than ever, and they would come and rout him out and ask him what he was doing there; and when he answered, 'Nothing,' he had merely come out for a stroll (it was then four o'clock in the morning), they looked as though they did not believe him, and two plain-clothes constables came home with him to see if he really did live where he said he did. They saw him go in with his key, and then they took up a position opposite and watched the house.

He thought he would light the fire when he got inside, and make himself some breakfast, just to pass away the time; but he did not seem able to handle anything from a scuttleful of coals to a teaspoon without dropping it or falling over it, and making such a noise that he was in mortal fear that it would wake Mrs G. up, and that she would think it was burglars and open the window and call 'Police!' and then these two detectives would rush in and handcuff him, and march him off to the police-court.

He was in a morbidly nervous state by this time, and he pictured the trial, and his trying to explain the circumstances to the jury, and nobody believing him, and his being sentenced to twenty years' penal servitude, and his mother dying of a broken heart. So he gave up trying to get breakfast, and wrapped himself up in his overcoat and sat in the easy-chair till Mrs G. came down at half-past seven.

He said he had never got up too early since that morning: it had been such a warning to him.

We had been sitting huddled up in our rugs while George had been telling me this true story, and on his finishing it I set to work to wake up Harris with a scull. The third prod did it: and he turned over on the other side, and said he would be down in a minute, and that he would have his lace-up boots. We soon let him know where he was, however, by the aid of the hitcher, and he sat up suddenly, sending Montmorency, who had been sleeping the sleep of the just right on the middle of his chest, sprawling across the boat.

Then we pulled up the canvas, and all four of us poked our heads out over the off-side, and looked down at the water and shivered. The idea, overnight, had been that we should get up early in the morning, fling off our rugs and shawls, and, throwing back the canvas, spring into the river with a joyous shout, and revel in a long delicious swim. Somehow, now the morning had come, the notion seemed less tempting. The water looked damp and chilly: the wind felt cold.

'Well, who's going to be first in?' said Harris at last.

There was no rush for precedence. George settled the matter so far as he was concerned by retiring into the boat and pulling on his socks. Montmorency gave vent to an involuntary howl, as if merely thinking of the thing had given him the horrors; and Harris said it would be so difficult to get into the boat again, and went back and sorted out his trousers.

I did not altogether like to give in, though I did not relish the plunge. There might be snags about, or weeds, I thought. I meant to compromise matters by going down to the edge and just throwing the water over myself; so I took a towel and crept out on the bank and wormed my way along on to the branch of a tree that dipped down into the water.

It was bitterly cold. The wind cut like a knife. I thought I would not throw the water over myself after all. I would go back into the boat and dress; and I turned to do so; and, as I turned, the silly branch gave way, and I and the towel went in together with a tremendous splash, and I was out mid-stream with a gallon of Thames water inside me before I knew what had happened.

'By Jove! old J.'s gone in,' I heard Harris say, as I came blowing to the surface. 'I didn't think he'd have the pluck to do it. Did you?'

'Is it all right?' sung out George.

'Lovely,' I spluttered back. 'You are duffers not to come in. I wouldn't have missed this for worlds. Why won't you try it? It only wants a little determination.'

But I could not persuade them.

Rather an amusing thing happened while dressing that morning. I was very cold when I got back into the boat, and, in my hurry to get my shirt on, I accidentally jerked it into the water. It made me awfully wild, especially as George burst out laughing. I could not see anything to laugh at, and I told George so, and he only laughed the more. I never saw a man laugh so much. I quite lost my temper with him at last, and I pointed out to him what a drivelling maniac of an imbecile idiot he was; but he only roared the louder. And then, just as I was landing the shirt, I noticed that it was not my shirt at all, but George's, which I had mistaken for mine; whereupon the humour of the thing struck me for the first time, and *I* began to laugh. And the more I looked from George's wet shirt to George, roaring with laughter, the more I was amused, and I laughed so much that I had to let the shirt fall back into the water again.

'Ar'n't you going to get it out?' said George, between his shrieks.

I could not answer him at all for a while, I was laughing so, but, at last, between my peals I managed to jerk out:

'It isn't my shirt—it's *yours!*'

I never saw a man's face change from lively to severe so suddenly in all my life before.

'What!' he yelled, springing up. 'You silly cuckoo! Why can't you be more careful what you're doing? Why the deuce don't you go and dress on the bank? You're not fit to be in a boat, you're not. Gimme the hitcher.'

I tried to make him see the fun of the thing, but he could not. George is very dense at seeing a joke sometimes.

Harris proposed that we should have scrambled eggs for breakfast. He said he would cook them. It seemed, from his account, that he was very good at doing scrambled eggs. He often did them at picnics and when out on yachts. He was quite famous for them. People who had once tasted his scrambled eggs, so we gathered from his conversation, never cared for any other food afterwards, but pined away and died when they could not get them.

It made our mouths water to hear him talk about the things, and we handed him out the stove and the frying-pan and all the eggs that had not smashed and gone over everything in the hamper, and begged him to begin.

He had some trouble in breaking the eggs—or rather not so much trouble in breaking them exactly as in getting them into the frying-pan when broken, and keeping them off his trousers, and preventing them from running up his sleeve; but he fixed some half-a-dozen into the pan at last, and then squatted down by the side of the stove and chivied them about with a fork.

It seemed harassing work, so far as George and I could judge. Whenever he went near the pan he burned himself, and then he would drop everything and dance round the stove, flicking his fingers about and cursing the things. Indeed, every time George and I looked round at him he was sure to be performing this feat. We thought at first that it was a necessary part of the culinary arrangements.

We did not know what scrambled eggs were, and we fanced that it must be some Red Indian or Sandwich Islands' sort of dish that required dances and incantations for its proper cooking. Montmorency went and put his nose over it once, and the fat spluttered up and scalded him, and then *he* began dancing and cursing. Altogether it was one of the most interesting and exciting operations I have ever witnessed. George and I were both quite sorry when it was over.

The result was not altogether the success that Harris had antici-pated. There seemed so little to show for the business. Six eggs had gone into the frying-pan, and all that came out was a teaspoonful of burnt and unappetizing looking mess.

Harris said it was the fault of the frying-pan, and thought it would have gone better if we had had a fish-kettle and a gas-stove; and we decided not to attempt the dish again until we had those aids to housekeeping by us.

The sun had got more powerful by the time we had finished breakfast, and the wind had dropped, and it was as lovely a morning as one could desire. Little was in sight to remind us of the nineteenth century; and, as we looked out upon the river in the morning sunlight, we could almost fancy that the centuries between us and that ever-to-be-famous June morning of 1215 had been drawn aside, and that we, English yeomen's sons in homespun cloth, with dirk at belt, were waiting there to witness the writing of that stupendous page of history, the meaning whereof was to be translated to the common people some four hundred and odd years later by one Oliver Cromwell, who had deeply studied it.

It is a fine summer morning—sunny, soft, and still. But through the air there runs a thrill of coming stir. King John has slept at Duncroft Hall, and all the day before the little town of Staines has echoed to the clang of armed men, and the clatter of great horses over its rough stones, and the shouts of captains, and the grim oaths and surly jests of bearded bowmen, billmen, pikemen, and strange-speaking foreign spearmen.

Gay-cloaked companies of knights and squires have ridden in, all travel-stained and dusty. And all the evening long the timid towns-men's doors have had to be quick opened to let in rough groups of soldiers, for whom there must be found both board and lodging, and the best of both, or woe betide the house and all within; for the sword is judge and jury, plaintiff and executioner, in these tempestuous times, and pays for what it takes by sparing those from whom it takes it, if it pleases it to do so.

Round the camp-fire in the market-place gather still more of the Barons' troops, and eat and drink deep, and bellow forth roystering drinking songs, and gamble and quarrel as the evening grows and deepens into night. The firelight sheds quaint shadows on their piled-up arms and on their uncouth forms. The children of the town steal round to watch them, wondering; and brawny country wenches, laughing, draw near to bandy ale-house jest and jibe with the swaggering troopers so unlike the village swains, who, now despised, stand apart behind, with vacant grins upon their broad, peering faces.

And out from the fields around, glitter the faint lights of more distant camps, as here some great lord's followers lie mustered, and there false John's French mercenaries hover like crouching wolves without the town.

And so, with sentinel in each dark street, and twinkling watch-fires on each height around, the night has worn away, and over this fair valley of old Thames has broken the morning of the great day that is to close so big with the fate of ages yet unborn.

Ever since grey dawn, in the lower of the two islands, just above where we are standing, there has been great clamour, and the sound of many workmen. The great pavilion brought there yester eve is being raised, and carpenters are busy nailing tiers of seats, while 'prentices from London town are there with many-coloured stuffs and silks and cloth of gold and silver.

And now, lo! down upon the road that winds along the river's bank from Staines there come towards us, laughing and talking together in deep guttural bass, a half-a-score of stalwart halbert-men—Barons' men, these—and halt at a hundred yards or so above us, on the other bank, and lean upon their arms, and wait.

And so, from hour to hour, march up along the road ever fresh groups and bands of armed men, their casques and breastplates flashing back the long low lines of morning sunlight, until, as far as eye can reach, the way seems thick with glittering steel and prancing steeds. And shouting horsemen are galloping from group to group, and little banners are fluttering lazily in the warm breeze, and every now and then there is a deeper stir as the ranks make way on either side, and some great Baron on his war-horse, with his guard of squires around him, passes along to take his station at the head of his serfs and vassals.

And up the slope of Cooper's Hill, just opposite, are gathered the wondering rustics and curious townsfolk, who have run from Staines, and none are quite sure what the bustle is about, but each one has a different version of the great event that they have come to see; and some say that much good to all the people will come from this day's work; but the old men shake their heads, for they have heard such tales before.

And all the river down to Staines is dotted with small craft and boats and tiny coracles—which last are growing out of favour now, and are used only by the poorer folk. Over the rapids, where in after years trim Bell Weir lock will stand, they have been forced or dragged by their study rowers, and now are crowding up as near as they dare come to the great covered barges, which lie in readiness to bear King John to where the fateful Charter waits his signing.

It is noon, and we and all the people have been waiting patient for many an hour, and the rumour has run round that slippery John has again escaped from the Barons' grasp, and has stolen away from Duncroft Hall with his mercenaries at his heels, and will soon be doing other work than signing charters for his people's liberty.

Not so! This time the grip upon him has been one of iron, and he has slid and wriggled in vain. Far down the road a little cloud of dust has risen, and draws nearer and grows larger, and the pattering of many hoofs grows louder, and in and out between the scattered groups of drawn-up men, there pushes on its way a brilliant cavalcade of gay-dressed lords and knights. And front and rear, and either flank, there ride the yeomen of the Barons, and in the midst King John.

He rides to where the barges lie in readiness, and the great Barons step forth from their ranks to meet him. He greets them with a smile and laugh, and pleasant honeyed words, as though it were some feast in his honour to which he had been invited. But as he rises to dismount, he casts one hurried glance from his own French mercenaries drawn up in the rear to the grim ranks of the Barons' men that hem him in.

Is it too late? One fierce blow at the unsuspecting horseman at his side, one cry to his French troops, one desperate charge upon the unready lines before him, and these rebellious Barons might rue the day they dared to thwart his plans! A bolder hand might have turned the game even at that point. Had it been a Richard there! the cup of liberty might have been dashed from England's lips, and the taste of freedom held back for a hundred years.

But the heart of King John sinks before the stern faces of the English fighting men, and the arm of King John drops back on to his rein, and he dismounts and takes his seat in the foremost barge. And the Barons follow in, with each mailed hand upon the sword-hilt, and the word is given to let go.

Slowly the heavy, bright-decked barges leave the shore of Runningmede. Slowly against the swift current they work their ponderous way, till, with a low grumble, they grate against the bank of the little island that from this day will bear the name of Magna Charta Island.* And King John has stepped upon the shore, and we wait in breathless silence till a great shout cleaves the air, and the great cornerstone in England's temple of liberty has, now we know, been firmly laid.

CHAPTER XII

Henry VIII and Anne Boleyn—Disadvantages of living in same house with pair of lovers—A trying time for the English nation—A night search for the picturesque—Homeless and houseless—Harris prepares to die—An angel comes along—Effect of sudden joy on Harris—A little supper—Lunch—High price for mustard—A fearful battle— Maidenhead—Sailing—Three fishers—We are cursed.

I was sitting on the bank, conjuring up this scene to myself, when George remarked that when I was quite rested, perhaps I would not mind helping to wash up; and, thus recalled from the days of the glorious past to the prosaic present, with all its misery and sin, I slid down into the boat and cleaned out the frying-pan with a stick of wood and a tuft of grass, polishing it up finally with George's wet shirt.

We went over to Magna Charta Island, and had a look at the stone which stands in the cottage there and on which the great Charter is said to have been signed; though, as to whether it really was signed there, or, as some say, on the other bank at 'Runningmede,' I decline to commit myself. As far as my own personal opinion goes, however, I am inclined to give weight to the popular island theory. Certainly, had I been one of the Barons, at the time, I should have strongly urged upon my comrades the advisability of our getting such a slippery customer as King John on to the island, where there was less chance of surprises and tricks.

There are the ruins of an old priory in the grounds of Ankerwyke House, which is close to Picnic Point, and it was round about the grounds of this old priory that Henry VIII is said to have waited for and met Anne Boleyn. He also used to meet her at Hever Castle in Kent, and also somewhere near St Albans. It must have been difficult for the people of England in those days to have found a spot where these thoughtless young folk were *not* spooning.

Have you ever been in a house where there are a couple courting? It is most trying. You think you will go and sit in the drawing-room, and you march off there. As you open the door, you hear a noise as if somebody had suddenly recollected something, and, when you get in, Emily is over by the window, full of interest in the opposite side of the road, and your friend, John Edward, is at the other end of the room with his whole soul held in thrall by photographs of other people's relatives.

'Oh!' you say, pausing at the door, 'I didn't know anybody was here.'

'Oh! didn't you?' says Emily, coldly, in a tone which implies that she does not believe you.

You hang about for a bit, then you say:

'It's very dark. Why don't you light the gas?'

John Edward says, 'Oh!' he hadn't noticed it; and Emily says that papa does not like the gas lit in the afternoon.

You tell them one or two items of news, and give them your views and opinions on the Irish question;* but this does not appear to interest them. All they remark on any subject is, 'Oh!' 'Is it?' 'Did he?' 'Yes,' and 'You don't say so!' And, after ten minutes of such style of conversation, you edge up to the door, and slip out, and are surprised to find that the door immediately closes behind you, and shuts itself, without your having touched it.

Half an hour later, you think you will try a pipe in the conservatory. The only chair in the place is occupied by Emily; and John Edward, if the language of clothes can be relied upon, has evidently been sitting on the floor. They do not speak, but they give you a look that says all that can be said in a civilised community; and you back out promptly and shut the door behind you.

You are afraid to poke your nose into any room in the house now; so, after walking up and down the stairs for a while, you go and sit in your own bedroom. This becomes uninteresting, however, after a time, and so you put on your hat and stroll out into the garden. You walk down the path, and as you pass the summer-house you glance in, and there are those two young idiots, huddled up into one corner of it; and they see you, and are evidently under the idea that, for some wicked purpose of your own, you are following them about.

'Why don't they have a special room for this sort of thing, and make people keep to it?' you mutter; and you rush back to the hall and get your umbrella and go out.

It must have been much like this when that foolish boy Henry VIII was courting his little Anne. People in Buckinghamshire would have come upon them unexpectedly when they were mooning round Windsor and Wraysbury, and have exclaimed, 'Oh! you here!' and Henry would have blushed and said, 'Yes; he'd just come over to see a man;' and Anne would have said, 'Oh, I'm so glad to see you! Isn't it funny? I've just met Mr Henry VIII in the lane, and he's going the same way I am.'

Then those people would have gone away and said to themselves: 'Oh! we'd better get out of here while this billing and cooing is on. We'll go down to Kent.'

And they would go to Kent, and the first thing they would see in Kent, when they got there, would be Henry and Anne fooling round Hever Castle.

'Oh, drat this!' they would have said. 'Here, let's go away. I can't stand any more of it. Let's go to St Albans—nice quiet place, St Albans.'

And when they reached St Albans, there would be that wretched couple, kissing under the Abbey walls. Then these folks would go and be pirates until the marriage was over.

From Picnic Point to Old Windsor lock is a delightful bit of the river. A shady road, dotted here and there with dainty little cottages, runs by the bank up to the 'Bells of Ouseley,' a picturesque inn, as most up-river inns are, and a place where a very good glass of ale may be drunk—so Harris says; and on a matter of this kind you can take Harris's word. Old Windsor is a famous spot in its way. Edward the Confessor had a palace here, and here the great Earl Godwin was proved guilty by the justice of that age of having encompassed the death of the King's brother. Earl Godwin broke a piece of bread and held it in his hand.

'If I am guilty,' said the Earl, 'may this bread choke me when I eat it!'

Then he put the bread into his mouth and swallowed it, and it choked him, and he died.

After you pass Old Windsor, the river is somewhat uninteresting, and does not become itself again until you are nearing Boveney.

George and I towed up past the Home Park, which stretches along the right bank from Albert to Victoria Bridge; and as we were passing Datchet, George asked me if I remembered our first trip up the river, and when we landed at Datchet at ten o'clock at night, and wanted to go to bed.

I answered that I did remember it. It will be some time before I forget it.

It was the Saturday before the August Bank Holiday. We were tired and hungry, we same three, and when we got to Datchet we took out the hamper, the two bags, and the rugs and coats, and such like things, and started off to look for diggings. We passed a very pretty little hotel, with clematis and creeper over the porch; but there was no honeysuckle about it, and, for some reason, or other, I had got my mind fixed on honeysuckle, and I said:

'Oh, don't let's go in there! Let's go on a bit further, and see if there isn't one with honeysuckle over it.'

So we went on till we came to another hotel. That was a very nice hotel, too, and it had honeysuckle on it, round at the side; but Harris did not like the look of a man who was leaning against the front door. He said he didn't look a nice man at all, and he wore ugly boots: so we went on further. We went a goodish way without coming across any more hotels, and then we met a man, and asked him to direct us to a few.

He said:

'Why, you are coming away from them. You must turn right round and go back, and then you will come to the Stag.'

We said:

'Oh, we had been there, and didn't like it—no honeysuckle over it.'

'Well, then,' he said, 'there's the Manor House, just opposite. Have you tried that?'

Harris replied that we did not want to go there—didn't like the looks of a man who was stopping there—Harris did not like the colour of his hair, didn't like his boots, either.

'Well, I don't know what you'll do, I'm sure,' said our informant; 'because they are the only two inns in the place.'

'No other inns!' exclaimed Harris.

'None,' replied the man.

'What on earth are we to do?' cried Harris.

Then George spoke up. He said Harris and I could get an hotel built for us, if we liked, and have some people made to put in. For his part, he was going back to the Stag.

The greatest minds never realise their ideals in any matter; and Harris and I sighed over the hollowness of all earthly desires, and followed George.

We took our traps into the Stag and laid them down in the hall.

The landlord came up and said:

'Good evening, gentlemen.'

'Oh, good evening,' said George; 'we want three beds, please.'

'Very sorry, sir,' said the landlord; 'but I'm afraid we can't manage it.'

'Oh, well, never mind,' said George, 'two will do. Two of us can sleep in one bed, can't we?' he continued, turning to Harris and me.

Harris said, 'Oh, yes;' he thought George and I could sleep in one bed very easily.

'Very sorry, sir,' again repeated the landlord: 'but we really haven't got a bed vacant in the whole house. In fact, we are putting two, and even three gentlemen in one bed, as it is.'

This staggered us for a bit.

But Harris, who is an old traveller, rose to the occasion, and, laughing cheerily, said:

'Oh, well, we can't help it. We must rough it. You must give us a shake-down in the billiard-room.'

'Very sorry, sir. Three gentlemen sleeping on the billiard-table already, and two in the coffee-room. Can't possibly take you in to-night.'

We picked up our things, and went over to the Manor House. It was a pretty little place. I said I thought I should like it better than the other house; and Harris said, 'Oh, yes,' it would be all right, and we needn't look at the man with the red hair; besides, the poor fellow couldn't help having red hair.

Harris spoke quite kindly and sensibly about it.

The people at the Manor House did not wait to hear us talk. The landlady met us on the doorstep with the greeting that we were the fourteenth party she had turned away within the last hour and a half. As for our meek suggestions of stables, billiard-room, or coal-cellars, she laughed them all to scorn: all these nooks had been snatched up long ago.

Did she know of any place in the whole village where we could get shelter for the night?

'Well, if we didn't mind roughing it—she did not recommend it, mind—but there was a little beershop half a mile down the Eton road——'

We waited to hear no more; we caught up the hamper and the bags, and the coats and rugs, and parcels, and ran. The distance seemed more like a mile than half a mile, but we reached the place at last, and rushed, panting, into the bar.

The people at the beershop were rude. They merely laughed at us. There were only three beds in the whole house, and they had seven single gentlemen and two married couples sleeping there already. A kind-hearted bargeman, however, who happened to be in the tap-room, thought we might try the grocer's, next door to the Stag, and we went back.

The grocer's was full. An old woman we met in the shop then kindly took us along with her for a quarter of a mile, to a lady friend of hers, who occasionally let rooms to gentlemen.

This old woman walked very slowly, and we were twenty minutes getting to her lady friend's. She enlivened the journey by describing to us, as we trailed along, the various pains she had in her back.

Her lady friend's rooms were let. From there we were recommended to No. 27. No. 27 was full, and sent us to No. 32, and 32 was full.

Then we went back into the high road, and Harris sat down on the hamper and said he would go no further. He said it seemed a quiet spot, and he would like to die there. He requested George and me to kiss his mother for him, and to tell all his relations that he forgave them and died happy.

At that moment an angel came by in the disguise of a small boy (and I cannot think of any more effective disguise an angel could have assumed), with a can of beer in one hand, and in the other something at the end of a string, which he let down on to every flat stone he came across, and then pulled up again, this producing a peculiarly un-attractive sound, suggestive of suffering.

We asked this heavenly messenger (as we discovered him after-wards to be) if he knew of any lonely house, whose occupants were few and feeble (old ladies or paralysed gentlemen preferred), who could be easily frightened into giving up their beds for the night to three desperate men; or, if not this, could he recommend us to an empty pigsty, or a disused limekiln, or anything of that sort. He did not know of any such place—at least, not one handy; but he said that, if we liked to come with him, his mother had a room to spare, and could put us up for the night.

We fell upon his neck there in the moonlight and blessed him, and it would have made a very beautiful picture if the boy himself had not been so overpowered by our emotion as to be unable to sustain himself under it, and sunk to the ground, letting us all down on top of him. Harris was so overcome with joy that he fainted, and had to seize the boy's beer-can and half empty it before he could recover consciousness, and then he started off at a run, and left George and me to bring on the luggage.

It was a little four-roomed cottage where the boy lived, and his mother—good soul!—gave us hot bacon for supper, and we ate it all—five pounds—and a jam tart afterwards, and two pots of tea, and then we went to bed. There were two beds in the room; one was a 2ft.6in. truckle bed, and George and I slept in that, and kept in by tying ourselves together with a sheet; and the other was the little boy's bed, and Harris had that all to himself, and we found him, in the morning, with two feet of bare leg sticking out at the bottom, and George and I used it to hang the towels on while we bathed.

We were not so uppish about what sort of hotel we would have, next time we went to Datchet.

To return to our present trip: nothing exciting happened, and we tugged steadily on to a little below Monkey Island, where we drew up and lunched. We tackled the cold beef for lunch, and then we found that we had forgotten to bring any mustard. I don't think I ever in my life, before or since, felt I wanted mustard as badly as I felt I wanted it then. I don't care for mustard as a rule, and it is very seldom that I take it at all, but I would have given worlds for it then.

I don't know how many worlds there may be in the universe, but anyone who had brought me a spoonful of mustard at that precise moment could have had them all. I grow reckless like that when I want a thing and can't get it.

Harris said he would have given worlds for mustard too. It would have been a good thing for anybody who had come up to that spot with a can of mustard, then: he would have been set up in worlds for the rest of his life.

But there! I daresay both Harris and I would have tried to back out of the bargain after we had got the mustard. One makes these extravagant offers in moments of excitement, but, of course, when one comes to think of it, one sees how absurdly out of proportion they are with the value of the required article. I heard a man, going up a mountain in Switzerland, once say he would give worlds for a glass of beer, and, when he came to a little shanty where they kept it, he kicked up a most fearful row because they charged him five francs for a bottle of Bass. He said it was a scandalous imposition, and he wrote to the *Times* about it.

It cast a gloom over the boat, there being no mustard. We ate our beef in silence. Existence seemed hollow and uninteresting. We thought of the happy days of childhood, and sighed. We brightened up a bit, however, over the apple-tart, and, when George drew out a tin of pine-apple from the bottom of the hamper, and rolled it into the middle of the boat, we felt that life was worth living after all.

We are very fond of pine-apple, all three of us. We looked at the picture on the tin; we thought of the juice. We smiled at one another, and Harris got a spoon ready.

Then we looked for the knife to open the tin with. We turned out everything in the hamper. We turned out the bags. We pulled up the boards at the bottom of the boat. We took everything out on to the bank and shook it. There was no tin-opener to be found.

Then Harris tried to open the tin with a pocket-knife, and broke the knife and cut himself badly; and George tried a pair of scissors, and the scissors flew up, and nearly put his eye out. While they were dressing their wounds, I tried to make a hole in the thing with the spiky end of the hitcher, and the hitcher slipped and jerked me out between the boat and the bank into two feet of muddy water, and the tin rolled over, uninjured, and broke a teacup.

Then we all got mad. We took that tin out on the bank, and Harris went up into a field and got a big sharp stone, and I went back into the boat and brought out the mast, and George held the tin and Harris held the sharp end of his stone against the top of it, and I took the mast and poised it high up in the air, and gathered up all my strength and brought it down.

It was George's straw hat that saved his life that day. He keeps that hat now (what is left of it), and, of a winter's evening, when the pipes are lit and the boys are telling stretchers about the dangers they have passed through, George brings it down and shows it round, and the stirring tale is told anew, with fresh exaggerations every time.

Harris got off with merely a flesh wound.

After that, I took the tin off myself, and hammered at it with the mast till I was worn out and sick at heart, whereupon Harris took it in hand.

We beat it out flat; we beat it back square; we battered it into every form known to geometry—but we could not make a hole in it. Then George went at it, and knocked it into a shape, so strange, so weird, so unearthly in its wild hideousness, that he got frightened and threw away the mast. Then we all three sat round it on the grass and looked at it.

There was one great dent across the top that had the appearance of a mocking grin, and it drove us furious, so that Harris rushed at the thing, and caught it up, and flung it far into the middle of the river, and as it sank we hurled our curses at it, and we got into the boat and rowed away from the spot, and never paused till we reached Maidenhead.

Maidenhead itself is too snobby to be pleasant. It is the haunt of the river swell and his overdressed female companion. It is the town of showy hotels, patronised chiefly by dudes and ballet girls. It is the witch's kitchen from which go forth those demons of the river —steam-launches. The *London Journal* duke always has his 'little place' at Maidenhead; and the heroine of the three-volume novel always dines there when she goes out on the spree with somebody else's husband.

We went through Maidenhead quickly, and then eased up, and took leisurely that grand reach beyond Boulter's and Cookham locks. Cliveden Woods still wore their dainty dress of spring, and rose up, from the water's edge, in one long harmony of blended shades of fairy green. In its unbroken loveliness this is, perhaps, the sweetest stretch of all the river, and lingeringly we slowly drew our little boat away from its deep peace.

We pulled up in the backwater, just below Cookham, and had tea; and, when we were through the lock, it was evening. A stiffish breeze had sprung up—in our favour, for a wonder; for, as a rule on the river, the wind is always dead against you whatever way you go. It is against you in the morning, when you start for a day's trip, and you pull a long distance, thinking how easy it will be to come back with the sail. Then, after tea, the wind veers round, and you have to pull hard in its teeth all the way home.

When you forget to take the sail at all, then the wind is consistently in your favour both ways. But there! this world is only a probation, and man was born to trouble as the sparks fly upward.*

This evening, however, they had evidently made a mistake, and had put the wind round at our back instead of in our face. We kept very quiet about it, and got the sail up quickly before they found it out, and then we spread ourselves about the boat in thoughtful attitudes, and the sail bellied out, and strained, and grumbled at the mast, and the boat flew.

I steered.

There is no more thrilling sensation I know of than sailing. It comes as near to flying as man has got to yet—except in dreams. The wings of the rushing wind seem to be bearing you onward, you know not where. You are no longer the slow, plodding, puny thing of clay, creeping tortuously upon the ground; you are a part of Nature! Your heart is throbbing against hers! Her glorious arms are round you, raising you up against her heart! Your spirit is at one with hers; your limbs grow light! The voices of the air are singing to you. The earth seems far away and little; and the clouds, so close above your head, are brothers, and you stretch your arms to them.

We had the river to ourselves, except that, far in the distance, we could see a fishing-punt, moored in mid-stream, on which three fishermen sat; and we skimmed over the water, and passed the wooded banks, and no one spoke.

I was steering.

As we drew nearer, we could see that the three men fishing seemed old and solemn-looking men. They sat on three chairs in the punt, and watched intently their lines. And the red sunset threw a mystic light upon the waters, and tinged with fire the towering woods, and made a golden glory of the piled-up clouds. It was an hour of deep enchantment, of ecstatic hope and longing. The little sail stood out against the purple sky, the gloaming lay around us, wrapping the world in rainbow shadows; and, behind us, crept the night.

We seemed like knights of some old legend, sailing across some mystic lake into the unknown realm of twilight, unto the great land of the sunset.

We did not go into the realm of twilight; we went slap into that punt, where those three old men were fishing. We did not know what had happened at first, because the sail shut out the view, but from the nature of the language that rose up upon the evening air, we gathered that we had come into the neighbourhood of human beings, and that they were vexed and discontented.

Harris let the sail down, and then we saw what had happened. We had knocked those three old gentlemen off their chairs into a general heap at the bottom of the boat, and they were now slowly and painfully sorting themselves out from each other, and picking fish off themselves; and as they worked, they cursed us—not with a common cursory curse, but with long, carefully-thought-out, comprehensive curses, that embraced the whole of our career, and went away into the distant future, and included all our relations, and covered everything connected with us—good, substantial curses.

Harris told them they ought to be grateful for a little excitement, sitting there fishing all day, and he also said that he was shocked and grieved to hear men their age give way to temper so.

But it did not do any good.

George said he would steer, after that. He said a mind like mine ought not to be expected to give itself away in steering boats—better let a mere commonplace human being see after that boat, before we jolly well all got drowned; and he took the lines, and brought us up to Marlow.

And at Marlow we left the boat by the bridge, and went and put up for the night at the 'Crown.'

CHAPTER XIII

Marlow—Bisham Abbey—The Medmenham Monks—Montmorency thinks he will murder an old Tom cat—But eventually decides that he will let it live—Shameful conduct of a fox terrier at the Civil Service Stores—Our departure from Marlow—An imposing procession—The steam launch, useful receipts for annoying and hindering it—We decline to drink the river—A peaceful dog—Strange disappearance of Harris and a pie.

MARLOW is one of the pleasantest river centres I know of. It is a bustling, lively little town; not very picturesque on the whole, it is true, but there are many quaint nooks and corners to be found in it, nevertheless—standing arches in the shattered bridge of Time, over which our fancy travels back to the days when Marlow Manor owned Saxon Algar for its lord, ere conquering William seized it to give to Queen Matilda, ere it passed to the Earls of Warwick or to worldly-wise Lord Paget, the councillor of four successive sovereigns.

There is lovely country round about it, too, if, after boating, you are fond of a walk, while the river itself is at its best here. Down to Cookham, past the Quarry Woods and the meadows, is a lovely reach. Dear old Quarry Woods! with your narrow, climbing paths, and little winding glades, how scented to this hour you seem with memories of sunny summer days! How haunted are your shadowy vistas with the ghosts of laughing faces! how from your whispering leaves there softly fall the voices of long ago!

From Marlow up to Sonning is even fairer yet. Grand old Bisham Abbey, whose stone walls have rung to the shouts of the Knights Templars, and which, at one time, was the home of Anne of Cleves and at another of Queen Elizabeth, is passed on the right bank just half a mile above Marlow Bridge. Bisham Abbey is rich in melo-dramatic properties. It contains a tapestry bed-chamber, and a secret room hid high up in the thick walls. The ghost of the Lady Hoby, who beat her little boy to death, still walks there at night, trying to wash its ghostly hands clean in a ghostly basin.

Warwick, the king-maker, rests there, careless now about such trivial things as earthly kings and earthly kingdoms; and Salisbury, who did good service at Poitiers.* Just before you come to the abbey, and right on the river's bank, is Bisham Church, and, perhaps, if any tombs are worth inspecting, they are the tombs and monu-ments in Bisham Church. It was while floating in his boat under the Bisham beeches that Shelley, who was then living at Marlow (you can see his house now, in West street), composed *The Revolt of Islam.**

By Hurley Weir, a little higher up, I have often thought that I could stay a month without having sufficient time to drink in all the beauty of the scene. The village of Hurley, five minutes' walk from the lock, is as old a little spot as there is on the river, dating, as it does, to quote the quaint phraseology of those dim days, 'from the times of King Sebert and King Offa.' Just past the weir (going up) is Danes' Field, where the invading Danes once encamped, during their march to Gloucestershire; and a little further still, nestling by a sweet corner of the stream, is what is left of Medmenham Abbey.

The famous Medmenham monks, or 'Hell Fire Club,' as they were commonly called, and of whom the notorious Wilkes* was a member, were a fraternity whose motto was, 'Do as you please,' and that invitation still stands over the ruined doorway of the abbey. Many years before this bogus abbey, with its congregation of irreverent jesters, was founded, there stood upon this same spot a monastery of a sterner kind, whose monks were of a somewhat different type to the revellers that were to follow them, five hundred years afterwards.

The Cistercian monks, whose abbey stood there in the thirteenth century, wore no clothes but rough tunics and cowls, and ate no flesh, nor fish, nor eggs. They lay upon straw, and they rose at midnight to mass. They spent the day in labour, reading, and prayer; and over all their lives there fell a silence as of death, for no one spoke.

A grim fraternity, passing grim lives in that sweet spot, that God had made so bright! Strange that Nature's voices all around them —the soft singing of the waters, the whisperings of the river grass, the music of the rushing wind—should not have taught them a truer meaning of life than this. They listened there, through the long days, in silence, waiting for a voice from heaven; and all day long and through the solemn night it spoke to them in myriad tones, and they heard it not.

From Medmenham to sweet Hambleden lock the river is full of peaceful beauty, but, after it passes Greenlands, the rather uninteresting looking river residence of my newsagent—a quiet unassuming old gentleman, who may often be met with about these regions, during the summer months, sculling himself along in easy vigorous style, or chatting genially to some old lock-keeper, as he passes through—until well the other side of Henley, it is somewhat bare and dull.

We got up tolerably early on the Monday morning at Marlow, and went for a bathe before breakfast; and, coming back, Montmorency made an awful ass of himself. The only subject on which Montmorency and I have any serious difference of opinion is cats. I like cats; Montmorency does not.

When I meet a cat, I say, 'Poor Pussy!' and stoop down and tickle the side of its head; and the cat sticks up its tail in a rigid, cast-iron manner, arches its back, and wipes its nose up against my trousers;

and all is gentleness and peace. When Montmorency meets a cat, the whole street knows about it; and there is enough bad language wasted in ten seconds to last an ordinarily respectable man all his life, with care.

I do not blame the dog (contenting myself, as a rule, with merely clouting his head or throwing stones at him), because I take it that it is his nature. Fox-terriers are born with about four times as much original sin in them as other dogs are, and it will take years and years of patient effort on the part of us Christians to bring about any appreciable reformation in the rowdiness of the fox-terrier nature.

I remember being in the lobby of the Haymarket Stores one day, and all round about me were dogs, waiting for the return of their owners, who were shopping inside. There were a mastiff, and one or two collies, and a St Bernard, a few retrievers and Newfoundlands, a boar-hound, a French poodle, with plenty of hair round its head, but mangy about the middle; a bull-dog, a few Lowther Arcade* sort of animals, about the size of rats, and a couple of Yorkshire tykes.

There they sat, patient, good, and thoughtful. A solemn peace-fulness seemed to reign in that lobby. An air of calmness and resignation—of gentle sadness pervaded the room.

Then a sweet young lady entered, leading a meek-looking little fox-terrier, and left him, chained up there, between the bull-dog and the poodle. He sat and looked about him for a minute. Then he cast up his eyes to the ceiling, and seemed, judging from his expression, to be thinking of his mother. Then he yawned. Then he looked round at the other dogs, all silent, grave, and dignified.

He looked at the bull-dog, sleeping dreamlessly on his right. He looked at the poodle, erect and haughty, on his left. Then, without a word of warning, without the shadow of a provocation, he bit that poodle's near fore-leg, and a yelp of agony rang through the quiet shades of that lobby.

The result of his first experiment seemed highly satisfactory to him, and he determined to go on and make things lively all round. He sprang over the poodle and vigorously attacked a collie, and the collie woke up, and immediately commenced a fierce and noisy contest with the poodle. Then Foxey came back to his own place, and caught the bull-dog by the ear, and tried to throw him away; and the bull-dog, a curiously impartial animal, went for everything he could reach, including the hall-porter, which gave that dear little terrier the opportunity to enjoy an uninterrupted fight of his own with an equally willing Yorkshire tyke.

Anyone who knows canine nature need hardly be told that, by this time, all the other dogs in the place were fighting as if their hearths and homes depended on the fray. The big dogs fought each other indiscriminately; and the little dogs fought among themselves, and filled up their spare time by biting the legs of the big dogs.

The whole lobby was a perfect pandemonium, and the din was terrific. A crowd assembled outside in the Haymarket, and asked if it was a vestry meeting; or, if not, who was being murdered, and why? Men came with poles and ropes, and tried to separate the dogs, and the police were sent for.

And in the midst of the riot that sweet young lady returned, and snatched up that sweet little dog of hers (he had laid the tyke up for a month, and had on the expression, now, of a new-born lamb) into her arms, and kissed him, and asked him if he was killed, and what those great nasty brutes of dogs had been doing to him; and he nestled up against her, and gazed up into her face with a look that seemed to say: 'Oh, I'm so glad you've come to take me away from this disgraceful scene!'

She said that the people at the Stores had no right to allow great savage things like those other dogs to be put with respectable people's dogs, and that she had a great mind to summon somebody.

Such is the nature of fox-terriers; and, therefore, I do not blame Montmorency for his tendency to row with cats; but he wished he had not given way to it that morning.

We were, as I have said, returning from a dip, and half-way up the High Street a cat darted out from one of the houses in front of us, and began to trot across the road. Montmorency gave a cry of joy—the cry of a stern warrior who sees his enemy given over to his hands—the sort of cry Cromwell might have uttered when the Scots came down the hill—and flew after his prey.

His victim was a large black Tom. I never saw a larger cat, nor a more disreputable-looking cat. It had lost half its tail, one of its ears, and a fairly appreciable proportion of its nose. It was a long, sinewy-looking animal. It had a calm, contented air about it.

Montmorency went for that poor cat at the rate of twenty miles an hour; but the cat did not hurry up—did not seem to have grasped the idea that its life was in danger. It trotted quietly on until its would-be assassin was within a yard of it, and then it turned round and sat down in the middle of the road, and looked at Montmorency with a gentle, inquiring expression, that said:

'Yes! You want me?'

Montmorency does not lack pluck; but there was something about the look of that cat that might have chilled the heart of the boldest dog. He stopped abruptly, and looked back at Tom.

Neither spoke; but the conversation that one could imagine was clearly as follows:—

THE CAT: 'Can I do anything for you?'

MONTMORENCY: 'No—no, thanks.'

THE CAT: 'Don't you mind speaking, if you really want anything, you know.'

MONTMORENCY (*backing down the High Street*): 'Oh, no—not at all—certainly—don't you trouble. I—I am afraid I've made a mistake. I thought I knew you. Sorry I disturbed you.'

THE CAT: 'Not at all—quite a pleasure. Sure you don't want anything, now?'

MONTMORENCY (*still backing*): 'Not at all, thanks—not at all —very kind of you. Good morning.'

THE CAT: 'Good-morning.'

Then the cat rose, and continued his trot; and Montmorency, fitting what he calls his tail carefully into its groove, came back to us, and took up an unimportant position in the rear.

To this day, if you say the word 'Cats!' to Montmorency, he will visibly shrink and look up piteously at you, as if to say:

'Please don't.'

We did our marketing after breakfast, and revictualled the boat for three days. George said we ought to take vegetables—that it was unhealthy not to eat vegetables. He said they were easy enough to cook, and that he would see to that; so we got ten pounds of potatoes, a bushel of peas, and a few cabbages. We got a beafsteak pie, a couple of gooseberry tarts, and a leg of mutton from the hotel; and fruit, and cakes, and bread and butter, and jam, and bacon and eggs, and other things we foraged round about the town for.

Our departure from Marlow I regard as one of our greatest successes. It was dignified and impressive, without being osten-tatious. We had insisted at all the shops we had been to that the things should be sent with us then and there. None of your 'Yes, sir, I will send them off at once: the boy will be down there before you are, sir!' and then fooling about on the landing-stage, and going back to the shop twice to have a row about them, for us. We waited while the basket was packed, and took the boy with us.

We went to a good many shops, adopting this principle at each one; and the consequence was that, by the time we had finished, we had as fine a collection of boys with baskets following us around as heart could desire; and our final march down the middle of the High Street, to the river, must have been as imposing a spectacle as Marlow had seen for many a long day.

The order of the procession was as follows:—

Montmorency, carrying a stick.

Two disreputable-looking curs, friends of
Montmorency's.

George, carrying coats and rugs, and smoking
a short pipe.

Harris, trying to walk with easy grace,
while carrying a bulged-out Gladstone bag in one
hand and a bottle of lime-juice in the other.

Greengrocer's boy and baker's boy,
with baskets.

Boots from the hotel, carrying hamper.

Confectioner's boy, with basket.

Grocer's boy, with basket.

Long-haired dog.

Cheesemonger's boy, with basket.

Odd man, carrying a bag.

Bosom companion of odd man, with his hands in his
pockets, smoking a short clay.

Fruiterer's boy, with basket.

Myself, carrying three hats and a pair of boots, and
trying to look as if I didn't know it.

Six small boys, and four stray dogs.

When we got down to the landing-stage, the boatman said:

'Let me see, sir; was yours a steam-launch or a house-boat?'

On our informing him it was a double-sculling skiff, he seemed surprised.

We had a good deal of trouble with steam launches that morning. It was just before the Henley week,* and they were going up in large numbers; some by themselves, some towing houseboats. I do hate steam launches: I suppose every rowing man does. I never see a steam launch but I feel I should like to lure it to a lonely part of the river, and there, in the silence and the solitude, strangle it.

There is a blatant bumptiousness about a steam launch that has the knack of rousing every evil instinct in my nature, and I yearn for the good old days, when you could go about and tell people what you thought of them with a hatchet and a bow and arrows. The expression on the face of the man who, with his hands in his pockets, stands by the stern, smoking a cigar, is sufficient to excuse a breach of the peace by itself; and the lordly whistle for you to get out of the way would, I am confident, ensure a verdict of 'justifiable homicide' from any jury of river men.

They used to *have to* whistle for us to get out of their way. If I may do so, without appearing boastful, I think I can honestly say that our one small boat, during that week, caused more annoyance and delay and aggravation to the steam launches that we came across than all the other craft on the river put together.

'Steam launch, coming!' one of us would cry out, on sighting the enemy in the distance; and, in an instant, everything was got ready to receive her. I would take the lines, and Harris and George would sit down beside me, all of us with our backs to the launch, and the boat would drift out quietly into mid-stream.

On would come the launch, whistling, and on we would go, drifting. At about a hundred yards off, she would start whistling like mad, and the people would come and lean over the side, and roar at us; but we never heard them! Harris would be telling us an anecdote about his mother, and George and I would not have missed a word of it for worlds.

Then that launch would give one final shriek of a whistle that would nearly burst the boiler, and she would reverse her engines, and blow off steam, and swing round and get aground; everyone on board of it would rush to the bow and yell at us, and the people on the bank would stand and shout to us, and all the other passing boats would stop and join in, till the whole river for miles up and down was in a state of frantic commotion. And then Harris would break off in the most interesting part of his narrative, and look up with mild surprise, and say to George:

'Why, George, bless us, if here isn't a steam launch!'

And George would answer:

'Well, do you know, I *thought* I heard something!'

Upon which we would get nervous and confused, and not know how to get the boat out of the way, and the people in the launch would crowd round and instruct us:

'Pull your right—you, you idiot! back with your left. No, not *you*—the other one—leave the lines alone, can't you—now, both together. NOT *that* way. Oh, you——'

Then they would lower a boat and come to our assistance; and, after quarter of an hour's effort, would get us clean out of their way, so that they could go on; and we would thank them so much, and ask them to give us a tow. But they never would.

Another good way we discovered of irritating the aristocratic type of steam launch, was to mistake them for a beanfeast,* and ask them if they were Messrs Cubit's lot or the Bermondsey Good Templars,* and could they lend us a saucepan.

Old ladies, not accustomed to the river, are always intensely nervous of steam launches. I remember going up once from Staines to Windsor—a stretch of water peculiarly rich in these mechanical monstrosities—with a party containing three ladies of this description. It was very exciting. At the first glimpse of every steam launch that came in view, they insisted on landing and sitting down on the bank until it was out of sight again. They said they were very sorry, but that they owed it to their families not to be fool-hardy.

We found ourselves short of water at Hambledon Lock; so we took our jar and went up to the lock-keeper's house to beg for some.

George was our spokesman. He put on a winning smile, and said:

'Oh, please could you spare us a little water?'

'Certainly,' replied the old gentleman; 'take as much as you want, and leave the rest.'

'Thank you so much,' murmured George, looking about him. 'Where—where do you keep it?'

'It's always in the same place my boy,' was the stolid reply: 'just behind you.'

'I don't see it,' said George, turning round.

'Why, bless us, where's your eyes?' was the man's comment, as he twisted George round and pointed up and down the stream. 'There's enough of it to see, ain't there?'

'Oh!' exclaimed George, grasping the idea; 'but we can't drink the river, you know!'

'No; but you can drink *some* of it,' replied the old fellow. 'It's what *I've* drunk for the last fifteen years.'

George told him that his appearance, after the course, did not seem a sufficiently good advertisement for the brand; and that he would prefer it out of a pump.

We got some from a cottage a little higher up. I daresay *that* was only river water, if we had known. But we did not know, so it was all right. What the eye does not see, the stomach does not get upset over.

We tried river water once, later on in the season, but it was not a success. We were coming down stream, and had pulled up to have tea in a backwater near Windsor. Our jar was empty, and it was a case of going without our tea or taking water from the river. Harris was for chancing it. He said it must be all right if we boiled the water. He said that the various germs of poison present in the water would be killed by the boiling. So we filled our kettle with Thames backwater, and boiled it; and very careful we were to see that it did boil.

We had made the tea, and were just settling down comfortably to drink it, when George, with his cup half-way to his lips, paused and exclaimed:

'What's that?'

'What's what?' asked Harris and I.

'Why that!' said George, looking westward.

Harris and I followed his gaze, and saw, coming down towards us on the sluggish current, a dog. It was one of the quietest and peacefullest dogs I have ever seen. I never met a dog who seemed more contented—more easy in its mind. It was floating dreamily on its back, with its four legs stuck up straight into the air. It was what I should call a full-bodied dog, with a well-developed chest. On he came, serene, dignified, and calm, until he was abreast of our boat, and there, among the rushes, he eased up, and settled down cosily for the evening.

George said he didn't want any tea, and emptied his cup into the water. Harris did not feel thirsty, either, and followed suit. I had drunk half mine, but I wished I had not.

I asked George if he thought I was likely to have typhoid.

He said: 'Oh, no;' he thought I had a very good chance indeed of escaping it. Anyhow, I should know in about a fortnight, whether I had or had not.

We went up the backwater to Wargrave. It is a short cut, leading out of the right-hand bank about half a mile above Marsh Lock, and is well worth taking, being a pretty, shady little piece of stream, besides saving nearly half a mile of distance.

Of course, its entrance is studded with posts and chains, and surrounded with notice boards, menacing all kinds of torture, imprisonment, and death to everyone who dares set scull upon its waters—I wonder some of these riparian boors don't claim the air of the river and threaten everyone with forty shillings fine who breathes it—but the posts and chains a little skill will easily avoid; and as for the boards, you might, if you have five minutes to spare, and there is nobody about, take one or two of them down and throw them into the river.

Half-way up the backwater, we got out and lunched; and it was during this lunch that George and I received rather a trying shock.

Harris received a shock, too; but I do not think Harris's shock could have been anything like so bad as the shock that George and I had over the business.

You see, it was in this way: we were sitting in a meadow, about ten yards from the water's edge, and we had just settled down comfortably to feed. Harris had the beefsteak pie between his knees, and was carving it, and George and I were waiting with our plates ready.

'Have you got a spoon there?' says Harris; 'I want a spoon to help the gravy with.'

The hamper was close behind us, and George and I both turned round to reach one out. We were not five seconds getting it. When we looked round again, Harris and the pie were gone!

It was a wide, open field. There was not a tree or a bit of hedge for hundreds of yards. He could not have tumbled into the river, because we were on the water side of him, and he would have had to climb over us to do it.

George and I gazed all about. Then we gazed at each other.

'Has he been snatched up to heaven?' I queried.

'They'd hardly have taken the pie too,' said George.

There seemed weight in this objection, and we discarded the heavenly theory.

'I suppose the truth of the matter is,' suggested George, descending to the commonplace and practicable, 'that there has been an earthquake.'

And then he added, with a touch of sadness in his voice: 'I wish he hadn't been carving that pie.'

With a sigh, we turned our eyes once more towards the spot where Harris and the pie had last been seen on earth; and there, as our blood froze in our veins and our hair stood up on end, we saw Harris's head—and nothing but his head—sticking bolt upright among the tall grass, the face very red, and bearing upon it an expression of great indignation!

George was the first to recover.

'Speak!' he cried, 'and tell us whether you are alive or dead—and where is the rest of you?'

'Oh, don't be a stupid ass!' said Harris's head, 'I believe you did it on purpose.'

'Did what?' exclaimed George and I.

'Why, put me to sit here—darn silly trick! Here, catch hold of the pie.'

And out of the middle of the earth, as it seemed to us, rose the pie—very much mixed up and damaged; and, after it, scrambled Harris—tumbled, grubby and wet.

He had been sitting, without knowing it, on the very verge of a small gully, the long grass hiding it from view; and in leaning a little back he had shot over, pie and all.

He said he had never felt so surprised in all his life, as when he first felt himself going, without being able to conjecture in the slightest what had happened. He thought at first that the end of the world had come.

Harris believes to this day that George and I planned it all beforehand. Thus does unjust suspicion follow even the most blameless; for, as the poet says, 'Who shall escape calumny?'*

Who, indeed!

CHAPTER XIV

Wargrave—Waxworks—Sonning—Our stew—Montmorency is sar-
castic—Fight between Montmorency and the tea-kettle—George's banjo
studies—Meet with discouragement—Difficulties in the way of the
musical amateur—Learning to play the bagpipes—Harris feels sad after
supper—George and I go for a walk—Return hungry and wet—There is
a strangeness about Harris—Harris and the swans, a remarkable story
—Harris has a troubled night.

WE caught a breeze, after lunch, which took us gently up past
Wargrave and Shiplake. Mellowed in the drowsy sunlight of a
summer's afternoon, Wargrave, nestling where the river bends,
makes a sweet old picture as you pass it, and one that lingers long
upon the retina of memory.

The 'George and Dragon' at Wargrave boasts a sign, painted on
the one side by Leslie, R.A., and on the other by Hodgson* of that
ilk. Leslie has depicted the fight; Hodgson has imagined the scene,
'After the Fight'—George, the work done, enjoying his pint of beer.

Day, the author of *Sandford and Merton*, lived and—more credit to
the place still—was killed at Wargrave. In the church is a memorial to
Mrs Sarah Hill, who bequeathed £1 annually, to be divided at Easter,
between two boys and two girls who 'have never been undutiful to
their parents; who have never been known to swear or to tell
untruths, to steal, or to break windows.' Fancy giving up all that for
five shillings a year! It is not worth it.

It is rumoured in the town that once, many years ago, a boy
appeared who really never had done these things—or at all events,
which was all that was required or could be expected, had never been
known to do them—and thus won the crown of glory. He was
exhibited for three weeks afterwards in the Town Hall, under a glass
case.

What has become of the money since no one knows. They say it is
always handed over to the nearest wax-works show.

Shiplake is a pretty village, but it cannot be seen from the river,
being upon the hill. Tennyson was married in Shiplake Church.

The river up to Sonning winds in and out through many islands,
and is very placid, hushed, and lonely. Few folk, except at twilight, a
pair or two of rustic lovers, walk along its banks. 'Arry and Lord

Fitznoodle have been left behind at Henley, and dismal, dirty Reading is not yet reached. It is a part of the river in which to dream of bygone days, and vanished forms and faces, and things that might have been, but are not, confound them.

We got out at Sonning, and went for a walk round the village. It is the most fairy-like little nook on the whole river. It is more like a stage village than one built of bricks and mortar. Every house is smothered in roses, and now, in early June, they were bursting forth in clouds of dainty splendour. If you stop at Sonning, put up at the 'Bull,' behind the church. It is a veritable picture of an old country inn, with green, square courtyard in front, where, on seats beneath the trees, the old men group of an evening to drink their ale and gossip over village politics; with low, quaint rooms and latticed windows, and awkward stairs and winding passages.

We roamed about sweet Sonning for an hour or so, and then, it being too late to push on past Reading, we decided to go back to one of the Shiplake islands, and put up there for the night. It was still early when we got settled, and George said that, as we had plenty of time, it would be a splendid opportunity to try a good, slap-up supper. He said he would show us what could be done up the river in the way of cooking, and suggested that, with the vegetables and the remains of the cold beef and general odds and ends, we should make an Irish stew.

It seemed a fascinating idea. George gathered wood and made a fire, and Harris and I started to peel the potatoes. I should never have thought that peeling potatoes was such an undertaking. The job turned out to be the biggest thing of its kind that I had ever been in. We began cheerfully, one might almost say skittishly, but our light-heartedness was gone by the time the first potato was finished. The more we peeled, the more peel there seemed to be left on; by the time we had got all the peel off and all the eyes out, there was no potato left—at least none worth speaking off. George came and had a look at it—it was about the size of a pea-nut. He said:

'Oh, that won't do! You're wasting them. You must scrape them.'

So we scraped them, and that was harder work than peeling. They are such an extraordinary shape, potatoes—all bumps and warts and hollows. We worked steadily for five-and-twenty minutes, and did four potatoes. Then we struck. We said we should require the rest of the evening for scraping ourselves.

I never saw such a thing as potato-scraping for making a fellow in a mess. It seemed difficult to believe that the potato-scrapings in which Harris and I stood, half smothered, could have come off four potatoes. It shows you what can be done with economy and care.

George said it was absurd to have only four potatoes in an Irish stew, so we washed half-a-dozen or so more, and put them in without peeling. We also put in a cabbage and about half a peck of peas. George stirred it all up, and then he said that there seemed to be a lot of room to spare, so we overhauled both the hampers, and picked out all the odds and ends and the remnants, and added them to the stew. There were half a pork pie and a bit of cold boiled bacon left, and we put them in. Then George found half a tin of potted salmon, and he emptied that into the pot.

He said that was the advantage of Irish stew: you got rid of such a lot of things. I fished out a couple of eggs that had got cracked, and we put those in. George said they would thicken the gravy.

I forget the other ingredients, but I know nothing was wasted; and I remember that, towards the end, Montmorency, who had evinced great interest in the proceedings throughout, strolled away with an earnest and thoughtful air, reappearing, a few minutes afterwards, with a dead water-rat in his mouth, which he evidently wished to present as his contribution to the dinner: whether in a sarcastic spirit, or with a genuine desire to assist, I cannot say.

We had a discussion as to whether the rat should go in or not. Harris said that he thought it would be all right, mixed up with the other things, and that every little helped; but George stood up for precedent. He said he had never heard of water-rats in Irish stew, and he would rather be on the safe side, and not try experiments.

Harris said:

'If you never try a new thing, how can you tell what it's like? It's men such as you that hamper the world's progress. Think of the man who first tried German sausage!'

It was a great success, that Irish stew. I don't think I ever enjoyed a meal more. There was something so fresh and piquant about it. One's palate gets so tired of the old hackneyed things: here was a dish with a new flavour, with a taste like nothing else on earth.

And it was nourishing, too. As George said, there was good stuff in it. The peas and potatoes might have been a bit softer, but we all had good teeth, so that did not matter much: and as for the gravy, it was a poem—a little too rich, perhaps, for a weak stomach, but nutritious.

We finished up with tea and cherry tart. Montmorency had a fight with the kettle during tea-time, and came off a poor second.

Throughout the trip, he had manifested great curiosity concerning the kettle. He would sit and watch it, as it boiled, with a puzzled expression, and would try and rouse it every now and then by growling at it. When it began to splutter and steam, he regarded it as a challenge, and would want to fight it, only, at that precise moment, some one would always dash up and bear off his prey before he could get at it.

To-day he determined he would be beforehand. At the first sound the kettle made, he rose, growling, and advanced towards it in a threatening attitude. It was only a little kettle, but it was full of pluck, and it up and spit at him.

'Ah! would ye!' growled Montmorency, showing his teeth; 'I'll teach ye to cheek a hard-working respectable dog; ye miserable, long-nosed, dirty-looking scoundrel, ye. Come on!'

And he rushed at that poor little kettle, and seized it by the spout.

Then, across the evening stillness, broke a blood-curdling yelp, and Montmorency left the boat, and did a constitutional three times round the island at the rate of thirty-five miles an hour, stopping every now and then to bury his nose in a bit of cool mud.

From that day Montmorency regarded the kettle with a mixture of awe, suspicion, and hate. Whenever he saw it he would growl and back at a rapid rate, with his tail shut down, and the moment it was put upon the stove he would promptly climb out of the boat, and sit on the bank, till the whole tea business was over.

George got out his banjo after supper, and wanted to play it, but Harris objected: he said he had got a headache, and did not feel strong enough to stand it. George thought the music might do him good —said music often soothed the nerves and took away a headache; and he twanged two or three notes, just to show Harris what it was like.

Harris said he would rather have the headache.

George has never learned to play the banjo to this day. He has had too much all-round discouragement to meet. He tried on two or three evenings, while we were up the river, to get a little practice, but it was never a success. Harris's language used to be enough to unnerve any man; added to which, Montmorency would sit and howl steadily, right through the performance. It was not giving the man a fair chance.

'What's he want to howl like that for when I'm playing?' George would exclaim indignantly, while taking aim at him with a boot.

'What do you want to play like that for when he is howling?' Harris would retort, catching the boot. 'You let him alone. He can't help howling. He's got a musical ear, and your playing *makes* him howl.'

So George determined to postpone study of the banjo until he reached home. But he did not get much opportunity even there. Mrs P. used to come up and say she was very sorry—for herself, she liked to hear him—but the lady upstairs was in a very delicate state, and the doctor was afraid it might injure the child.

Then George tried taking it out with him late at night, and practising round the square. But the inhabitants complained to the police about it, and a watch was set for him one night, and he was captured. The evidence against him was very clear, and he was bound over to keep the peace for six months.

He seemed to lose heart in the business after that. He did make one or two feeble efforts to take up the work again when the six months had elapsed, but there was always the same coldness—the same want of sympathy on the part of the world to fight against; and, after awhile, he despaired altogether, and advertised the instrument for sale at a great sacrifice—'owner having no further use for same'—and took to learning card tricks instead.

It must be disheartening work learning a musical instrument. You would think that Society, for its own sake, would do all it could to assist a man to acquire the art of playing a musical instrument. But it doesn't!

I knew a young fellow once, who was studying to play the bagpipes, and you would be surprised at the amount of opposition he had to contend with. Why, not even from the members of his own family did he receive what you could call active encouragement. His father was dead against the business from the beginning, and spoke quite unfeelingly on the subject.

My friend used to get up early in the morning to practise, but he had to give that plan up, because of his sister. She was somewhat religiously inclined, and she said it seemed such an awful thing to begin the day like that.

So he sat up at night instead, and played after the family had gone to bed, but that did not do, as it got the house such a bad name. People, going home late, would stop outside to listen, and then put it about all over the town, the next morning, that a fearful murder had been committed at Mr Jefferson's the night before; and would describe how they had heard the victim's shrieks and the brutal oaths and curses of the murderer, followed by the prayer for mercy, and the last dying gurgle of the corpse.

So they let him practise in the day-time, in the back-kitchen with all the doors shut; but his more successful passages could generally be heard in the sitting-room, in spite of these precautions, and would affect his mother almost to tears.

She said it put her in mind of her poor father (he had been swallowed by a shark, poor man, while bathing off the coast of New Guinea—where the connection came in, she could not explain).

Then they knocked up a little place for him at the bottom of the garden, about quarter of a mile from the house, and made him take the machine down there when he wanted to work it; and sometimes a visitor would come to the house who knew nothing of the matter, and they would forget to tell him all about it, and caution him, and he would go out for a stroll round the garden and suddenly get within earshot of those bagpipes, without being prepared for it, or knowing what it was. If he were a man of strong mind, it only gave him fits; but a person of mere average intellect it usually sent mad.

There is, it must be confessed, something very sad about the early efforts of an amateur in bagpipes. I have felt that myself when listening to my young friend. They appear to be a trying instrument to perform upon. You have to get enough breath for the whole tune before you start—at least, so I gathered from watching Jefferson.

He would begin magnificently with a wild, full, come-to-the-battle sort of a note, that quite roused you. But he would get more and more piano as he went on, and the last verse generally collapsed in the middle with a splutter and a hiss.

You want to be in good health to play the bagpipes.

Young Jefferson only learnt to play one tune on those bagpipes: but I never heard any complaints about the insufficiency of his repertoire—none whatever. This tune was 'The Campbells are Coming, Hooray—Hooray!' so he said, though his father always held that it was 'The Blue Bells of Scotland.' Nobody seemed quite sure what it was exactly, but they all agreed that it sounded Scotch.

Strangers were allowed three guesses, and most of them guessed a different tune each time.

Harris was disagreeable after supper,—I think it must have been the stew that had upset him: he is not used to high living,—so George and I left him in the boat, and settled for a mouch round Henley. He said he should have a glass of whisky and a pipe, and fix things up for the night. We were to shout when we returned, and he would row over from the island and fetch us.

'Don't go to sleep, old man,' we said as we started.

'Not much fear of that while this stew's on,' he grunted, as he pulled back to the island.

Henley was getting ready for the regatta, and was full of bustle. We met a goodish number of men we knew about the town, and in their pleasant company the time slipped by somewhat quickly; so that it was nearly eleven o'clock before we set off on our four-mile walk home—as we had learned to call our little craft by this time.

It was a dismal night, coldish, with a thin rain falling; and as we trudged through the dark, silent fields, talking low to each other, and wondering if we were going right or not, we thought of the cosy boat, with the bright light streaming through the tight-drawn canvas; of Harris and Montmorency, and the whisky, and wished that we were there.

We conjured up the picture of ourselves inside, tired and a little hungry; of the gloomy river and the shapeless trees; and, like a giant glow-worm underneath them, our dear old boat, so snug and warm and cheerful. We could see ourselves at supper there, pecking away at cold meat, and passing each other chunks of bread; we could hear the cheery clatter of our knives, the laughing voices, filling all the space, and overflowing through the opening out into the night. And we hurried on to realise the vision.

We struck the tow-path at length, and that made us happy; because prior to this we had not been sure whether we were walking towards the river or away from it, and when you are tired and want to go to bed uncertainties like that worry you. We passed Shiplake as the clock was striking the quarter to twelve; and then George said, thoughtfully:

'You don't happen to remember which of the islands it was, do you?'

'No,' I replied, beginning to grow thoughtful too, 'I don't. How many are there?'

'Only four,' answered George. 'It will be all right, if he's awake.'

'And if not?' I queried; but we dismissed that train of thought.

We shouted when we came opposite the first island, but there was no response; so we went to the second, and tried there, and obtained the same result.

'Oh! I remember now,' said George; 'it was the third one.'

And we ran on hopefully to the third one, and hallooed.

No answer!

The case was becoming serious. It was now past midnight. The hotels at Shiplake and Henley would be crammed; and we could not go round, knocking up cottagers and householders in the middle of the night, to know if they let apartments! George suggested walking back to Henley and assaulting a policeman, and so getting a night's lodging in the station-house. But then there was the thought, 'Suppose he only hits us back and refuses to lock us up!'

We could not pass the whole night fighting policemen. Besides, we did not want to overdo the thing and get six months.

We despairingly tried what seemed in the darkness to be the fourth island, but met with no better success. The rain was coming down fast now, and evidently meant to last. We were wet to the skin, and cold and miserable. We began to wonder whether there were only four islands or more, or whether we were near the islands at all, or whether we were anywhere within a mile of where we ought to be, or in the wrong part of the river altogether; everything looked so strange and different in the darkness. We began to understand the sufferings of the Babes in the Wood.

Just when we had given up all hope—yes, I know that is always the time that things do happen in novels and tales; but I can't help it. I resolved, when I began to write this book, that I would be strictly truthful in all things; and so I will be, even if I have to employ hackneyed phrases for the purpose.

It *was* just when we had given up all hope, and I must therefore say so. Just when we had given up all hope, then, I suddenly caught sight, a little way below us, of a strange, weird sort of glimmer flickering among the trees on the opposite bank. For an instant I thought of ghosts: it was such a shadowy, mysterious light. The next moment it flashed across me that it was our boat, and I sent up such a yell across the water that made the night seem to shake in its bed.

We waited breathless for a minute, and then—oh! divinest music of the darkness!—we heard the answering bark of Montmorency. We shouted back loud enough to wake the Seven Sleepers*—I never could understand myself why it should take more noise to wake seven sleepers than one—and, after what seemed an hour, but what was really, I suppose, about five minutes, we saw the lighted boat creeping slowly over the blackness, and heard Harris's sleepy voice asking where we were.

There was an unaccountable strangeness about Harris. It was something more than mere ordinary tiredness. He pulled the boat against a part of the bank from which it was quite impossible for us to get into it, and immediately went to sleep. It took us an immense amount of screaming and roaring to wake him up again and put some sense into him; but we succeeded at last, and got safely on board.

Harris had a sad expression on him, so we noticed, when we got into the boat. He gave you the idea of a man who had been through trouble. We asked him if anything had happened, and he said—

'Swans!'

It seemed we had moored close to a swan's nest, and, soon after George and I had gone, the female swan came back, and kicked up a row about it. Harris had chivied her off, and she had gone away, and fetched up her old man. Harris said he had had quite a fight with these two swans; but courage and skill had prevailed in the end, and he had defeated them.

Half-an-hour afterwards they returned with eighteen other swans! It must have been a fearful battle, so far as we could understand Harris's account of it. The swans had tried to drag him and Montmorency out of the boat and drown them; and he had defended himself like a hero for four hours, and had killed the lot, and they had all paddled away to die.

'How many swans did you say there were?' asked George.

'Thirty-two,' replied Harris, sleepily.

'You said eighteen just now,' said George.

'No, I didn't,' grunted Harris; 'I said twelve. Think I can't count?'

What were the real facts about these swans we never found out. We questioned Harris on the subject in the morning, and he said, 'What swans?' and seemed to think that George and I had been dreaming.

Oh, how delightful it was to be safe in the boat, after our trials and fears! We ate a hearty supper, George and I, and we should have had some toddy after it, if we could have found the whisky, but we could not. We examined Harris as to what he had done with it; but he did not seem to know what we meant by 'whisky,' or what we were talking about at all. Montmorency looked as if he knew something, but said nothing.

I slept well that night, and should have slept better if it had not been for Harris. I have a vague recollection of having been woke up at least a dozen times during the night by Harris wandering about the boat with the lantern, looking for his clothes. He seemed to be worrying about his clothes all night.

Twice he routed up George and myself to see if we were lying on his trousers. George got quite wild the second time.

'What the thunder do you want your trousers for, in the middle of the night?' he asked indignantly. 'Why don't you lie down, and go to sleep?'

I found him in trouble, the next time I awoke, because he could not find his socks; and my last hazy remembrance is of being rolled over on my side, and of hearing Harris muttering something about its being an extraordinary thing where his umbrella could have got to.

CHAPTER XV

Household duties—Love of work—The old river hand, what he does and what he tells you he has done—Scepticism of the new generation—Early boating recollections—Rafting—George does the thing in style—The old boatman, his method—So calm, so full of peace—The beginner—Punting—A sad accident—Pleasures of friendship—Sailing, my first experience—Possible reason why we were not drowned.

WE woke late the next morning, and, at Harris's earnest desire, partook of a plain breakfast, with 'non dainties.' Then we cleaned up, and put everything straight (a continual labour, which was beginning to afford me a pretty clear insight into a question that had often posed me—namely, how a woman with the work of only one house on her hands manages to pass away her time), and, at about ten, set out on what we had determined should be a good day's journey.

We agreed that we would pull this morning, as a change from towing; and Harris thought the best arrangement would be that

George and I should scull, and he steer. I did not chime in with this idea at all; I said I thought Harris would have been showing a more proper spirit if he had suggested that he and George should work, and let me rest a bit. It seemed to me that I was doing more than my fair share of the work on this trip, and I was beginning to feel strongly on the subject.

It always does seem to me that I am doing more work than I should do. It is not that I object to the work, mind you; I like work: it fascinates me. I can sit and look at it for hours. I love to keep it by me: the idea of getting rid of it nearly breaks my heart.

You cannot give me too much work; to accumulate work has almost become a passion with me: my study is so full of it now, that there is hardly an inch of room for any more. I shall have to throw out a wing soon.

And I am careful of my work, too. Why, some of the work that I have by me now has been in my possession for years and years, and there isn't a finger-mark on it. I take a great pride in my work; I take it down now and then and dust it. No man keeps his work in a better state of preservation than I do.

But, though I crave for work, I still like to be fair. I do not ask for more than my proper share.

But I get it without asking for it—at least, so it appears to me—and this worries me.

George says he does not think I need trouble myself on the subject. He thinks it is only my over-scrupulous nature that makes me fear I am having more than my due; and that, as a matter of fact, I don't have half as much as I ought. But I expect he only says this to comfort me.

In a boat, I have always noticed that it is the fixed idea of each member of the crew that he is doing everything. Harris's notion was, that it was he alone who had been working, and that both George and I had been imposing upon him. George, on the other hand, ridiculed the idea of Harris's having done anything more than eat and sleep, and had a cast-iron opinion that it was he—George himself—who had done all the labour worth speaking of.

He said he had never been out with such a couple of lazy skulks as Harris and I.

That amused Harris.

'Fancy old George talking about work!' he laughed; 'why, about half-an-hour of it would kill him. Have you ever seen George work?' he added, turning to me.

I agreed with Harris that I never had—most certainly not since we had started on this trip.

'Well, I don't see how *you* can know much about it, one way or the other,' George retorted on Harris; 'for I'm blest if you haven't been asleep half the time. Have you ever seen Harris fully awake, except at meal-time?' asked George, addressing me.

Truth compelled me to support George. Harris had been very little good in the boat, so far as helping was concerned, from the beginning.

'Well, hang it all, I've done more than old J., anyhow,' rejoined Harris.

'Well, you couldn't very well have done less,' added George.

'I suppose J. thinks he is the passenger,' continued Harris.

And that was their gratitude to me for having brought them and their wretched old boat all the way up from Kingston, and for having superintended and managed everything for them, and taken care of them, and slaved for them. It is the way of the world.

We settled the present difficulty by arranging that Harris and George should scull up past Reading, and that I should tow the boat on from there. Pulling a heavy boat against a strong stream has few attractions for me now. There was a time, long ago, when I used to clamour for the hard work: now I like to give the youngsters a chance.

I notice that most of the old river hands are similarly retiring, whenever there is any stiff pulling to be done. You can always tell the old river hand by the way in which he stretches himself out upon the cushions at the bottom of the boat, and encourages the rowers by telling them anecdotes about the marvellous feats he performed last season.

'Call what you're doing hard work!' he drawls, between his contented whiffs, addressing the two perspiring novices, who have been grinding away steadily up stream for the last hour and a half; 'why, Jim Biffles and Jack and I, last season, pulled up from Marlow to Goring in one afternoon—never stopped once. Do you remember that, Jack?'

Jack, who has made himself a bed up in the prow of all the rugs and coats he can collect, and who has been lying there asleep for the last two hours, partially wakes up on being thus appealed to, and recollects all about the matter, and also remembers that there was an unusually strong stream against them all the way—likewise a stiff wind.

'About thirty-four miles, I suppose, it must have been,' adds the first speaker, reaching down another cushion to put under his head.

'No—no; don't exaggerate, Tom,' murmurs Jack, reprovingly; 'thirty-three at the outside.'

And Jack and Tom, quite exhausted by this conversational effort, drop off to sleep once more. And the two simple-minded youngsters at the sculls feel quite proud of being allowed to row such wonderful oarsmen as Jack and Tom, and strain away harder than ever.

When I was a young man, I used to listen to these tales from my elders, and take them in, and swallow them, and digest every word of them, and then come up for more; but the new generation do not seem to have the simple faith of the old times. We—George, Harris, and myself—took a 'raw'un' up with us once last season, and we plied him with the customary stretchers about the wonderful things we had done all the way up.

We gave him all the regular ones—the time-honoured lies that have done duty up the river with every boating-man for years past— and added seven entirely original ones that we had invented for ourselves, including a really quite likely story, founded, to a certain extent, on an all but true episode, which had actually happened in a modified degree some years ago to friends of ours—a story that a mere child could have believed without injuring itself, much.

And that young man mocked at them all, and wanted us to repeat the feats then and there, and to bet us ten to one that we didn't.

We got to chatting about our rowing experiences this morning, and to recounting stories of our first efforts in the art of oarsmanship. My own earliest boating recollection is of five of us contributing threepence each and taking out a curiously constructed craft on the Regent's Park lake, drying ourselves subsequently in the park-keeper's lodge.

After that, having acquired a taste for the water, I did a good deal of rafting in various suburban brickfields*—an exercise providing more interest and excitement than might be imagined, especially when you are in the middle of the pond and the proprietor of the materials of which the raft is constructed suddenly appears on the bank, with a big stick in his hand.

Your first sensation on seeing this gentleman is that, somehow or other, you don't feel equal to company and conversation, and that, if you could do so without appearing rude, you would rather avoid meeting him; and your object is, therefore, to get off on the opposite side of the pond to which he is, and to go home quietly and quickly, pretending not to see him. He, on the contrary, is yearning to take you by the hand, and talk to you.

It appears that he knows your father, and is intimately acquainted with yourself, but this does not draw you towards him. He says he'll teach you to take his boards and make a raft of them; but, seeing that you know how to do this pretty well already, the offer, though doubtless kindly meant, seems a superfluous one on his part, and you are reluctant to put him to any trouble by accepting it.

His anxiety to meet you, however, is proof against all your coolness, and the energetic manner in which he dodges up and down the pond so as to be on the spot to greet you when you land is really quite flattering.

If he be of a stout and short-winded build, you can easily avoid his advances; but, when he is of the youthful and long-legged type, a meeting is inevitable. The interview is, however, extremely brief, most of the conversation being on his part, your remarks being mostly of an exclamatory and monosyllabic order, and as soon as you can tear yourself away you do so.

I devoted some three months to rafting, and, being then as proficient as there was any need to be at that branch of the art, I determined to go in for rowing proper, and joined one of the Lea boating clubs.

Being out in a boat on the river Lea, especially on Saturday afternoons, soon makes you smart at handling a craft, and spry at escaping being run down by roughs or swamped by barges; and it also affords plenty of opportunity for acquiring the most prompt and graceful method of lying down flat at the bottom of the boat so as to avoid being chucked out into the river by passing tow-lines.

But it does not give you style. It was not till I came to the Thames that I got style. My style of rowing is very much admired now. People say it is so quaint.

George never went near the water until he was sixteen. Then he and eight other gentlemen of about the same age went down in a body to Kew one Saturday, with the idea of hiring a boat there, and pulling to Richmond and back; one of their number, a shock-headed youth, named Joskins, who had once or twice taken out a boat on the Serpentine, told them it was jolly fun, boating!

The tide was running out pretty rapidly when they reached the landing-stage, and there was a stiff breeze blowing across the river, but this did not trouble them at all, and they proceeded to select their boat.

There was an eight-oared racing outrigger drawn up on the stage; that was the one that took their fancy. They said they'd have that one, please. The boatman was away, and only his boy was in charge. The boy tried to damp their ardour for the outrigger, and showed them two or three very comfortable-looking boats of the family-party build, but those would not do at all; the outrigger was the boat they thought they would look best in.

So the boy launched it, and they took off their coats and prepared to take their seats. The boy suggested that George, who, even in those days, was always the heavy man of any party, should be number four. George said he should be happy to be number four, and promptly stepped into bow's place, and sat down with his back to the stern. They got him into his proper position at last, and then the others followed.

A particularly nervous boy was appointed cox, and the steering principle explained to him by Joskins. Joskins himself took stroke. He told the others that it was simple enough; all they had to do was to follow him.

They said they were ready, and the boy on the landing stage took a boat-hook and shoved him off.

What then followed George is unable to describe in detail. He has a confused recollection of having, immediately on starting, received a violent blow in the small of the back from the butt-end of number five's scull, at the same time that his own seat seemed to disappear from under him by magic, and leave him sitting on the boards. He also noticed, as a curious circumstance, that number two was at the same instant lying on his back at the bottom of the boat, with his legs in the air, apparently in a fit.

They passed under Kew Bridge, broadside, at the rate of eight miles an hour. Joskins being the only one who was rowing. George, on recovering his seat, tried to help him, but, on dipping his oar into the water, it immediately, to his intense surprise, disappeared under the boat, and nearly took him with it.

And then 'cox' threw both rudder lines overboard, and burst into tears.

How they got back George never knew, but it took them just forty minutes. A dense crowd watched the entertainment from Kew Bridge with much interest, and everybody shouted out to them different directions. Three times they managed to get the boat back through the arch, and three times they were carried under it again, and every time 'cox' looked up and saw the bridge above him he broke out into renewed sobs.

George said he little thought that afternoon that he should ever come to really like boating.

Harris is more accustomed to sea rowing than to river work, and says that, as an exercise, he prefers it. I don't. I remember taking a small boat out at Eastbourne last summer: I used to do a good deal of sea rowing years ago, and I thought I should be all right; but I found I had forgotten the art entirely. When one scull was deep down underneath the water, the other would be flourishing wildly about in the air. To get a grip of the water with both at the same time I had to stand up. The parade was crowded with nobility and gentry, and I had to pull past them in this ridiculous fashion. I landed half-way down the beach, and secured the services of an old boatman to take me back.

I like to watch an old boatman rowing, especially one who has been hired by the hour. There is something so beautifully calm and restful about his method. It is so free from that fretful haste, that vehement striving, that is every day becoming more and more the bane of nineteenth-century life. He is not for ever straining himself to pass all the other boats. If another boat overtakes him and passes him it does not annoy him; as a matter of fact, they all do overtake him and pass him—all those that are going his way. This would trouble and irritate some people; the sublime equanimity of the hired boatman under the ordeal affords us a beautiful lesson against ambition and uppishness.

Plain practical rowing of the get-the-boat-along order is not a very difficult art to acquire, but it takes a good deal of practice before a man feels comfortable when rowing past girls. It is the 'time' that worries a youngster. 'It's jolly funny,' he says, as for the twentieth time within five minutes he disentangles his sculls from yours; 'I can get on all right when I'm by myself!'

To see two novices try to keep time with one another is very amusing. Bow finds it impossible to keep pace with stroke, because stroke rows in such an extraordinary fashion. Stroke is intensely indignant at this, and explains that what he has been endeavouring to do for the last ten minutes is to adapt his method to bow's limited capacity. Bow, in turn, then becomes insulted, and requests stroke not to trouble his head about him (bow), but to devote his mind to setting a sensible stroke.

'Or, shall *I* take stroke?' he adds, with the evident idea that that would at once put the whole matter right.

They splash along for another hundred yards with still moderate success, and then the whole secret of their trouble bursts upon stroke like a flash of inspiration.

'I tell you what it is: you've got my sculls,' he cries, turning to bow; 'pass yours over.'

'Well, do you know, I've been wondering how it was I couldn't get on with these,' answers bow, quite brightening up, and most willingly assisting in the exchange. '*Now* we shall be all right.'

But they are not—not even then. Stroke has to stretch his arms nearly out of their sockets to reach his sculls now; while bow's pair, at each recovery, hit him a violent blow in the chest. So they change back again, and come to the conclusion that the man has given them the wrong set altogether; and over their mutual abuse of this man they become quite friendly and sympathetic.

George said he had often longed to take to punting for a change. Punting is not as easy as it looks. As in rowing, you soon learn how to get along and handle the craft, but it takes long practice before you can do this with dignity and without getting the water all up your sleeve.

One young man I knew had a very sad accident happen to him the first time he went punting. He had been getting on so well that he had grown quite cheeky over the business, and was walking up and down the punt, working his pole with a careless grace that was quite fascinating to watch. Up he would march to the head of the punt, plant his pole, and then run along right to the other end, just like an old punter. Oh! it was grand.

And it would all have gone on being grand if he had not unfortunately, while looking round to enjoy the scenery, taken just one step more than there was any necessity for, and walked off the punt altogether. The pole was firmly fixed in the mud, and he was left clinging to it while the punt drifted away. It was an undignified position for him. A rude boy on the bank immediately yelled out to a lagging chum to 'hurry up and see a real monkey on a stick.'

I could not go to his assistance because, as ill-luck would have it, we had not taken the proper precaution to bring out a spare pole with us. I could only sit and look at him. His expression as the pole slowly sank with him I shall never forget; there was so much thought in it.

I watched him gently let down into the water, and saw him scramble out, sad and wet. I could not help laughing, he looked such a ridiculous figure. I continued to chuckle to myself about it for some time, and then it was suddenly forced in upon me that really I had got very little to laugh at when I came to think of it. Here was I, alone in a punt, without a pole, drifting helplessly down mid-stream—possibly towards a weir.

I began to feel very indignant with my friend for having stepped overboard and gone off in that way. He might, at all events, have left me the pole.

I drifted on for about a quarter of a mile, and then I came in sight of a fishing-punt moored in mid-stream, in which sat two old fisher-men. They saw me bearing down upon them, and they called out to me to keep out of their way.

'I can't,' I shouted back.

'But you don't try,' they answered.

I explained the matter to them when I got nearer, and they caught me and lent me a pole. The weir was just fifty yards below. I am glad they happened to be there.

The first time I went punting was in company with three other fellows; they were going to show me how to do it. We could not all start together, so I said I would go down first and get out the punt, and then I could potter about and practice a bit until they came.

I could not get a punt out that afternoon, they were all engaged; so I had nothing else to do but to sit down on the bank, watching the river, and waiting for my friends.

I had not been sitting there long before my attention became attracted to a man in a punt who, I noticed with some surprise, wore a jacket and cap exactly like mine. He was evidently a novice at punting, and his performance was most interesting. You never knew what was going to happen when he put the pole in; he evidently did not know himself. Sometimes he shot up stream and sometimes he shot down stream, and at other times he simply spun round and came up the other side of the pole. And with every result he seemed equally surprised and annoyed.

The people about the river began to get quite absorbed in him after a while, and to make bets with one another as to what would be the outcome of his next push.

In the course of time my friends arrived on the opposite bank, and they stopped and watched him too. His back was towards them, and they only saw his jacket and cap. From this they immediately jumped to the conclusion that it was I, their beloved companion, who was making an exhibition of himself, and their delight knew no bounds. They commenced to chaff him unmercifully.

I did not grasp their mistake at first, and I thought, 'How rude of them to go on like that, with a perfect stranger, too!' But before I could call out and reprove them, the explanation of the matter occurred to me, and I withdrew behind a tree.

Oh, how they enjoyed themselves, ridiculing that young man! For five good minutes they stood there, shouting ribaldry at him, deriding him, mocking him, jeering at him. They peppered him with stale jokes, and even made a few new ones and threw at him. They hurled at him all the private family jokes belonging to our set, and which must have been perfectly unintelligible to him. And then, unable to stand their brutal jibes any longer, he turned round on them, and they saw his face!

I was glad to notice that they had sufficient decency left in them to look very foolish. They explained to him that they had thought he was some one they knew. They said they hoped he would not deem them capable of so insulting any one except a personal friend of their own.

Of course their having mistaken him for a friend excused it. I remember Harris telling me once of a bathing experience he had at Boulogne. He was swimming about there near the beach, when he felt himself suddenly seized by the neck from behind, and forcibly plunged under water. He struggled violently, but whoever had got hold of him seemed to be a perfect Hercules in strength, and all his efforts to escape were unavailing. He had given up kicking, and was trying to turn his thoughts upon solemn things, when his captor released him.

He regained his feet, and looked round for his would-be murderer.

The assassin was standing close by him, laughing heartily, but the moment he caught sight of Harris's face, as it emerged from the water, he started back and seemed quite concerned.

'I really beg your pardon,' he stammered, confusedly, 'but I took you for a friend of mine!'

Harris thought it was lucky for him the man had not mistaken him for a relation, or he would probably have been drowned outright.

Sailing is a thing that wants knowledge and practice too—though, as a boy, I did not think so. I had an idea it came natural to a body, like rounders and touch.* I knew another boy who held this view likewise, and so, one windy day, we thought we would try the sport. We were stopping down at Yarmouth, and we decided we would go for a trip up the Yare. We hired a sailing boat at the yard by the bridge, and started off.

'It's rather a rough day,' said the man to us, as we put off: 'better take in a reef and luff sharp when you get round the bend.'

We said we would make a point of it, and left him with a cheery 'Good-morning,' wondering to ourselves how you 'luffed,' and where we were to get a 'reef' from, and what we were to do with it when we had got it.

We rowed until we were out of sight of the town, and then, with a wide stretch of water in front of us, and the wind blowing a perfect hurricane across it, we felt that the time had come to commence operations.

Hector—I think that was his name—went on pulling while I unrolled the sail. It seemed a complicated job, but I accomplished it at length, and then came the question, which was the top end?

By a sort of natural instinct, we, of course, eventually decided that the bottom was the top, and set to work to fix it upside-down. But it was a long time before we could get it up, either that way or any other way. The impression on the mind of the sail seemed to be that we were playing at funerals, and that I was the corpse and itself was the winding-sheet.

When it found that this was not the idea, it hit me over the head with the boom, and refused to do anything.

'Wet it,' said Hector; 'drop it over and get it wet.'

He said people in ships always wetted the sails before they put them up. So I wetted it; but that only made matters worse than they were before. A dry sail clinging to your legs and wrapping itself round your head is not pleasant, but, when the sail is sopping wet, it becomes quite vexing.

We did get the thing up at last, the two of us together. We fixed it, not exactly upside down—more sideways like—and we tied it up to the mast with the painter, which we cut off for the purpose.

That the boat did not upset I simply state as a fact. Why it did not upset I am unable to offer any reason. I have often thought about the matter since, but I have never succeeded in arriving at any satisfactory explanation of the phenomenon.

Possibly the result may have been brought about by the natural obstinacy of all things in this world. The boat may possibly have come to the conclusion, judging from a cursory view of our behaviour, that we had come out for a morning's suicide, and had thereupon determined to disappoint us. That is the only suggestion I can offer.

By clinging like grim death to the gunwale, we just managed to keep inside the boat, but it was exhausting work. Hector said that pirates and other seafaring people generally lashed the rudder to something or other, and hauled in the main top-jib, during severe squalls, and thought we ought to try to do something of the kind; but I was for letting her have her head to the wind.

As my advice was by far the easiest to follow, we ended by adopting it, and contrived to embrace the gunwale and give her her head.

The boat travelled up stream for about a mile at a pace I have never sailed at since, and don't want to again. Then, at a bend, she heeled over till half her sail was under water. Then she righted herself by a miracle and flew for a long low bank of soft mud.

That mud-bank saved us. The boat ploughed its way into the middle of it and then stuck. Finding that we were once more able to move according to our ideas, instead of being pitched and thrown about like peas in a bladder, we crept forward, and cut down the sail.

We had had enough sailing. We did not want to overdo the thing and get a surfeit of it. We had had a sail—a good all-round exciting, interesting sail—and now we thought we would have a row, just for a change like.

We took the sculls and tried to push the boat off the mud, and, in doing so, we broke one of the sculls. After that we proceeded with great caution, but they were a wretched old pair, and the second one cracked almost easier than the first, and left us helpless.

The mud stretched out for about a hundred yards in front of us, and behind us was the water. The only thing to be done was to sit and wait until someone came by.

It was not the sort of day to attract people out on the river, and it was three hours before a soul came in sight. It was an old fisherman who, with immense difficulty, at last rescued us, and we were towed back in an ignominious fashion to the boat-yard.

What between tipping the man who had brought us home, and paying for the broken sculls, and for having been out four hours and a half, it cost us a pretty considerable number of weeks' pocket-money, that sail. But we learned experience, and they say that is always cheap at any price.

CHAPTER XVI

Reading—We are towed by steam launch—Irritating behaviour of small boats—How they get in the way of steam launches—George and Harris again shirk their work—Rather a hackneyed story—Streatley and Goring.

WE came in sight of Reading about eleven. The river is dirty and dismal here. One does not linger in the neighbourhood of Reading. The town itself is a famous old place, dating from the dim days of King Ethelred, when the Danes anchored their warships in the Kennet, and started from Reading to ravage all the land of Wessex; and here Ethelred and his brother Alfred fought and defeated them, Ethelred doing the praying and Alfred the fighting.

In later years, Reading seems to have been regarded as a handy place to run down to, when matters were becoming unpleasant in London. Parliament generally rushed off to Reading whenever there was a plague on at Westminster; and, in 1625, the Law followed suit, and all the courts were held at Reading. It must have been worth while having a mere ordinary plague now and then in London to get rid of both the lawyers and the Parliament.

During the Parliamentary struggle, Reading was besieged by the Earl of Essex, and, a quarter of a century later, the Prince of Orange routed King James's troops there.

Henry I lies buried at Reading, in the Benedictine abbey founded by him there, the ruins of which may still be seen; and, in this same abbey, great John of Gaunt was married to the Lady Blanche.

At Reading lock we came up with a steam launch, belonging to some friends of mine, and they towed us up to within about a mile of Streatley. It is very delightful being towed up by a launch. I prefer it myself to rowing. The run would have been more delightful still, if it had not been for a lot of wretched small boats that were continually getting in the way of our launch, and, to avoid running down which, we had to be continually easing and stopping. It is really most annoying, the manner in which these rowing boats get in the way of one's launch up the river; something ought to be done to stop it.

And they are so confoundedly impertinent, too, over it. You can whistle till you nearly burst your boiler before they will trouble themselves to hurry. I would have one or two of them run down now and then, if I had my way, just to teach them all a lesson.

The river becomes very lovely from a little above Reading. The railway rather spoils it near Tilehurst, but from Mapledurham up to Streatley it is glorious. A little above Mapledurham lock you pass Hardwick House, where Charles I played bowls. The neighbourhood of Pangbourne, where the quaint little Swan Inn stands, must be as familiar to the *habitués* of the Art Exhibitions as it is to its own inhabitants.

My friends' launch cast us loose just below the grotto, and then Harris wanted to make out that it was my turn to pull. This seemed to me most unreasonable. It had been arranged in the morning that I should bring the boat up to three miles above Reading. Well, here we were, ten miles above Reading! Surely it was now their turn again.

I could not get either George or Harris to see the matter in its proper light, however; so, to save argument, I took the sculls. I had not been pulling for more than a minute or so, when George noticed something black floating on the water, and we drew up to it. George leant over, as we neared it, and laid hold of it. And then he drew back with a cry, and a blanched face.

It was the dead body of a woman. It lay very lightly on the water, and the face was sweet and calm. It was not a beautiful face; it was too prematurely aged-looking, too thin and drawn, to be that; but it was a gentle, lovable face, in spite of its stamp of pinch and poverty, and upon it was that look of restful peace that comes to the faces of the sick sometimes when at last the pain has left them.

Fortunately for us—we having no desire to be kept hanging about coroners' courts—some men on the bank had seen the body too, and now took charge of it from us.

We found out the woman's story afterwards. Of course it was the old, old vulgar tragedy. She had loved and been deceived—or had deceived herself. Anyhow, she had sinned—some of us do now and then—and her family and friends, naturally shocked and indignant, had closed their doors against her.

Left to fight the world alone, with the millstone of her shame around her neck, she had sunk ever lower and lower. For a while she had kept both herself and the child on the twelve shillings a week that twelve hours' drudgery a day procured her, paying six shillings out of it for the child, and keeping her own body and soul together on the remainder.

Six shillings a week does not keep body and soul together very unitedly. They want to get away from each other when there is only such a very slight bond as that between them; and one day, I suppose, the pain and the dull monotony of it all had stood before her eyes plainer than usual, and the mocking spectre had frightened her. She had made one last appeal to friends, but, against the chill wall of their respectability, the voice of the erring outcast fell unheeded; and then she had gone to see her child—had held it in her arms and kissed it, in a weary, dull sort of way, and without betraying any particular emotion of any kind, and had left it, after putting into its hand a penny box of chocolate she had bought it, and afterwards, with her last few shillings, had taken a ticket and come down to Goring.

It seemed that the bitterest thoughts of her life must have centred about the wooded reaches and the bright green meadows around Goring; but women strangely hug the knife that stabs them, and, perhaps, amidst the gall, there may have mingled also sunny memories of sweetest hours, spent upon those shadowed deeps over which the great trees bend their branches down so low.

She had wandered about the woods by the river's brink all day, and then, when evening fell and the grey twilight spread its dusky robe upon the waters, she stretched her arms out to the silent river that had known her sorrow and her joy. And the old river had taken her into its gentle arms, and had laid her weary head upon its bosom, and had hushed away the pain.

Thus had she sinned in all things—sinned in living and in dying.

God help her! and all other sinners, if any more there be.

Goring on the left bank and Streatley on the right are both or either charming places to stay at for a few days. The reaches down to Pangbourne woo one for a sunny sail or for a moonlight row, and the country round about is full of beauty. We had intended to push on to Wallingford that day, but the sweet smiling face of the river here lured us to linger for a while; and so we left our boat at the bridge, and went up into Streatley, and lunched at the 'Bull,' much to Montmorency's satisfaction.

They say that the hills on each side of the stream here once joined and formed a barrier across what is now the Thames, and that then the river ended there above Goring in one vast lake. I am not in a position either to contradict or affirm this statement. I simply offer it.

It is an ancient place, Streatley, dating back, like most river-side towns and villages, to British and Saxon times. Goring is not nearly so pretty a little spot to stop at as Streatley, if you have your choice; but it is passing fair enough in its way, and is nearer the railway in case you want to slip off without paying your hotel bill.

CHAPTER XVII

Washing day—Fish and fishers—On the art of angling—A conscientious fly-fisher—A fishy story.

WE stayed two days at Streatley, and got our clothes washed. We had tried washing them ourselves, in the river, under George's superintendence, and it had been a failure. Indeed, it had been more than a failure, because we were worse off after we had washed our clothes than we were before. Before we had washed them, they had been very, very dirty, it is true; but they were just wearable. *After* we had washed them—well, the river between Reading and Henley was much cleaner, after we had washed our clothes in it, than it was before. All the dirt contained in the river between Reading and Henley, we collected, during that wash, and worked it into our clothes.

The washerwoman at Streatley said she felt she owed it to herself to charge us just three times the usual prices for that wash. She said it had not been like washing, it had been more in the nature of excavating.

We paid the bill without a murmur.

The neighbourhood of Streatley and Goring is a great fishing centre. There is some excellent fishing to be had there. The river abounds in pike, roach, dace, gudgeon, and eels, just here; and you can sit and fish for them all day.

Some people do. They never catch them. I never knew anybody catch anything, up the Thames, except minnows and dead cats, but that has nothing to do, of course, with fishing! The local fisherman's guide doesn't say a word about catching anything. All it says is the place is 'a good station for fishing;' and, from what I have seen of the district, I am quite prepared to bear out this statement.

There is no spot in the world where you can get more fishing, or where you can fish for a longer period. Some fishermen come here and fish for a day, and others stop and fish for a month. You can hang on and fish for a year, if you want to: it will be all the same.

The *Angler's Guide to the Thames* says that 'jack and perch are also to be had about here,' but there the *Angler's Guide* is wrong. Jack and perch may *be* about there. Indeed, I know for a fact that they are. You can *see* them there in shoals, when you are out for a walk along the banks: they come and stand half out of the water with their mouths open for biscuits. And, if you go for a bathe, they crowd round, and get in your way and irritate you. But they are not to be 'had' by a bit of worm on the end of a hook, nor anything like it—not they!

I am not a good fisherman myself. I devoted a considerable amount of attention to the subject at one time, and was getting on, as I thought, fairly well; but the old hands told me that I should never be any real good at it, and advised me to give it up. They said that I was an extremely neat thrower, and that I seemed to have plenty of gumption for the thing, and quite enough constitutional laziness. But they were sure I should never make anything of a fisherman. I had not got sufficient imagination.

They said that as a poet, or a shilling shocker,* or a reporter, or anything of that kind, I might be satisfactory, but that, to gain any position as a Thames angler, would require more play of fancy, more power of invention than I appeared to possess.

Some people are under the impression that all that is required to make a good fisherman is the ability to tell lies easily and without blushing; but this is a mistake. Mere bald fabrication is useless; the veriest tyro can manage that. It is in the circumstantial detail, the embellishing touches of probability, the general air of scrupulous—almost of pedantic—veracity, that the experienced angler is seen.

Anybody can come in and say, 'Oh, I caught fifteen dozen perch yesterday evening;' or 'Last Monday I landed a gudgeon, weighing eighteen pounds, and measuring three feet from the tip to the tail.'

There is no art, no skill, required for that sort of thing. It shows pluck, but that is all.

No; your accomplished angler would scorn to tell a lie, that way. His method is a study in itself.

He comes in quietly with his hat on, appropriates the most comfortable chair, lights his pipe, and commences to puff in silence. He lets the youngsters brag away for a while, and then, during a momentary lull, he removes the pipe from his mouth, and remarks, as he knocks the ashes out against the bars:

'Well, I had a haul on Tuesday evening that it's not much good my telling anybody about.'

'Oh! why's that?' they ask.

'Because I don't expect anybody would believe me if I did,' replies the old fellow calmly, and without even a tinge of bitterness in his tone, as he refills his pipe, and requests the landlord to bring him three of Scotch, cold.

There is a pause after this, nobody feeling sufficiently sure of himself to contradict the old gentleman. So he has to go on by himself without any encouragement.

'No,' he continues thoughtfully; 'I shouldn't believe it myself if anybody told it to me, but it's a fact, for all that. I had been sitting there all the afternoon and had caught literally nothing—except a few dozen dace and a score of jack; and I was just about giving it up as a bad job when I suddenly felt a rather smart pull at the line. I thought it was another little one, and I went to jerk it up. Hang me, if I could move the rod! It took me half-an-hour—half-an-hour, sir!—to land that fish; and every moment I thought the line was going to snap! I reached him at last, and what do you think it was? A sturgeon! a forty pound sturgeon! taken on a line, sir! Yes, you may well look surprised—I'll have another three of Scotch, landlord, please.'

And then he goes on to tell of the astonishment of everybody who saw it; and what his wife said, when he got home, and of what Joe Buggles thought about it.

I asked the landlord of an inn up the river once, if it did not injure him, sometimes, listening to the tales that the fishermen about there told him; and he said:

'Oh, no; not now, sir. It did used to knock me over a bit at first, but, lor love you! me and the missus we listens to 'em all day now. It's what you're used to, you know. It's what you're used to.'

I knew a young man once, he was a most conscientious fellow and, when he took to fly-fishing, he determined never to exaggerate his hauls by more than twenty-five per cent.

'When I have caught forty fish,' said he, 'then I will tell people that I have caught fifty, and so on. But I will not lie any more than that, because it is sinful to lie.'

But the twenty-five per cent plan did not work well at all. He never was able to use it. The greatest number of fish he ever caught in one day was three, and you can't add twenty-five per cent to three—at least, not in fish.

So he increased his percentage to thirty-three-and-a-third; but that, again, was awkward, when he had only caught one or two; so, to simplify matters, he made up his mind to just double the quantity.

He stuck to this arrangement for a couple of months, and then he grew dissatisfied with it. Nobody believed him when he told them that he only doubled, and he, therefore, gained no credit that way whatever, while his moderation put him at a disadvantage among the other anglers. When he had really caught three small fish, and said he had caught six, it used to make him quite jealous to hear a man, whom he knew for a fact had only caught one, going about telling people he had landed two dozen.

So, eventually, he made one final arrangement with himself, which he has religiously held to ever since, and that was to count each fish that he caught as ten, and to assume ten to begin with. For example, if he did not catch any fish at all, then he said he had caught ten fish— you could never catch less than ten fish by his system; that was the foundation of it. Then, if by any chance he really did catch one fish, he called it twenty, while two fish would count thirty, three forty, and so on.

It is a simple and easily worked plan, and there has been some talk lately of its being made use of by the angling fraternity in general.

Indeed, the Committee of the Thames Anglers' Association did recommend its adoption about two years ago, but some of the older members opposed it. They said they would consider the idea if the number were doubled, and each fish counted as twenty.

If ever you have an evening to spare, up the river, I should advise you to drop into one of the little village inns, and take a seat in the tap-room. You will be nearly sure to meet one or two old rod-men, sipping their toddy there, and they will tell you enough fishy stories, in half an hour, to give you indigestion for a month.

George and I—I don't know what had become of Harris; he had gone out and had a shave, early in the afternoon, and had then come back and spent full forty minutes in pipeclaying his shoes, we had not seen him since—George and I, therefore, and the dog, left to ourselves, went for a walk to Wallingford on the second evening, and, coming home, we called in at a little river-side inn, for a rest, and other things.

We went into the parlour and sat down. There was an old fellow there, smoking a long clay pipe, and we naturally began chatting.

He told us that it had been a fine day to-day, and we told him that it had been a fine day yesterday, and then we all told each other that we thought it would be a fine day to-morrow; and George said the crops seemed to be coming up nicely.

After that it came out, somehow or other, that we were strangers in the neighbourhood, and that we were going away the next morning.

Then a pause ensued in the conversation, during which our eyes wandered round the room. They finally rested upon a dusty old glass-case, fixed very high up above the chimney-piece, and containing a trout. It rather fascinated me, that trout; it was such a monstrous fish. In fact, at first glance, I thought it was a cod.

'Ah!' said the old gentleman, following the direction of my gaze, 'fine fellow that, ain't he?'

'Quite uncommon,' I murmured; and George asked the old man how much he thought it weighed.

'Eighteen pounds six ounces,' said our friend, rising and taking down his coat. 'Yes,' he continued, 'it wur sixteen year ago, come the third o' next month, that I landed him. I caught him just below the bridge with a minnow. They told me he wur in the river, and I said I'd have him, and so I did. You don't see many fish that size about here now, I'm thinking. Good-night, gentlemen, good-night.'

And out he went, and left us alone.

We could not take our eyes off the fish after that. It really was a remarkably fine fish. We were still looking at it, when the local carrier, who had just stopped at the inn, came to the door of the room with a pot of beer in his hand, and he also looked at the fish.

'Good-sized trout, that,' said George, turning round to him.

'Ah! you may well say that, sir,' replied the man; and then, after a pull at his beer, he added, 'Maybe you wasn't here, sir, when that fish was caught?'

'No,' we told him. We were strangers in the neighbourhood.

'Ah!' said the carrier, 'then, of course, how should you? It was nearly five years ago that I caught that trout.'

'Oh! was it you who caught it, then?' said I.

'Yes, sir,' replied the genial old fellow. 'I caught him just below the lock—leastways, what was the lock then—one Friday afternoon; and the remarkable thing about it is that I caught him with a fly. I'd gone out pike fishing, bless you, never thinking of a trout, and when I saw that whopper on the end of my line, blest if it didn't quite take me aback. Well, you see, he weighed twenty-six pound. Good-night, gentlemen, good-night.'

Five minutes afterwards, a third man came in, and described how *he* had caught it early one morning, with bleak; and then he left, and a stolid, solemn-looking, middle-aged individual came in, and sat down over by the window.

None of us spoke for a while; but, at length, George turned to the new comer, and said:

'I beg your pardon, I hope you will forgive the liberty that we—perfect strangers in the neighbourhood—are taking, but my friend here and myself would be so much obliged if you would tell us how you caught that trout up there.'

'Why, who told you I caught that trout!' was the surprised query.

We said that nobody had told us so, but somehow or other we felt instinctively that it was he who had done it.

'Well, it's a most remarkable thing—most remarkable,' answered the stolid stranger, laughing; 'because, as a matter of fact, you are quite right. I did catch it. But fancy your guessing it like that. Dear me, it's really a most remarkable thing.'

And then he went on, and told us how it had taken him half an hour to land it, and how it had broken his rod. He said he had weighed it carefully when he reached home, and it had turned the scale at thirty-four pounds.

He went in his turn, and when he was gone, the landlord came in to us. We told him the various histories we had heard about his trout, and he was immensely amused, and we all laughed very heartily.

'Fancy Jim Bates and Joe Muggles and Mr Jones and old Billy Maunders all telling you that they had caught it. Ha! ha! ha! Well, that is good,' said the honest old fellow, laughing heartily. 'Yes, they are the sort to give it *me*, to put up in *my* parlour, if *they* had caught it, they are! Ha! ha! ha!'

And then he told us the real history of the fish. It seemed that he had caught it himself, years ago, when he was quite a lad; not by any art or skill, but by that unaccountable luck that appears to always wait upon a boy when he plays the wag from school, and goes out fishing on a sunny afternoon, with a bit of string tied on to the end of a tree.

He said that bringing home that trout had saved him from a whacking, and that even his schoolmaster had said it was worth the rule-of-three and practice put together.

He was called out of the room at this point, and George and I again turned our gaze upon the fish.

It really was a most astonishing trout. The more we looked at it, the more we marvelled at it.

It excited George so much that he climbed up on the back of a chair to get a better view of it.

And then the chair slipped, and George clutched wildly at the trout-case to save himself, and down it came with a crash, George and the chair on top of it.

'You haven't injured the fish, have you?' I cried in alarm, rushing up.

'I hope not,' said George, rising cautiously and looking about.

But he had. That trout lay shattered into a thousand fragments—I say a thousand, but they may have only been nine hundred. I did not count them.

We thought it strange and unaccountable that a stuffed trout should break up into little pieces like that.

And so it would have been strange and unaccountable, if it had been a stuffed trout, but it was not.

That trout was plaster-of-Paris.

CHAPTER XVIII

Locks—George and I are photographed—Wallingford—Dorchester—
Abingdon—A family man—A good spot for drowning—A difficult bit of
water—Demoralizing effect of river air.

WE left Streatley early the next morning, and pulled up to Culham,
and slept under the canvas, in the backwater there.

The river is not extraordinarily interesting between Streatley and
Wallingford. From Cleeve you get a stretch of six and a half miles
without a lock. I believe this is the longest uninterrupted stretch
anywhere above Teddington, and the Oxford Club make use of it for
their trial eights.

But however satisfactory this absence of locks may be to rowing-
men, it is to be regretted by the mere pleasure-seeker.

For myself, I am fond of locks. They pleasantly break the
monotony of the pull. I like sitting in the boat and slowly rising out of
the cool depths up into new reaches and fresh views; or sinking down,
as it were, out of the world, and then waiting, while the gloomy gates
creak, and the narrow strip of daylight between them widens till the
fair smiling river lies full before you, and you push your little boat out
from its brief prison on to the welcoming waters once again.

They are picturesque little spots, these locks. The stout old lock-
keeper, or his cheerful-looking wife, or bright-eyed daughter, are
pleasant folk to have a passing chat with.[1] You meet other boats there,
and river gossip is exchanged. The Thames would not be the
fairyland it is without its flower-decked locks.

Talking of locks reminds me of an accident George and I very
nearly had one summer's morning at Hampton Court.

It was a glorious day, and the lock was crowded; and, as is a
common practice up the river, a speculative photographer was taking
a picture of us all as we lay upon the rising waters.

I did not catch what was going on at first, and was, therefore,
extremely surprised at noticing George hurriedly smooth out his
trousers, ruffle up his hair, and stick his cap on in a rakish manner at

[1] Or rather *were*. The Conservancy* of late seems to have constituted itself into a
society for the employment of idiots. A good many of the new lock-keepers, especially in
the more crowded portions of the river, are excitable, nervous old men, quite unfitted for
their post.

the back of his head, and then, assuming an expression of mingled affability and sadness, sit down in a graceful attitude, and try to hide his feet.

My first idea was that he had suddenly caught sight of some girl he knew, and I looked about to see who it was. Everybody in the lock seemed to have been suddenly struck wooden. They were all standing or sitting about in the most quaint and curious attitudes I have ever seen off a Japanese fan. All the girls were smiling. Oh, they did look so sweet! And all the fellows were frowning, and looking stern and noble.

And then, at last, the truth flashed across me, and I wondered if I should be in time. Ours was the first boat, and it would be unkind of me to spoil the man's picture, I thought.

So I faced round quickly, and took up a position in the prow, where I leant with careless grace upon the hitcher, in an attitude suggestive of agility and strength. I arranged my hair with a curl over the forehead, and threw an air of tender wistfulness into my expression, mingled with a touch of cynicism, which I am told suits me.

As we stood, waiting for the eventful moment, I heard someone behind call out:

'Hi! look at your nose.'

I could not turn round to see what was the matter, and whose nose it was that was to be looked at. I stole a side-glance at George's nose! It was all right—at all events, there was nothing wrong with it that could be altered. I squinted down at my own, and that seemed all that could be expected also.

'Look at your nose, you stupid ass!' came the same voice again, louder.

And then another voice cried:

'Push your nose out, can't you, you—you two with the dog!'

Neither George nor I dared to turn round. The man's hand was on the cap, and the picture might be taken any moment. Was it us they were calling to? What was the matter with our noses? Why were they to be pushed out?

But now the whole lock started yelling, and a stentorian voice from the back shouted:

'Look at your boat, sir; you in the red and black caps. It's your two corpses that will get taken in that photo, if you ain't quick.'

We looked then, and saw that the nose of our boat had got fixed under the woodwork of the lock, while the in-coming water was rising all around it, and tilting it up. In another moment we should be over. Quick as thought, we each seized an oar, and a vigorous blow against the side of the lock with the butt-ends released the boat, and sent us sprawling on our backs.

We did not come out well in that photograph, George and I. Of course, as was to be expected, our luck ordained it, that the man should set his wretched machine in motion at the precise moment that we were both lying on our backs with a wild expression of 'Where am I? and what is it?' on our faces, and our four feet waving madly in the air.

Our feet were undoubtedly the leading article in that photograph. Indeed, very little else was to be seen. They filled up the foreground entirely. Behind them, you caught glimpses of the other boats, and bits of the surrounding scenery; but everything and everybody else in the lock looked so utterly insignificant and paltry compared with our feet, and all the other people felt quite ashamed of themselves, and refused to subscribe to the picture.

The owner of one steam launch, who had bespoke six copies, rescinded the order on seeing the negative. He said he would take them if anybody could show him his launch, but nobody could. It was somewhere behind George's right foot.

There was a good deal of unpleasantness over the business. The photographer thought we ought to take a dozen copies each, seeing that the photo was about nine-tenths us, but we declined. We said we had no objection to being photo'd full-length, but we preferred being taken the right way up.

Wallingford, six miles above Streatley, is a very ancient town, and has been an active centre for the making of English history. It was a rude, mud-built town in the time of the Britons, who squatted there, until the Roman legions evicted them; and replaced their clay-baked walls by mighty fortifications, the trace of which Time has not yet succeeded in sweeping away, so well those old-world masons knew how to build.

But Time, though he halted at Roman walls, soon crumbled Romans to dust; and on the ground, in later years, fought savage Saxons and huge Danes, until the Normans came.

It was a walled and fortified town up to the time of the

Parliamentary War, when it suffered a long and bitter siege from Fairfax. It fell at last, and then the walls were razed.

From Wallingford up to Dorchester the neighbourhood of the river grows more hilly, varied, and picturesque. Dorchester stands half a mile from the river. It can be reached by paddling up the Thame, if you have a small boat; but the best way is to leave the river at Day's lock, and to take a walk across the fields. Dorchester is a delightfully peaceful old place, nestling in stillness and silence and drowsiness.

Dorchester, like Wallingford, was a city in ancient British times; it was then called Caer Doren, 'the city on the water.' In more recent times the Romans formed a great camp here, the fortifications surrounding which now seem like low, even hills. In Saxon days it was the capital of Wessex. It is very old, and it was very strong and great once. Now it sits aside from the stirring world, and nods and dreams.

Round Clifton Hampden, itself a wonderfully pretty village, old-fashioned, peaceful, and dainty with flowers, the river scenery is rich and beautiful. If you stay the night on land at Clifton, you cannot do better than put up at the 'Barley Mow.' It is, without exception, I should say, the quaintest, most old-world inn up the river. It stands on the right of the bridge, quite away from the village. Its low-pitched gables and thatched roof and latticed windows give it quite a story-book appearance, while inside it is even still more once-upon-a-timeyfied.

It would not be a good place for the heroine of a modern novel to stay at. The heroine of a modern novel is always 'divinely tall,' and she is ever 'drawing herself up to her full height.' At the 'Barley Mow' she would bump her head against the ceiling each time she did this.

It would also be a bad house for a drunken man to put up at. There are too many surprises in the way of unexpected steps down into this room and up into that; and as for getting upstairs to his bedroom, or ever finding his bed when he got up, either operation would be an utter impossibility to him.

We were up early the next morning, as we wanted to be in Oxford by the afternoon. It is surprising how early one *can* get up, when camping out. One does not yearn for 'just another five minutes' nearly so much, lying wrapped up in a rug on the boards of a boat, with a Gladstone bag for a pillow, as one does in a feather-bed. We had finished breakfast, and were through Clifton lock by half-past eight.

From Clifton to Culham the river banks are flat, monotonous, and uninteresting, but, after you get through Culham lock—the coldest and deepest lock on the river—the landscape improves.

At Abingdon, the river passes by the streets. Abingdon is a typical country town of the smaller order—quiet, eminently respectable, clean, and desperately dull. It prides itself on being old, but whether it can compare in this respect with Wallingford and Dorchester seems doubtful. A famous abbey stood here once, and within what is left of its sanctified walls they brew bitter ale nowadays.

In St Nicholas Church, at Abingdon, there is a monument to John Blackwall and his wife Jane, who both, after leading a happy married life, died on the very same day, August 21, 1625; and in St Helen's Church, it is recorded that W. Lee, who died in 1637, 'had in his lifetime issue from his loins two hundred lacking but three.' If you work this out you will find that Mr W. Lee's family numbered one hundred and ninety-seven. Mr W. Lee—five times Mayor of Abingdon—was, no doubt, a benefactor to his generation, but I hope there are not many of his kind about in this overcrowded nineteenth century.

From Abingdon to Nuneham Courtenay is a lovely stretch. Nuneham Park is well worth a visit. It can be viewed on Tuesdays and Thursdays. The house contains a fine collection of pictures and curiosities, and the grounds are very beautiful.

The pool under Sandford lasher, just behind the lock, is a very good place to drown yourself in. The undercurrent is terribly strong, and if you once get down into it you are all right. An obelisk marks the spot where two men have already been drowned, while bathing there; and the steps of the obelisk are generally used as a diving-board by young men now who wish to see if the place really *is* dangerous.

Iffley lock and mill, a mile before you reach Oxford, is a favourite subject with the river-loving brethren of the brush. The real article, however, is rather disappointing, after the pictures. Few things, I have noticed, come quite up to the pictures of them, in this world.

We passed through Iffley lock at about half-past twelve, and then, having tidied up the boat and made all ready for landing, we set to work on our last mile.

Between Iffley and Oxford is the most difficult bit of the river I know. You want to be born on that bit of water, to understand it. I have been over it a fairish number of times, but I have never been able to get the hang of it. The man who could row a straight course from Oxford to Iffley ought to be able to live comfortably, under one roof, with his wife, his mother-in-law, his elder sister, and the old servant who was in the family when he was a baby.

First the current drives you on to the right bank, and then on to the left, then it takes you out into the middle, turns you round three times, and carries you up stream again, and always ends by trying to smash you up against a college barge.

Of course, as a consequence of this, we got in the way of a good many other boats, during the mile, and they in ours, and, of course, as a consequence of that, a good deal of bad language occurred.

I don't know why it should be, but everybody is always so exceptionally irritable on the river. Little mishaps, that you would hardly notice on dry land, drive you nearly frantic with rage, when they occur on the water. When Harris or George makes an ass of himself on dry land, I smile indulgently; when they behave in a chuckle-head way on the river, I use the most blood-curdling language to them. When another boat gets in my way, I feel I want to take an oar and kill all the people in it.

The mildest tempered people, when on land, become violent and blood-thirsty when in a boat. I did a little boating once with a young lady. She was naturally of the sweetest and gentlest disposition imaginable, but on the river it was quite awful to hear her.

'Oh, drat the man!' she would exclaim, when some unfortunate sculler would get in her way; 'why don't he look where he's going?'

And, 'Oh, bother the silly old thing!' she would say indignantly, when the sail would not go up properly. And she would catch hold of it, and shake it quite brutally.

Yet, as I have said, when on shore she was kind-hearted and amiable enough.

The air of the river has a demoralising effect upon one's temper, and this it is, I suppose, which causes even barge men to be sometimes rude to one another, and to use language which, no doubt, in their calmer moments they regret.

CHAPTER XIX

Oxford—Montmorency's idea of Heaven—The hired up-river boat, its beauties and advantages—The 'Pride of the Thames'—The weather changes—The river under different aspects—Not a cheerful evening— Yearnings for the unattainable—The cheery chat goes round—George performs upon the banjo—A mournful melody—Another wet day— Flight—A little supper and a toast.

WE spent two very pleasant days at Oxford. There are plenty of dogs in the town of Oxford. Montmorency had eleven fights on the first day, and fourteen on the second, and evidently thought he had got to heaven.

Among folk too constitutionally weak, or too constitutionally lazy, whichever it may be, to relish up-stream work, it is a common practice to get a boat at Oxford, and row down. For the energetic, however, the up-stream journey is certainly to be preferred. It does not seem good to be always going with the current. There is more satisfaction in squaring one's back, and fighting against it, and winning one's way forward in spite of it—at least, so I feel, when Harris and George are sculling and I am steering.

To those who do contemplate making Oxford their starting-place, I would say, take your own boat—unless, of course, you can take someone else's without any possible danger of being found out. The boats that, as a rule, are let for hire on the Thames above Marlow, are very good boats. They are fairly water-tight; and so long as they are handled with care, they rarely come to pieces, or sink. There are places in them to sit down on, and they are complete with all the necessary arrangements—or nearly all—to enable you to row them and steer them.

But they are not ornamental. The boat you hire up the river above Marlow is not the sort of boat in which you can flash about and give yourself airs. The hired up-river boat very soon puts a stop to any nonsense of that sort on the part of its occupants. That is its chief— one may say, its only recommendation.

The man in the hired up-river boat is modest and retiring. He likes to keep on the shady side, underneath the trees, and to do most of his travelling early in the morning or late at night, when there are not many people about on the river to look at him.

When the man in the hired up-river boat sees anyone he knows, he gets out on to the bank, and hides behind a tree.

I was one of a party who hired an up-river boat one summer, for a few days' trip. We had none of us ever seen the hired up-river boat before; and we did not know what it was when we did see it.

We had written for a boat—a double sculling skiff; and when we went down with our bags to the yard, and gave our names, the man said:

'Oh, yes; you're the party that wrote for a double sculling skiff. It's all right. Jim, fetch round *The Pride of the Thames.*'

The boy went, and re-appeared five minutes afterwards, struggling with an antediluvian chunk of wood, that looked as though it had been recently dug out of somewhere, and dug out carelessly, so as to have been unnecessarily damaged in the process.

My own idea, on first catching sight of the object, was that it was a Roman relic of some sort,—relic of *what* I do not know, possibly of a coffin.

The neighbourhood of the upper Thames is rich in Roman relics, and my surmise seemed to me a very probable one; but our serious young man, who is a bit of a geologist, pooh-poohed my Roman relic theory, and said it was clear to the meanest intellect (in which category he seemed to be grieved that he could not conscientiously include mine) that the thing the boy had found was the fossil of a whale; and he pointed out to us various evidences proving that it must have belonged to the preglacial period.

To settle the dispute, we appealed to the boy. We told him not to be afraid, but to speak the plain truth: Was it the fossil of a pre-Adamite whale, or was it an early Roman coffin?

The boy said it was *The Pride of the Thames.*

We thought this a very humorous answer on the part of the boy at first, and somebody gave him twopence as a reward for his ready wit; but when he persisted in keeping up the joke, as we thought, too long, we got vexed with him.

'Come, come, my lad!' said our captain sharply, 'don't let us have any nonsense. You take your mother's washing-tub home again, and bring us a boat.'

The boat-builder himself came up then, and assured us, on his word, as a practical man, that the thing really was a boat—was, in fact, *the* boat, the 'double sculling skiff' selected to take us on our trip down the river.

We grumbled a good deal. We thought he might, at least, have had it whitewashed or tarred—had *something* done to it to distinguish it from a bit of a wreck; but he could not see any fault in it.

He even seemed offended at our remarks. He said he had picked us out the best boat in all his stock, and he thought we might have been more grateful.

He said it, *The Pride of the Thames*, had been in use, just as it now stood (or rather as it now hung together), for the last forty years, to *his* knowledge, and nobody had complained of it before, and he did not see why we should be the first to begin.

We argued no more.

We fastened the so-called boat together with some pieces of string, got a bit of wall-paper and pasted over the shabbier places, said our prayers, and stepped on board.

They charged us thirty-five shillings for the loan of the remnant for six days; and we could have bought the thing out-and-out for four-and-sixpence at any sale of drift-wood round the coast.

The weather changed on the third day,—Oh! I am talking about our present trip now,—and we started from Oxford upon our homeward journey in the midst of a steady drizzle.

The river—with the sunlight flashing from its dancing wavelets, gilding gold the grey-green beech-trunks, glinting through the dark, cool wood paths, chasing shadows o'er the shallows, flinging diamonds from the mill-wheels, throwing kisses to the lilies, wantoning with the weirs' white waters, silvering moss-grown walls and bridges, brightening every tiny townlet, making sweet each lane and meadow, lying tangled in the rushes, peeping, laughing, from each inlet, gleaming gay on many a far sail, making soft the air with glory—is a golden fairy stream.

But the river—chill and weary, with the ceaseless rain-drops falling on its brown and sluggish waters, with a sound as of a woman, weeping low in some dark chamber; while the woods, all dark and silent, shrouded in their mists of vapour, stand like ghosts upon the margin; silent ghosts with eyes reproachful, like the ghosts of evil actions, like the ghosts of friends neglected—is a spirit-haunted water through the land of vain regrets.

Sunlight is the life-blood of Nature. Mother Earth looks at us with such dull, soulless eyes, when the sunlight has died away from out of her. It makes us sad to be with her then; she does not seem to know us

or to care for us. She is as a widow who has lost the husband she loved, and her children touch her hand, and look up into her eyes, but gain no smile from her.

We rowed on all that day through the rain, and very melancholy work it was. We pretended, at first, that we enjoyed it. We said it was a change, and that we liked to see the river under all its different aspects. We said we could not expect to have it all sunshine, nor should we wish it. We told each other that Nature was beautiful, even in her tears.

Indeed, Harris and I were quite enthusiastic about the business, for the first few hours. And we sang a song about a gipsy's life, and how delightful a gipsy's existence was!—free to storm and sunshine, and to every wind that blew!—and how he enjoyed the rain, and what a lot of good it did him; and how he laughed at people who didn't like it.

George took the fun more soberly, and stuck to the umbrella.

We hoisted the cover before we had lunch, and kept it up all the afternoon, just leaving a little space in the bow, from which one of us could paddle and keep a look-out. In this way we made nine miles, and pulled up for the night a little below Day's lock.

I cannot honestly say that we had a merry evening. The rain poured down with quiet persistency. Everything in the boat was damp and clammy. Supper was not a success. Cold veal pie, when you don't feel hungry, is apt to cloy. I felt I wanted whitebait and a cutlet; Harris babbled of soles and white-sauce, and passed the remains of his pie to Montmorency, who declined it, and, apparently insulted by the offer, went and sat over at the other end of the boat by himself.

George requested that we would not talk about these things, at all events until he had finished his cold boiled beef without mustard.

We played penny nap after supper. We played for about an hour and a half, by the end of which time George had won fourpence —George always is lucky at cards—and Harris and I had lost exactly twopence each.

We thought we would give up gambling then. As Harris said, it breeds an unhealthy excitement when carried too far. George offered to go on and give us our revenge; but Harris and I decided not to battle any further against Fate.

After that, we mixed ourselves some toddy, and sat round and talked. George told us about a man he had known, who had come up the river two years ago, and who had slept out in a damp boat on just such another night as that was, and it had given him rheumatic fever, and nothing was able to save him, and he had died in great agony ten days afterwards. George said he was quite a young man, and was engaged to be married. He said it was one of the saddest things he had ever known.

And that put Harris in mind of a friend of his, who had been in the Volunteers, and who had slept out under canvas one wet night down at Aldershot, 'on just such another night as this,' said Harris; and he had woke up in the morning a cripple for life. Harris said he would introduce us both to the man when we got back to town; it would make our hearts bleed to see him.

This naturally led to some pleasant chat about sciatica, fevers, chills, lung diseases, and bronchitis; and Harris said how very awkward it would be if one of us were taken seriously ill in the night, seeing how far away we were from a doctor.

There seemed to be a desire for something frolicksome to follow upon this conversation, and in a weak moment I suggested that George should get out his banjo, and see if he could not give us a comic song.

I will say for George that he did not want any pressing. There was no nonsense about having left his music at home, or anything of that sort. He at once fished out his instrument, and commenced to play 'Two Lovely Black Eyes.'

I had always regarded 'Two Lovely Black Eyes' as rather a commonplace tune until that evening. The rich vein of sadness that George extracted from it quite surprised me.

The desire that grew upon Harris and myself, as the mournful strains progressed, was to fall upon each other's necks and weep; but by great effort we kept back the rising tears, and listened to the wild yearnful melody in silence.

When the chorus came we even made a desperate effort to be merry. We re-filled our glasses and joined in; Harris, in a voice trembling with emotion, leading, and George and I following a few words behind:

> 'Two lovely black eyes;
> Oh! what a surprise!
> Only for telling a man he was wrong,
> Two——'

There we broke down. The unutterable pathos of George's accompaniment to that 'two' we were, in our then state of depression, unable to bear. Harris sobbed like a little child, and the dog howled till I thought his heart or his jaw must surely break.

George wanted to go on with another verse. He thought that when he had got a little more into the tune, and could throw more 'abandon,' as it were, into the rendering, it might not seem so sad. The feeling of the majority, however, was opposed to the experiment.

There being nothing else to do, we went to bed—that is, we undressed ourselves, and tossed about at the bottom of the boat for some three or four hours. After which, we managed to get some fitful slumber until five a.m., when we all got up and had breakfast.

The second day was exactly like the first. The rain continued to pour down, and we sat, wrapped up in our mackintoshes, underneath the canvas, and drifted slowly down.

One of us—I forget which one now, but I rather think it was myself—made a few feeble attempts during the course of the morning to work up the old gipsy foolishness about being children of Nature and enjoying the wet; but it did not go down well at all. That—

'I care not for the rain, not I!'

was so painfully evident, as expressing the sentiments of each of us, that to sing it seemed unnecessary.

On one point we were all agreed, and that was that, come what might, we would go through with this job to the bitter end. We had come out for a fortnight's enjoyment on the river, and a fortnight's enjoyment on the river we meant to have. If it killed us! well, that would be a sad thing for our friends and relations, but it could not be helped. We felt that to give in to the weather in a climate such as ours would be a most disastrous precedent.

'It's only two days more,' said Harris, 'and we are young and strong. We may get over it all right, after all.'

At about four o'clock we began to discuss our arrangements for the evening. We were a little past Goring then, and we decided to paddle on to Pangbourne, and put up there for the night.

'Another jolly evening!' murmured George.

We sat and mused on the prospect. We should be in at Pangbourne by five. We should finish dinner at, say, half-past six. After that we could walk about the village in the pouring rain until bed-time; or we could sit in a dimly-lit bar-parlour and read the almanac.

'Why, the Alhambra* would be almost more lively,' said Harris, venturing his head outside the cover for a moment and taking a survey of the sky.

'With a little supper at the——¹ to follow,' I added, half unconsciously.

'Yes, it's almost a pity we've made up our minds to stick to this boat,' answered Harris; and then there was silence for awhile.

'If we *hadn't* made up our minds to contract our certain deaths in this bally old coffin,' observed George, casting a glance of intense malevolence over the boat, 'it might be worth while to mention that there's a train leaves Pangbourne, I know, soon after five, which would just land us in town in comfortable time to get a chop, and then go on to the place you mentioned afterwards.'

Nobody spoke. We looked at one another, and each one seemed to see his own mean and guilty thoughts reflected in the faces of the others. In silence, we dragged out and overhauled the Gladstone. We looked up the river and down the river; not a soul was in sight!

Twenty minutes later, three figures, followed by a shamed-looking dog, might have been seen creeping stealthily from the boat-house at the 'Swan' towards the railway station, dressed in the following neither neat nor gaudy costume:

Black leather shoes, dirty; suit of boating flannels, very dirty; brown felt hat, much battered; mackintosh, very wet; umbrella.

We had deceived the boatman at Pangbourne. We had not had the face to tell him that we were running away from the rain. We had left the boat, and all it contained, in his charge, with instructions that it was to be ready for us at nine the next morning. If, we said—*if* anything unforeseen should happen, preventing our return, we would write to him.

We reached Paddington at seven, and drove direct to the restaurant I have before described, where we partook of a light meal, left Montmorency, together with suggestions for a supper to be ready at half-past ten, and then continued our way to Leicester Square.

¹ A capital little out-of-the-way restaurant, in the neighbourhood of——, where you can get one of the best-cooked and cheapest little French dinners or suppers that I know of, with an excellent bottle of Beaune, for three-and-six; and which I am not going to be idiot enough to advertise.

We attracted a good deal of attention at the Alhambra. On our presenting ourselves at the pay-box we were gruffly directed to go round to Castle Street, and were informed that we were half-an-hour behind our time.

We convinced the man, with some difficulty, that we were *not* 'the world-renowned contortionists from the Himalaya Mountains,' and he took our money and let us pass.

Inside we were a still greater success. Our fine bronzed countenances and picturesque clothes were followed round the place with admiring gaze. We were the cynosure of every eye.

It was a proud moment for us all.

We adjourned soon after the first ballet, and wended our way back to the restaurant, where supper was already awaiting us.

I must confess to enjoying that supper. For about ten days we seemed to have been living, more or less, on nothing but cold meat, cake, and bread and jam. It had been a simple, a nutritious diet; but there had been nothing exciting about it, and the odour of Burgundy, and the smell of French sauces, and the sight of clean napkins and long loaves, knocked as a very welcome visitor at the door of our inner man.

We pegged and quaffed away in silence for a while, until the time came when, instead of sitting bolt upright, and grasping the knife and fork firmly, we leant back in our chairs and worked slowly and carelessly—when we stretched out our legs beneath the table, let our napkins fall, unheeded, to the floor, and found time to more critically examine the smoky ceiling than we had hitherto been able to do—when we rested our glasses at arm's-length upon the table, and felt good, and thoughtful, and forgiving.

Then Harris, who was sitting next the window, drew aside the curtain and looked out upon the street.

It glistened darkly in the wet, the dim lamps flickered with each gust, the rain splashed steadily into the puddles and trickled down the water-spouts into the running gutters. A few soaked wayfarers hurried past, crouching beneath their dripping umbrellas, the women holding up their skirts.

'Well,' said Harris, reaching his hand out for his glass, 'we have had a pleasant trip, and my hearty thanks for it to old Father Thames—but I think we did well to chuck it when we did. Here's to Three Men well out of a Boat!'

And Montmorency, standing on his hind legs, before the window, peering out into the night, gave a short bark of decided concurrence with the toast.

THREE MEN ON THE BUMMEL

To the gentle

GUIDE

WHO LETS ME EVER GO MY OWN WAY, YET BRINGS ME RIGHT——

To the laughter-loving

PHILOSOPHER,

WHO, IF HE HAS NOT RECONCILED ME TO BEARING THE TOOTH-
ACHE PATIENTLY, AT LEAST HAS TAUGHT ME THE COMFORT THAT
THIS EVEN WILL ALSO PASS——

To the good

FRIEND

WHO SMILES WHEN I TELL HIM OF MY TROUBLES, AND WHO,
WHEN I ASK FOR HELP, ANSWERS ONLY 'WAIT!'——

To the grave-faced

JESTER,

TO WHOM ALL LIFE IS BUT A VOLUME OF OLD HUMOUR——

To good master

TIME

THIS LITTLE WORK OF A POOR
PUPIL
IS DEDICATED

CHAPTER I

'WHAT we want,' said Harris, 'is a change.'

At this moment the door opened, and Mrs Harris put her head in to say that Ethelbertha had sent her to remind me that we must not be late getting home because of Clarence. Ethelbertha, I am inclined to think, is unnecessarily nervous about the children. As a matter of fact, there was nothing wrong with the child whatever. He had been out with his aunt that morning; and if he looks wistfully at a pastrycook's window she takes him inside and buys him cream buns and 'maids-of-honour' until he insists that he has had enough, and politely, but firmly, refuses to eat another anything. Then, of course, he wants only one helping of pudding at lunch, and Ethelbertha thinks he is sickening for something. Mrs Harris added that it would be as well for us to come upstairs soon, on our own account also, as otherwise we should miss Muriel's rendering of 'The Mad Hatter's Tea Party,' out of *Alice in Wonderland*. Muriel is Harris's second, age eight: she is a bright, intelligent child; but I prefer her myself in serious pieces. We said we would finish our cigarettes and follow almost immediately; we also begged her not to let Muriel begin until we arrived. She promised to hold the child back as long as possible, and went. Harris, as soon as the door was closed, resumed his interrupted sentence.

'You know what I mean,' he said, 'a complete change.'

The question was how to get it.

George suggested 'business.' It was the sort of suggestion George would make. A bachelor thinks a married woman doesn't know enough to get out of the way of a steam-roller. I knew a young fellow once, an engineer, who thought he would go to Vienna 'on business.' His wife wanted to know 'what business?' He told her it would be his duty to visit the mines in the neighbourhood of the Austrian capital, and to make reports. She said she would go with him; she was that sort of woman. He tried to dissuade her: he told her that a mine was no place for a beautiful woman. She said she felt that herself, and that therefore she did not intend to accompany him down the shafts; she would see him off in the morning, and then amuse herself until his return, looking round the Vienna shops, and buying a few things she might want. Having started the idea, he did not see very well how to get out of it; and for ten long summer days he did visit the mines in the neighbourhood of Vienna, and in the evening wrote reports about them, which she posted for him to his firm, who didn't want them.

I should be grieved to think that either Ethelbertha or Mrs Harris belonged to that class of wife, but it is as well not to overdo 'business'—it should be kept for cases of real emergency.

'No,' I said, 'the thing is to be frank and manly. I shall tell Ethelbertha that I have come to the conclusion a man never values happiness that is always with him. I shall tell her that, for the sake of learning to appreciate my own advantages as I know they should be appreciated, I intend to tear myself away from her and the children for at least three weeks. I shall tell her,' I continued, turning to Harris, 'that it is you who have shown me my duty in this respect; that it is to you we shall owe——'

Harris put down his glass rather hurriedly.

'If you don't mind, old man,' he interrupted, 'I'd really rather you didn't. She'll talk it over with my wife, and—well, I should not be happy, taking credit that I do not deserve.'

'But you do deserve it,' I insisted; 'it was your suggestion.'

'It was you gave me the idea,' interrupted Harris again. 'You know you said it was a mistake for a man to get into a groove, and that unbroken domesticity cloyed the brain.'

'I was speaking generally,' I explained.

'It struck me as very apt,' said Harris. 'I thought of repeating it to Clara; she has a great opinion of your sense, I know. I am sure that if——'

'We won't risk it,' I interrupted, in my turn; 'it is a delicate matter, and I see a way out of it. We will say George suggested the idea.'

There is a lack of genial helpfulness about George that it some-times vexes me to notice. You would have thought he would have welcomed the chance of assisting two old friends out of a dilemma; instead, he became disagreeable.

'You do,' said George, 'and I shall tell them both that my original plan was that we should make a party—children and all; that I should bring my aunt, and that we should hire a charming old château I know of in Normandy, on the coast, where the climate is peculiarly adapted to delicate children, and the milk such as you do not get in England. I shall add that you over-rode the suggestion, arguing we should be happier by ourselves.'

With a man like George kindness is of no use; you have to be firm.

'You do,' said Harris, 'and I, for one, will close with the offer. We will just take that château. You will bring your aunt—I will see to that,—and we will have a month of it. The children are all fond of you; J. and I will be nowhere. You've promised to teach Edgar fishing; and it is you who will have to play wild beasts. Since last Sunday Dick and Muriel have talked of nothing else but your hippopotamus. We will picnic in the woods—there will only be eleven of us,—and in the evenings we will have music and reci-tations. Muriel is master of six pieces already, as perhaps you know; and all the other children are quick studies.'

George climbed down—he has no real courage—but he did not do it gracefully. He said that if we were mean and cowardly and false-hearted enough to stoop to such a shabby trick, he supposed he couldn't help it; and that if I didn't intend to finish the whole bottle of claret myself, he would trouble me to spare him a glass. He also added, somewhat illogically, that it really did not matter, seeing both Ethelbertha and Mrs Harris were women of sense who would judge him better than to believe for a moment that the suggestion emanated from him.

This little point settled, the question was: What sort of a change?

Harris, as usual, was for the sea. He said he knew a yacht, just the very thing—one that we could manage by ourselves; no skulking lot of lubbers loafing about, adding to the expense and taking away from the romance. Give him a handy boy, he would sail it himself. We knew that yacht, and we told him so; we had been on it with Harris before. It smells of bilge-water and greens to the exclusion of all other scents; no ordinary sea air can hope to head against it. So far as sense of smell is concerned, one might be spending a week in Limehouse Hole.* There is no place to get out of the rain; the saloon is ten feet by four, and half of that is taken up by a stove, which falls to pieces when you go to light it. You have to take your bath on deck, and the towel blows overboard just as you step out of the tub. Harris and the boy do all the interesting work—the lugging and the reefing, the letting her go and the heeling her over, and all that sort of thing,—leaving George and myself to do the peeling of the potatoes and the washing up.

'Very well, then,' said Harris, 'let's take a proper yacht, with a skipper, and do the thing in style.'

That also I objected to. I know that skipper; his notion of yachting is to lie in what he calls the 'offing,' where he can be well in touch with his wife and family, to say nothing of his favourite public-house.

Years ago, when I was young and inexperienced, I hired a yacht myself. Three things had combined to lead me into this foolishness: I had had a stroke of unexpected luck; Ethelbertha had expressed a yearning for sea air; and the very next morning, in taking up casually at the club a copy of the *Sportsman*, I had come across the following advertisement:—

To YACHTSMEN.—Unique Opportunity.—'Rogue,' 28-ton Yawl.— Owner, called away suddenly on business, is willing to let this superbly-fitted 'greyhound of the sea' for any period, short or long. Two cabins and saloon; pianette, by Woffenkoff; new copper. Terms, 10 guineas a week.— Apply Pertwee and Co., 3A Bucklersbury.

It had seemed to me like the answer to a prayer. 'The new copper' did not interest me; what little washing we might want could wait, I thought. But the 'pianette by Woffenkoff' sounded alluring. I pictured Ethelbertha playing in the evening—something with a chorus, in which, perhaps, the crew, with a little training, might join—while our moving home bounded, 'greyhound-like,' over the silvery billows.

I took a cab and drove direct to 3A Bucklersbury. Mr Pertwee was an unpretentious-looking gentleman, who had an unostentatious office on the third floor. He showed me a picture in water-colours of the *Rogue* flying before the wind. The deck was at an angle of 95 to the ocean. In the picture no human beings were represented on the deck; I suppose they had slipped off. Indeed, I do not see how anyone could have kept on, unless nailed. I pointed out this disadvantage to the agent, who, however, explained to me that the picture represented the *Rogue* doubling something or other on the well-known occasion of her winning the Medway Challenge Shield. Mr Pertwee assumed that I knew all about the event, so that I did not like to ask any questions. Two specks near the frame of the picture, which at first I had taken for moths, represented, it appeared, the second and third winners in this celebrated race. A photograph of the yacht at anchor off Gravesend was less impressive, but suggested more stability. All answers to my inquiries being satisfactory, I took the thing for a fortnight. Mr Pertwee said it was fortunate I wanted it only for a fortnight—later on I came to agree with him,—the time fitting in exactly with another hiring. Had I required it for three weeks he would have been compelled to refuse me.

The letting being thus arranged, Mr Pertwee asked me if I had a skipper in my eye. That I had not was also fortunate—things seemed to be turning out luckily for me all round,—because Mr Pertwee felt sure I could not do better than keep on Mr Goyles, at present in charge—an excellent skipper, so Mr Pertwee assured me, a man who knew the sea as a man knows his own wife, and who had never lost a life.

It was still early in the day, and the yacht was lying off Harwich. I caught the ten forty-five from Liverpool Street, and by one o'clock was talking to Mr Goyles on deck. He was a stout man, and had a fatherly way with him. I told him my idea, which was to take the outlying Dutch islands and then creep up to Norway. He said 'Aye, aye, sir,' and appeared quite enthusiastic about the trip; said he should enjoy it himself. We came to the question of victualling, and he grew more enthusiastic. The amount of food suggested by Mr Goyles, I confess, surprised me. Had we been living in the days of Drake and the Spanish Main, I should have feared he was arranging for something illegal. However, he laughed in his fatherly way, and assured me we were not overdoing it. Anything left the crew would divide and take home with them—it seemed this was the custom. It appeared to me that I was providing for this crew for the winter, but I did not like to appear stingy, and said no more. The amount of drink required also surprised me. I arranged for what I thought we should need for ourselves, and then Mr Goyles spoke up for the crew. I must say that for him, he did think of his men.

'We don't want anything in the nature of an orgie, Mr Goyles,' I suggested.

'Orgie!' replied Mr Goyles; 'why they'll take that little drop in their tea.'

He explained to me that his motto was, Get good men and treat them well.

'They work better for you,' said Mr Goyles; 'and they come again.'

Personally, I didn't feel I wanted them to come again. I was beginning to take a dislike to them before I had seen them; I regarded them as a greedy and guzzling crew. But Mr Goyles was so cheerfully emphatic, and I was so inexperienced, that again I let him have his way. He also promised that even in this department he would see to it personally that nothing was wasted.

I also left him to engage the crew. He said he could do the thing, and would, for me, with the help of two men and a boy. If he was alluding to the clearing up of the victuals and drink, I think he was making an under-estimate; but possibly he may have been speaking of the sailing of the yacht.

I called at my tailors on the way home and ordered a yachting suit, with a white hat, which they promised to bustle up and have ready in time; and then I went home and told Ethelbertha all I had done. Her delight was clouded by only one reflection—would the dressmaker be able to finish a yachting costume for her in time? That is so like a woman.

Our honeymoon, which had taken place not very long before, had been somewhat curtailed, so we decided we would invite nobody, but have the yacht to ourselves. And thankful I am to Heaven that we did so decide. On Monday we put on all our clothes and started. I forget what Ethelbertha wore, but, whatever it may have been, it looked very fetching. My own costume was a dark blue, trimmed with a narrow white braid, which, I think, was rather effective.

Mr Goyles met us on deck, and told us that lunch was ready. I must admit Goyles had secured the services of a very fair cook. The capabilities of the other members of the crew I had no opportunity of judging. Speaking of them in a state of rest, however, I can say of them they appeared to be a cheerful crew.

My idea had been that so soon as the men had finished their dinner we would weigh anchor, while I, smoking a cigar, with Ethelbertha by my side, would lean over the gunwale and watch the white cliffs of the Fatherland sink imperceptibly into the horizon. Ethelbertha and I carried out our part of the programme, and waited, with the deck to ourselves.

'They seem to be taking their time,' said Ethelbertha.

'If, in the course of fourteen days,' I said, 'they eat half of what is on this yacht, they will want a fairly long time for every meal. We had better not hurry them, or they won't get through a quarter of it.'

'They must have gone to sleep,' said Ethelbertha, later on. 'It will be tea-time soon.'

They were certainly very quiet. I went for'ard, and hailed Captain Goyles down the ladder. I hailed him three times; then he came up slowly. He appeared to be a heavier and older man than when I had seen him last. He had a cold cigar in his mouth.

'When are you ready, Captain Goyles,' I said, 'we'll start.'

Captain Goyles removed the cigar from his mouth.

'Not to-day we won't, sir,' he replied, '*with* your permission.'

'Why, what's the matter with to-day?' I said. I know sailors are superstitious folk; I thought maybe a Monday might be considered unlucky.

'The day's all right,' answered Captain Goyles, 'it's the wind I'm a-thinking of. It don't look much like changing.'

'But do we want it to change?' I asked. 'It seems to me to be just where it should be, dead behind us.'

'Aye, aye,' said Captain Goyles, 'dead's the right word to use, for dead we'd all be, bar Providence, if we was to put out in this. You see, sir,' he explained, in answer to my look of surprise, 'this is what we call a "land wind," that is, it's a-blowing, as one might say, direct off the land.'

When I came to think of it the man was right; the wind was blowing off the land.

'It may change in the night,' said Captain Goyles, more hopefully; 'anyhow, it's not violent, and she rides well.'

Captain Goyles resumed his cigar, and I returned aft, and explained to Ethelbertha the reason for the delay. Ethelbertha, who appeared to be less high spirited than when we first boarded, wanted to know *why* we couldn't sail when the wind was off the land.

'If it was not blowing off the land,' said Ethelbertha, 'it would be blowing off the sea, and that would send us back into the shore again. It seems to me this is just the very wind we want.'

I said: 'That is your inexperience, love; it *seems* to be the very wind we want, but it is not. It's what we call a land wind, and a land wind is always very dangerous.'

Ethelbertha wanted to know *why* a land wind was very dangerous.

Her argumentativeness annoyed me somewhat; maybe I was feeling a bit cross; the monotonous rolling heave of a small yacht at anchor depresses an ardent spirit.

'I can't explain it to you,' I replied, which was true, 'but to set sail in this wind would be the height of foolhardiness, and I care for you too much, dear, to expose you to unnecessary risks.'

I thought this rather a neat conclusion, but Ethelbertha merely replied that she wished, under the circumstances, we hadn't come on board till Tuesday, and went below.

In the morning the wind veered round to the north; I was up early; and observed this to Captain Goyles.

'Aye, aye, sir,' he remarked; 'it's unfortunate, but it can't be helped.'

'You don't think it possible for us to start to-day?' I hazarded.

He did not get angry with me, he only laughed.

'Well, sir,' said he, 'if you was a-wanting to go to Ipswich, I should say as it couldn't be better for us, but our destination being, as you see, the Dutch coast—why there you are!'

I broke the news to Ethelbertha, and we agreed to spend the day on shore. Harwich is not a merry town, towards evening you might call it dull. We had some tea and watercress at Dovercourt, and then returned to the quay to look for Captain Goyles and the boat. We waited an hour for him. When he came he was more cheerful than we were; if he had not told me himself that he never drank anything but one glass of hot grog before turning in for the night, I should have said he was drunk.

The next morning the wind was in the south, which made Captain Goyles rather anxious, it appearing that it was equally unsafe to move or to stop where we were; our only hope was it would change before anything happened. By this time, Ethelbertha had taken a dislike to the yacht; she said that, personally, she would rather be spending a week in a bathing machine, seeing that a bathing machine was at least steady.

We passed another day in Harwich, and that night and the next, the wind still continuing in the south, we slept at the 'King's Head.'

On Friday the wind was blowing direct from the east. I met Captain Goyles on the Quay, and suggested that, under these circumstances, we might start. He appeared irritated at my persistence.

'If you knew a bit more, sir,' he said, 'you'd see for yourself that it's impossible. The wind's a-blowing direct off the sea.'

I said: 'Captain Goyles, tell me what is this thing I have hired? Is it a yacht or a house-boat?'

He seemed surprised at my question.

He said: 'It's a yawl.'

'What I mean is,' I said, 'can it be moved at all, or is it a fixture here? If it is a fixture,' I continued, 'tell me so frankly, then we will get some ivy in boxes and train over the port-holes, stick some flowers and an awning on deck, and make the thing look pretty. If, on the other hand, it can be moved——'

'Moved!' interrupted Captain Goyles. 'You get the right wind behind the *Rogue*——'

I said: 'What is the right wind?'

Captain Goyles looked puzzled.

'In the course of this week,' I went on, 'we have had wind from the north, from the south, from the east, from the west—with variations. If you can think of any other point of the compass from which it can blow, tell me, and I will wait for it. If not, and if that anchor has not grown into the bottom of the ocean, we will have it up to-day and see what happens.'

He grasped the fact that I was determined.

'Very well, sir,' he said, 'you're master and I'm man. I've only got one child as is still dependent on me, thank God, and no doubt your executors will feel it their duty to do the right thing by the old woman.'

His solemnity impressed me.

'Mr Goyles,' I said, 'be honest with me. Is there any hope, in any weather, of getting away from this damned hole?'

Captain Goyles's kindly geniality returned to him.

'You see, sir,' he said, 'this is a very peculiar coast. We'd be all right if we were once out, but getting away from it in a cockle-shell like that—well, to be frank, sir, it wants doing.'

I left Captain Goyles with the assurance that he would watch the weather as a mother would her sleeping babe; it was his own simile, and it struck me as rather touching. I saw him again at twelve o'clock; he was watching it from the window of the 'Chain and Anchor.'

At five o'clock that evening a stroke of luck occurred; in the middle of the High Street I met a couple of yachting friends, who had had to put in by reason of a strained rudder. I told them my story, and they appeared less surprised than amused. Captain Goyles and the two men were still watching the weather. I ran into the 'King's Head,' and prepared Ethelbertha. The four of us crept quietly down to the quay, where we found our boat. Only the boy was on board; my two friends took charge of the yacht, and by six o'clock we were scudding merrily up the coast.

We put in that night at Aldborough, and the next day worked up to Yarmouth, where, as my friends had to leave, I decided to abandon the yacht. We sold the stores by auction on Yarmouth sands early in the morning. I made a loss, but had the satisfaction of 'doing' Captain Goyles. I left the *Rogue* in charge of a local mariner, who, for a couple of sovereigns, undertook to see to its return to Harwich; and we came back to London by train. There may be yachts other than the *Rogue*, and skippers other than Mr Goyles, but that experience has prejudiced me against both.

George also thought a yacht would be a good deal of responsibility, so we dismissed the idea.

'What about the river?' suggested Harris. 'We have had some pleasant times on that.'

George pulled in silence at his cigar, and I cracked another nut.

'The river is not what it used to be,' said I; 'I don't know what, but there's a something—a dampness—about the river air that always starts my lumbago.'

'It's the same with me,' said George. 'I don't know how it is, but I never can sleep now in the neighbourhood of the river. I spent a week at Joe's place in the spring, and every night I woke up at seven o'clock and never got a wink afterwards.'

'I merely suggested it,' observed Harris. 'Personally, I don't think it good for me, either; it touches my gout.'

'What suits me best,' I said, 'is mountain air. What say you to a walking tour in Scotland?'

'It's always wet in Scotland,' said George. 'I was three weeks in Scotland the year before last, and was never dry once all the time— not in that sense.'

'It's fine enough in Switzerland,' said Harris.

"They would never stand our going to Switzerland by ourselves,' I objected. 'You know what happened last time. It must be some place where no delicately nurtured woman or child could possibly live; a country of bad hotels and comfortless travelling; where we shall have to rough it, to work hard, to starve perhaps——'

'Easy!' interrupted George, 'easy, there! Don't forget I'm coming with you.'

'I have it!' exclaimed Harris; 'a bicycle tour!'

George looked doubtful.

'There's a lot of uphill about a bicycle tour,' said he, 'and the wind is against you.'

'So there is downhill, and the wind behind you,' said Harris.

'I've never noticed it,' said George.

'You won't think of anything better than a bicycle tour,' persisted Harris.

I was inclined to agree with him.

'And I'll tell you where,' continued he; 'through the Black Forest.'

'Why, that's *all* uphill,' said George.

'Not all,' retorted Harris; 'say two-thirds. And there's one thing you've forgotten.'

He looked round cautiously, and sunk his voice to a whisper.

'There are little railways going up those hills, little cogwheel things that——'

The door opened, and Mrs Harris appeared. She said that Ethelbertha was putting on her bonnet, and that Muriel, after waiting, had given 'The Mad Hatter's Tea Party' without us.

'Club, to-morrow, at four,' whispered Harris to me, as he rose, and I passed it on to George as we went upstairs.

CHAPTER II

A delicate business—What Ethelbertha might have said—What she did say—What Mrs Harris said—What we told George—We will start on Wednesday—George suggests the possibility of improving our minds—Harris and I are doubtful—Which man on a tandem does the most work?—The opinion of the man in front—Views of the man behind—How Harris lost his wife—The luggage question—The wisdom of my late Uncle Podger—Beginning of story about a man who had a bag.

I OPENED the ball with Ethelbertha that same evening. I commenced by being purposely a little irritable. My idea was that Ethelbertha would remark upon this. I should admit it, and account for it by over brain pressure. This would naturally lead to talk about my health in general, and the evident necessity there was for my taking prompt and vigorous measures. I thought that with a little tact I might even manage so that the suggestion should come from Ethelbertha herself. I imagined her saying: 'No, dear, it is change you want; complete change. Now be persuaded by me, and go away for a month. No, do not ask me to come with you. I know you would rather that I did, but I will not. It is the society of other men you need. Try and persuade George and Harris to go with you. Believe me, a highly strung brain such as yours demands occasional relaxation from the strain of domestic surroundings. Forget for a little while that children want music lessons, and boots, and bicycles, with tincture of rhubarb three times a day; forget there are such things in life as cooks, and house decorators, and next-door dogs, and butchers' bills. Go away to some green corner of the earth, where all is new and strange to you, where your overwrought mind will gather peace and fresh ideas. Go away for a space and give me time to miss you, and to reflect upon your goodness and virtue, which, continually present with me, I may, human-like, be apt to forget, as one, through use, grows indifferent to the blessing of the sun and the beauty of the moon. Go away, and come back refreshed in mind and body, a brighter, better man—if that be possible—than when you went away.'

But even when we obtain our desires, they never come to us garbed as we would wish. To begin with, Ethelbertha did not seem to remark that I was irritable; I had to draw her attention to it. I said:

'You must forgive me, I'm not feeling quite myself to-night.'

She said: 'Oh! I have not noticed anything different; what's the matter with you?'

'I can't tell you what it is,' I said; 'I've felt it coming on for weeks.'

'It's that whisky,' said Ethelbertha. 'You never touch it except when we go to the Harris's. You know you can't stand it; you have not a strong head.'

'It isn't the whisky,' I replied; 'it's deeper than that. I fancy it's more mental than bodily.'

'You've been reading those criticisms again,' said Ethelbertha, more sympathetically; 'why don't you take my advice and put them on the fire?'

'And it isn't the criticisms,' I answered; 'they've been quite flattering of late—one or two of them.'

'Well, what is it?' said Ethelbertha; 'there must be something to account for it.'

'No, there isn't,' I replied; 'that's the remarkable thing about it; I can only describe it as a strange feeling of unrest that seems to have taken possession of me.'

Ethelbertha glanced across at me with a somewhat curious expression, I thought; but as she said nothing, I continued the argument myself.

'This aching monotony of life, these days of peaceful, uneventful felicity, they appal one.'

'I should not grumble at them,' said Ethelbertha; 'we might get some of the other sort, and like them still less.'

'I'm not so sure of that,' I replied. 'In a life of continuous joy, I can imagine even pain coming as a welcome variation. I wonder sometimes whether the saints in heaven do not occasionally feel the continual serenity a burden. To myself, a life of endless bliss, uninterrupted by a single contrasting note, would, I feel, grow maddening. I suppose,' I continued, 'I am a strange sort of man; I can hardly understand myself at times. There are moments,' I added, 'when I hate myself.'

Often a little speech like this, hinting at hidden depths of indescribable emotion, has touched Ethelbertha, but to-night she appeared strangely unsympathetic. With regard to heaven and its possible effect upon me, she suggested my not worrying myself about that, remarking it was always foolish to go half-way to meet trouble that might never come; while as to my being a strange sort of fellow, that, she supposed, I could not help, and if other people were willing to put up with me, there was an end of the matter. The monotony of life, she added, was a common experience; there she could sympathise with me.

'You don't know how I long,' said Ethelbertha, 'to get away occasionally, even from you; but I know it can never be, so I do not brood upon it.'

I had never heard Ethelbertha speak like this before; it astonished and grieved me beyond measure.

'That's not a very kind remark to make,' I said, 'not a wifely remark.'

'I know it isn't,' she replied; 'that is why I have never said it before. You men never can understand,' continued Ethelbertha, 'that, however fond a woman may be of a man, there are times when he palls upon her. You don't know how I long to be able sometimes to put on my bonnet and go out, with nobody to ask me where I am going, why I am going, how long I am going to be, and when I shall be back. You don't know how I sometimes long to order a dinner that I should like and that the children would like, but at the sight of which you would put on your hat and be off to the Club. You don't know how much I feel inclined sometimes to invite some woman here that I like, and that I know you don't; to go and see the people that *I* want to see, to go to bed when *I* am tired, and to get up when *I* feel I want to get up. Two people living together are bound both to be continually sacrificing their own desires to the other one. It is sometimes a good thing to slacken the strain a bit.'

On thinking over Ethelbertha's words afterwards, I have come to see their wisdom; but at the time I admit I was hurt and indignant.

'If your desire,' I said, 'is to get rid of me——'

'Now, don't be an old goose,' said Ethelbertha; 'I only want to get rid of you for a little while, just long enough to forget there are one or two corners about you that are not perfect, just long enough to let me remember what a dear fellow you are in other respects, and to look forward to your return, as I used to look forward to your coming in the old days when I did not see you so often as to become, perhaps, a little indifferent to you, as one grows indifferent to the glory of the sun, just because he is there every day.'

I did not like the tone that Ethelbertha took. There seemed to be a frivolity about her, unsuited to the theme into which we had drifted.

That a woman should contemplate cheerfully an absence of three or four weeks from her husband appeared to me to be not altogether nice, not what I call womanly; it was not like Ethelbertha at all. I was worried, I felt I didn't want to go on this trip at all. If it had not been for George and Harris, I would have abandoned it. As it was, I could not see how to change my mind with dignity.

'Very well, Ethelbertha,' I replied, 'it shall be as you wish. If you desire a holiday from my presence, you shall enjoy it; but if it be not impertinent curiosity on the part of a husband, I should like to know what you propose doing in my absence?'

'We will take that house at Folkestone,' answered Ethelbertha, 'and I'll go down there with Kate. And if you want to do Clara Harris a good turn,' added Ethelbertha, 'you'll persuade Harris to go with you, and then Clara can join us. We three used to have some very jolly times together before you men ever came along, and it would be just delightful to renew them. Do you think,' continued Ethelbertha, 'that you could persuade Mr Harris to go with you?'

I said I would try.

'There's a dear boy,' said Ethelbertha; 'try hard. You might get George to join you.'

I replied there was not much advantage in George's coming, seeing he was a bachelor, and that, therefore, nobody would be much benefited by his absence. But a woman never understands satire. Ethelbertha merely remarked it would look unkind leaving him behind. I promised to put it to him.

I met Harris at the Club in the afternoon, and asked him how he had got on.

He said, 'Oh, that's all right; there's no difficulty about getting away.'

But there was that about his tone that suggested incomplete satisfaction, so I pressed him for further details.

'She was as sweet as milk about it,' he continued; 'said it was an excellent idea of George's, and that she thought it would do me good.'

'That's seems all right,' I said; 'what's wrong about that?'

'There's nothing wrong about that,' he answered, 'but that wasn't all. She went on to talk of other things.'

'I understand,' I said.

'There's that bath-room fad of hers,' he continued.

'I've heard of it,' I said; 'she has started Ethelbertha on the same idea.'

'Well, I've had to agree to that being put in hand at once; I couldn't argue any more when she was so nice about the other thing. That will cost me a hundred pounds, at the very least.'

'As much as that?' I asked.

'Every penny of it,' said Harris; 'the estimate alone is sixty.'

I was sorry to hear him say this.

'Then there's the kitchen stove,' continued Harris; 'everything that has gone wrong in the house for the last two years has been the fault of that kitchen stove.'

'I know,' I said. 'We have been in seven houses since we were married, and every kitchen stove has been worse than the last. Our present one is not only incompetent; it is spiteful. It knows when we are giving a party, and goes out of its way to do its worst.'

'*We* are going to have a new one,' said Harris, but he did not say it proudly. 'Clara thought it would be such a saving of expense, having the two things done at the same time. I believe,' said Harris, 'if a woman wanted a diamond tiara, she would explain that it was to save the expense of a bonnet.'

'How much do you reckon the stove is going to cost you?' I asked. I felt interested in the subject.

'I don't know,' answered Harris; 'another twenty, I suppose. Then we talked about the piano. Could you ever notice,' said Harris, 'any difference between one piano and another?'

'Some of them seem to be a bit louder than others,' I answered; 'but one gets used to that.'

'Ours is all wrong about the treble,' said Harris. 'By the way, what *is* the treble?'

'It's the shrill end of the thing,' I explained; 'the part that sounds as if you'd trod on its tail. The brilliant selections always end up with a flourish on it.'

'They want more of it,' said Harris; 'our old one hasn't got enough of it. I'll have to put it in the nursery, and get a new one for the drawing-room.'

'Anything else?' I asked.

'No,' said Harris; 'she didn't seem able to think of anything else.'

'You'll find when you get home,' I said, 'she has thought of one other thing.'

'What's that?' said Harris.

'A house at Folkestone for the season.'

'What should she want a house at Folkestone for?' said Harris.

'To live in,' I suggested, 'during the summer months.'

'She's going to her people in Wales,' said Harris, 'for the holidays, with the children; we've had an invitation.'

'Possibly,' I said, 'she'll go to Wales before she goes to Folkestone, or maybe she'll take Wales on her way home; but she'll want a house at Folkestone for the season, notwithstanding. I may be mistaken—I hope for your sake that I am—but I feel a presentiment that I'm not.'

'This trip,' said Harris, 'is going to be expensive.'

'It was an idiotic suggestion,' I said, 'from the beginning.'

'It was foolish of us to listen to him,' said Harris; 'he'll get us into real trouble one of these days.'

'He always was a muddler,' I agreed.

'So headstrong,' added Harris.

We heard his voice at that moment in the hall, asking for letters.

'Better not say anything to him,' I suggested; 'it's too late to go back now.'

'There would be no advantage in doing so,' replied Harris. 'I should have to get that bath-room and piano in any case now.'

He came in looking very cheerful.

'Well,' he said, 'is it all right? Have you managed it?'

There was that about his tone I did not altogether like; I noticed Harris resented it also.

'Managed what?' I said.

'Why, to get off,' said George.

I felt the time was come to explain things to George.

'In married life,' I said, 'the man proposes, the woman submits. It is her duty; all religion teaches it.'

George folded his hands and fixed his eyes on the ceiling.

'We may chaff and joke a little about these things,' I continued; 'but when it comes to practice, that is what always happens. We have mentioned to our wives that we are going. Naturally, they are grieved; they would prefer to come with us; failing that, they would have us remain with them. But we have explained to them our wishes on the subject, and—there's an end of the matter.'

George said, 'Forgive me; I did not understand. I am only a bachelor. People tell me this, that, and the other, and I listen.'

I said, 'That is where you do wrong. When you want information come to Harris or myself; we will tell you the truth about these questions.'

George thanked us, and we proceeded with the business in hand.

'When shall we start?' said George.

'So far as I am concerned,' replied Harris, 'the sooner the better.'

His idea, I fancy, was to get away before Mrs H. thought of other things. We fixed the following Wednesday.

'What about route?' said Harris.

'I have an idea,' said George. 'I take it you fellows are naturally anxious to improve your minds?'

I said, 'We don't want to become monstrosities. To a reasonable degree, yes, if it can be done without much expense and with little personal trouble.'

'It can,' said George. 'We know Holland and the Rhine. Very well, my suggestion is that we take the boat to Hamburg, see Berlin and Dresden, and work our way to the Schwarzwald, through Nuremberg and Stuttgart.'

'There are some pretty bits in Mesopotamia, so I've been told,' murmured Harris.

George said Mesopotamia was too much out of our way, but that the Berlin-Dresden route was quite practicable. For good or evil, he persuaded us into it.

'The machines, I suppose,' said George, 'as before. Harris and I on the tandem, J.——'

'I think not,' interrupted Harris, firmly. 'You and J. on the tandem, I on the single.'

'All the same to me,' agreed George. 'J. and I on the tandem, Harris——'

'I do not mind taking my turn,' I interrupted, 'but I am not going to carry George *all* the way; the burden should be divided.'

'Very well,' agreed Harris, 'we'll divide it. But it must be on the distinct understanding that he works.'

'That he what?' said George.

'That he works,' repeated Harris, firmly; 'at all events, uphill.'

'Great Scott!' said George; 'don't you want *any* exercise?'

There is always unpleasantness about this tandem. It is the theory of the man in front that the man behind does nothing; it is equally the theory of the man behind that he alone is the motive power, the man in front merely doing the puffing. The mystery will never be solved. It is annoying when Prudence is whispering to you on the one side not to overdo your strength and bring on heart disease; while Justice into the other ear is remarking, 'Why should you do it all? This isn't a cab. He's not your passenger': to hear him grunt out:

'What's the matter—lost your pedals?'

Harris, in his early married days, made much trouble for himself on one occasion, owing to this impossibility of knowing what the person behind is doing. He was riding with his wife through Holland. The roads were stony, and the machine jumped a good deal.

'Sit tight,' said Harris, without turning his head.

What Mrs Harris thought he said was, 'Jump off.' Why she should have thought he said 'Jump off,' when he said 'Sit tight,' neither of them can explain.

Mrs Harris puts it this way, 'If you had said, "Sit tight," why should I have jumped off?'

Harris puts it, 'If I had wanted you to jump off, why should I have said "Sit tight!"?'

The bitterness is past, but they argue about the matter to this day.

Be the explanation what it may, however, nothing alters the fact that Mrs Harris did jump off, while Harris pedalled away hard, under the impression she was still behind him. It appears that at first she thought he was riding up the hill merely to show off. They were both young in those days, and he used to do that sort of thing. She expected him to spring to earth on reaching the summit, and lean in a careless and graceful attitude against the machine, waiting for her. When, on the contrary, she saw him pass the summit and proceed rapidly down a long and steep incline, she was seized, first with surprise, secondly with indignation, and lastly with alarm. She ran to the top of the hill and shouted, but he never turned his head. She watched him disappear into a wood a mile and a half distant, and then sat down and cried. They had had a slight difference that morning, and she wondered if he had taken it seriously and intended desertion. She had no money; she knew no Dutch. People passed, and seemed sorry for her; she tried to make them understand what had happened. They gathered that she had lost something, but could not grasp what. They took her to the nearest village, and found a policeman for her. He concluded from her pantomime that some man had stolen her bicycle. They put the telegraph into operation, and discovered in a village four miles off an unfortunate boy riding a lady's machine of an obsolete pattern. They brought him to her in a cart, but as she did not appear to want either him or his bicycle they let him go again, and resigned themselves to bewilderment.

Meanwhile, Harris continued his ride with much enjoyment. It seemed to him that he had suddenly become a stronger, and in every way more capable cyclist. Said he to what he thought was Mrs Harris:

'I haven't felt this machine so light for months. It's this air, I think; it's doing me good.'

Then he told her not to be afraid, and he would show her how fast he *could* go. He bent down over the handles, and put his heart into his work. The bicycle bounded over the road like a thing of life; farmhouses and churches, dogs and chickens came to him and passed. Old folks stood and gazed at him, the children cheered him.

In this way he sped merrily onward for about five miles. Then, as he explains it, the feeling began to grow upon him that something was wrong. He was not surprised at the silence; the wind was blowing strongly, and the machine was rattling a good deal. It was a sense of void that came upon him. He stretched out his hand behind him, and felt; there was nothing there but space. He jumped, or rather fell off, and looked back up the road; it stretched white and straight through the dark wood, and not a living soul could be seen upon it. He remounted, and rode back up the hill. In ten minutes he came to where the road broke into four; there he dismounted and tried to remember which fork he had come down.

While he was deliberating a man passed, sitting sideways on a horse. Harris stopped him, and explained to him that he had lost his wife. The man appeared to be neither surprised nor sorry for him. While they were talking another farmer came along, to whom the first man explained the matter, not as an accident, but as a good story. What appeared to surprise the second man most was that Harris should be making a fuss about the thing. He could get no sense out of either of them, and cursing them he mounted his machine again, and took the middle road on chance. Half way up, he came upon a party of two young women with one young man between them. They appeared to be making the most of him. He asked them if they had seen his wife. They asked him what she was like. He did not know enough Dutch to describe her properly; all he could tell them was she was a very beautiful woman, of medium size. Evidently this did not satisfy them, the description was too general; any man could say that, and by this means perhaps get possession of a wife that did not belong to him. They asked him how she was dressed; for the life of him he could not recollect.

I doubt if any man could tell how any woman was dressed ten minutes after he had left her. He recollected a blue skirt, and then there was something that carried the dress on, as it were, up to the neck. Possibly, this may have been a blouse; he retained a dim vision of a belt; but what sort of a blouse? Was it green, or yellow, or blue? Had it a collar, or was it fastened with a bow? Were there feathers in her hat, or flowers? Or was it a hat at all? He dared not say, for fear of making a mistake and being sent miles after the wrong party. The two young women giggled, which in his then state of mind irritated Harris. The young man, who appeared anxious to get rid of him, suggested the police station at the next town. Harris made his way there. The police gave him a piece of paper, and told him to write down a full description of his wife, together with details of when and where he had lost her. He did not know where he had lost her; all he could tell them was the name of the village where he had lunched. He knew he had her with him then, and that they had started from there together.

The police looked suspicious; they were doubtful about three matters: Firstly, was she really his wife? Secondly, had he really lost her? Thirdly, why had he lost her? With the aid of a hotel-keeper, however, who spoke a little English, he overcame their scruples. They promised to act, and in the evening they brought her to him in a covered waggon, together with a bill for expenses. The meeting was not a tender one. Mrs Harris is not a good actress, and always has great difficulty in disguising her feelings. On this occasion, she frankly admits, she made no attempt to disguise them.

The wheel business settled, there arose the everlasting luggage question.

'The usual list, I suppose,' said George, preparing to write.

That was wisdom I had taught them; I had learned it myself years ago from my Uncle Podger.

'Always before beginning to pack,' my Uncle would say, 'make a list.'

He was a methodical man.

'Take a piece of paper'—he always began at the beginning—'put

down on it everything you can possibly require; then go over it and
see that it contains nothing you can possibly do without. Imagine
yourself in bed; what have you got on? Very well, put it down
—together with a change. You get up; what do you do? Wash
yourself. What do you wash yourself with? Soap; put down soap. Go
on till you have finished. Then take your clothes. Begin at your feet;
what do you wear on your feet? Boots, shoes, socks; put them down.
Work up till you get to your head. What else do you want besides
clothes? A little brandy; put it down. A corkscrew; put it down. Put
down everything, then you don't forget anything.'

That is the plan he always pursued himself. The list made, he
would go over it carefully, as he always advised, to see that he had
forgotten nothing. Then he would go over it again, and strike out
everything it was possible to dispense with.

Then he would lose the list.

Said George: 'Just sufficient for a day or two we will take with us
on our bikes. The bulk of our luggage we must send on from town to
town.'

'We must be careful,' I said; 'I knew a man once——'

Harris looked at his watch.

'We'll hear about him on the boat,' said Harris; 'I have got to meet
Clara at Waterloo Station in half an hour.'

'It won't take half an hour,' I said; 'it's a true story, and——'

'Don't waste it,' said George: 'I am told there are rainy evenings in
the Black Forest; we may be glad of it. What we have to do now is to
finish this list.'

Now I come to think of it, I never did get off that story; something
always interrupted it. And it really was true.

CHAPTER III

Harris's one fault—Harris and the Angel—A patent bicycle lamp—The ideal saddle—The 'Overhauler'—His eagle eye—His method—His cheery confidence—His simple and inexpensive tastes—His appearance —How to get rid of him—George as prophet—The gentle art of making oneself disagreeable in a foreign tongue—George as a student of human nature—He proposes an experiment—His prudence—Harris's support secured, upon conditions.

ON Monday afternoon Harris came round; he had a cycling paper in his hand.

I said: 'If you take my advice, you will leave it alone.'

Harris said: 'Leave what alone?'

I said: 'That brand-new, patent, revolution in cycling, record-breaking, Tomfoolishness, whatever it may be, the advertisement of which you have there in your hand.'

He said: 'Well, I don't know; there will be some steep hills for us to negotiate; I guess we shall want a good brake.'

I said: 'We shall want a brake, I agree; what we shall not want is a mechanical surprise that we don't understand, and that never acts when it is wanted.'

'This thing,' he said, 'acts automatically.'

'You needn't tell me,' I said. 'I know exactly what it will do, by instinct. Going uphill it will jam the wheel so effectively that we shall have to carry the machine bodily. The air at the top of the hill will do it good, and it will suddenly come right again. Going downhill it will start reflecting what a nuisance it has been. This will lead to remorse, and finally to despair. It will say to itself: "I'm not fit to be a brake. I don't help these fellows; I only hinder them. I'm a curse, that's what I am;" and, without a word of warning, it will "chuck" the whole business. That is what that brake will do. Leave it alone. You are a good fellow,' I continued, 'but you have one fault.'

'What?' he asked, indignantly.

'You have too much faith,' I answered. 'If you read an advertisement, you go away and believe it. Every experiment that every fool has thought of in connection with cycling you have tried. Your guardian angel appears to be a capable and conscientious spirit, and hitherto she has seen you through; take my advice and don't try her too far. She must have had a busy time since you started cycling. Don't go on till you make her mad.'

He said: 'If every man talked like that there would be no advancement made in any department of life. If nobody ever tried a new thing the world would come to a standstill. It is by——'

'I know all that can be said on that side of the argument,' I interrupted. 'I agree in trying new experiments up to thirty-five; *after* thirty-five I consider a man is entitled to think of himself. You and I have done our duty in this direction, you especially. You have been blown up by a patent gas lamp——'

He said: 'I really think, you know, that was my fault; I think I must have screwed it up too tight.'

I said: 'I am quite willing to believe that if there was a wrong way of handling the thing that is the way you handled it. You should take that tendency of yours into consideration; it bears upon the argument. Myself, I did not notice what you did; I only know we were riding peacefully and pleasantly along the Whitby Road, discussing the Thirty Years' War, when your lamp went off like a pistol-shot. The start sent me into the ditch; and your wife's face, when I told her there was nothing the matter and that she was not to worry, because the two men would carry you upstairs, and the doctor would be round in a minute bringing the nurse with him, still lingers in my memory.'

He said: 'I wish you had thought to pick up the lamp. I should like to have found out what was the cause of its going off like that.'

I said: 'There was not time to pick up the lamp. I calculate it would have taken two hours to have collected it. As to its "going off," the mere fact of its being advertised as the safest lamp ever invented would of itself, to anyone but you, have suggested accident. Then there was that electric lamp,' I continued.

'Well, that really did give a fine light,' he replied; 'you said so yourself.'

I said: 'It gave a brilliant light in the King's Road, Brighton, and frightened a horse. The moment we got into the dark beyond Kemp Town it went out, and you were summoned for riding without a light. You may remember that on sunny afternoons you used to ride about with that lamp shining for all it was worth. When lighting-up time came it was naturally tired, and wanted a rest.'

'It was a bit irritating, that lamp,' he murmured; 'I remember it.'

I said: 'It irritated me; it must have been worse for you. Then there are saddles,' I went on—I wished to get this lesson home to him. 'Can you think of any saddle ever advertised that you have *not* tried?'

He said: 'It has been an idea of mine that the right saddle is to be found.'

I said: 'You give up that idea; this is an imperfect world of joy and sorrow mingled. There may be a better land where bicycle saddles are made out of rainbow, stuffed with cloud; in this world the simplest thing is to get used to something hard. There was that saddle you bought in Birmingham; it was divided in the middle, and looked like a pair of kidneys.'

He said: 'You mean that one constructed on anatomical principles.'

'Very likely,' I replied. 'The box you bought it in had a picture on the cover, representing a sitting skeleton—or rather that part of a skeleton which does sit.'

He said: 'It was quite correct; it showed you the true position of the——'

I said: 'We will not go into details; the picture always seemed to me indelicate.'

He said: 'Medically speaking, it was right.'

'Possibly,' I said, 'for a man who rode in nothing but his bones. I only know that I tried it myself and that to a man who wore flesh it was agony. Every time you went over a stone or rut it nipped you; it was like riding on an irritable lobster. You rode that for a month.'

'I thought it only right to give it a fair trial,' he answered.

I said: 'You gave your family a fair trial also; if you will allow me the use of slang. Your wife told me that never in the whole course of your married life had she known you so bad tempered, so un-Christian like, as you were that month. Then you remember that other saddle, the one with the spring under it.'

He said: 'You mean "the Spiral."'

I said: 'I mean the one that jerked you up and down like a Jack-in-the-box; sometimes you came down again in the right place, and sometimes you didn't. I am not referring to these matters merely to recall painful memories, but I want to impress you with the folly of trying experiments at your time of life.'

He said: 'I wish you wouldn't harp so much on my age. A man at thirty-four——'

'A man at what?'

He said: 'If you don't want the thing, don't have it. If your machine runs away with you down a mountain, and you and George get flung through a church roof, don't blame me.'

'I cannot promise for George,' I said; 'a little thing will sometimes irritate him, as you know. If such an accident as you suggest happen, he may be cross, but I will undertake to explain to him that it was not your fault.'

'Is the thing all right?' he asked.

'The tandem,' I replied, 'is well.'

He said: 'Have you overhauled it?'

I said: 'I have not, nor is anyone else going to overhaul it. The thing is now in working order, and it is going to remain in working order till we start.'

I have had experience of this 'overhauling.' There was a man at Folkestone; I used to meet him on the Lees. He proposed one evening we should go for a long bicycle ride together on the following day, and I agreed. I got up early, for me; I made an effort, and was pleased with myself. He came half an hour late: I was waiting for him in the garden. It was a lovely day. He said:—

'That's a good–looking machine of yours. How does it run?'

'Oh, like most of them!' I answered; 'easily enough in the morning; goes a little stiffly after lunch.'

He caught hold of it by the front wheel and the fork, and shook it violently.

I said: 'Don't do that; you'll hurt it.'

I did not see why he should shake it; it had not done anything to him. Besides, if it wanted shaking, I was the proper person to shake it. I felt much as I should had he started whacking my dog.

He said: 'This front wheel wobbles.'

I said: 'It doesn't if you don't wobble it.' It didn't wobble, as a matter of fact—nothing worth calling a wobble.

He said: 'This is dangerous; have you got a screw-hammer?'

I ought to have been firm, but I thought that perhaps he really did know something about the business. I went to the tool shed to see what I could find. When I came back he was sitting on the ground with the front wheel between his legs. He was playing with it, twiddling it round between his fingers; the remnant of the machine was lying on the gravel path beside him.

He said: 'Something has happened to this front wheel of yours.'

'It looks like it, doesn't it?' I answered. But he was the sort of man that never understands satire.

He said: 'It looks to me as if the bearings were all wrong.'

I said: 'Don't you trouble about it any more; you will make yourself tired. Let us put it back and get off.'

He said: 'We may as well see what is the matter with it, now it is out.' He talked as though it had dropped out by accident.

Before I could stop him he had unscrewed something somewhere, and out rolled all over the path some dozen or so little balls.

'Catch 'em!' he shouted; 'catch 'em! We mustn't lose any of them.' He was quite excited about them.

We grovelled round for half an hour, and found sixteen. He said he hoped we had got them all, because, if not, it would make a serious difference to the machine. He said there was nothing you should be more careful about in taking a bicycle to pieces than seeing you did not lose any of the balls. He explained that you ought to count them as you took them out and see that exactly the same number went back in place. I promised, if ever I took a bicycle to pieces I would remember his advice.

I put the balls for safety in my hat, and I put my hat upon the doorstep. It was not a sensible thing to do, I admit. As a matter of fact, it was a silly thing to do. I am not as a rule addle-headed; his influence must have affected me.

He then said that while he was about it he would see to the chain for me, and at once began taking off the gear-case. I did try to persuade him from that. I told him what an experienced friend of mind once said to me solemnly:—

'If anything goes wrong with your gear-case, sell the machine and buy a new one; it comes cheaper.'

He said: 'People talk like that who understand nothing about machines. Nothing is easier than taking off a gear-case.'

I had to confess he was right. In less than five minutes he had the gear-case in two pieces, lying on the path, and was grovelling for screws. He said it was always a mystery to him the way screws disappeared.

We were still looking for the screws when Ethelbertha came out. She seemed surprised to find us there; she said she thought we had started hours ago.

He said: 'We shan't be long now. I'm just helping your husband to overhaul this machine of his. It's a good machine; but they all want going over occasionally.'

Ethelbertha said: 'If you want to wash yourselves when you have done you might go into the back kitchen, if you don't mind; the girls have just finished the bedrooms.'

She told me that if she met Kate they would probably go for a sail; but that in any case she would be back to lunch. I would have given a sovereign to be going with her. I was getting heartily sick of standing about watching this fool breaking up my bicycle.

Common sense continued to whisper to me: 'Stop him, before he does any more mischief. You have a right to protect your own property from the ravages of a lunatic. Take him by the scruff of the neck, and kick him out of the gate!'

But I am weak when it comes to hurting other people's feelings, and I let him muddle on.

He gave up looking for the rest of the screws. He said screws had a knack of turning up when you least expected them; and that now he would see to the chain. He tightened it till it would not move; next he loosened it until it was twice as loose as it was before. Then he said we had better think about getting the front wheel back into its place again.

I held the fork open, and he worried with the wheel. At the end of ten minutes I suggested he should hold the forks, and that I should handle the wheel; and we changed places. At the end of his first minute he dropped the machine, and took a short walk round the croquet lawn, with his hands pressed together between his thighs. He explained as he walked that the thing to be careful about was to avoid getting your fingers pinched between the forks and the spokes of the wheel. I replied I was convinced, from my own experience, that there was much truth in what he said. He wrapped himself up in a couple of dusters, and we commenced again. At length we did get the thing into position; and the moment it was in position he burst out laughing.

I said: 'What's the joke?'

He said: 'Well, I am an ass!'

It was the first thing he had said that made me respect him. I asked him what had led him to the discovery.

He said: 'We've forgotten the balls!'

I looked for my hat; it was lying topsy-turvy in the middle of the path, and Ethelbertha's favourite hound was swallowing the balls as fast as he could pick them up.

'He will kill himself,' said Ebbson—I have never met him since that day, thank the Lord; but I think his name was Ebbson—'they are solid steel.'

I said: 'I am not troubling about the dog. He has had a bootlace and a packet of needles already this week. Nature's the best guide; puppies seem to require this kind of stimulant. What I am thinking about is my bicycle.'

He was of a cheerful disposition. He said: 'Well, we must put back all we can find, and trust to Providence.'

We found eleven. We fixed six on one side and five on the other, and half an hour later the wheel was in its place again. It need hardly be added that it really did wobble now; a child might have noticed it. Ebbson said it would do for the present. He appeared to be getting a bit tired himself. If I had let him, he would, I believe, at this point have gone home. I was determined now, however, that he should stop and finish; I had abandoned all thoughts of a ride. My pride in the machine he had killed. My only interest lay now in seeing him scratch and bump and pinch himself. I revived his drooping spirits with a glass of beer and some judicious praise. I said:

'Watching you do this is of real use to me. It is not only your skill and dexterity that fascinates me, it is your cheery confidence in yourself, your inexplicable hopefulness, that does me good.'

Thus encouraged, he set to work to refix the gear-case. He stood the bicycle against the house, and worked from the off side. Then he stood it against a tree, and worked from the near side. Then I held it for him, while he lay on the ground with his head between the wheels, and worked at it from below, and dropped oil upon himself. Then he took it away from me, and doubled himself across it like a pack-saddle, till he lost his balance and slid over on to his head. Three times he said:

'Thank Heaven, that's right at last!'

And twice he said:

'No, I'm damned if it is after all!'

What he said the third time I try to forget.

Then he lost his temper and tried bullying the thing. The bicycle, I was glad to see, showed spirit; and the subsequent proceedings degenerated into little else than a rough-and-tumble fight between him and the machine. One moment the bicycle would be on the gravel-path, and he on top of it; the next, the position would be reversed—he on the gravel-path, the bicycle on him. Now he would be standing flushed with victory, the bicycle firmly fixed between his legs. But his triumph would be short-lived. By a sudden, quick movement it would free itself, and, turning upon him, hit him sharply over the head with one of its handles.

At a quarter to one, dirty and dishevelled, cut and bleeding, he said: 'I think that will do;' and rose and wiped his brow.

The bicycle looked as if it also had had enough of it. Which had received most punishment it would have been difficult to say. I took him into the back kitchen, where, so far as was possible without soda and proper tools, he cleaned himself, and sent him home.

The bicycle I put into a cab and took round to the nearest repairing shop. The foreman of the works came up and looked at it.

'What do you want me to do with that?' said he.

'I want you,' I said, 'so far as is possible, to restore it.'

'It's a bit far gone,' said he; 'but I'll do my best.'

He did his best, which came to two pounds ten. But it was never the same machine again; and at the end of the season I left it in an agent's hands to sell. I wished to deceive nobody; I instructed the man to advertise it as a last year's machine. The agent advised me not to mention any date. He said:

'In this business it isn't a question of what is true and what isn't; it's a question of what you can get people to believe. Now, between you and me, it don't look like a last year's machine; so far as looks are concerned, it might be a ten-year old. We'll say nothing about date; we'll just get what we can.'

I left the matter to him, and he got me five pounds, which he said was more than he had expected.

There are two ways you can get exercise out of a bicycle: you can 'overhaul' it, or you can ride it. On the whole, I am not sure that a man who takes his pleasure overhauling does not have the best of the bargain. He is independent of the weather and the wind; the state of the roads troubles him not. Give him a screw-hammer, a bundle of rags, an oil-can, and something to sit down upon, and he is happy for the day. He has to put up with certain disadvantages, of course; there is no joy without alloy. He himself always looks like a tinker, and his machine always suggests the idea that, having stolen it, he has tried to disguise it; but as he rarely gets beyond the first milestone with it, this, perhaps, does not much matter. The mistake some people make is in thinking they can get both forms of sport out of the same machine. This is impossible; no machine will stand the double strain. You must make up your mind whether you are going to be an 'overhauler' or a rider. Personally, I prefer to ride, therefore I take care to have near me nothing than can tempt me to overhaul. When anything happens to my machine, I wheel it to the nearest repairing shop. If I am too far from the town or village to walk, I sit by the roadside and wait till a cart comes along. My chief danger, I always find, is from the wandering overhauler. The sight of a broken-down machine is to the overhauler as a wayside corpse to a crow; he swoops down upon it with a friendly yell of triumph. At first, I used to try politeness. I would say:

'It is nothing; don't you trouble. You ride on, and enjoy yourself, I beg it of you as a favour; please go away.'

Experience has taught me, however, that courtesy is of no use in such an extremity. Now I say:

'You go away, and leave the thing alone, or I will knock your silly head off.'

And if you look determined, and have a good stout cudgel in your hand, you can generally drive him off.

George came in later in the day. He said:

'Well, do you think everything will be ready?'

I said: 'Everything will be ready by Wednesday, except, perhaps, you and Harris.'

He said: 'Is the tandem all right?'

'The tandem,' I said, 'is well.'

He said: 'You don't think it wants overhauling?'

I replied: 'Age and experience have taught me that there are few matters concerning which a man does well to be positive. Consequently, there remain to me now but a limited number of questions upon which I feel any degree of certainty. Among such still-unshaken beliefs, however, is the conviction that that tandem does not want overhauling. I also feel a presentiment that, provided my life is spared, no human between now and Wednesday morning is going to overhaul it.'

George said: 'I should not show temper over the matter, if I were you. There will come a day, perhaps not far distant, when that bicycle, with a couple of mountains between it and the nearest repairing shop, will, in spite of your chronic desire for rest, *have* to be overhauled. Then you will clamour for people to tell you where you put the oil can, and what you have done with the screw-hammer. Then, while you exert yourself holding the thing steady against a tree, you will suggest that somebody else should clean the chain and pump the back wheel.'

I felt there was justice in George's rebuke—also a certain amount of prophetic wisdom. I said:

'Forgive me if I seemed unresponsive. The truth is, Harris was round here this morning——'

George said: 'Say no more; I understand. Besides, what I came to talk to you about was another matter. Look at that.'

He handed me a small book bound in red cloth.

It was a guide to English conversation for the use of German travellers. It commenced 'On a Steam-boat,' and terminated 'At the Doctor's'; its longest chapter being devoted to conversation in a railway carriage, among, apparently, a compartment load of quarrelsome and ill-mannered lunatics: 'Can you not get further away from me, sir?'—'It is impossible, madam; my neighbour, here, is very stout.'—'Shall we not endeavour to arrange our legs?'—'Please have the goodness to keep your elbows down'—'Pray do not inconvenience yourself, madam, if my shoulder is of any accommodation to you,' whether intended to be said sarcastically or not, there was nothing to indicate—'I really must request you to move a little, madam, I can hardly breathe,' the author's idea being, presumably, that by this time the whole party was mixed up together on the floor. The chapter concluded with the phrase, 'Here we are at our destination, God be thanked! (*Gott sei dank!*)' a pious exclamation, which under the circumstances must have taken the form of a chorus.

At the end of the book was an appendix, giving the German traveller hints concerning the preservation of his health and comfort during his sojourn in English towns, chief among such hints being advice to him to always travel with a supply of disinfectant powder, to always lock his bedroom door at night, and to always carefully count his small change.

'It is not a brilliant publication,' I remarked, handing the book back to George; 'it is not a book that personally I would recommend to any

German about to visit England; I think it would get him disliked. But I have read books published in London for the use of English travellers abroad every whit as foolish. Some educated idiot, misunderstanding seven languages, would appear to go about writing these books for the misinformation and false guidance of modern Europe.'

'You cannot deny,' said George, 'that these books are in large request. They are bought by the thousand, I know. In every town in Europe there must be people going about talking this sort of thing.'

'Maybe,' I replied; 'but fortunately nobody understands them. I have noticed, myself, men standing on railway platforms and at street corners reading aloud from such books. Nobody knows what language they are speaking; nobody has the slightest knowledge of what they are saying. This is, perhaps, as well; were they understood they would probably be assaulted.'

George said: 'Maybe you are right; my idea is to see what would happen if they were understood. My proposal is to get to London early on Wednesday morning, and spend an hour or two going about and shopping with the aid of this book. There are one or two little things I want—a hat and a pair of bedroom slippers, among other articles. Our boat does not leave Tilbury till twelve, and that just gives us time. I want to try this sort of talk where I can properly judge of its effect. I want to see how the foreigner feels when he is talked to in this way.'

It struck me as a sporting idea. In my enthusiasm I offered to accompany him, and wait outside the shop. I said I thought that Harris would like to be in it, too—or rather outside.

George said that was not quite his scheme. His proposal was that Harris and I should accompany him into the shop. With Harris, who looks formidable, to support him, and myself at the door to call the police if necessary, he said he was willing to adventure the thing.

We walked round to Harris's, and put the proposal before him. He examined the book, especially the chapters dealing with the purchase of shoes and hats. He said:

'If George talks to any bootmaker or any hatter the things that are put down here, it is not support he will want; it is carrying to the hospital that he will need.'

That made George angry.

'You talk,' said George, 'as though I were a foolhardy boy without any sense. I shall select from the more polite and less irritating speeches; the grosser insults I shall avoid.'

This being clearly understood, Harris gave in his adhesion; and our start was fixed for early Wednesday morning.

CHAPTER IV

Why Harris considers alarm clocks unnecessary in a family—Social instincts of the young—A child's thoughts about the morning—The sleepless watchman—The mystery of him—His over anxiety—Night thoughts—The sort of work one does before breakfast—The good sheep and the bad—Disadvantages of being virtuous—Harris's new stove begins badly—The daily out-going of my Uncle Podger—The elderly city man considered as a racer—We arrive in London—We talk the language of the traveller.

GEORGE came down on Tuesday evening, and slept at Harris's place. We thought this a better arrangement than his own suggestion, which was that we should call for him on our way and 'pick him up.' Picking George up in the morning means picking him out of bed to begin with, and shaking him awake—in itself an exhausting effort with which to commence the day; helping him find his things and finish his packing; and then waiting for him while he eats his breakfast, a tedious entertainment from the spectator's point of view, full of wearisome repetition.

I knew that if he slept at 'Beggarbush' he would be up in time; I have slept there myself, and I know what happens. About the middle of the night, as you judge, though in reality it may be somewhat later, you are startled out of your sleep by what sounds like a rush of cavalry along the passage, just outside your door. Your half-awakened intelligence fluctuates between burglars, the Day of Judgment, and a gas explosion. You sit up in bed and listen intently. You are not kept waiting long; the next moment a door is violently slammed, and somebody, or something, is evidently coming downstairs on a tea-tray.

'I told you so,' says a voice outside, and immediately some hard substance, a head one would say from the ring of it, rebounds against the panel of your door.

By this time you are charging madly round the room for your clothes. Nothing is where you put it overnight, the articles most essential have disappeared entirely; and meanwhile the murder, or revolution, or whatever it is, continues unchecked. You pause for a moment, with your head under the wardrobe, where you think you can see your slippers, to listen to a steady, monotonous thumping upon a distant door. The victim, you presume, has taken refuge there; they mean to have him out and finish him. Will you be in time? The knocking ceases, and a voice, sweetly reassuring in its gentle plaintiveness, asks meekly:

'Pa, may I get up?'

You do not hear the other voice, but the responses are:

'No, it was only the bath—no, she ain't really hurt,—only wet, you know. Yes, ma, I'll tell 'em what you say. No, it was a pure accident. Yes; good-night, papa.'

Then the same voice, exerting itself so as to be heard in a distant part of the house, remarks:

'You've got to come upstairs again. Pa says it isn't time yet to get up.'

You return to bed, and lie listening to somebody being dragged upstairs, evidently against their will. By a thoughtful arrangement, the spare rooms at 'Beggarbush' are exactly underneath the nurseries. The same somebody, you conclude, still offering the most creditable opposition, is being put back into bed. You can follow the contest with much exactitude, because every time the body is flung down upon the spring mattress, the bedstead, just above your head, makes a sort of jump; while every time the body succeeds in struggling out again, you are aware by the thud upon the floor. After a time the struggle wanes, or maybe the bed collapses; and you drift back into sleep. But the next moment, or what seems to be the next moment, you again open your eyes under the consciousness of a presence. The door is being held ajar, and four solemn faces, piled one on top of the other, are peering at you, as though you were some natural curiosity kept in this particular room. Seeing you awake, the top face, walking calmly over the other three, comes in and sits on the bed in a friendly attitude.

'Oh!' it says, 'we didn't know you were awake. I've been awake some time.'

'So I gather,' you reply, shortly.

'Pa doesn't like us to get up too early,' it continues. 'He says everybody else in the house is liable to be disturbed if we get up. So, of course, we mustn't.'

The tone is that of gentle resignation. It is instinct with the spirit of virtuous pride, arising from the consciousness of self-sacrifice.

'Don't you call this being up?' you suggest.

'Oh, no; we're not really up, you know, because we're not properly dressed.' The fact is self-evident. 'Pa's always very tired in the morning,' the voice continues; 'of course, that's because he works hard all day. Are you ever tired in the morning?'

At this point he turns and notices, for the first time, that the three other children have also entered, and are sitting in a semi-circle on the floor. From their attitude it is clear they have mistaken the whole thing for one of the slower forms of entertainment, some comic lecture or conjuring exhibition, and are waiting patiently for you to get out of bed and do something. It shocks him, the idea of their being in the guest's bedchamber. He peremptorily orders them out. They do not answer him, they do not argue; in dead silence, and with one accord, they fall upon him. All you can see from the bed is a confused tangle of waving arms and legs, suggestive of an intoxicated octopus trying to find bottom. Not a word is spoken; that seems to be the etiquette of the thing. If you are sleeping in your pyjamas, you spring from the bed, and only add to the confusion; if you are wearing a less showy garment, you stop where you are and shout commands, which are utterly unheeded. The simplest plan is to leave it to the eldest boy. He does get them out after a while, and closes the door upon them. It re-opens immediately, and one, generally Muriel, is shot back into the room. She enters as from a catapult. She is handicapped by having long hair, which can be used as a convenient handle. Evidently aware of this natural disadvantage, she clutches it herself tightly in one hand, and punches with the other. He opens the door again, and cleverly uses her as a batttering-ram against the wall of those without. You can hear the dull crash as her head enters among them, and scatters them. When the victory is complete, he comes back and resumes his seat on the bed. There is no bitterness about him; he has forgotten the whole incident.

'I like the morning,' he says, 'don't you?'

'Some mornings,' you agree, 'are all right; others are not so peaceful.'

He takes no notice of your exception; a far-away look steals over his somewhat ethereal face.

'I should like to die in the morning,' he says; 'everything is so beautiful then.'

'Well,' you answer, 'perhaps you will, if your father ever invites an irritable man to come and sleep here, and doesn't warn him before-hand.'

He descends from his contemplative mood, and becomes himself again.

'It's jolly in the garden,' he suggests; 'you wouldn't like to get up and have a game of cricket, would you?'

It was not the idea with which you went to bed, but now, as things have turned out, it seems as good a plan as lying there hopelessly awake; and you agree.

You learn, later in the day, that the explanation of the proceeding is that you, unable to sleep, woke up early in the morning, and thought you would like a game of cricket. The children, taught to be ever courteous to guests, felt it their duty to humour you. Mrs Harris remarks at breakfast that at least you might have seen to it that the children were properly dressed before you took them out; while Harris points out to you, pathetically, how, by your one morning's example and encouragement, you have undone his labour of months.

On this Wednesday morning, George, it seems, clamoured to get up at a quarter-past five, and persuaded them to let him teach them cycling tricks round the cucumber frames on Harris's new wheel. Even Mrs Harris, however, did not blame George on this occasion; she felt intuitively the idea could not have been entirely his.

It is not that the Harris children have the faintest notion of avoiding blame at the expense of a friend and comrade. One and all they are honesty itself in accepting responsibility for their own misdeeds. It simply is, that is how the thing presents itself to their understanding. When you explain to them that you had no original intention of getting up at five o'clock in the morning to play cricket on the croquet lawn, or to mimic the history of the early Church by shooting with a cross-bow at dolls tied to a tree; that as a matter of fact, left to your own initiative, you would have slept peacefully till roused in Christian fashion with a cup of tea at eight, they are firstly astonished, secondly apologetic, and thirdly sincerely contrite. In the present instance, waiving the purely academic question whether the awakening of George at a little before five was due to natural instinct on his part, or to the accidental passing of a home-made boomerang through his bedroom window, the dear children frankly admitted that the blame for his uprising was their own. As the eldest boy said:

'We ought to have remembered that Uncle George had a long day before him, and we ought to have dissuaded him from getting up. I blame myself entirely.'

But an occasional change of habit does nobody any harm; and besides, as Harris and I agreed, it was good training for George. In the Black Forest we should be up at five every morning; that we had determined on. Indeed, George himself had suggested half-past four, but Harris and I had argued that five would be early enough as an average; that would enable us to be on our machines by six, and to break the back of our journey before the heat of the day set in. Occasionally we might start a little earlier, but not as a habit.

I myself was up that morning at five. This was earlier than I had intended. I had said to myself on going to sleep, 'Six o'clock, sharp!'

There are men I know who can wake themselves at any time to the minute. They say to themselves, literally, as they lay their heads upon the pillow, 'Four-thirty,' 'Four-forty-five,' or 'Five-fifteen,' as the case may be; and as the clock strikes they open their eyes. It is very wonderful this; the more one dwells upon it, the greater the mystery grows. Some Ego within us, acting quite independently of our conscious self, must be capable of counting the hours while we sleep. Unaided by clock or sun, or any other medium known to our five senses, it keeps watch through the darkness. At the exact moment it whispers 'Time!' and we awake. The work of an old riverside fellow I once talked with called him to be out of bed each morning half-an-hour before high tide. He told me that never once had he overslept himself by a minute. Latterly, he never even troubled to work out the tide for himself. He would lie down tired, and sleep a dreamless sleep, and each morning at a different hour this ghostly watchman, true as the tide itself, would silently call him. Did the man's spirit haunt through the darkness the muddy river stairs; or had it knowledge of the ways of Nature? Whatever the process, the man himself was unconscious of it.

In my own case my inward watchman is, perhaps, somewhat out of practice. He does his best; but he is over-anxious; he worries himself, and loses count. I say to him, maybe, 'Five-thirty, please'; and he wakes me with a start at half-past two. I look at my watch. He suggests that, perhaps, I forgot to wind it up. I put it to my ear; it is still going. He thinks, maybe, something has happened to it; he is confident himself it is half-past five, if not a little later. To satisfy him, I put on a pair of slippers and go downstairs to inspect the dining-room clock. What happens to a man when he wanders about the house in the middle of the night, clad in a dressing-gown and a pair of slippers, there is no need to recount; most men know by experience. Everything—especially everything with a sharp corner —takes a cowardly delight in hitting him. When you are wearing a pair of stout boots, things get out of your way; when you venture among furniture in woolwork slippers and no socks, it comes at you and kicks you. I return to bed bad tempered, and refusing to listen to his further absurd suggestion that all the clocks in the house have entered into a conspiracy against me, take half an hour to get to sleep again. From four to five he wakes me every ten minutes. I wish I had never said a word to him about the thing. At five o'clock he goes to sleep himself, worn out, and leaves it to the girl, who does it half an hour later than usual.

On this particular Wednesday he worried me to such an extent, that I got up at five simply to be rid of him. I did not know what to do with myself. Our train did not leave till eight; all our luggage had been packed and sent on the night before, together with the bicycles, to Fenchurch Street Station. I went into my study; I thought I would put in an hour's writing. The early morning, before one has break-fasted, is not, I take it, a good season for literary effort. I wrote three paragraphs of a story, and then read them over to myself. Some unkind things have been said about my work; but nothing has yet been written which would have done justice to those three para-graphs. I threw them into the waste-paper basket, and sat trying to remember what, if any, charitable institutions provided pensions for decayed authors.

To escape from this train of reflection, I put a golf-ball in my pocket, and selecting a driver, strolled out into the paddock. A couple of sheep were browsing there, and they followed and took a keen interest in my practice. The one was a kindly, sympathetic old party. I do not think she understood the game; I think it was my doing this innocent thing so early in the morning that appealed to her. At every stroke I made she bleated:

'Go—o—o—d, go—o—o—d ind—e—e—d!'

She seemed as pleased as if she had done it herself.

As for the other one, she was a cantankerous, disagreeable old thing, as discouraging to me as her friend was helpful.

'Ba—a—ad, da—a—a—m ba—a—a—d!' was her comment on almost every stroke. As a matter of fact, some were really excellent strokes; but she did it just to be contradictory, and for the sake of irritating. I could see that.

By a most regrettable accident, one of my swiftest balls struck the good sheep on the nose. And at that the bad sheep laughed—laughed distinctly and undoubtedly, a husky, vulgar laugh; and, while her friend stood glued to the ground, too astonished to move, she changed her note for the first time and bleated:

'Go—o—o—d, ve—e—ry go—o—o—d! Be—e—e—est sho—o—o—ot he—e—e's ma—a—a—de!'

I would have given half-a-crown if it had been she I had hit instead of the other one. It is ever the good and amiable who suffer in this world.

I had wasted more time than I had intended in the paddock, and when Ethelbertha came to tell me it was half-past seven, and that breakfast was on the table, I remembered that I had not shaved. It vexes Ethelbertha my shaving quickly. She fears that to outsiders it may suggest a poor-spirited attempt at suicide, and that in consequence it may get about the neighbourhood that we are not happy together. As a further argument, she has also hinted that my appearance is not of the kind that can be trifled with.

On the whole, I was just as glad not to be able to take a long farewell of Ethelbertha; I did not want to risk her breaking down. But I should have liked more opportunity to say a few farewell words of advice to the children, especially as regards my fishing rod, which they will persist in using for cricket stumps; and I hate having to run for a train. Quarter of a mile from the station I overtook George and Harris; they were also running. In their case—so Harris informed me, jerkily, while we trotted side by side—it was the new kitchen stove that was to blame. This was the first morning they had tried it, and from some cause or other it had blown up the kidneys and scalded the cook. He said he hoped that by the time we returned they would have got more used to it.

We caught the train by the skin of our teeth, as the saying is, and reflecting upon the events of the morning, as we sat gasping in the carriage, there passed vividly before my mind the panorama of my Uncle Podger, as on two hundred and fifty days in the year he would start from Ealing Common by the nine-thirteen train to Moorgate Street.

From my Uncle Podger's house to the railway station was eight minutes' walk. What my uncle always said was:

'Allow yourself a quarter of an hour, and take it easily.'

What he always did was to start five minutes before the time and run. I do not know why, but this was the custom of the suburb. Many stout City gentlemen lived at Ealing in those days—I believe some live there still—and caught early trains to Town. They all started late; they all carried a black bag and a newspaper in one hand, and an umbrella in the other; and for the last quarter of a mile to the station, wet or fine, they all ran.

Folks with nothing else to do, nursemaids chiefly and errand boys, with now and then a perambulating costermonger added, would gather on the common of a fine morning to watch them pass, and cheer the most deserving. It was not a showy spectacle. They did not run well, they did not even run fast; but they were earnest, and they did their best. The exhibition appealed less to one's sense of art than to one's natural admiration for conscientious effort.

Occasionally a little harmless betting would take place among the crowd.

'Two to one agin the old gent in the white weskit!'

'Ten to one on old Blowpipes, bar he don't roll over hisself 'fore 'e gets there!'

'Heven money on the Purple Hemperor!'—a nickname bestowed by a youth of entomological tastes upon a certain retired military neighbour of my uncle's,—a gentleman of imposing appearance when stationary, but apt to colour highly under exercise.

My uncle and the others would write to the *Ealing Press* complaining bitterly concerning the supineness of the local police; and the editor would add spirited leaders upon the Decay of Courtesy among the Lower Orders, especially throughout the Western Suburbs. But no good ever resulted.

It was not that my uncle did not rise early enough; it was that troubles came to him at the last moment. The first thing he would do after breakfast would be to lose his newspaper. We always knew when

Uncle Podger had lost anything, by the expression of astonished indignation with which, on such occasions, he would regard the world in general. It never occurred to my Uncle Podger to say to himself:

'I am a careless old man. I lose everything: I never know where I have put anything. I am quite incapable of finding it again for myself. In this respect I must be a perfect nuisance to everybody about me. I must set to work and reform myself.'

On the contrary, by some peculiar course of reasoning, he had convinced himself that whenever he lost a thing it was everybody else's fault in the house but his own.

'I had it in my hand here not a minute ago!' he would exclaim.

From his tone you would have thought he was living surrounded by conjurers, who spirited away things from him merely to irritate him.

'Could you have left it in the garden?' my aunt would suggest.

'What should I want to leave it in the garden for? I don't want a paper in the garden; I want the paper in the train with me.'

'You haven't put it in your pocket?'

'God bless the woman! Do you think I should be standing here at five minutes to nine looking for it if I had it in my pocket all the while? *Do* you think I'm a fool?'

Here somebody would exclaim, 'What's this?' and hand him from somewhere a paper neatly folded.

'I do wish people would leave my things alone,' he would growl, snatching at it savagely.

He would open his bag to put it in, and then glancing at it, he would pause, speechless with sense of injury.

'What's the matter?' aunt would ask.

'The day before yesterday's!' he would answer, too hurt even to shout, throwing the paper down upon the table.

If only sometimes it had been yesterday's it would have been a change. But it was always the day before yesterday's; except on Tuesday; then it would be Saturday's.

We would find it for him eventually; as often as not he was sitting on it. And then he would smile, not genially, but with the weariness that comes to a man who feels that fate has cast his lot among a band of hopeless idiots.

'All the time, right in front of your noses——!' He would not finish the sentence; he prided himself on his self-control.

This settled, he would start for the hall, where it was the custom of my Aunt Maria to have the children gathered, ready to say good-bye to him.

My aunt never left the house herself, if only to make a call next door, without taking a tender farewell of every inmate. One never knew, she would say, what might happen.

One of them, of course, was sure to be missing; and the moment this was noticed all the other six, without an instant's hesitation, would scatter with a whoop to find it. Immediately they were gone it would turn up by itself from somewhere quite near, always with the most reasonable explanation for its absence; and would at once start off after the others to explain to them that it was found. In this way, five minutes at least would be taken up in everybody's looking for everybody else, which was just sufficient time to allow my uncle to find his umbrella and lose his hat. Then, at last, the group reassembled in the hall, the drawing-room clock would commence to strike nine. It possessed a cold, penetrating chime that always had the effect of confusing my uncle. In his excitement he would kiss some of the children twice over, pass by others, forget whom he had kissed and whom he hadn't, and have to begin all over again. He used to say he believed they mixed themselves up on purpose, and I am not prepared to maintain that the charge was altogether false. To add to his troubles, one child always had a sticky face; and that child would always be the most affectionate.

If things were going too smoothly, the eldest boy would come out with some tale about all the clocks in the house being five minutes slow, and of his having been late for school the previous day in consequence. This would send my uncle rushing impetuously down to the gate, where he would recollect that he had with him neither his bag nor his umbrella. All the children that my aunt could not stop would charge after him, two of them struggling for the umbrella, the others surging round the bag. And when they returned we would discover on the hall table the most important thing of all that he had forgotten, and wonder what he would say about it when he came home.

We arrived at Waterloo a little after nine, and at once proceeded to put George's experiment into operation. Opening the book at the chapter entitled 'At the Cab Rank,' we walked up to a hansom, raised our hats, and wished the driver 'Good-morning.'

This man was not to be outdone in politeness by any foreigner, real or imitation. Calling to a friend named 'Charles' to 'hold the steed,' he sprang from his box, and returned to us a bow that would have done credit to Mr Turveydrop* himself. Speaking apparently in the name of the nation, he welcomed us to England, adding a regret that Her Majesty was not at the moment in London.

We could not reply to him in kind. Nothing of this sort had been anticipated by the book. We called him 'coachman,' at which he again bowed to the pavement, and asked him if he would have the goodness to drive us to the Westminster Bridge road.

He laid his hand upon his heart, and said the pleasure would be his.

Taking the third sentence in the chapter, George asked him what his fare would be.

The question, as introducing a sordid element into the conversation, seemed to hurt his feelings. He said he never took money from distinguished strangers; he suggested a souvenir—a diamond scarf pin, a gold snuffbox, some little trifle of that sort by which he could remember us.

As a small crowd had collected, and as the joke was drifting rather too far in the cabman's direction, we climbed in without further parley, and were driven away amid cheers. We stopped the cab at a boot shop a little past Astley's Theatre that looked the sort of place we wanted. It was one of those overfed shops that the moment their shutters are taken down in the morning disgorge their goods all round them. Boxes of boots stood piled on the pavement or in the gutter opposite. Boots hung in festoons about its doors and windows. Its sun-blind was as some grimy vine, bearing bunches of black and brown boots. Inside, the shop was a bower of boots. The man, when we entered, was busy with a chisel and hammer opening a new crate full of boots.

George raised his hat, and said 'Good-morning.'

The man did not even turn round. He struck me from the first as a disagreeable man. He grunted something which might have been 'Good-morning,' or might not, and went on with his work.

George said, 'I have been recommended to your shop by my friend, Mr X.'

In response, the man should have said, 'Mr X. is a most worthy gentleman; it will give me the greatest pleasure to serve any friend of his.'

What he did say was, 'Don't know him; never heard of him.'

This was disconcerting. The book gave three or four methods of buying boots; George had carefully selected the one centred round 'Mr X,' as being of all the most courtly. You talked a good deal with the shopkeeper about this 'Mr X,' and then, when by this means friendship and understanding had been established, you slid naturally and gracefully into the immediate object of your coming, namely, your desire for boots, 'cheap and good.' This gross, material man cared, apparently, nothing for the niceties of retail dealing. It was necessary with such a one to come to business with brutal directness. George abandoned 'Mr X,' and turning back to a previous page, took a sentence at random. It was not a happy selection; it was a speech that would have been superfluous made to any bootmaker. Under the present circumstances, threatened and stifled as we were on every side by boots, it possessed the dignity of positive imbecility. It ran:—

'One has told me that you have here boots for sale.'

For the first time the man put down his hammer and chisel, and looked at us. He spoke slowly, in a thick and husky voice. He said:

'What d'ye think I keep boots for—to smell 'em?'

He was one of those men that begin quietly and grow more angry as they proceed, their wrongs apparently working within them like yeast.

'What d'ye think I am,' he continued, 'a boot collector? What d'ye think I'm running this shop for—my health? D'ye think I love the boots, and can't bear to part with a pair? D'ye think I hang 'em about here to look at 'em? Ain't there enough of 'em? Where d'ye think you are—in an international exhibition of boots? What d'ye think these boots are—a historical collection? Did you ever hear of a man keeping a boot shop and not selling boots? D'ye think I decorate the shop with 'em to make it look pretty? What d'ye take me for—a prize idiot?'

I have always maintained that these conversation books are never of any real use. What we wanted was some English equivalent for the well-known German idiom: 'Behalten Sie Ihr Haar auf.'*

Nothing of the sort was to be found in the book from beginning to end. However, I will do George the credit to admit he chose the very best sentence that was to be found therein and applied it. He said:

'I will come again, when, perhaps, you will have some more boots to show me. Till then, adieu!'

With that we returned to our cab and drove away, leaving the man standing in the centre of his boot-bedecked doorway addressing remarks to us. What he said, I did not hear, but the passers-by appeared to find it interesting.

George was for stopping at another boot shop and trying the experiment afresh; he said he really did want a pair of bedroom slippers. But we persuaded him to postpone their purchase until our arrival in some foreign city, where the tradespeople are no doubt more inured to this sort of talk, or else more naturally amiable. On the subject of the hat, however, he was adamant. He maintained that without that he could not travel, and, accordingly, we pulled up at a small shop in the Blackfriars Road.

The proprietor of this shop was a cheery, bright-eyed little man, and he helped us rather than hindered us.

When George asked him in the words of the book, 'Have you any hats?' he did not get angry; he just stopped and thoughtfully scratched his head.

'Hats,' said he. 'Let me think. Yes'—here a smile of positive pleasure broke over his genial countenance—'yes, now I come to think of it, I believe I have a hat. But, tell me, why do you ask me?'

George explained to him that he wished to purchase a cap, a travelling cap, but the essence of the transaction was that it was to be a 'good cap.'

The man's face fell.

'Ah,' he remarked, 'there, I am afraid, you have me. Now, if you had wanted a bad cap, not worth the price asked for it; a cap good for nothing but to clean windows with, I could have found you the very thing. But a good cap—no; we don't keep them. But wait a minute,' he continued, on seeing the disappointment that spread over George's expressive countenance, 'don't be in a hurry. I have a cap here'—he went to a drawer and opened it—'it is not a good cap, but it is not so bad as most of the caps I sell.'

He brought it forward, extended on his palm.

'What do you think of that?' he asked. 'Could you put up with that?'

George fitted it on before the glass, and, choosing another remark from the book, said:

'This hat fits me sufficiently well, but, tell me, do you consider that it becomes me?'

The man stepped back and took a bird's-eye view.

'Candidly,' he replied, 'I can't say that it does.'

He turned from George, and addressed himself to Harris and myself.

'Your friend's beauty,' said he, 'I should describe as elusive. It is there, but you can easily miss it. Now, in that cap, to my mind, you do miss it.'

At that point it occurred to George that he had had sufficient fun with this particular man. He said:

'That is all right. We don't want to lose the train. How much?'

Answered the man, 'The price of that cap, sir, which, in my opinion, is twice as much as it is worth, is four-and-six. Would you like it wrapped up in brown paper, sir, or in white?'

George said he would take it as it was, paid the man four-and-six in silver, and went out. Harris and I followed.

At Fenchurch Street we compromised with our cabman for five shillings. He made us another courtly bow, and begged us to remember him to the Emperor of Austria.

Comparing views in the train, we agreed that we had lost the game by two points to one; and George, who was evidently disappointed, threw the book out of window.

We found our luggage and the bicycles safe on the boat, and with the tide at twelve dropped down the river.

CHAPTER V

A necessary digression—Introduced by story containing moral—One of the charms of this book—The Journal that did not command success—Its boast: 'Instruction combined with Amusement'—Problem: say what should be considered instructive and what amusing—A popular game—Expert opinion on English law—Another of the charms of this book—A hackneyed tune—Yet a third charm of this book—The sort of wood it was where the maiden lived—Description of the Black Forest.

A STORY is told of a Scotchman who, loving a lassie, desired her for his wife. But he possessed the prudence of his race. He had noticed in his circle many an otherwise promising union result in disappointment and dismay, purely in consequence of the false estimate formed by bride or bridegroom concerning the imagined perfectability of the other. He determined that in his own case no collapsed ideal should be possible. Therefore, it was that his proposal took the following form:

'I'm but a puir lad, Jennie; I hae nae siller to offer ye, and nae land.'

'Ah, but ye hae yoursel', Davie!'

'An' I'm wishfu' it wa' onything else, lassie. I'm nae but a puir ill-seasoned loon, Jennie.'

'Na, na; there's mony a lad mair ill-looking than yoursel', Davie.'

'I hae na seen him, lass, and I'm just a-thinkin' I shouldna' care to.'

'Better a plain man, Davie, that ye can depend a' than ane that would be a speirin' at the lassies, a bringin' trouble into the hame wi' his flouting ways.'

'Dinna ye reckon on that, Jennie; it's nae the bonniest Bubbly Jock that mak's the most feathers to fly in the kailyard.* I was ever a lad to run after the petticoats, as is weel kent; an' it's a weary handfu' I'll be to ye, I'm thinkin'.'

'Ah, but ye hae a kind heart, Davie! an' ye love me weel. I'm sure on't.'

'I like ye weel enoo', Jennie, though I canna say how long the feeling may bide wi' me; an' I'm kind enoo' when I hae my ain way, an' naethin' happens to put me oot. But I hae the deevil's ain temper, as my mither can tell ye, an' like my puir fayther, I'm a thinkin', I'll grow nae better as I grow mair auld.'

'Ay, but ye're sair hard upon yersel', Davie. Ye're an honest lad. I ken ye better than ye ken yersel', an' ye'll mak a guid hame for me.'

'Maybe, Jennie! But I hae my doots. It's a sair thing for wife an' bairns when the guid man canna keep awa' frae the glass; an' when the scent of the whusky comes to me it's just as though I hae'd the throat o' a Loch Tay salmon; it just gaes doon an' doon, an' there's nae filling o' me.'

'Ay, but ye're a guid man when ye're sober, Davie.'

'Maybe I'll be that, Jennie, if I'm nae disturbed.'

'An' ye'll bide wi' me, Davie, an' work for me?'

'I see nae reason why I shouldna bide wi' ye, Jennie; but dinna ye clack aboot work to me, for I just canna bear the thoct o't.'

'Anyhow, ye'll do your best, Davie? As the minister says, nae man can do mair than that.'

'An' it's a puir best that mine'll be, Jennie, and I'm nae sae sure ye'll hae ower muckle even o' that. We're a' weak, sinfu' creatures,

Jennie, an' ye'd hae some deefficulty to find a man weaker or mair sinfu' than mysel'.'

'Weel, weel, ye hae a truthfu' tongue, Davie. Mony a lad will mak fine promises to a puir lassie, only to break 'em an' her heart wi' 'em. Ye speak me fair, Davie, and I'm thinkin' I'll just tak ye, an' see what comes o't.'

Concerning what did come of it, the story is silent, but one feels that under no circumstances had the lady any right to complain of her bargain. Whether she ever did or did not—for women do not invariably order their tongues according to logic, nor men either for the matter of that—Davie, himself, must have had the satisfaction of reflecting that all reproaches were undeserved.

I wish to be equally frank with the reader of this book. I wish here conscientiously to set forth its shortcomings. I wish no one to read this book under a misapprehension.

There will be no useful information in this book.

Anyone who should think that with the aid of this book he would be able to make a tour through Germany and the Black Forest would probably lose himself before he got to the Nore. That, at all events, would be the best thing that could happen to him. The farther away from home he got, the greater only would be his difficulties.

I do not regard the conveyance of useful information as my *forte*. This belief was not inborn with me; it has been driven home upon me by experience.

In my early journalistic days, I served upon a paper, the forerunner of many very popular periodicals of the present day. Our boast was that we combined instruction with amusement; as to what should be regarded as affording amusement and what instruction, the reader judged for himself. We gave advice to people about to marry—long, earnest advice that would, had they followed it, have made our circle of readers the envy of the whole married world. We told our subscribers how to make fortunes by keeping rabbits, giving facts and figures. The thing that must have surprised them was that we ourselves did not give up journalism and start rabbit-farming. Often and often have I proved conclusively from authoritative sources how a man starting a rabbit farm with twelve selected rabbits and a little judgment must, at the end of three years, be in receipt of an income of two thousand a year, rising rapidly; he simply could not help himself. He might not want the money. He might not know what to do with it when he had it. But there it was for him. I have never met a rabbit farmer myself worth two thousand a year, though I have known many start with the twelve necessary, assorted rabbits. Something has always gone wrong somewhere; maybe the continued atmosphere of a rabbit farm saps the judgment.

We told our readers how many bald-headed men there were in Iceland, and for all we knew our figures may have been correct; how many red herrings placed tail to mouth it would take to reach from London to Rome, which must have been useful to anyone desirous of laying down a line of red herrings from London to Rome, enabling him to order in the right quantity at the beginning; how many words the average woman spoke in a day; and other such like items of information calculated to make them wise and great beyond the readers of other journals.

We told them how to cure fits in cats. Personally I do not believe, and I did not believe then, that you can cure fits in cats. If I had a cat subject to fits I should advertise it for sale, or even give it away. But our duty was to supply information when asked for. Some fool wrote, clamouring to know; and I spent the best part of a morning seeking knowledge on the subject. I found what I wanted at length at the end of an old cookery book. What it was doing there I have never been able to understand. It had nothing to do with the proper subject of the book whatever; there was no suggestion that you could make any-thing savoury out of a cat, even when you had cured it of its fits. The authoress had just thrown in this paragraph out of pure generosity. I can only say that I wish she had left it out; it was the cause of a deal of angry correspondence and of the loss of four subscribers to the paper, if not more. The man said the result of following our advice had been two pounds worth of damage to his kitchen crockery, to say nothing of a broken window and probable blood poisoning to himself; added to which the cat's fits were worse than before. And yet it was a simple enough recipe. You held the cat between your legs, gently, so as not to hurt it, and with a pair of scissors made a sharp, clean cut in its tail. You did not cut off any part of the tail; you were to be careful not to do that; you only made an incision.

As we explained to the man, the garden or the coal cellar would have been the proper place for the operation; no one but an idiot would have attempted to perform it in a kitchen, and without help.

We gave them hints on etiquette. We told them how to address peers and bishops; also how to eat soup. We instructed shy young men how to acquire easy grace in drawing-rooms. We taught dancing to both sexes by the aid of diagrams. We solved their religious doubts for them, and supplied them with a code of morals that would have done credit to a stained-glass window.

The paper was not a financial success, it was some years before its time, and the consequence was that our staff was limited. My own department, I remember, included 'Advice to Mothers'—I wrote that with the assistance of my landlady, who, having divorced one husband and buried four children, was, I considered, a reliable authority on all domestic matters; 'Hints on Furnishing and House-hold Decorations—with Designs'; a column of 'Literary Counsel to Beginners'—I sincerely hope my guidance was of better service to them than it has ever proved to myself; and our weekly article, 'Straight Talks to Young Men,' signed 'Uncle Henry.' A kindly, genial old fellow was 'Uncle Henry,' with wide and varied experi-ence, and a sympathetic attitude towards the rising generation. He had been through trouble himself in his far back youth, and knew most things. Even to this day I read 'Uncle Henry's' advice, and, though I say it who should not, it still seems to me good, sound advice. I often think that had I followed 'Uncle Henry's' counsel closer I would have been wiser, made fewer mistakes, felt better satisfied with myself than is now the case.

A quiet, weary little woman, who lived in a bed-sitting room off the Tottenham Court Road, and who had a husband in a lunatic asylum, did our 'Cooking Column,' 'Hints on Education'—we were full of hints,—and a page and a half of 'Fashionable Intelligence,' written in the pertly personal style which even yet has not altogether disappeared, so I am informed, from modern journalism: 'I must tell you about the *divine* frock I wore at "Glorious Goodwood"'* last week. Prince C.—but there, I really must *not* repeat all the things the silly fellow says; he is *too* foolish—and the *dear* Countess, I fancy, was just the *weeish* bit jealous'—and so on.

Poor little woman! I see her now in the shabby grey alpaca, with the inkstains on it. Perhaps a day at 'Glorious Goodwood,' or anywhere else in the fresh air, might have put some colour into her cheeks.

Our proprietor—one of the most unashamedly ignorant men I ever met—I remember his gravely informing a correspondent once that Ben Jonson had written *Rabelais** to pay for his mother's funeral, and only laughing good-naturedly when his mistakes were pointed out to him—wrote with the aid of a cheap encyclopædia the pages devoted to 'General Information,' and did them on the whole remarkably well; while our office boy, with an excellent pair of scissors for his assistant, was responsible for our supply of 'Wit and Humour.'

It was hard work, and the pay was poor; what sustained us was the consciousness that we were instructing and improving our fellow men and women. Of all games in the world, the one most universally and eternally popular is the game of school. You collect six children, and put them on a doorstep, while you walk up and down with the book and cane. We play it when babies, we play it when boys and girls, we play it when men and women, we play it as, lean and slippered,* we totter towards the grave. It never palls upon, it never wearies us. Only one thing mars it: the tendency of one and all of the other six children to clamour for their turn with the book and the cane. The reason, I am sure, that journalism is so popular a calling, in spite of its many drawbacks, is this: each journalist feels he is the boy walking up and down with the cane. The Government, the Classes, and the Masses, Society, Art, and Literature, are the other children sitting on the door-step. He instructs and improves them.

But I digress. It was to excuse my present permanent disinclination to be the vehicle of useful information that I recalled these matters. Let us now return.

Somebody, signing himself 'Balloonist,' had written to ask concerning the manufacture of hydrogen gas. It is an easy thing to manufacture—at least, so I gathered after reading up the subject at the British Museum; yet I did warn 'Balloonist,' whoever he might be, to take all necessary precaution against accident. What more could I have done? Ten days afterwards a florid-faced lady called at the office, leading by the hand what, she explained, was her son, aged twelve. The boy's face was unimpressive to a degree positively remarkable. His mother pushed him forward and took off his hat, and then I perceived the reason for this. He had no eyebrows whatever, and of his hair nothing remained but a scrubby dust, giving to his head the appearance of a hard-boiled egg, skinned and sprinkled with black pepper.

'That was a handsome lad this time last week, with naturally curly hair,' remarked the lady. She spoke with a rising inflection, suggestive of the beginning of things.

'What has happened to him?' asked our chief.

'This is what's happened to him,' retorted the lady. She drew from her muff a copy of our last week's issue, with my article on hydrogen gas scored in pencil, and flung it before his eyes. Our chief took it and read it through.

'He was "Balloonist"?' queried the chief.

'He was "Balloonist,"' admitted the lady, 'the poor innocent child, and now look at him!'

'Maybe it'll grow again,' suggested our chief.

'Maybe it will,' retorted the lady, her key continuing to rise, 'and maybe it won't. What I want to know is what you are going to do for him.'

Our chief suggested a hair wash. I thought at first she was going to fly at him; but for the moment she confined herself to words. It appears she was not thinking of a hair wash, but of compensation. She also made observations on the general character of our paper, its utility, its claim to public support, the sense and wisdom of its contributors.

'I really don't see that it is our fault,' urged the chief—he was a mild-mannered man; 'he asked for information, and he got it.'

'Don't you try to be funny about it,' said the lady (he had not meant to be funny, I am sure; levity was not his failing) 'or you'll get something that *you* haven't asked for. Why, for two pins,' said the lady, with a suddenness that sent us both flying like scuttled chickens behind our respective chairs, 'I'd come round and make your head like it!' I take it, she meant like the boy's. She also added observations upon our chief's personal appearance, that were distinctly in bad taste. She was not a nice woman by any means.

Myself, I am of the opinion that had she brought the action she threatened, she would have had no case; but our chief was a man who had had experience of the law, and his principle was always to avoid it. I have heard him say:

'If a man stopped me in the street and demanded of me my watch, I should refuse to give it to him. If he threatened to take it by force, I feel I should, though not a fighting man, do my best to protect it. If, on the other hand, he should assert his intention of trying to obtain it by means of an action in any court of law, I should take it out of my pocket and hand it to him, and think I had got off cheaply.'

He squared the matter with the florid-faced lady for a five-pound note, which must have represented a month's profits on the paper; and she departed, taking her damaged offspring with her. After she was gone, our chief spoke kindly to me. He said:

'Don't think I am blaming you in the least; it is not your fault, it is Fate. Keep to moral advice and criticism—there you are distinctly good; but don't try your hand any more on "Useful Information." As I have said, it is not your fault. Your information is correct enough —there is nothing to be said against that; it simply is that you are not lucky with it.'

I would that I had followed his advice always; I would have saved myself and other people much disaster. I see no reason why it should be, but so it is. If I instruct a man as to the best route between London and Rome, he loses his luggage in Switzerland, or is nearly ship-wrecked off Dover. If I counsel him in the purchase of a camera, he gets run in by the German police for photographing fortresses. I once took a deal of trouble to explain to a man how to marry his deceased wife's sister at Stockholm. I found out for him the time the boat left Hull and the best hotels to stop at. There was not a single mistake from beginning to end in the information with which I supplied him; no hitch occurred anywhere; yet now he never speaks to me.

Therefore it is that I have come to restrain my passion for the giving of information; therefore it is that nothing in the nature of practical instruction will be found, if I can help it, within these pages.

There will be no description of towns, no historical reminiscences, no architecture, no morals.

I once asked an intelligent foreigner what he thought of London.

He said, 'It is a very big town.'

I said, 'What struck you most about it?'

He replied, 'The people.'

I said, 'Compared with other towns—Paris, Rome, Berlin—what did you think of it?'

He shrugged his shoulders. 'It is bigger,' he said; 'what more can one say?'

One anthill is very much like another. So many avenues, wide or narrow, where the little creatures swarm in strange confusion; these bustling by, important; these halting to pow-wow with one another.

These struggling with big burdens; those but basking in the sun. So many granaries stored with food; so many cells where the little things sleep, and eat, and love; the corner where lie their little white bones. This hive is larger, the next smaller. This nest lies on the sand, and another under the stones. This was built but yesterday, while that was fashioned ages ago, some say even before the swallows came; who knows?

Nor will there be found herein folk-lore or story.

Every valley where lie homesteads has its song. I will tell you the plot; you can turn it into verse and set it to music of your own.

There lived a lass, and there came a lad, who loved and rode away.

It is a monotonous song, written in many languages; for the young man seems to have been a mighty traveller. Here in sentimental Germany they remember him well. So also the dwellers of the Blue Alsatian Mountains remember his coming among them; while, if my memory serves me truly, he likewise visited the Banks of Allan Water. A veritable Wandering Jew is he; for still the foolish girls listen, so they say, to the dying away of his hoof-beats.

In this land of many ruins, that long while ago were voice-filled homes, linger many legends; and here again, giving you the essentials, I leave you to cook the dish for yourself. Take a human heart or two, assorted; a bundle of human passions—there are not many of them, half a dozen at the most; season with a mixture of good and evil; flavour the whole with the sauce of death, and serve up where and when you will. 'The Saint's Cell,' 'The Haunted Keep,' 'The Dungeon Grave,' 'The Lover's Leap'—call it what you will, the stew's the same.

Lastly, in this book there will be no scenery. This is not laziness on my part; it is self-control. Nothing is easier to write than scenery; nothing more difficult and unnecessary to read. When Gibbon* had to trust to travellers' tales for a description of the Hellespont, and the Rhine was chiefly familiar to English students through the medium of Cæsar's *Commentaries*,* it behoved every globe-trotter, for whatever distance, to describe to the best of his ability the things that he had seen. Dr Johnson, familiar with little else than the view down Fleet Street, could read the description of a Yorkshire moor with pleasure and with profit. To a cockney who had never seen higher ground than the Hog's Back in Surrey, an account of Snowdon must have appeared exciting. But we, or rather the steam-engine and the camera for us, have changed all that. The man who plays tennis every year at the foot of the Matterhorn, and billiards on the summit of the Rigi, does not thank you for an elaborate and painstaking description of the Grampian Hills. To the average man, who has seen a dozen oil paintings, a hundred photographs, a thousand pictures in the illustrated journals, and a couple of panoramas of Niagara, the word-painting of a waterfall is tedious.

An American friend of mind, a cultured gentleman, who loved poetry well enough for its own sake, told me that he had obtained a more correct and more satisfying idea of the Lake district from an eighteenpenny book of photographic views than from all the works of Coleridge, Southey, and Wordsworth put together. I also remember his saying concerning this subject of scenery in literature, that he would thank an author as much for writing an eloquent description of what he had just had for dinner. But this was in reference to another argument; namely, the proper province of each art. My friend maintaining that just as canvas and colour were the wrong mediums for story telling, so word-painting was, at its best, but a clumsy method of conveying impressions that could much better be received through the eye.

As regards the question, there also lingers in my memory very distinctly a hot school afternoon. The class was for English literature, and the proceedings commenced with the reading of a certain lengthy, but otherwise unobjectionable, poem. The author's name, I am ashamed to say, I have forgotten, together with the title of the poem. The reading finished, we closed our books, and the Professor, a kindly, white-haired old gentleman, suggested our giving in our own words an account of what we had just read.

'Tell me,' said the Professor, encouragingly, 'what it is all about.'

'Please, sir,' said the first boy—he spoke with bowed head and evident reluctance, as though the subject were one which, left to himself, he would never have mentioned,—'it is about a maiden.'

'Yes,' agreed the Professor; 'but I want you to tell me in your own words. We do not speak of a maiden, you know; we say a girl. Yes, it is about a girl. Go on.'

'A girl,' repeated the top boy, the substitution apparently, increasing his embarrassment, 'who lived in a wood.'

'What sort of a wood?' asked the Professor.

The first boy examined his inkpot carefully, and then looked at the ceiling.

'Come,' urged the Professor, growing impatient, 'you have been reading about this wood for the last ten minutes. Surely you can tell me something concerning it.'

'The gnarly trees, their twisted branches'—recommenced the top boy.

'No, no,' interrupted the Professor; 'I do not want you to repeat the poem. I want you to tell me in your own words what sort of a wood it was where the girl lived.'

The Professor tapped his foot impatiently; the top boy made a dash for it.

'Please, sir, it was the usual sort of wood.'

'Tell him what sort of a wood,' said he, pointing to the second lad.

The second boy said it was a 'green wood.' This annoyed the Professor still more; he called the second boy a blockhead, though really I cannot see why, and passed on to the third, who, for the last minute, had been sitting apparently on hot plates, with his right arm waving up and down like a distracted semaphore signal. He would have had to say it the next second, whether the Professor had asked him or not; he was red in the face, holding his knowledge in.

'A dark and gloomy wood,' shouted the third boy, with much relief to his feelings.

'A dark and gloomy wood,' repeated the Professor, with evident approval. 'And why was it dark and gloomy?'

The third boy was still equal to the occasion.

'Because the sun could not get inside it.'

The Professor felt he had discovered the poet of the class.

'Because the sun could not get into it, or, better, because the sunbeams could not penetrate. And why could not the sunbeams penetrate there?'

'Please, sir, because the leaves were too thick.'

'Very well,' said the Professor. 'The girl lived in a dark and gloomy wood, through the leafy canopy of which the sunbeams were unable to pierce. Now, what grew in this wood?' He pointed to the fourth boy.

'Please, sir, trees, sir.'

'And what else?'

'Toadstools, sir.' This after a pause.

The Professor was not quite sure about the toadstools, but on referring to the text he found that the boy was right; toadstools had been mentioned.

'Quite right,' admitted the Professor, 'toadstools grew there. And what else? What do you find underneath trees in a wood?'

'Please, sir, earth, sir.'

'No; no; what grows in a wood besides trees?'

'Oh, please, sir, bushes, sir.'

'Bushes; very good. Now we are getting on. In this wood there were trees and bushes. And what else?'

He pointed to a small boy near the bottom, who having decided that the wood was too far off to be of any annoyance to him, individually, was occupying his leisure playing noughts and crosses against himself. Vexed and bewildered, but feeling it necessary to add something to the inventory, he hazarded blackberries. This was a mistake; the poet had not mentioned blackberries.

'Of course, Klobstock would think of something to eat,' commented the Professor, who prided himself on his ready wit. This raised a laugh against Klobstock, and pleased the Professor.

'You,' continued he, pointing to a boy in the middle; 'what else was there in this wood besides trees and bushes?'

'Please, sir, there was a torrent there.'

'Quite right; and what did the torrent do?'

'Please, sir, it gurgled.'

'No; no. Streams gurgle, torrents——?'

'Roar, sir.'

'It roared. And what made it roar?'

This was a poser. One boy—he was not our prize intellect, I admit—suggested the girl. To help us the Professor put his question in another form:

'When did it roar?'

Our third boy, again coming to the rescue, explained that it roared when it fell down among the rocks. I think some of us had a vague idea that it must have been a cowardly torrent to make such a noise about a little thing like this; a pluckier torrent, we felt, would have got up and gone on, saying nothing about it. A torrent that roared every time it fell upon a rock we deemed a poor spirited torrent; but the Professor seemed quite content with it.

'And what lived in this wood beside the girl?' was the next question.

'Please, sir, birds, sir.'

'Yes, birds lived in this wood. What else?'

Birds seemed to have exhausted our ideas.

'Come,' said the Professor, 'what are those animals with tails, that run up trees?'

We thought for a while, then one of us suggested cats.

This was an error; the poet had said nothing about cats; squirrels was what the Professor was trying to get.

I do not recall much more about this wood in detail. I only recollect that the sky was introduced into it. In places where there occurred an opening among the trees you could by looking up see the sky above you; very often there were clouds in this sky, and occasionally, if I remember rightly, the girl got wet.

I have dwelt upon this incident, because it seems to me suggestive of the whole question of scenery in literature. I could not at the time, I cannot now, understand why the top boy's summary was not sufficient. With all due deference to the poet, whoever he may have been, one cannot but acknowledge that his wood was, and could not be otherwise than, 'the usual sort of a wood.'

I could describe the Black Forest to you at great length. I could translate to you Hebel,* the poet of the Black Forest. I could write pages concerning its rocky gorges and its smiling valleys, its pine-clad slopes, its rock-crowned summits, its foaming rivulets (where the tidy German has not condemned them to flow respectably through wooden troughs or drainpipes), its white villages, its lonely farmsteads.

But I am haunted by the suspicion you might skip all this. Were you sufficiently conscientious—or weak-minded enough—not to do so, I should, all said and done, succeed in conveying to you only an impression much better summed up in the simple words of the unpretentious guide book:

'A picturesque, mountainous district, bounded on the south and the west by the plain of the Rhine, towards which its spurs descend precipitately. Its geological formation consists chiefly of variegated sandstone and granite; its lower heights being covered with extensive pine forests. It is well watered with numerous streams, while its populous valleys are fertile and well cultivated. The inns are good; but the local wines should be partaken of by the stranger with discretion.'

CHAPTER VI

Why we went to Hanover—Something they do better abroad—The art of polite foreign conversation, as taught in English schools—A true history, now told for the first time—The French joke, as provided for the amusement of British youth—Fatherly instincts of Harris—The road-waterer, considered as an artist—Patriotism of George—What Harris ought to have done—What he did—We save Harris's life—A sleepless city—The cab-horse as a critic.

WE arrived at Hamburg on Friday, after a smooth and uneventful voyage; and from Hamburg we travelled to Berlin by way of Hanover. It is not the most direct route. I can only account for our visit to Hanover as the nigger accounted to the magistrate for his appearance in the Deacon's poultry-yard.

'Yes, sar, what the constable sez is quite true, sar; I was dar, sar.'

'Oh, so you admit it? And what were you doing with a sack, pray, in Deacon Abraham's poultry-yard at twelve o'clock at night?'

'I'se gwine ter tell yer, sar; yes, sar. I'd been to Massa Jordan's wid a sack of melons. Yes, sar; an' Massa Jordan he wuz very 'greeable, an' axed me for ter come in.'

'Well?'

'Yes, sar, very 'greeable man is Massa Jordan. An' dar we sat a talking an' a talking——'

'Very likely. What we want to know is what you were doing in the Deacon's poultry-yard?'

'Yes, sar, dat's what I'se cumming to. It wuz ver' late 'fore I left Massa Jordan's, an' den I sez ter mysel', sez I, now yer jest step out with yer best leg foremost, Ulysses, case yer gets into trouble wid de ole woman. Ver' talkative woman she is, sar, very——'

'Yes, never mind her; there are other people very talkative in this town besides your wife. Deacon Abraham's house is half a mile out of your way home from Mr Jordan's. How did you get there?'

'Dat's what I'm a-gwine ter explain, sar.'

'I am glad of that. And how do you propose to do it?'

'Well, I'se thinkin', sar, I must ha' digressed.'

I take it we digressed a little.

At first, for some reason or other, Hanover strikes you as an uninteresting town, but it grows upon you. It is in reality two towns; a place of broad, modern, handsome streets and tasteful gardens; side by side with a sixteenth century town, where old timbered houses overhang the narrow lanes; where through low archways one catches glimpses of galleried courtyards, once often thronged, no doubt, with troops of horse, or blocked with lumbering coach and six, waiting its rich merchant owner, and his fat placid Frau, but where now children and chickens scuttle at their will; while over the carved balconies hang dingy clothes a-drying.

A singularly English atmosphere hovers over Hanover, especially on Sundays, when its shuttered shops and clanging bells give to it the suggestion of a sunnier London. Nor was this British Sunday atmosphere apparent only to myself, else I might have attributed it to imagination; even George felt it. Harris and I, returning from a short stroll with our cigars after lunch on the Sunday afternoon, found him peacefully slumbering in the smoke-room's easiest chair.

'After all,' said Harris, 'there is something about the British Sunday that appeals to the man with English blood in his veins. I should be sorry to see it altogether done away with, let the new generation say what it will.'

And taking one each end of the ample settee, we kept George company.

To Hanover one should go, they say, to learn the best German. The disadvantage is that outside Hanover, which is only a small province, nobody understands this best German. Thus you have to decide whether to speak good German and remain in Hanover, or bad German and travel about. Germany being separated by so many centuries into a dozen principalities, is unfortunate in possessing a variety of dialects. Germans from Posen wishful to converse with men of Wurtemburg, have to talk as often as not in French or English; and young ladies who have received an expensive education in Westphalia surprise and disappoint their parents by being unable to understand a word said to them in Mechlenberg. An English-speaking foreigner, it is true, would find himself equally nonplussed among the Yorkshire wolds, or in the purlieus of Whitechapel; but the cases are not on all fours. Throughout Germany it is not only in the country districts and among the uneducated that dialects are maintained. Every province has practically its own language, of which it is proud and retentive. An educated Bavarian will admit to you that, academically speaking, the North German is more correct; but he will continue to speak South German and to teach it to his children.

In the course of the century, I am inclined to think that Germany will solve her difficulty in this respect by speaking English. Every boy and girl in Germany, above the peasant class, speaks English. Were English pronunciation less arbitrary, there is not the slightest doubt but that in the course of a very few years, comparatively speaking, it would become the language of the world. All foreigners agree that, grammatically, it is the easiest language of any to learn. A German, comparing it with his own language, where every word in every sentence is governed by at least four distinct and separate rules, tells you that English has no grammar. A good many English people would seem to have come to the same conclusion; but they are wrong. As a matter of fact, there is an English grammar, and one of these days our schools will recognise the fact, and it will be taught to our children, penetrating maybe even into literary and journalistic circles. But at present we appear to agree with the foreigner that it is a quantity neglectable. English pronunciation is the stumbling-block to our progress. English spelling would seem to have been designed chiefly as a disguise to pronunciation. It is a clever idea, calculated to check presumption on the part of the foreigner; but for that he would learn it in a year.

For they have a way of teaching languages in Germany that is not our way; and the consequence is that when the German youth or maiden leaves the gymnasium or high school at fifteen, 'it' (as in German one conveniently may say) can understand and speak the tongue it has been learning. In England we have a method that for obtaining the least possible result at the greatest possible expenditure of time and money is perhaps unequalled. An English boy who has been through a good middle-class school in England can talk to a Frenchman, slowly and with difficulty, about female gardeners and aunts; conversation which, to a man possessed perhaps of neither, is liable to pall. Possibly, if he be a bright exception, he may be able to tell the time, or make a few guarded observations concerning the weather. No doubt he could repeat a goodly number of irregular verbs by heart; only, as a matter of fact, few foreigners care to listen to their own irregular verbs, recited by young Englishmen. Likewise he might be able to remember a choice selection of grotesquely involved

French idioms, such as no modern Frenchman has ever heard or understands when he does hear.

The explanation is that, in nine cases out of ten, he has learnt French from an 'Ahn's First-Course.' The history of this famous work is remarkable and instructive. The book was originally written for a joke, by a witty Frenchman who had resided for some years in England. He intended it as a satire upon the conversational powers of British society. From this point of view it was distinctly good. He submitted it to a London publishing firm. The manager was a shrewd man. He read the book through. Then he sent for the author.

'This book of yours,' said he to the author, 'is very clever. I have laughed over it myself till the tears came.'

'I am delighted to hear you say so,' replied the pleased Frenchman. 'I tried to be truthful without being unnecessarily offensive.'

'It is most amusing,' concurred the manager; 'and yet published as harmless joke, I feel it would fail.'

The author's face fell.

'Its humour,' proceeded the manager, 'would be denounced as forced and extravagant. It would amuse the thoughtful and intelligent, but from a business point of view that portion of the public are never worth consideration. But I have an idea,' continued the manager. He glanced round the room to be sure they were alone, and leaning forward sunk his voice to a whisper. 'My notion is to publish it as a serious work for the use of schools!'

The author stared, speechless.

'I know the English schoolman,' said the manager; 'this book will appeal to him. It will exactly fit in with his method. Nothing sillier, nothing more useless for the purpose will he ever discover. He will smack his lips over the book, as a puppy licks up blacking.'

The author, sacrificing art to greed, consented. They altered the title and added a vocabulary, but left the book otherwise as it was.

The result is known to every schoolboy. 'Ahn' became the palladium of English philological education. If it no longer retain its ubiquity, it is because something even less adaptable to the object in view has been since invented.

Lest, in spite of all, the British schoolboy should obtain, even from the like of 'Ahn,' some glimmering of French, the British educational method further handicaps him by bestowing upon him the assistance of, what is termed in the prospectus, 'A native gentleman.' This native French gentleman, who, by-the-by, is generally a Belgian, is no doubt a most worthy person, and can, it is true, understand and speak his own language with tolerable fluency. There his qualifications cease. Invariably he is a man with a quite remarkable inability to teach anybody anything. Indeed, he would seem to be chosen not so much as an instructor as an amuser of youth. He is always a comic figure. No Frenchman of a dignified appearance would be engaged for any English school. If he possess by nature a few harmless peculiarities, calculated to cause merriment, so much the more is he esteemed by his employers. The class naturally regards him as an animated joke. The two to four hours a week that are deliberately wasted on this ancient farce, are looked forward to by the boys as a merry interlude in an otherwise monotonous existence. And then, when the proud parent takes his son and heir to Dieppe merely to discover that the lad does not know enough to call a cab, he abuses not the system but its innocent victim.

I confine my remarks to French, because that is the only language we attempt to teach our youth. An English boy who could speak German would be looked down upon as unpatriotic. Why we waste time in teaching even French according to this method I have never been able to understand. A perfect unacquaintance with a language is respectable. But putting aside comic journalists and lady novelists, for whom it is a business necessity, this smattering of French which we are so proud to possess only serves to render us ridiculous.

In the German school the method is somewhat different. One hour every day is devoted to the same language. The idea is not to give the lad time between each lesson to forget what he learned at the last; the idea is for him to get on. There is no comic foreigner provided for his amusement. The desired language is taught by a German schoolmaster who knows it inside and out as thoroughly as he knows his own. Maybe this system does not provide the German youth with that perfection of foreign accent for which the British tourist is in every land remarkable, but it has other advantages. The boy does not call his master 'froggy,' or 'sausage,' nor prepare for the French or English hour any exhibition of homely wit whatever. He just sits there, and for his own sake tries to learn that foreign tongue with as little trouble to everybody concerned as possible. When he has left school he can talk, not about pen-knives and gardeners and aunts merely, but about European politics, history,

Shakespeare, or the musical glasses, according to the turn the conversation may take.

Viewing the German people from an Anglo-Saxon standpoint, it may be that in this book I shall find occasion to criticise them: but on the other hand, there is much that we might learn from them; and in the matter of common sense, as applied to education, they can give us ninety-nine in a hundred, and beat us with one hand.

The beautiful wood of the Eilenriede bounds Hanover on the south and west, and here occurred a sad drama in which Harris took a prominent part.

We were riding our machines through this wood on the Monday afternoon in the company of many other cyclists, for it is a favourite resort with the Hanoverians on a sunny afternoon, and its shady pathways are then filled with happy, thoughtful folk. Among them rode a young and beautiful girl on a machine that was new. She was evidently a novice on the bicycle. One felt instinctively that there would come a moment when she would require help, and Harris, with his accustomed chivalry, suggested we should keep near her. Harris, as he occasionally explains to George and to myself, has daughters of his own, or, to speak more correctly, a daughter, who as the years progress will no doubt cease practising catherine wheels, in the front garden, and will grow up into a beautiful and respectable young lady. This naturally gives Harris an interest in all beautiful girls up to the age of thirty-five or thereabouts; they remind him, so he says, of home.

We had ridden for about two miles, when we noticed, a little ahead of us in a space where five ways met, a man with a hose, watering the roads. The pipe, supported at each joint by a pair of tiny wheels, writhed after him as he moved, suggesting a gigantic worm, from whose open neck, as the man, gripping it firmly in both hands, pointing it now this way, and now that, now elevating it, now depressing it, poured a strong stream of water at the rate of about a gallon a second.

'What a much better method than ours,' observed Harris, enthusiastically. Harris is inclined to be chronically severe on all British institutions. 'How much simpler, quicker, and more economical! You see, one man by this method can in five minutes water a stretch of road that would take us with our clumsy lumbering cart half an hour to cover.'

George, who was riding behind me on the tandem, said, 'Yes, and it is also a method by which with a little carelessness a man could cover a good many people in a good deal less time than they could get out of the way.'

George, the opposite to Harris, is British to the core. I remember George quite patriotically indignant with Harris once for suggesting the introduction of the guillotine into England.

'It is so much neater,' said Harris.

'I don't care if it is,' said George; 'I'm an Englishman; hanging is good enough for me.'

'Our water-cart may have its disadvantages,' continued George, 'but it can only make you uncomfortable about the legs, and you can avoid it. This is the sort of machine with which a man can follow you round the corner and upstairs.'

'It fascinates me to watch them,' said Harris. 'They are so skilful. I have seen a man from the corner of a crowded square in Strassburg cover every inch of ground, and not so much as wet an apron string. It is marvellous how they judge their distance. They will send the water up to your toes, and then bring it over your head so that it falls around your heels. They can——'

'Ease up a minute,' said George.

I said: 'Why?'

He said, 'I am going to get off and watch the rest of this show from behind a tree. There may be great performers in this line, as Harris says; this particular artist appears to me to lack something. He has just soused a dog, and now he's busy watering a sign-post. I am going to wait till he has finished.'

'Nonsense,' said Harris; 'he won't wet you.'

'That is precisely what I am going to make sure of,' answered George, saying which he jumped off, and, taking up a position behind a remarkably fine elm, pulled out and commenced filling his pipe.

I did not care to take the tandem on by myself, so I stepped off and joined him, leaving the machine against a tree. Harris shouted something or other about our being a disgrace to the land that gave us birth, and rode on.

The next moment I heard a woman's cry of distress. Glancing round the stem of the tree, I perceived that it proceeded from the young and elegant lady before mentioned, whom, in our interest concerning the road-waterer, we had forgotten. She was riding her machine steadily and straightly through a drenching shower of water from the hose. She appeared to be too paralysed either to get off or turn her wheel aside. Every instant she was becoming wetter, while the man with the hose, who was either drunk or blind, continued to pour water upon her with utter indifference. A dozen voices yelled imprecations upon him, but he took no heed whatever.

Harris, his fatherly nature stirred to its depths, did at this point what, under the circumstances, was quite the right and proper thing to do. Had he acted throughout with the same coolness and judgment he then displayed, he would have emerged from that incident the hero of the hour, instead of, as happened, riding away followed by insult and threat. Without a moment's hesitation he spurted at the man, sprang to the ground, and, seizing the hose by the nozzle, attempted to wrest it away.

What he ought to have done, what any man retaining his common sense would have done the moment he got his hands upon the thing, was to turn off the tap. Then he might have played football with the man, or battledore and shuttlecock as he pleased; and the twenty or thirty people who had rushed forward to assist would have only applauded. His idea, however, as he explained to us afterwards, was to take away the hose from the man, and, for punishment, turn it upon the fool himself. The waterman's idea appeared to be the same, namely, to retain the hose as a weapon with which to soak Harris. Of course, the result was that, between them, they soused every dead and living thing within fifty yards, except themselves. One furious man, too drenched to care what more happened to him, leapt into the arena and also took a hand. The three among them proceeded to sweep the compass with that hose. They pointed it to heaven, and the water descended upon the people in the form of an equinoctial storm. They pointed it downwards, and sent the water in rushing streams that took people off their feet, or caught them about the waist line, and doubled them up.

Not one of them would loosen his grip upon the hose, not one of them thought to turn the water off. You might have concluded they were struggling with some primeval force of nature. In forty-five seconds, so George said, who was timing it, they had swept that circus bare of every living thing except one dog, who, dripping like a water nymph, rolled over by the force of water, now on this side, now on that, still gallantly staggered again and again to its feet to bark defiance at what it evidently regarded as the powers of hell let loose.

Men and women left their machines upon the ground, and flew into the woods. From behind every tree of importance, peeped out wet, angry heads.

At last, there arrived upon the scene one man of sense. Braving all things, he crept to the hydrant, where still stood the iron key, and screwed it down. And then from forty trees began to creep more or less soaked human beings, each one with something to say.

At first I fell to wondering whether a stretcher or a clothes basket would be the more useful for the conveyance of Harris's remains back to the hotel. I consider that George's promptness on that occasion saved Harris's life. Being dry, and therefore able to run quicker, he was there before the crowd. Harris was for explaining things, but George cut him short.

'You get on that,' said George, handing him his bicycle, 'and go. They don't know we belong to you, and you may trust us implicitly not to reveal the secret. We'll hang about behind, and get in their way. Ride zig-zag in case they shoot.'

I wish this book to be a strict record of fact, unmarred by exaggeration, and therefore I have shown my description of this incident to Harris, lest anything beyond bald narrative may have crept into it. Harris maintains it is exaggerated, but admits that one or two people may have been 'sprinkled.' I have offered to turn a street hose on him at a distance of five-and-twenty yards, and take his opinion afterwards, as to whether 'sprinkled' is the adequate term, but he has declined the test. Again, he insists there could not have been more than half a dozen people, at the outside, involved in the catastrophe, that forty is a ridiculous misstatement. I have offered to return with him to Hanover and make strict inquiry into the matter, and this offer he has likewise declined. Under these circumstances, I maintain that mine is a true and restrained narrative of an event that is, by a certain number of Hanoverians, remembered with bitterness unto this very day.

We left Hanover that same evening, and arrived at Berlin in time for supper and an evening stroll. Berlin is a disappointing town; its centre overcrowded, its outlying parts lifeless; its one famous street, Unter den Linden, an attempt to combine Oxford Street with the Champs Élysées, singularly unimposing, being much too wide for its size; its theatres dainty and charming, where acting is considered of more importance than scenery or dress, where long runs are unknown, successful pieces being played again and again, but never consecutively, so that for a week running you may go to the same Berlin theatre and see a fresh play every night; its opera house unworthy of it; its two music halls, with an unnecessary suggestion of vulgarity and commonness about them, ill-arranged and much too large for comfort. In the Berlin cafés and restaurants, the busy time is from midnight on till three. Yet most of the people who frequent them are up again at seven. Either the Berliner has solved the great problem of modern life, how to do without sleep, or, with Carlyle,* he must be looking forward to eternity.

Personally, I know of no other town where such late hours are the vogue, except St Petersburg. But your St Petersburger does not get up early in the morning. At St Petersburg, the music halls, which it is the fashionable thing to attend *after* the theatre—a drive to them taking half an hour in a swift sleigh—do not practically begin till twelve. Through the Neva at four o'clock in the morning you have to literally push your way; and the favourite trains for travellers are those starting about five o'clock in the morning. These trains save the Russian the trouble of getting up early. He wishes his friends 'Good-night,' and drives down to the station comfortably after supper, without putting the house to any inconvenience.

Potsdam, the Versailles to Berlin, is a beautiful little town, situated among lakes and woods. Here in the shady ways of its quiet, far-stretching park of Sans Souci, it is easy to imagine lean, snuffy Frederick 'bummeling' with shrill Voltaire.

Acting on my advice, George and Harris consented not to stay long in Berlin; but to push on to Dresden. Most that Berlin has to show can be seen better elsewhere, and we decided to be content with a drive through the town. The hotel porter introduced us to a Droschke* driver, under whose guidance, so he assured us, we should see everything worth seeing in the shortest possible time. The man himself, who called for us at nine o'clock in the morning, was all that could be desired. He was bright, intelligent, and well-informed; his German was easy to understand, and he knew a little English with which to eke it out on occasion. With the man himself there was no fault to be found, but his horse was the most unsympathetic brute I have ever sat behind.

He took a dislike to us the moment he saw us. I was the first to come out of the hotel. He turned his head, and looked me up and down with a cold, glassy eye; and then he looked across at another horse, a friend of his that was standing facing him. I knew what he said. He had an expressive head, and he made no attempt to disguise his thought. He said:

'Funny things one does come across in the summer time, don't one?'

George followed me out the next moment, and stood behind me. The horse again turned his head and looked. I have never known a horse that could twist himself as this horse did. I have seen a camelopard* do tricks with his neck that compelled one's attention, but this animal was more like the thing one dreams of after a dusty day at Ascot, followed by a dinner with six old chums. If I had seen his eyes looking at me from between his own hind legs, I doubt if I should have been surprised. He seemed more amused with George, if anything, than with myself. He turned to his friend again.

'Extraordinary, isn't it?' he remarked; 'I suppose there must be some place where they grow them'; and then he commenced licking flies off his own left shoulder. I began to wonder whether he had lost his mother when young, and had been brought up by a cat.

George and I climbed in, and sat waiting for Harris. He came a moment later. Myself, I thought he looked rather neat. He wore a white flannel knickerbocker suit, which he had had made specially for bicycling in hot weather; his hat may have been a trifle out of the common, but it did keep the sun off.

The horse gave one look at him, said 'Gott im Himmel!'* as plainly as ever horse spoke, and started off down Friedrich Strasse at a brisk walk, leaving Harris and the driver standing on the pavement. His owner called to him to stop, but he took no notice. They ran after us, and overtook us at the corner of the Dorotheen Strasse. I could not catch what the man said to the horse, he spoke quickly and excitedly; but I gathered a few phrases, such as:

'Got to earn my living somehow, haven't I?' 'Who asked for your opinion?' 'Aye, little you care so long as you can guzzle.'

The horse cut the conversation short by turning up the Dorotheen Strasse on his own account. I think what he said was:

'Come on then; don't talk so much. Let's get the job over, and, where possible, let's keep to the back streets.'

Opposite the Brandenburger Tor* our driver hitched the reins to the whip, climbed down, and came round to explain things to us. He pointed out the Tiergarten,* and then descanted to us of the Reichstag House.* He informed us of its exact height, length, and breadth, after the manner of guides. Then he turned his attention to the Gate. He said it was constructed of sandstone, in imitation of the 'Properleer' in Athens.*

At this point the horse, which had been occupying its leisure licking its own legs, turned round its head. It did not say anything, it just looked.

The man began again nervously. This time he said it was an imitation of the 'Propeyedliar.'

Here the horse proceeded up the Linden, and nothing would persuade him not to proceed up the Linden. His owner expostulated with him, but he continued to trot on. From the way he hitched his shoulders as he moved, I somehow felt he was saying:

'They've seen the Gate, haven't they? Very well, that's enough. As for the rest, you don't know what you're talking about, and they wouldn't understand you if you did. You talk German.'

It was the same throughout the length of the Linden. The horse consented to stand still sufficiently long to enable us to have a good look at each sight, and to hear the name of it. All explanation and description he cut short by the simple process of moving on.

'What these fellows want,' he seemed to say to himself, 'is to go home and tell people they have seen these things. If I am doing them an injustice, if they are more intelligent than they look, they can get better information than this old fool of mine is giving them from the guide book. Who wants to know how high a steeple is? You don't remember it the next five minutes when you are told, and if you do it is because you have got nothing else in your head. He just tires me with his talk. Why doesn't he hurry up, and let us all get home to lunch?'

Upon reflection, I am not sure that wall-eyed old brute had not sense on its side. Anyhow, I know there have been occasions, with a guide, when I would have been glad of its interference.

But one is apt to 'sin one's mercies,' as the Scotch say, and at the time we cursed that horse instead of blessing it.

CHAPTER VII

*George wonders—German love of order—'The Band of the Schwarz-
wald Blackbirds will perform at seven'—The china dog—Its superiority
over all other dogs—The German and the solar system—A tidy country
—The mountain valley as it ought to be, according to the German
idea—How the waters come down in Germany—The scandal of Dresden—Harris gives an entertainment—It is unappreciated—George and
the aunt of him—George, a cushion, and three damsels.*

AT a point between Berlin and Dresden, George, who had, for the
last quarter of an hour or so, been looking very attentively out of the
window, said:

'Why, in Germany, is it the custom to put the letter-box up a tree?
Why do they not fix it to the front door as we do? I should hate having
to climb up a tree to get my letters. Besides, it is not fair to the
postman. In addition to being most exhausting, the delivery of letters
must to a heavy man, on windy nights, be positively dangerous work.
If they will fix it to a tree, why not fix it lower down, why always
among the topmost branches? But, maybe, I am misjudging the
country,' he continued, a new idea occurring to him. 'Possibly the
Germans, who are in many matters ahead of us, have perfected a
pigeon post. Even so, I cannot help thinking they would have been
wiser to train the birds, while they were about it, to deliver the letters
nearer the ground. Getting your letters out of those boxes must be
tricky work even to the average middle-aged German.'

I followed his gaze out of window. I said:

'Those are not letter-boxes, they are birds' nests. You must
understand this nation. The German loves birds, but he likes tidy
birds. A bird left to himself, builds his nest just anywhere. It is not a
pretty object, according to the German notion of prettiness. There is
not a bit of paint on it anywhere, not a plaster image all round, not
even a flag. The nest finished, the bird proceeds to live outside it. He
drops things on the grass; twigs, ends of worms, all sorts of things. He
is indelicate. He makes love, quarrels with his wife, and feeds the
children quite in public. The German householder is shocked. He
says to the bird:

'"For many things I like you. I like to look at you. I like to hear you
sing. But I don't like your ways. Take this little box, and put your

rubbish inside where I can't see it. Come out when you want to sing; but let your domestic arrangements be confined to the interior. Keep to the box, and don't make the garden untidy." '

In Germany one breathes in love of order with the air, in Germany the babies beat time with their rattles, and the German bird has come to prefer the box, and to regard with contempt the few uncivilised outcasts who continue to build their nests in trees and hedges. In course of time every German bird, one is confident, will have his proper place in a full chorus. This promiscuous and desultory warbling of his must, one feels, be irritating to the precise German mind; there is no method in it. The music-loving German will organise him. Some stout bird with a specially well-developed crop will be trained to conduct him, and, instead of wasting himself in a wood at four o'clock in the morning, he will, at the advertised time, sing in a beer garden, accompanied by a piano. Things are drifting that way.

Your German likes nature, but his idea of nature is a glorified Welsh Harp.* He takes great interest in his garden. He plants seven rose trees on the north side and seven on the south, and if they do not grow up all the same size and shape it worries him so that he cannot sleep of nights. Every flower he ties to a stick. This interferes with his view of the flower, but he has the satisfaction of knowing it is there, and that it is behaving itself. The lake is lined with zinc, and once a week he takes it up, carries it into the kitchen, and scours it. In the geometrical centre of the grass plot, which is sometimes as large as a tablecloth and is generally railed round, he places a china dog. The Germans are very fond of dogs, but as a rule they prefer them of china. The china dog never digs holes in the lawn to bury bones, and never scatters a flower-bed to the winds with his hind legs. From the German point of view, he is the ideal dog. He stops where you put him, and he is never where you do not want him. You can have him perfect in all points, according to the latest requirements of the Kennel Club; or you can indulge your own fancy and have something unique. You are not, as with other dogs, limited to breed. In china, you can have a blue dog or a pink dog. For a little extra, you can have a double-headed dog.

On a certain fixed date in the autumn the German stakes his flowers and bushes to the earth, and covers them with Chinese matting; and on a certain fixed date in the spring he uncovers them, and stands them up again. If it happens to be an exceptionally fine autumn, or an exceptionally late spring, so much the worse for the unfortunate vegetable. No true German would allow his arrangements to be interfered with by so unruly a thing as the solar system. Unable to regulate the weather, he ignores it.

Among trees, your German's favourite is the poplar. Other, disorderly, nations may sing the charms of the rugged oak, the spreading chestnut, or the waving elm. To the Germans all such, with their wilful, untidy ways, are eyesores. The poplar grows where it is planted, and how it is planted. It has no improper rugged ideas of its own. It does not want to wave or to spread itself. It just grows straight and upright as a German tree should grow; and so gradually the German is rooting out all other trees, and replacing them with poplars.

Your German likes the country, but he prefers it as the lady thought she would the noble savage, more dressed. He likes his walk through the wood—to a restaurant. But the pathway must not be too steep, it must have a brick gutter running down one side of it to drain it, and every twenty yards or so it must have its seat on which he can rest and mop his brow; for your German would no more think of sitting on the grass than would an English bishop dream of rolling down One Tree Hill. He likes his view from the summit of the hill, but he likes to find there a stone tablet telling him what to look at, and a table and bench at which he can sit to partake of the frugal beer and 'Belegte-Semmel'* he has been careful to bring with him. If, in addition, he can find a police notice posted on a tree, forbidding him to do something or other, that gives him an extra sense of comfort and security.

Your German is not averse even to wild scenery, provided it be not too wild. But if he consider it too savage, he sets to work to tame it. I remember, in the neighbourhood of Dresden, discovering a picturesque and narrow valley leading down towards the Elbe. The winding roadway ran beside a mountain torrent, which for a mile or so fretted and foamed over rocks and boulders between wood-covered banks. I followed it enchanted until, turning a corner, I suddenly came across a gang of eighty or a hundred workmen. They were busy tidying up that valley, and making that stream respectable. All the stones that were impeding the course of the water they were carefully picking out and carting away. The bank on either side they were bricking up and cementing. The overhanging trees and bushes, the tangled vines and creepers they were rooting up and trimming down. A little further I came upon the finished work —the mountain valley, as it ought to be, according to German ideas. The water, now a broad, sluggish stream, flowed over a level, gravelly bed, between two walls, crowned with stone coping. At every hundred yards it gently descended down three shallow wooden platforms. For a space on either side the ground had been cleared, and at regular intervals young poplars planted. Each sapling was protected by a shield of wickerwork and bossed by an iron rod. In the course of a couple of years it is the hope of the local council to have 'finished' that valley throughout its entire length, and made it fit for a tidy-minded lover of German nature to walk in. There will be a seat every fifty yards, a police notice every hundred, and a restaurant every half-mile.

They are doing the same from the Memel to the Rhine. They are just tidying up the country. I remember well the Wehrthal. It was once the most romantic ravine to be found in the Black Forest. The last time I walked down it some hundreds of Italian workmen were encamped there hard at work, training the wild little Wehr the way it should go, bricking the banks for it here, blasting rocks for it there, making cement steps for it down which it can travel soberly and without fuss.

For in Germany there is no nonsense talked about untrammelled nature. In Germany nature has got to behave herself, and not set a bad example to the children. A German poet, noticing waters coming down as Southey* describes, somewhat inexactly, the waters coming down at Lodore, would be too shocked to stop and write alliterative verse about them. He would hurry away, and at once report them to the police. Then their foaming and their shrieking would be of short duration.

'Now then, now then, what's all this about?' the voice of German authority would say severely to the waters. 'We can't have this sort of thing, you know. Come down quietly, can't you? Where do you think you are?'

And the local German council would provide those waters with zinc pipes and wooden troughs, and a corkscrew staircase, and show them how to come down sensibly, in the German manner.

It is a tidy land is Germany.

We reached Dresden on the Wednesday evening, and stayed there over the Sunday.

Taking one consideration with another, Dresden, perhaps, is the most attractive town in Germany; but it is a place to be lived in for a while rather than visited. Its museums and galleries, its palaces and gardens, its beautiful and historically rich environment, provide pleasure for a winter, but bewilder for a week. It has not the gaiety of Paris or Vienna, which quickly palls; its charms are more solidly German, and more lasting. It is the Mecca of the musician. For five shillings, in Dresden, you can purchase a stall at the opera house, together, unfortunately, with a strong disinclination ever again to take the trouble of sitting out a performance in any English, French, or American opera house.

The chief scandal of Dresden still centres round August the Strong,* 'the Man of Sin,' as Carlyle always called him, who is popularly reputed to have cursed Europe with over a thousand children. Castles where he imprisoned this discarded mistress or that—one of them, who persisted in her claim to a better title, for forty years, it is said, poor lady! The narrow rooms where she ate her heart out and died are still shown. Chateaux, shameful for this deed of infamy or that, lie scattered round the neighbourhood like bones about a battlefield; and most of your guide's stories are such as the 'young person' educated in Germany had best not hear. His life-sized portrait hangs in the fine Zwinger, which he built as an arena for his wild beast fights when the people grew tired of them in the market-place; a beetle-browed, frankly animal man, but with the culture and taste that so often wait upon animalism. Modern Dresden undoubtedly owes much to him.

But what the stranger in Dresden stares at most is, perhaps, its electric trams. These huge vehicles flash through the streets at from ten to twenty miles an hour, taking curves and corners after the manner of an Irish car driver. Everybody travels by them, excepting only officers in uniform, who must not. Ladies in evening dress, going to ball or opera, porters with their baskets, sit side by side. They are all-important in the streets, and everything and everybody makes haste to get out of their way. If you do not get out of their way, and you still happen to be alive when picked up, then on your recovery you are fined for having been in their way. This teaches you to be wary of them.

One afternoon Harris took a 'bummel' by himself. In the evening, as we sat listening to the band at the Belvedere, Harris said, *à propos* of nothing in particular, 'These Germans have no sense of humour.'

'What makes you think that?' I asked.

'Why, this afternoon,' he answered, 'I jumped on one of those electric tramcars. I wanted to see the town, so I stood outside on the little platform—what do you call it?'

'The Stehplatz,' I suggested.

'That's it,' said Harris. 'Well, you know the way they shake you about, and how you have to look out for the corners, and mind yourself when they stop and when they start?'

I nodded.

'There were about half a dozen of us standing there,' he continued, 'and, of course, I am not experienced. The thing started suddenly, and that jerked me backwards. I fell against a stout gentleman, just behind me. He could not have been standing very firmly himself, and he, in his turn, fell back against a boy who was carrying a trumpet in a green baize case. They never smiled, neither the man nor the boy with the trumpet; they just stood there and looked sulky. I was going to say I was sorry, but before I could get the words out the tram eased up, for some reason or other, and that, of course, shot me forward again, and I butted into a white-haired old chap, who looked to me like a professor. Well, *he* never smiled, never moved a muscle.'

'Maybe, he was thinking of something else,' I suggested.

'That could not have been the case with them all,' replied Harris, 'and in the course of that journey, I must have fallen against every one of them at least three times. You see,' explained Harris, 'they knew when the corners were coming, and in which direction to brace themselves. I, as a stranger, was naturally at a disadvantage. The way I rolled and staggered about that platform, clutching wildly now at this man and now at that, must have been really comic. I don't say it was high-class humour, but it would have amused most people. Those Germans seemed to see no fun in it whatever—just seemed anxious, that was all. There was one man, a little man, who stood with his back against the brake; I fell against him five times, I counted them. You would have expected the fifth time would have dragged a laugh out of him, but it didn't; he merely looked tired. They are a dull lot.'

George also had an adventure at Dresden. There was a shop near the Altmarkt, in the window of which were exhibited some cushions for sale. The proper business of the shop was handling of glass and china; the cushions appeared to be in the nature of an experiment. They were very beautiful cushions, hand-embroidered on satin. We often passed the shop, and every time George paused and examined those cushions. He said he thought his aunt would like one.

George has been very attentive to this aunt of his during the journey. He has written her quite a long letter every day, and from every town we stop at he sends her off a present. To my mind, he is overdoing the business, and more than once I have expostulated with him. His aunt will be meeting other aunts, and talking to them; the whole class will become disorganised and unruly. As a nephew, I object to the impossible standard that George is setting up. But he will not listen.

Therefore it was that on the Saturday he left us after lunch, saying he would go round to that shop and get one of those cushions for his aunt. He said he would not be long, and suggested our waiting for him.

We waited for what seemed to me rather a long time. When he rejoined us he was empty handed, and looked worried. We asked him where his cushion was. He said he hadn't got a cushion, said he had changed his mind, said he didn't think his aunt would care for a cushion. Evidently something was amiss. We tried to get at the bottom of it, but he was not communicative. Indeed, his answers after our twentieth question or thereabouts became quite short.

In the evening, however, when he and I happened to be alone, he broached the subject himself. He said:

'They are somewhat peculiar in some things, these Germans.'

I said: 'What has happened?'

'Well,' he answered, 'there was that cushion I wanted.'

'For your aunt,' I remarked.

'Why not?' he returned. He was huffy in a moment; I never knew a man so touchy about an aunt. 'Why shouldn't I send a cushion to my aunt?'

'Don't get excited,' I replied. 'I am not objecting; I respect you for it.'

He recovered his temper, and went on:

'There were four in the window, if you remember, all very much alike, and each one labelled in plain figures twenty marks. I don't pretend to speak German fluently, but I can generally make myself understood with a little effort, and gather the sense of what is said to me, provided they don't gabble. I went into the shop. A young girl came up to me; she was a pretty, quiet little soul, one might almost say, demure; not at all the sort of girl from whom you would have expected such a thing. I was never more surprised in all my life.'

'Surprised about what?' I said.

George always assumes you know the end of the story while he is telling you the beginning; it is an annoying method.

'At what happened,' replied George; 'at what I am telling you. She smiled and asked me what I wanted. I understood that all right; there could have been no mistake about that. I put down a twenty mark piece on the counter and said:

'"Please give me a cushion."

'She stared at me as if I had asked for a feather bed. I thought, maybe, she had not heard, so I repeated it louder. If I had chucked her under the chin she could not have looked more surprised or indignant.

'She said she thought I must be making a mistake.

'I did not want to begin a long conversation and find myself stranded. I said there was no mistake. I pointed to my twenty mark piece, and repeated for the third time that I wanted a cushion, "a twenty mark cushion."

'Another girl came up, an elder girl; and the first girl repeated to her what I had just said: she seemed quite excited about it. The second girl did not believe her—did not think I looked the sort of man who would want a cushion. To make sure, she put the question to me herself.

'"Did you say you wanted a cushion?" she asked.

'"I have said it three times," I answered. "I will say it again—I want a cushion."

'She said: "Then you can't have one."

'I was getting angry by this time. If I hadn't really wanted the thing I should have walked out of the shop; but there the cushions were in the window, evidently for sale. I didn't see *why* I couldn't have one.

'I said: "I will have one!" It is a simple sentence. I said it with determination.

'A third girl came up at this point, the three representing, I fancy, the whole force of the shop. She was a bright-eyed, saucy-looking little wench, this last one. On any other occasion I might have been pleased to see her; now, her coming only irritated me. I didn't see the need of three girls for this business.

'The first two girls started explaining the thing to the third girl, and before they were half-way through the third girl began to giggle—she was the sort of girl who would giggle at anything. That done, they fell to chattering like Jenny Wrens, all three together; and between every half-dozen words they looked across at me; and the more they looked at me the more the third girl giggled; and before they had finished they were all three giggling, the little idiots; you might have thought I was a clown, giving a private performance.

'When she was steady enough to move, the third girl came up to me; she was still giggling. She said:

'"If you get it, will you go?"

'I did not quite understand her at first, and she repeated it.

'"This cushion. When you've got it, will you go—away—at once?"

'I was only too anxious to go. I told her so. But I added I was not going without it. I had made up my mind to have that cushion now if I stopped in the shop all night for it.

'She rejoined the other two girls. I thought they were going to get me the cushion and have done with the business. Instead of that, the strangest thing possible happened. The two other girls got behind the first girl, all three still giggling, Heaven knows what about, and pushed her towards me. They pushed her close up to me, and then, before I knew what was happening, she put her hands on my shoulders, stood up on tiptoe, and kissed me. After which, burying her face in her apron, she ran off, followed by the second girl. The third girl opened the door for me, and so evidently expected me to go, that in my confusion I went, leaving my twenty marks behind me. I don't say I minded the kiss, though I did not particularly want it, while I did want the cushion. I don't like to go back to the shop. I cannot understand the thing at all.'

I said: 'What did you ask for?'

He said: 'A cushion.'

I said: 'That is what you wanted, I know. What I mean is, what was the actual German word you said.'

He replied: 'A Kuss.'

I said: 'You have nothing to complain of. It is somewhat confusing.

A "Kuss" sounds as if it ought to be a cushion, but it is not; it is a kiss, while a "Kissen" is a cushion. You muddled up the two words —people have done it before. I don't know much about this sort of thing myself; but you asked for a twenty mark kiss, and from your description of the girl some people might consider the price reasonable. Anyhow, I should not tell Harris. If I remember rightly, he also has an aunt.'

George agreed with me it would be better not.

CHAPTER VIII

Mr and Miss Jones, of Manchester—The benefits of cocoa—A hint to the Peace Society—The window as a mediæval argument—The favourite Christian recreation—The language of the guide—How to repair the ravages of time—George tries a bottle—The fate of the German beer drinker—Harris and I resolve to do a good action—The usual sort of statue—Harris and his friends—A pepperless Paradise—Women and towns.

WE were on our way to Prague, and were waiting in the great hall of the Dresden Station until such time as the powers-that-be should permit us on to the platform. George, who had wandered to the bookstall, returned to us with a wild look in his eyes. He said:

'I've seen it.'

I said, 'Seen what?'

He was too excited to answer intelligently. He said:

'It's here. It's coming this way, both of them. If you wait you'll see it for yourselves. I'm not joking; it's the real thing.'

As is usual about this period, some paragraphs, more or less serious, had been appearing in the papers concerning the sea-serpent, and I thought for the moment he must be referring to this. A moment's reflection, however, told me that here, in the middle of Europe, three hundred miles from the coast, such a thing was impossible. Before I could question him further, he seized me by the arm.

'Look!' he said; 'now am I exaggerating?'

A turned my head and saw what, I suppose, few living Englishmen have ever seen before—the travelling Britisher according to the

Continental idea, accompanied by his daughter. They were coming towards us in the flesh and blood, unless we were dreaming, alive and concrete—the English 'Milor' and the English 'Mees,' as for generations they have been portrayed in the Continental comic press and upon the Continental stage. They were perfect in every detail. The man was tall and thin, with sandy hair, a huge nose, and long Dundreary whiskers.* Over a pepper-and-salt suit he wore a light overcoat, reaching almost to his heels. His white helmet was ornamented with a green veil; a pair of opera-glasses hung at his side, and in his lavender-gloved hand he carried an alpenstock* a little taller than himself. His daughter was long and angular. Her dress I cannot describe: my grandfather, poor gentleman, might have been able to do so; it would have been more familiar to him. I can only say that it appeared to me unnecessarily short, exhibiting a pair of ankles—if I may be permitted to refer to such points—that, from an artistic point of view, called rather for concealment. Her hat made me think of Mrs Hemans;* but why I cannot explain. She wore side-spring boots—'prunella,' I believe, used to be the trade name —mittens, and pince-nez. She also carried an alpenstock (there is not a mountain within a hundred miles of Dresden) and a black bag strapped to her waist. Her teeth stuck out like a rabbit's, and her figure was that of a bolster on stilts.

Harris rushed for his camera, and of course could not find it; he never can when he wants it. Whenever we see Harris scuttling up and down like a lost dog shouting, 'Where's my camera? What the dickens have I done with my camera? Don't either of you remember where I put my camera?'—then we know that for the first time that day he has come across something worth photographing. Later on, he remembered it was in his bag; that is where it would be on an occasion like this.

They were not content with appearance; they acted the thing to the letter. They walked gaping round them at every step. The gentleman had an open Baedeker* in his hand, and the lady carried a phrase book. They talked French that nobody could understand, and German that they could not translate themselves! The man poked at officials with his alpenstock to attract their attention, and the lady, her eye catching sight of an advertisement of somebody's cocoa, said 'Shocking!' and turned the other way.

Really, there was some excuse for her. One notices, even in

England, the home of the proprieties, that the lady who drinks cocoa appears, according to the poster, to require very little else in this world; a yard or so of art muslin at the most. On the Continent she dispenses, so far as one can judge, with every other necessity of life. Not only is cocoa food and drink to her, it should be clothes also, according to the idea of the cocoa manufacturer. But this by the way.

Of course, they immediately became the centre of attraction. By being able to render them some slight assistance, I gained the advantage of five minutes' conversation with them. They were very affable. The gentleman told me his name was Jones, and that he came from Manchester, but he did not seem to know what part of Manchester, or where Manchester was. I asked him where he was going to, but he evidently did not know. He said it depended. I asked him if he did not find an alpenstock a clumsy thing to walk about with through a crowded town; he admitted that occasionally it did get in the way. I asked him if he did not find a veil interfere with his view of things; he explained that you only wore it when the flies became troublesome. I enquired of the lady if she did not find the wind blow cold; she said she had noticed it, especially at the corners. I did not ask these questions one after another as I have here put them down; I mixed them up with general conversation, and we parted on good terms.

I have pondered much upon the apparition, and have come to a definite opinion. A man I met later at Frankfort, and to whom I described the pair, said he had seen them himself in Paris, three weeks after the termination of the Fashoda incident;* while a traveller for some English steel works whom we met in Strassburg remembered having seen them in Berlin during the excitement caused by the Transvaal question.* My conclusion is that they were actors out of work, hired to do this thing in the interest of international peace. The French Foreign Office, wishful to allay the anger of the Parisian mob clamouring for war with England; secured this admirable couple and sent them round the town. You cannot be amused at a thing, and at the same time want to kill it. The French nation saw the English citizen and citizeness—no caricature, but the living reality—and their indignation exploded in laughter. The success of the stratagem prompted them later on to offer their services to the German Government, with the beneficial results that we all know.

Our own Government might learn the lesson. It might be as well to keep near Downing Street a few small, fat Frenchmen, to be sent round the country when occasion called for it, shrugging their shoulders and eating frog sandwiches; or a file of untidy, lank-haired Germans might be retained, to walk about, smoking long pipes, saying 'So.' The public would laugh and exclaim, 'War with such? It would be too absurd.' Failing the Government, I recommend the scheme to the Peace Society.

Our visit to Prague we were compelled to lengthen somewhat. Prague is one of the most interesting towns in Europe. Its stones are saturated with history and romance; its every suburb must have been a battlefield. It is the town that conceived the Reformation and hatched the Thirty Years' War. But half Prague's troubles, one imagines, might have been saved to it, had it possessed windows less large and temptingly convenient. The first of these mighty catastrophes it set rolling by throwing the seven Catholic councillors from the windows of its Rathaus* on to the pikes of the Hussites below. Later, it gave the signal for the second by again throwing the Imperial councillors from the windows of the old Burg in the Hradschin—Prague's second 'Fenstersturz.'* Since, other fateful questions have been decided in Prague; one assumes from their having been concluded without violence that such must have been discussed in cellars. The window, as an argument, one feels, would always have proved too strong a temptation to any true-born Praguer.

In the Teynkirche stands the worm-eaten pulpit from which preached John Huss.* One may hear from the selfsame desk to-day the voice of a Papist priest, while in far-off Constance a rude block of stone, half ivy hidden, marks the spot where Huss and Jerome died burning at the stake. History is fond of her little ironies. In this same Teynkirche lies buried Tycho Brahe, the astronomer, who made the common mistake of thinking the earth, with its eleven hundred creeds and one humanity, the centre of the universe; but who otherwise observed the stars clearly.

Through Prague's dirty, palace-bordered alleys must have pressed often in hot haste blind Ziska and open-minded Wallenstein—they have dubbed him 'The Hero' in Prague; and the town is honestly proud of having owned him for citizen. In his gloomy palace in the Waldstein-Platz they show as a sacred spot the cabinet where he prayed, and seem to have persuaded themselves he really had a soul.

Its steep, winding ways must have been choked a dozen times, now by Sigismund's flying legions, followed by fierce-killing Taborites,* and now by pale Protestants pursued by the victorious Catholics of Maximilian. Now Saxons, now Bavarians, and now French; now the saints of Gustavus Adolphus, and now the steel fighting machines of Frederick the Great, have thundered at its gates and fought upon its bridges.*

The Jews have always been an important feature of Prague. Occasionally they have assisted the Christians in their favourite occupation of slaughtering one another, and the great flag suspended from the vaulting of the Altneuschule testifies to the courage with which they helped Catholic Ferdinand to resist the Protestant Swedes. The Prague Ghetto was one of the first to be established in Europe, and in the tiny synagogue, still standing, the Jew of Prague has worshipped for eight hundred years, his women folk devoutly listening, without, at the ear holes provided for them in the massive walls. A Jewish cemetery adjacent, 'Bethchajim, or the House of Life,' seems as though it were bursting with its dead. Within its narrow acre it was the law of centuries that here or nowhere must the bones of Israel rest. So the worn and broken tombstones lie piled in close confusion, as though tossed and tumbled by the struggling host beneath.

The Ghetto walls have long been levelled, but the living Jews of Prague still cling to their fœtid lanes, though these are being rapidly replaced by fine new streets that promise to eventually transform this quarter into the handsomest part of the town.

At Dresden they advised us not to talk German in Prague. For years racial animosity between the German minority and Czech majority has raged throughout Bohemia, and to be mistaken for a German in certain streets of Prague is inconvenient to a man whose staying powers in a race are not what once they were. However, we did talk German in certain streets in Prague; it was a case of talking German or nothing. The Czech dialect is said to be of great antiquity and of highly scientific cultivation. Its alphabet contains forty-two letters, suggestive to a stranger of Chinese. It is not a language to be picked up in a hurry. We decided that on the whole there would be less risk to our constitution in keeping to German, and as a matter of fact no harm came to us. The explanation I can only surmise. The Praguer is an exceedingly acute person; some subtle falsity of accent, some slight grammatical inaccuracy, may have crept into our German, revealing to him the fact that, in spite of all appearances to the contrary, we were no true-born Deutscher. I do not assert this; I put it forward as a possibility.

To avoid unnecessary danger, however, we did our sight-seeing with the aid of a guide. No guide I have ever come across is perfect. This one had two distinct failings. His English was decidedly weak. Indeed, it was not English at all. I do not know what you would call it. It was not altogether his fault; he had learnt English from a Scotch lady. I understand Scotch fairly well—to keep abreast of modern English literature this is necessary,—but to understand broad Scotch talked with a Slavonic accent, occasionally relieved by German modifications, taxes the intelligence. For the first hour it was difficult to rid one's self of the conviction that the man was choking. Every moment we expected him to die on our hands. In the course of the morning we grew accustomed to him, and rid ourselves of the instinct to throw him on his back every time he opened his mouth, and tear his clothes from him. Later, we came to understand a part of what he said, and this led to the discovery of his second failing.

It would seem he had lately invented a hair-restorer, which he had persuaded a local chemist to take up and advertise. Half his time he had been pointing out to us, not the beauties of Prague, but the benefits likely to accrue to the human race from the use of this concoction; and the conventional agreement with which, under the impression he was waxing eloquent concerning views and architecture, we had met his enthusiasm he had attributed to sympathetic interest in this wretched wash of his.

The result was that now there was no keeping him away from the subject. Ruined palaces and crumbling churches he dismissed with curt reference as mere frivolities, encouraging a morbid taste for the decadent. His duty, as he saw it, was not to lead us to dwell upon the ravages of time, but rather to direct our attention to the means of repairing them. What had we to do with broken-headed heroes, or bald-headed saints? Our interest should be surely in the living world; in the maidens with their flowing tresses, or the flowing tresses they might have, by judicious use of 'Kophkeo,' in the young men with their fierce moustaches—as pictured on the label.

Unconsciously, in his own mind, he had divided the world into two sections. The Past ('Before Use'), a sickly, disagreeable-looking, uninteresting world. The Future ('After Use') a fat, jolly, God-bless-everybody sort of world; and this unfitted him as a guide to scenes of mediæval history.

He sent us each a bottle of the stuff to our hotel. It appeared that in the early part of our converse with him we had, unwittingly, clamoured for it. Personally, I can neither praise it nor condemn it. A long series of disappointments has disheartened me; added to which a permanent atmosphere of paraffin, however faint, is apt to cause remark, especially in the case of a married man. Now, I never try even the sample.

I gave my bottle to George. He asked for it to send to a man he knew in Leeds. I learnt later that Harris had given him his bottle also, to send to the same man.

A suggestion of onions has clung to this tour since we left Prague. George has noticed it himself. He attributes it to the prevalence of garlic in European cooking.

It was in Prague that Harris and I did a kind and friendly thing to George. We had noticed for some time past that George was getting too fond of Pilsener beer. This German beer is an insidious drink, especially in hot weather; but it does not do to imbibe too freely of it. It does not get into your head, but after a time it spoils your waist. I always say to myself on entering Germany:

'Now, I will drink no German beer. The white wine of the country, with a little soda-water; perhaps occasionally a glass of Ems or potash. But beer, never—or, at all events, hardly ever.'

It is a good and useful resolution, which I recommend to all travellers. I only wish I could keep to it myself. George, although I urged him, refused to bind himself by any such hard and fast limit. He said that in moderation German beer was good.

'One glass in the morning,' said George, 'one in the evening, or even two. That will do no harm to anyone.'

Maybe he was right. It was his half-dozen glasses that troubled Harris and myself.

'We ought to do something to stop it,' said Harris; 'it is becoming serious.'

'It's hereditary, so he has explained to me,' I answered. 'It seems his family have always been thirsty.'

'There is Apollinaris water,' replied Harris, 'which, I believe, with a little lemon squeezed into it, is practically harmless. What I am thinking about is his figure. He will lose all his natural elegance.'

We talked the matter over, and, Providence aiding us, we fixed upon a plan. For the ornamentation of the town a new statue had just been cast. I forget of whom it was a statue. I only remember that in the essentials it was the usual sort of street statue, representing the usual sort of gentleman, with the usual stiff neck, riding the usual sort of horse—the horse that always walks on its hind legs, keeping its front paws for beating time. But in detail it possessed individuality. Instead of the usual sword or bâton, the man was holding, stretched out in his hand, his own plumed hat; and the horse, instead of the usual waterfall for a tail, possessed a somewhat attenuated appendage that somehow appeared out of keeping with his ostentatious behaviour. One felt that a horse with a tail like that would not have pranced so much.

It stood in a small square not far from the further end of the Karlsbrücke, but it stood there only temporarily. Before deciding finally where to fix it, the town authorities had resolved, very sensibly, to judge by practical test where it would look best. Accordingly, they had made three rough copies of the statue—mere wooden profiles, things that would not bear looking at closely, but which, viewed from a little distance, produced all the effect that was necessary. One of these they had set up at the approach to the Franz-Josefsbrücke, a second stood in the open space behind the theatre, and the third in the centre of the Wenzelsplatz.

'If George is not in the secret of this thing,' said Harris—we were walking by ourselves for an hour, he having remained behind in the hotel to write a letter to his aunt,—'if he has not observed these statues, then by their aid we will make a better and a thinner man of him, and that this very evening.'

So during dinner we sounded him, judiciously; and finding him ignorant of the matter, we took him out, and led him by side-streets to the place where stood the real statue. George was for looking at it and passing on, as is his way with statues, but we insisted on his pulling up and viewing the thing conscientiously. We walked him round that statue four times, and showed it to him from every possible point of view. I think, on the whole, we rather bored him with the thing, but our object was to impress it upon him. We told him the history of the man that rode upon the horse, the name of the artist who had made the statue, how much it weighed, how much it measured. We worked that statue into his system. By the time we had done with him he knew more about that statue, for the time being, than he knew about anything else. We soaked him in that statue, and only let him go at last on the condition that he would come again with us in the morning, when we could all see it better, and for such purpose we saw to it that he made a note in his pocket-book of the place where the statue stood.

Then we accompanied him to his favourite beer hall, and sat beside him, telling him anecdotes of men who, unaccustomed to German beer, and drinking too much of it, had gone mad and developed homicidal mania; of men who had died young through drinking German beer; of lovers that German beer had been the means of parting for ever from beautiful girls.

At ten o'clock we started to walk back to the hotel. It was a stormy-looking night, with heavy clouds drifting over a light moon. Harris said:

'We won't go back the same way we came; we'll walk back by the river. It is lovely in the moonlight.'

Harris told a sad history, as we walked, about a man he once knew, who is now in a home for harmless imbeciles. He said he recalled the story because it was on just such another night as this that he was walking with that man the very last time he ever saw the poor fellow. They were strolling down the Thames Embankment, Harris said, and the man frightened him then by persisting that he saw the statue of the Duke of Wellington at the corner of Westminster Bridge, when, as everybody knows, it stands in Piccadilly.

It was at this exact instant that we came in sight of the first of these wooden copies. It occupied the centre of a small, railed-in square a little above us on the opposite side of the way. George suddenly stood still and leant against the wall of the quay.

'What's the matter?' I said; 'feeling giddy?'

He said: 'I do, a little. Let's rest here a moment.'

He stood there with his eyes glued to the thing. He said, speaking huskily:

'Talking of statues, what always strikes me is how very much one statue is like another statue.'

Harris said: 'I cannot agree with you there—pictures, if you like. Some pictures are very like other pictures, but with a statue there is always something distinctive. Take that statue we saw early in the evening,' continued Harris, 'before we went into the concert hall. It represented a man sitting on a horse. In Prague you will see other statues of men on horses, but nothing at all like that one.'

'Yes, they are,' said George; 'they are all alike. It's always the same horse, and it's always the same man. They are all exactly alike. It's idiotic nonsense to say they are not.'

He appeared to be angry with Harris.

'What makes you think so?' I asked.

'What makes me think so?' retorted George, now turning upon me. 'Why, look at that damned thing over there!'

I said: 'What damned thing?'

'Why, that thing,' said George; 'look at it! There is the same horse with half a tail, standing on its hind legs; the same man without his hat; the same——'

Harris said: 'You are talking now about the statue we saw in the Ringplatz.'

'No, I'm not,' replied George; 'I'm talking about the statue over there.'

'What statue?' said Harris.

George looked at Harris; but Harris is a man who might, with care, have been a fair amateur actor. His face merely expressed friendly sorrow, mingled with alarm. Next, George turned his gaze on me. I endeavoured, so far as lay with me, to copy Harris's expression, adding to it on my own account a touch of reproof.

'Will you have a cab?' I said as kindly as I could to George. 'I'll run and get one.'

'What the devil do I want with a cab?' he answered, ungraciously. 'Can't you fellows understand a joke? It's like being out with a couple of confounded old women,' saying which, he started off across the bridge, leaving us to follow.

'I am so glad that was only a joke of yours,' said Harris, on our overtaking him. 'I knew a case of softening of the brain that began——'

'Oh, you're a silly ass!' said George, cutting him short; 'you know everything.'

He was really most unpleasant in his manner.

We took him round by the riverside of the theatre. We told him it was the shortest way, and, as a matter of fact, it was. In the open space behind the theatre stood the second of these wooden apparitions. George looked at it, and again stood still.

'What's the matter?' said Harris, kindly. 'You are not ill, are you?'

'I don't believe this is the shortest way,' said George.

'I assure you it is,' persisted Harris.

'Well, I'm going the other,' said George; and he turned and went, we, as before, following him.

Along the Ferdinand Strasse Harris and I talked about private lunatic asylums, which, Harris said, were not well managed in England. He said a friend of his, a patient in a lunatic asylum——

George said, interrupting: 'You appear to have a large number of friends in lunatic asylums.'

He said it in a most insulting tone, as though to imply that that is where one would look for the majority of Harris's friends. But Harris did not get angry; he merely replied, quite mildly:

'Well, it really is extraordinary, when one comes to think of it, how many of them have gone that way sooner or later. I get quite nervous sometimes, now.'

At the corner of the Wenzelsplatz, Harris, who was a few steps ahead of us, paused.

'It's a fine street, isn't it?' he said, sticking his hands in his pockets, and gazing up at it admiringly.

George and I followed suit. Two hundred yards away from us, in its very centre, was the third of these ghostly statues. I think it was the best of the three—the most like, the most deceptive. It stood boldly outlined against the wild sky: the horse on its hind legs, with its curiously attenuated tail; the man bareheaded, pointing with his plumed hat to the now entirely visible moon.

'I think, if you don't mind,' said George—he spoke with almost a pathetic ring in his voice, his aggressiveness had completely fallen from him,—'that I will have that cab, if there's one handy.'

'I thought you were looking queer,' said Harris, kindly. 'It's your head, isn't it?'

'Perhaps it is,' answered George.

'I have noticed it coming on,' said Harris; 'but I didn't like to say anything to you. You fancy you see things, don't you?'

'No, no; it isn't that,' replied George, rather quickly. 'I don't know what it is.'

'I do,' said Harris, solemnly, 'and I'll tell you. It's this German beer that you are drinking. I have known a case where a man——'

'Don't tell me about him just now,' said George. 'I dare say it's true, but somehow I don't feel I want to hear about him.'

'You are not used to it,' said Harris.

'I shall give it up from to-night,' said George. 'I think you must be right; it doesn't seem to agree with me.'

We took him home, and saw him to bed. He was very gentle and quite grateful.

One evening later on, after a long day's ride, followed by a most satisfactory dinner, we started him on a big cigar, and, removing things from his reach, told him of this strategem that for his good we had planned.

'How many copies of that statue did you say we saw?' asked George, after we had finished.

'Three,' replied Harris.

'Only three?' said George. 'Are you sure?'

'Positive,' replied Harris. 'Why?'

'Oh, nothing!' answered George.

But I don't think he quite believed Harris.

From Prague we travelled to Nuremberg, through Carlsbad. Good Germans, when they die, go, they say, to Carlsbad, as good Americans to Paris. This I doubt, seeing that it is a small place with no convenience for a crowd. In Carlsbad, you rise at five, the fashionable hour for promenade, when the band plays under the Colonnade, and the Sprudel is filled with a packed throng over a mile long, being from six to eight in the morning. Here you may hear more languages spoken than the Tower of Babel could have echoed. Polish Jews and Russian princes, Chinese mandarins and Turkish pashas, Norwegians looking as if they had stepped out of Ibsen's plays,* women from the Boulevards, Spanish grandees and English countesses, mountaineers from Montenegro and millionaires from Chicago, you will find every dozen yards. Every luxury in the world Carlsbad provides for its visitors, with the one exception of pepper. That you cannot get within five miles of the town for money; what you can get there for love is not worth taking away. Pepper, to the liver brigade that forms four-fifths of Carlsbad's customers, is poison; and, prevention being better than cure, it is carefully kept out of the neighbourhood. 'Pepper parties' are formed in Carlsbad to journey to some place without the boundary, and there indulge in pepper orgies.

Nuremberg, if one expects a town of mediæval appearance, disappoints. Quaint corners, picturesque glimpses, there are in plenty; but everywhere they are surrounded and intruded upon by the modern, and even what is ancient is not nearly so ancient as one thought it was. After all, a town, like a woman, is only as old as it looks; and Nuremberg is still a comfortable-looking dame, its age somewhat difficult to conceive under its fresh paint and stucco in the blaze of the gas and the electric light. Still, looking closely, you may see its wrinkled walls and grey towers.

CHAPTER IX

Harris breaks the Law—The helpful man: The dangers that beset him— George sets forth upon a career of crime—Those to whom Germany would come as a boon and a blessing—The English Sinner: His disappointments —The German Sinner: His exceptional advantages—What you may not do with your bed—An inexpensive vice—The German dog: His simple goodness—The misbehaviour of the beetle—A people that go the way they ought to go—The German small boy: His love of legality—How to go astray with a perambulator—The German student: His chastened wilfulness.

ALL three of us, by some means or another, managed, between Nuremberg and the Black Forest, to get into trouble.

Harris led off at Stuttgart by insulting an official. Stuttgart is a charming town, clean and bright, a smaller Dresden. It has the additional attraction of containing little that one need to go out of one's way to see: a medium-sized picture gallery, a small museum of antiquities, and half a palace, and you are through with the entire thing and can enjoy yourself. Harris did not know it was an official he was insulting. He took it for a fireman (it looked like a fireman), and he called it a 'dummer Esel.'

In Germany you are not permitted to call an official a 'silly ass,' but undoubtedly this particular man was one. What had happened was this: Harris in the Stadtgarten,* anxious to get out, and seeing a gate open before him, had stepped over a wire into the street. Harris maintains he never saw it, but undoubtedly there was hanging to the wire a notice, 'Durchgang Verboten!' The man, who was standing near the gate, stopped Harris, and pointed out to him this notice. Harris thanked him, and passed on. The man came after him, and explained that treatment of the matter in such off-hand way could not be allowed; what was necessary to put the business right was that Harris should step back over the wire into the garden. Harris pointed out to the man that the notice said 'going through forbidden,' and that, therefore, by re-entering the garden that way he would be infringing the law a second time. The man saw this for himself, and suggested that to get over the difficulty Harris should go back into the garden by the proper entrance, which was round the corner, and afterwards immediately come out again by the same gate. Then it was that Harris called the man a silly ass. That delayed us a day, and cost Harris forty marks.

I followed suit at Carlsruhe, by stealing a bicycle. I did not mean to steal the bicycle; I was merely trying to be useful. The train was on the point of starting when I noticed, as I thought, Harris's bicycle still in the goods van. No one was about to help me. I jumped into the van and hauled it out, only just in time. Wheeling it down the platform in triumph, I came across Harris's bicycle, standing against a wall behind some milk-cans. The bicycle I had secured was not Harris's, but some other man's.

It was an awkward situation. In England, I should have gone to the stationmaster and explained my mistake. But in Germany they are not content with your explaining a little matter of this sort to one man: they take you round and get you to explain it to about half a dozen; and if any one of the half dozen happens not to be handy, or not to have time just then to listen to you, they have a habit of leaving you over for the night to finish your explanation the next morning. I thought I would just put the thing out of sight, and then, without making any fuss or show, take a short walk. I found a wood shed, which seemed just the very place, and was wheeling the bicycle into it when, unfortunately, a red-hatted railway official, with the airs of a retired field-marshal, caught sight of me and came up. He said:

'What are you doing with that bicycle?'

I said: 'I am going to put it in this wood shed out of the way.' I tried to convey by my tone that I was performing a kind and thoughtful action, for which the railway officials ought to thank me; but he was unresponsive.

'Is it your bicycle?' he said.

'Well, not exactly,' I replied.

'Whose is it?' he asked, quite sharply.

'I can't tell you,' I answered. 'I don't know whose bicycle it is.'

'Where did you get it from?' was his next question. There was a suspiciousness about his tone that was almost insulting.

'I got it,' I answered, with as much calm dignity as at the moment I could assume, 'out of the train. The fact is,' I continued, frankly, 'I have made a mistake.'

He did not allow me time to finish. He merely said he thought so too, and blew a whistle.

Recollection of the subsequent proceedings is not, so far as I am concerned, amusing. By a miracle of good luck—they say Providence watches over certain of us—the incident happened in Carlsruhe, where I possess a German friend, an official of some importance. Upon what would have been my fate had the station not been in Carlsruhe, or had my friend been from home, I do not care to dwell; as it was I got off, as the saying is, by the skin of my teeth. I should like to add that I left Carlsruhe without a stain upon my character, but that would not be the truth. My going scot free is regarded in police circles there to this day as a grave miscarriage of justice.

But all lesser sin sinks into insignificance beside the lawlessness of George. The bicycle incident had thrown us all into confusion, with the result that we lost George altogether. It transpired subsequently that he was waiting for us outside the police court; but this at the time we did not know. We thought, maybe, he had gone on to Baden by himself; and anxious to get away from Carlsruhe, and not, perhaps, thinking out things too clearly, we jumped into the next train that came up and proceeded thither. When George, tired of waiting, returned to the station, he found us gone and he found his luggage gone. Harris had his ticket; I was acting as banker to the party, so that he had in his pocket only some small change. Excusing himself upon these grounds, he thereupon commenced deliberately a career of crime that, reading it later, as set forth baldly in the official summons, made the hair of Harris and myself almost to stand on end.

German travelling, it may be explained, is somewhat complicated. You buy a ticket at the station you start from for the place you want to go to. You might think this would enable you to get there, but it does not. When your train comes up, you attempt to swarm into it; but the guard magnificently waves you away. Where are your credentials? You show him your ticket. He explains to you that by itself that is of no service whatever; you have only taken the first step towards travelling; you must go back to the booking-office and get in addition what is called a 'Schnellzug ticket.'* With this you return, thinking your troubles over. You are allowed to get in, so far so good. But you must not sit down anywhere, and you must not stand still, and you must not wander about. You must take another ticket, this time what is called a 'Platz ticket,'* which entitles you to a place for a certain distance.

What a man could do who persisted in taking nothing but the one ticket, I have often wondered. Would he be entitled to run behind the train on the six-foot way? Or could he stick a label on himself and get into the goods van? Again, what could be done with the man who, having taken his Schnellzug ticket, obstinately refused, or had not the money to take a Platz ticket: would they let him lie in the umbrella rack, or allow him to hang himself out of the window?

To return to George, he had just sufficient money to take a third-class slow train ticket to Baden, and that was all. To avoid the inquisitiveness of the guard, he waited till the train was moving, and then jumped in.

That was his first sin:

    (*a*) Entering a train in motion;

    (*b*) After being warned not to do so by an official.

Second sin:

    (*a*) Travelling in train of superior class to that for which ticket was held.

    (*b*) Refusing to pay difference when demanded by an official. (George says he did not 'refuse'; he simply told the man he had not got it.)

Third sin:

    (*a*) Travelling in carriage of superior class to that for which ticket was held;

    (*b*) Refusing to pay difference when demanded by an official. (Again George disputes the accuracy of the report. He turned his pockets out, and offered the man all he had, which was about eightpence in German money. He offered to go into a third class, but there was no third class. He offered to go into the goods van, but they would not hear of it.)

Fourth sin:

    (*a*) Occupying seat, and not paying for same;

    (*b*) Loitering about corridor. (As they would not let him sit down without paying, and as he could not pay, it was difficult to see what else he could do.)

But explanations are held as no excuse in Germany; and his journey from Carlsruhe to Baden was one of the most expensive perhaps on record.

Reflecting upon the ease and frequency with which one gets into trouble here in Germany, one is led to the conclusion that this country would come as a boon and a blessing to the average young Englishman. To the medical student, to the eater of dinners at the Temple,* to the subaltern on leave, life in London is a wearisome proceeding. The healthy Briton takes his pleasure lawlessly, or it is no pleasure to him. Nothing that he may do affords to him any genuine satisfaction. To be in trouble of some sort is his only idea of bliss. Now, England affords him small opportunity in this respect; to get himself into a scrape requires a good deal of persistence on the part of the young Englishman.

I spoke on this subject one day with our senior churchwarden. It was the morning of the 10th of November, and we were both of us glancing, somewhat anxiously, through the police reports. The usual batch of young men had been summoned for creating the usual disturbance the night before at the Criterion.* My friend the churchwarden has boys of his own, and a nephew of mine, upon whom I am keeping a fatherly eye, is by a fond mother supposed to be in London for the sole purpose of studying engineering. No names we knew happened, by fortunate chance, to be in the list of those detained in custody, and, relieved, we fell to moralising upon the folly and depravity of youth.

'It is very remarkable,' said my friend the churchwarden, 'how the Criterion retains its position in this respect. It was just so when I was young; the evening always wound up with a row at the Criterion.'

'So meaningless,' I remarked.

'So monotonous,' he replied. 'You have no idea,' he continued, a dreamy expression stealing over his furrowed face, 'how unutterably tired one can become of the walk from Piccadilly Circus to the Vine Street Police Court. Yet, what else was there for us to do? Simply nothing. Sometimes we would put out a street lamp, and a man would come round and light it again. If one insulted a policeman, he simply took no notice. He did not even know he was being insulted; or, if he did, he seemed not to care. You could fight a Covent Garden porter, if you fancied yourself at that sort of thing. Generally speaking, the porter got the best of it; and when he did it cost you five shillings, and when he did not the price was half a sovereign. I could never see much excitement in that particular sport. I tried driving a hansom cab once. That has always been regarded as the acme of modern Tom and Jerryism.* I stole it late one night from outside a public-house in Dean Street, and the first thing that happened to me was that I was hailed in Golden Square by an old lady surrounded by three children, two of them crying and the third one half asleep. Before I could get away she had shot the brats into the cab, taken my number, paid me, so she said, a shilling over the legal fare, and directed me to an address a little beyond what she called North Kensington. As a matter of fact, the place turned out to be the other side of Willesden. The horse was tired, and the journey took us well over two hours. It was the slowest lark I ever remember being concerned in. I tried once or twice to persuade the children to let me take them back to the old lady: but every time I opened the trap-door to speak to them the youngest one, a boy, started screaming; and when I offered other drivers to transfer the job to them, most of them replied in the words of a song popular about that period: "Oh, George, don't you think you're going just a bit too far?" One man offered to take home to my wife any last message I might be thinking of, while another promised to organise a party to come and dig me out in the spring. When I mounted the dickey I had imagined myself driving a peppery old colonel to some lonesome and cabless region, half a dozen miles from where he wanted to go, and there leaving him upon the kerb-stone to swear. About that there might have been good sport or there might not, according to circumstances and the colonel. The idea of a trip to an outlying suburb in charge of a nursery full of helpless infants had never occurred to me. No, London,' concluded my friend the churchwarden with a sigh, 'affords but limited opportunity to the lover of the illegal.'

Now, in Germany, on the other hand, trouble is to be had for the asking. There are many things in Germany that you must not do that are quite easy to do. To any young Englishman yearning to get himself into a scrape, and finding himself hampered in his own country, I would advise a single ticket to Germany; a return, lasting as it does only a month, might prove a waste.

In the Police Guide of the Fatherland he will find set forth a list of the things the doing of which will bring to him interest and excitement. In Germany you must not hang your bed out of window. He might begin with that. By waving his bed out of window he could get into trouble before he had his breakfast. At home he might hang himself out of window, and nobody would mind much, provided he did not obstruct anybody's ancient lights or break away and injure any passer underneath.

In Germany you must not wear fancy dress in the streets. A Highlander of my acquaintance who came to pass the winter in Dresden spent the first few days of his residence there in arguing this question with the Saxon Government. They asked him what he was doing in those clothes. He was not an amiable man. He answered, he was wearing them. They asked him why he was wearing them. He replied, to keep himself warm. They told him frankly that they did not believe him, and sent him back to his lodgings in a closed landau. The personal testimony of the English Minister was necessary to assure the authorities that the Highland garb was the customary dress of many respectable, law-abiding British subjects. They accepted the statement, as diplomatically bound, but retain their private opinion to this day. The English tourist they have grown accustomed to; but a Leicestershire gentleman, invited to hunt with some German officers, on appearing outside his hotel, was promptly marched off, horse and all, to explain his frivolity at the police court.

Another thing you must not do in the streets of German towns is to feed horses, mules, or donkeys, whether your own or those belonging to other people. If a passion seizes you to feed somebody else's horse, you must make an appointment with the animal, and the meal must take place in some properly authorised place. You must not break glass or china in the street, nor, in fact, in any public resort whatever; and if you do, you must pick up all the pieces. What you are to do with the pieces when you have gathered them together I cannot say. The only thing I know for certain is that you are not permitted to throw them anywhere, to leave them anywhere, or apparently to part with them in any way whatever. Presumably, you are expected to carry them about with you until you die, and then be buried with them; or, maybe, you are allowed to swallow them.

In German streets you must not shoot with a crossbow. The German law-maker does not content himself with the misdeeds of the average man—the crime one feels one wants to do, but must not: he worries himself imagining all the things a wandering maniac might do. In Germany there is now law against a man standing on his head in the middle of the road; the idea has not occurred to them. One of these days a German statesman, visiting a circus and seeing acrobats, will reflect upon this omission. Then he will straightway set to work and frame a clause forbidding people from standing on their heads in the middle of the road, and fixing a fine. This is the charm of German law: misdemeanour in Germany has its fixed price. You are not kept awake all night, as in England, wondering whether you will get off with a caution, be fined forty shillings, or, catching the magistrate in an unhappy moment for yourself, get seven days. You know exactly what your fun is going to cost you. You can spread out your money on the table, open your Police Guide, and plan out your holiday to a fifty pfennig piece. For a really cheap evening, I would recommend walking on the wrong side of the pavement after because cautioned not to do so. I calculate that by choosing your district and keeping to the quiet side streets you could walk for a whole evening on the wrong side of the pavement at a cost of little over three marks.

In German towns you must not ramble about after dark 'in droves.' I am not quite sure how many constitute a 'drove,' and no official to whom I have spoken on this subject has felt himself competent to fix the exact number. I once put it to a German friend who was starting for the theatre with his wife, his mother-in-law, five children of his own, his sister and her *fiancé*, and two nieces, if he did not think he was running a risk under this by-law. He did not take my suggestion as a joke. He cast an eye over the group.

'Oh, I don't think so,' he said; 'you see, we are all one family.'

'The paragraph says nothing about its being a family drove or not,' I replied; 'it simply says "drove." I do not mean it in any uncomplimentary sense, but, speaking etymologically, I am inclined personally to regard your collection as a "drove." Whether the police will take the same view or not remains to be seen. I am merely warning you.'

My friend himself was inclined to pooh-pooh my fears; but his wife thinking it better not to run any risk of having the party broken up by the police at the very beginning of the evening, they divided, arranging to come together again in the theatre lobby.

Another passion you must restrain in Germany is that prompting you to throw things out of window. Cats are no excuse. During the first week of my residence in Germany I was awakened incessantly by cats. One night I got mad. I collected a small arsenal—two or three pieces of coal, a few hard pears, a couple of candle ends, an odd egg I found on the kitchen table, an empty soda-water bottle, and a few articles of that sort,—and, opening the window, bombarded the spot from where the noise appeared to come. I do not suppose I hit anything; I never knew a man who did hit a cat, even when he could see it, except, maybe, by accident when aiming at something else. I have known crack shots, winners of Queen's prizes—those sort of men,—shoot with shot-guns at cats fifty yards away, and never hit a hair. I have often thought that, instead of bull's-eyes, running deer, and that rubbish, the really superior marksman would be he who could boast that he had shot the cat.

But, anyhow, they moved off; maybe the egg annoyed them. I had noticed when I picked it up that it did not look a good egg; and I went back to bed again, thinking the incident closed. Ten minutes afterwards there came a violent ringing of the electric bell. I tried to ignore it, but it was too persistent, and, putting on my dressing gown, I went down to the gate. A policeman was standing there. He had all the things I had been throwing out of the window in a little heap in front of him, all except the egg. He had evidently been collecting them. He said:

'Are these things yours?'

I said: 'They were mine, but personally I have done with them. Anybody can have them—you can have them.'

He ignored my offer. He said:

'You threw these things out of window.'

'You are right,' I admitted; 'I did.'

'Why did you throw them out of window?' he asked. A German policeman has his code of questions arranged for him; he never varies them, and he never omits one.

'I threw them out of the window at some cats,' I answered.

'What cats?' he asked.

It was the sort of question a German policeman would ask. I

replied with as much sarcasm as I could put into my accent that I was ashamed to say I could not tell him what cats. I explained that, personally, they were strangers to me; but I offered, if the police would call all the cats in the district together, to come round and see if I could recognise them by their yaul.

The German policeman does not understand a joke, which is perhaps on the whole just as well, for I believe there is a heavy fine for joking with any German uniform; they call it 'treating an official with contumely.' He merely replied that it was not the duty of the police to help me recognise the cats; their duty was merely to fine me for throwing things out of window.

I asked what a man was supposed to do in Germany when woke up night after night by cats, and he explained that I could lodge an information against the owner of the cat, when the police would proceed to caution him, and, if necessary, order the cat to be destroyed. Who was going to destroy the cat, and what the cat would be doing during the process, he did not explain.

I asked him how he proposed I should discover the owner of the cat. He thought for a while, and then suggested that I might follow it home. I did not feel inclined to argue with him any more after that; I should only have said things that would have made the matter worse. As it was, that night's sport cost me twelve marks; and not a single one of the four German officials who interviewed me on the subject could see anything ridiculous in the proceedings from beginning to end.

But in Germany most human faults and follies sink into comparative insignificance beside the enormity of walking on the grass. Nowhere, and under no circumstances, may you at any time in Germany walk on the grass. Grass in Germany is quite a fetish. To put your foot on German grass would be as great a sacrilege as to dance a hornpipe on a Mohammedan's praying-mat. The very dogs respect German grass; no German dog would dream of putting a paw on it. If you see a dog scampering across the grass in Germany, you may know for certain that it is the dog of some unholy foreigner. In England, when we want to keep dogs out of places, we put up wire netting, six feet high, supported by buttresses, and defended on the top by spikes. In Germany, they put a notice-board in the middle of the place, 'Hunde verboten,'* and a dog that has German blood in its veins looks at that notice-board and walks away. In a German park I have seen a gardener step gingerly with felt boots on to a grass-plot, and, removing therefrom a beetle, place it gravely but firmly on the gravel; which done, he stood sternly watching the beetle, to see that it did not try to get back on the grass; and the beetle, looking utterly ashamed of itself, walked hurriedly down the gutter, and turned up the path marked 'Ausgang.'*

In German parks separate roads are devoted to the different orders of the community, and no one person, at peril of liberty and fortune, may go upon another person's road. There are special paths for 'wheel-riders' and special paths for 'foot-goers,' avenues for 'horse-riders,' roads for people in light vehicles, and roads for people in heavy vehicles; ways for children and for 'alone ladies.' That no particular route has yet been set aside for bald-headed men or 'new women'* has always struck me as an omission.

In the Grosse Garten in Dresden I once came across an old lady, standing, helpless and bewildered, in the centre of seven tracks. Each was guarded by a threatening notice, warning everybody off it by the person for whom it was intended.

'I am sorry to trouble you,' said the old lady, on learning I could speak English and read German, 'but would you mind telling me what I am and where I have to go?'

I inspected her carefully. I came to the conclusion that she was a 'grown up' and a 'foot-goer,' and pointed out her path. She looked at it, and seemed disappointed.

'But I don't want to go down there,' she said; 'mayn't I go this way?'

'Great heavens, no, madam!' I replied. 'That path is reserved for children.'

'But I wouldn't do them any harm,' said the old lady, with a smile. She did not look the sort of old lady who would have done them any harm.

'Madam,' I replied, 'if it rested with me, I would trust you down that path, though my own first-born were at the other end; but I can only inform you of the laws of this country. For you, a full-grown woman, to venture down that path is to go to certain fine, if not imprisonment. There is your path, marked plainly—*Nur für Fussgänger*,* and if you will follow my advice, you will hasten down it; you are not allowed to stand here and hesitate.'

'It doesn't lead a bit in the direction I want to go,' said the old lady.

'It leads in the direction you *ought* to want to go,' I replied, and we parted.

In the German parks there are special seats labelled, 'Only for grown-ups' (*Nur für Erwachsene*), and the German small boy, anxious to sit down, and reading that notice, passes by, and hunts for a seat on which children are permitted to rest; and there he seats himself, careful not to touch the woodwork with his muddy boots. Imagine a seat in Regent's or St James's Park labelled 'Only for grown-ups!' Every child for five miles round would be trying to get on that seat, and hauling other children off who were on. As for any 'grown-up,' he would never be able to get within half a mile of that seat for the crowd. The German small boy, who has accidentally sat down on such without noticing, rises with a start when his error is pointed out to him, and goes away with downcast head, blushing to the roots of his hair with shame and regret.

Not that the German child is neglected by a paternal Government. In German parks and public gardens special places (*Spielplätze*) are provided for him, each one supplied with a heap of sand. There he can play to his heart's content at making mud pies and building sand castles. To the German child a pie made of any other mud than this would appear an immoral pie. It would give to him no satisfaction: his soul would revolt against it.

'That pie,' he would say to himself, 'was not, as it should have been, made of Government mud specially set apart for the purpose; it was not manufactured in the place, planned and maintained by the Government for the making of mud pies. It can bring no real blessing with it; it is a lawless pie.' And until his father had paid the proper fine, and he had received his proper licking, his conscience would continue to trouble him.

Another excellent piece of material for obtaining excitement in Germany is the simple domestic perambulator. What you may do with a 'Kinderwagen,' as it is called, and what you may not, covers pages of German law; after the reading of which, you conclude that the man who can push a perambulator through a German town without breaking the law was meant for a diplomatist. You must not loiter with a perambulator, and you must not go too fast. You must not get in anybody's way with a perambulator, and if anybody gets in your way you must get out of their way. If you want to stop with a perambulator, you ·nust go to a place specially appointed where perambulators may stop; and when you get there you *must* stop. You must not cross the road with a perambulator; if you and the baby happen to live on the other side, that is your fault. You must not leave your perambulator anywhere, and only in certain places can you take it with you. I should say that in Germany you could go out with a perambulator and get into enough trouble in half an hour to last you for a month. Any young Englishman anxious for a row with the police could not do better than come over to Germany and bring his perambulator with him.

In Germany you must not leave your front door unlocked after ten o'clock at night, and you must not play the piano in your own house after eleven. In England I have never felt I wanted to play the piano myself, or to hear anyone else play it, after eleven o'clock at night; but that is a very different thing to being told that you must not play it. Here, in Germany, I never feel that I really care for the piano until eleven o'clock, then I could sit and listen to the 'Maiden's Prayer,' or the Overture to 'Zampa,'* with pleasure. To the law-loving German, on the other hand, music after eleven o'clock at night ceases to be music; it becomes sin, and as such gives him no satisfaction.

The only individual throughout Germany who ever dreams of taking liberties with the law is the German student, and he only to a certain well-defined point. By custom, certain privileges are permitted to him, but even these are strictly limited and clearly understood. For instance, the German student may get drunk and fall asleep in the gutter with no other penalty than that of having the next morning to tip the policeman who has found him and brought him home. But for this purpose he must choose the gutters of side-streets. The German student, conscious of the rapid approach of oblivion, uses all his remaining energy to get round the corner, where he may collapse without anxiety. In certain districts he may ring bells. The rent of flats in these localities is lower than in other quarters of the town; while the difficulty is further met by each family preparing for itself a secret code of bell-ringing by means of which it is known whether the summons is genuine or not. When visiting such a household late at night it is well to be acquainted with this code, or you may, if persistent, get a bucket of water thrown over you.

Also the German student is allowed to put out lights at night, but there is a prejudice against his putting out too many. The larky German student generally keeps count, contenting himself with half a dozen lights per night. Likewise, he may shout and sing as he walks home, up till half-past two; and at certain restaurants it is permitted to him to put his arm round the Fräulein's waist. To prevent any suggestion of unseemliness, the waitresses at restaurants frequented by students are always carefully selected from among a staid and elderly class of women, by reason of which the German student can enjoy the delights of flirtation without fear and without reproach to anyone.

They are a law-abiding people, the Germans.

CHAPTER X

Baden Baden from the visitor's point of view—Beauty of the early morning, as viewed from the preceding afternoon—Distance, as measured by the compass—Ditto, as measured by the leg—George in account with his conscience—A lazy machine—Bicycling, according to the poster: its restfulness—The poster cyclist: its costume; its method—The griffin as a household pet—A dog with proper self-respect—The horse that was abused.

FROM Baden, about which it need only be said that it is a pleasure resort singularly like other pleasure resorts of the same description, we started bicycling in earnest. We planned a ten days' tour, which, while completing the Black Forest, should include a spin down the Donau-Thal, which for the twenty miles from Tuttlingen to Sigmaringen is, perhaps, the finest valley in Germany; the Danube stream here winding its narrow way past old-world unspoilt villages; past ancient monasteries, nestling in green pastures, where still the barefooted and bare-headed friar, his rope girdle tight about his loins, shepherds, with crook in hand, his sheep upon the hill sides; through rocky woods; between sheer walls of cliff, whose every towering crag stands crowned with ruined fortress, church, or castle; together with a Blick* at the Vosges mountains, where half the population is bitterly pained if you speak to them in French, the other half being insulted when you address them in German, and the whole indignantly contemputuous at the first sound of English; a state of things that renders conversation with the stranger somewhat nervous work.

We did not succeed in carrying out our programme in its entirety, for the reason that human performance lags ever behind human intention. It is easy to say and believe at three o'clock in the afternoon that: 'We will rise at five, breakfast lightly at half-past, and start away at six.'

'Then we shall be well on our way before the heat of the day sets in,' remarks one.

'This time of the year, the early morning is really the best part of the day. Don't you think so?' adds another.

'Oh, undoubtedly.'

'So cool and fresh.'

'And the half-lights are so exquisite.'

The first morning one maintains one's vows. The party assembles at half-past five. It is very silent; individually, somewhat snappy; inclined to grumble with its food, also with most other things; the atmosphere charged with compressed irritability seeking its vent. In the evening the Tempter's voice is heard:

'I think if we got off by half-past six, sharp, that would be time enough?'

The voice of Virtue protests, faintly: 'It will be breaking our resolution.'

The Tempter replies: 'Resolutions were made for man, not man for resolutions.'* The devil can paraphrase Scripture* for his own purpose. 'Besides, it is disturbing the whole hotel; think of the poor servants.'

The voice of Virtue continues, but even feebler: 'But everybody gets up early in these parts.'

'They would not if they were not obliged to, poor things! Say breakfast at half-past six, punctual; that will be disturbing nobody.'

Thus Sin masquerades under the guise of Good, and one sleeps till six, explaining to one's conscience, who, however, doesn't believe it, that one does this because of unselfish consideration for others. I have known such consideration extend until seven of the clock.

Likewise, distance measured with a pair of compasses is not precisely the same as when measured by the leg.

'Ten miles an hour for seven hours, seventy miles. A nice easy day's work.'

'There are some stiff hills to climb?'

'The other side to come down. Say, eight miles an hour, and call it sixty miles. Gott im Himmel! if we can't average eight miles an hour, we had better go in bath-chairs.' It does seem somewhat impossible to do less, on paper.

But at four o'clock in the afternoon the voice of Duty rings less trumpet-toned:

'Well, I suppose we ought to be getting on.'

'Oh, there's no hurry! don't fuss. Lovely view from here, isn't it?'

'Very. Don't forget we are twenty-five miles from St Blasien.'

'How far?'

'Twenty-five miles, a little over if anything.'

'Do you mean to say we have only come thirty-five miles?'

'That's all.'

'Nonsense. I don't believe that map of yours.'

'It is impossible, you know. We have been riding steadily ever since the first thing this morning.'

'No, we haven't. We didn't get away till eight, to begin with.'

'Quarter to eight.'

'Well, quarter to eight; and every half-dozen miles we have stopped.'

'We have only stopped to look at the view. It's no good coming to see a country, and then not seeing it.'

'And we have had to pull up some stiff hills.'

'Besides, it has been an exceptionally hot day to-day.'

'Well, don't forget St Blasien is twenty-five miles off, that's all.'

'Any more hills?'

'Yes, two; up and down.'

'I thought you said it was downhill into St Blasien?'

'So it is for the last ten miles. We are twenty-five miles from St Blasien here.'

'Isn't there anywhere between here and St Blasien? What's that little place there on the lake?'

'It isn't St Blasien, or anywhere near it. There's a danger in beginning that sort of thing.'

'There's a danger in overworking oneself. One should study moderation in all things. Pretty little place, that Titisee, according to the map; looks as if there would be good air there.'

'All right, I'm agreeable. It was you fellows who suggested our making for St Blasien.'

'Oh, I'm not so keen on St Blasien! poky little place, down in a valley. This Titisee, I should say, was ever so much nicer.'

'Quite near, isn't it?'

'Five miles.'

General chorus: 'We'll stop at Titisee.'

George made discovery of this difference between theory and practice on the very first day of our ride.

'I thought,' said George—he was riding the single, Harris and I being a little ahead on the tandem—'that the idea was to train up the hills and ride down them.'

'So it is,' answered Harris, 'as a general rule. But the trains don't go up *every* hill in the Black Forest.'

'Somehow, I felt a suspicion that they wouldn't,' growled George; and for a while silence reigned.

'Besides,' remarked Harris, who had evidently been ruminating the subject, 'you would not wish to have nothing but downhill, surely. It would not be playing the game. One must take a little rough with one's smooth.'

Again there returned silence, broken after awhile by George, this time.

'Don't you two fellows over-exert yourselves merely on my account,' said George.

'How to you mean?' asked Harris.

'I mean,' answered George, 'that where a train does happen to be going up these hills, don't you put aside the idea of taking it for fear of outraging my finer feelings. Personally, I am prepared to go up all these hills in a railway train, even if it's not playing the game. I'll square the thing with my conscience; I've been up at seven every day for a week now, and I calculate it owes me a bit. Don't you consider me in the matter at all.'

We promised to bear this in mind, and again the ride continued in dogged dumbness, until it was again broken by George.

'What bicycle did you say this was of yours?' asked George.

Harris told him. I forget of what particular manufacture it happened to be; it is immaterial.

'Are you sure?' persisted George.

'Of course I am sure,' answered Harris. 'Why, what's the matter with it?'

'Well, it doesn't come up to the poster,' said George, 'that's all.'

'What poster?' asked Harris.

'The poster advertising this particular brand of cycle,' explained George. 'I was looking at one on a hoarding in Sloane Street only a day or two before we started. A man was riding this make of machine, a man with a banner in his hand; he wasn't doing any work, that was clear as daylight; he was just sitting on the thing and drinking in the air. The cycle was going of its own accord, and going well. This thing of yours leaves all the work to me. It is a lazy brute of a machine; if you don't shove, it simply does nothing. I should complain about it, if I were you.'

When one comes to think of it, few bicycles do realise the poster. On only one poster that I can recollect have I seen the rider represented as doing any work. But then this man was being pursued by a bull. In ordinary cases the object of the artist is to convince the hesitating neophyte that the sport of bicycling consists in sitting on a luxurious saddle, and being moved rapidly in the direction you wish to go by unseen heavenly powers.

Generally speaking, the rider is a lady, and then one feels that, for perfect bodily rest combined with entire freedom from mental anxiety, slumber upon a water-bed cannot compare with bicycle-riding upon a hilly road. No fairy travelling on a summer cloud could take things more easily than does the bicycle girl, according to the poster. Her costume for cycling in hot weather is ideal. Old-fashioned landladies might refuse her lunch, it is true; and a narrowminded police force might desire to secure her, and wrap her in a rug preliminary to summonsing her. But such she heeds not. Uphill and downhill, through traffic that might tax the ingenuity of a cat, over road surfaces calculated to break the average steam roller she passes, a vision of idle loveliness; her fair hair streaming to the wind, her sylph-like form poised airily, one foot upon the saddle, the other resting lightly upon the lamp. Sometimes she condescends to sit down on the saddle; then she puts her feet on the rests, lights a cigarette, and waves above her head a Chinese lantern.

Less often, it is a mere male thing that rides the machine. He is not so accomplished an acrobat as is the lady; but simple tricks, such as standing on the saddle and waving flags, drinking beer or beef-tea while riding, he can and does perform. Something, one supposes, he must do to occupy his mind: sitting still hour after hour on this machine, having no work to do, nothing to think about, must pall upon any man of active temperament. Thus it is that we see him rising on his pedals as he nears the top of some high hill to apostrophise the sun, or address poetry to the surrounding scenery.

Occasionally the poster pictures a pair of cyclists; and then one grasps the fact how much superior for purposes of flirtation is the modern bicycle to the old-fashioned parlour or the played-out garden gate. He and she mount their bicycles, being careful, of course, that such are of the right make. After that they have nothing to think about but the old sweet tale. Down shady lanes, through busy towns on market days, merrily roll the wheels of the 'Bermondsey Company's Bottom Bracket Britain's Best,' or of the 'Camberwell Company's Jointless Eureka.' They need no pedalling; they require no guiding. Give them their heads, and tell them what time you want to get home, and that is all they ask. While Edwin leans from his saddle to whisper the dear old nothings in Angelina's ear, while Angelina's face, to hide its blushes, is turned towards the horizon at the back, the magic bicyles pursue their even course.

And the sun is always shining, and the roads are always dry. No stern parent rides behind, no interfering aunt beside, no demon small boy brother is peeping round the corner, there never comes a skid. Ah me! Why were there no 'Britain's Best' nor 'Camberwell Eurekas' to be hired when *we* were young?

Or maybe the 'Britain's Best' or the 'Camberwell Eureka' stands leaning against a gate; maybe it is tired. It has worked hard all the afternoon, carrying these young people. Mercifully minded, they have dismounted, to give the machine a rest. They sit upon the grass beneath the shade of graceful boughs; it is long and dry grass. A stream flows by their feet. All is rest and peace.

That is ever the idea the cycle poster artist sets himself to convey—rest and peace.

But I am wrong in saying that no cyclist, according to the poster, ever works. Now I come to reflect, I have seen posters representing gentlemen on cycles working very hard—over-working themselves, one might almost say. They are thin and haggard with the toil, the perspiration stands upon their brow in beads; you feel that if there is another hill beyond the poster they must either get off or die. But this is the result of their own folly. This happens because they will persist in riding a machine of an inferior make. Were they riding a 'Putney Popular' or 'Battersea Bounder,' such as the sensible young man in the centre of the poster rides, then all this unnecessary labour would be saved to them. Then all required of them would be, as in gratitude bound, to look happy; perhaps, occasionally to back-pedal a little when the machine in its youthful buoyancy loses its head for a moment and dashes on too swiftly.

You tired young men, sitting dejectedly on milestones, too spent to heed the steady rain that soaks you through; you weary maidens, with the straight, damp hair, anxious about the time, longing to swear, not knowing how; you stout bald men, vanishing visibly as you pant and grunt along the endless road; you purple, dejected matrons, plying with pain the slow unwilling wheel; why did you not see to it that you bought a 'Britain's Best' or a 'Camberwell Eureka'? Why are these bicycles of inferior make so prevalent throughout the land?

Or is it with bicycling as with all other things: does Life at no point realise the Poster?

The one thing in Germany that never fails to charm and fascinate me is the German dog. In England one grows tired of the old breeds, one knows them all so well: the mastiff, the plum-pudding dog, the terrier (black, white or rough-haired, as the case may be, but always quarrelsome), the collie, the bulldog; never anything new. Now in Germany you get variety. You come across dogs the like of which you have never seen before: that until you hear them bark you do not know are dogs. It is all so fresh, so interesting. George stopped a dog in Sigmaringen and drew our attention to it. It suggested a cross between a codfish and a poodle. I would not like to be positive it was *not* a cross between a codfish and a poodle. Harris tried to photograph it, but it ran up a fence and disappeared through some bushes.

I do not know what the German breeder's idea is; at present he retains his secret. George suggests he is aiming at a griffin. There is much to bear out this theory, and indeed in one or two cases I have come across success on these lines would seem to have been almost achieved. Yet I cannot bring myself to believe that such are anything more than mere accidents. The German is practical, and I fail to see the object of a griffin. If mere quaintness of design be desired, is there not already the Dachshund! What more is needed? Besides, about a house, a griffin would be so inconvenient: people would be continually treading on its tail. My own idea is that what the Germans are trying for is a mermaid, which they will then train to catch fish.

For your German does not encourage laziness in any living thing.

He likes to see his dogs work, and the German dog loves work; of that there can be no doubt. The life of the English dog must be a misery to him. Imagine a strong, active, and intelligent being, of exceptionally energetic temperament, condemned to spend twenty-four hours a day in absolute idleness! How would you like it yourself? No wonder he feels misunderstood, yearns for the unattainable, and gets himself into trouble generally.

Now the German dog, on the other hand, has plenty to occupy his mind. He is busy and important. Watch him as he walks along harnessed to his milk cart. No churchwarden at collection time could feel or look more pleased with himself. He does not do any real work; the human being does the pushing, he does the barking; that is his idea of division of labour. What he says to himself is:

'The old man can't bark, but he can shove. Very well.'

The interest and the pride he takes in the business is quite beautiful to see. Another dog passing by makes, maybe, some jeering remark, casting discredit upon the creaminess of the milk. He stops suddenly, quite regardless of the traffic.

'I beg your pardon, what was that you said about our milk?'

'I said nothing about your milk,' retorts the other dog, in a tone of gentle innocence. 'I merely said it was a fine day, and asked the price of chalk.'

'Oh, you asked the price of chalk, did you? Would you like to know?'

'Yes, thanks; somehow I thought you would be able to tell me.'

'You are quite right, I can. It's worth——'

'Oh, do come along!' says the old lady, who is tired and hot, and anxious to finish her round.

'Yes, but hang it all; did you hear what he hinted about our milk?'

'Oh, never mind him! There's a tram coming round the corner: we shall all get run over.'

'Yes, but I do mind him; one has one's proper pride. He asked the price of chalk, and he's going to know it! It's worth just twenty times as much——'

'You'll have the whole thing over, I know you will,' cries the old lady, pathetically, struggling with all her feeble strength to haul him back. 'Oh dear, oh dear! I do wish I had left you at home.'

The tram is bearing down upon them; a cab-driver is shouting at them; another huge brute, hoping to be in time to take a hand, is dragging a bread cart, followed by a screaming child, across the road from the opposite side; a small crowd is collecting; and a policeman is hastening to the scene.

'It's worth,' says the milk dog, 'just twenty times as much as you'll be worth before I've done with you.'

'Oh, you think so, do you?'

'Yes, I do, you grandson of a French poodle, you cabbage-eating——'

'There! I knew you'd have it over,' says the poor milk-woman. 'I told him he'd have it over.'

But he is busy, and heeds her not. Five minutes later, when the traffic is renewed, when the bread girl has collected her muddy rolls, and the policeman has gone off with the name and address of everybody in the street, he consents to look behind him.

'It *is* a bit of an upset,' he admits. Then shaking himself free of care, he adds, cheerfully, 'But I guess I taught him the price of chalk. He won't interfere with us again, I'm thinking.'

'I'm sure I hope not,' says the old lady, regarding dejectedly the milky road.

But his favourite sport is to wait at the top of the hill for another dog, and then race down. On these occasions the chief occupation of the other fellow is to run about behind, picking up the scattered articles, loaves, caggages, or shirts, as they are jerked out. At the bottom of the hill, he stops and waits for his friend.

'Good race, wasn't it?' he remarks, panting, as the Human comes up, laden to the chin. 'I believe I'd have won it, too, if it hadn't been for that fool of a small boy. He was right in my way just as I turned the corner. *You noticed him?* Wish I had, beastly brat! What's he yelling like that for? *Because I knocked him down and ran over him?* Well, why didn't he get out of the way? It's disgraceful, the way people leave their children about for other people to tumble over. Halloa! did all those things come out? You couldn't have packed them very carefully; you should see to a thing like that. *You did not dream of my tearing down the hill twenty miles an hour?* Surely, you knew me better than to expect I'd let that old Schneider's dog pass me without an effort. But there, you never think. You're sure you've got them all? *You believe so?* I shouldn't "believe" if I were you; I should run back up the hill again and make sure. *You feel too tired?* Oh, all right! don't blame me if anything is missing, that's all.'

He is so self-willed. He is cock-sure that the correct turning is the second on the right, and nothing will persuade him that it is the third. He is positive he can get across the road in time, and will not be convinced until he sees the cart smashed up. Then he is very apologetic, it is true. But of what use is that? As he is usually of the size and strength of a young bull, and his human companion is generally a weak-kneed old man or woman, or a small child, he has his way. The greatest punishment his proprietor can inflict upon him is to leave him at home, and take the cart out alone. But your German is too kind-hearted to do this often.

That he is harnessed to the cart for anybody's pleasure but his own it is impossible to believe; and I am confident that the German peasant plans the tiny harness and fashions the little cart purely with the hope of gratifying his dog. In other countries—in Belgium, Holland and France—I have seen these draught dogs ill-treated and over-worked; but in Germany, never. Germans abuse animals shockingly. I have seen a German stand in front of his horse and call it every name he could lay his tongue to. But the horse did not mind it. I have seen a German, weary with abusing his horse, call to his wife to come out and assist him. When she came, he told her what the horse had done. The recital roused the woman's temper to almost equal heat with his own; and standing one each side of the poor beast, they both abused it. They abused its dead mother, they insulted its father; they made cutting remarks about its personal appearance, its intelligence, its moral sense, its general ability as a horse. The animal bore the torrent with exemplary patience for a while; then it did the best thing possible to do under the circumstances. Without losing its own temper, it moved quietly away. The lady returned to her washing, and the man followed it up the street, still abusing it.

A kinder-hearted people than the Germans there is no need for. Cruelty to animal or child is a thing almost unknown in the land. The whip with them is a musical instrument; its crack is heard from morning to night, but an Italian coachman that in the streets of Dresden I once saw use it was very nearly lynched by the indignant crowd. Germany is the only country in Europe where the traveller can settle himself comfortably in his hired carriage, confident that his gentle, willing friend between the shafts will be neither over-worked nor cruelly treated.

CHAPTER XI

*Black Forest House: and the sociability therein—Its perfume—George
positively declines to remain in bed after four o'clock in the morning—The
road one cannot miss—My peculiar extra instinct—An ungrateful
party—Harris as a scientist—His cheery confidence—The village: where
it was, and where it ought to have been—George: his plan—We
promenade à la Français—The German coachman asleep and
awake—The man who spreads the English language abroad.*

THERE was one night when, tired out and far from town or village, we
slept in a Black Forest farmhouse. The great charm about the Black
Forest house is its sociability. The cows are in the next room, the
horses are upstairs, the geese and ducks are in the kitchen, while the
pigs, the children, and the chickens live all over the place.

You are dressing, when you hear a grunt behind you.

'Good-morning! Don't happen to have any potato peelings in
here? No, I see you haven't; good-bye.'

Next there is a cackle, and you see the neck of an old hen stretched
round the corner.

'Fine morning, isn't it? You don't mind my bringing this worm of
mine in here, do you? It is so difficult in this house to find a room
where one can enjoy one's food with any quietness. From a chicken I
have always been a slow eater, and when a dozen—there, I thought
they wouldn't leave me alone. Now they'll all want a bit. You don't
mind my getting on the bed, do you? Perhaps here they won't notice
me.'

While you are dressing various shock heads peer in at the door;
they evidently regard the room as a temporary menagerie. You
cannot tell whether the heads belong to boys or girls; you can only
hope they are all male. It is of no use shutting the door, because there
is nothing to fasten it by, and the moment you are gone they push it
open again. You breakfast as the Prodigal Son is generally represented feeding: a pig or two drop in to keep you company; a party of
elderly geese criticise you from the door; you gather from their
whispers, added to their shocked expression, that they are talking
scandal about you. Maybe a cow will condescend to give a glance in.

This Noah's Ark arrangement it is, I suppose, that gives to the
Black Forest home its distinctive scent. It is not a scent you can liken

to any one thing. It is as if you took roses and Limburger cheese and hair oil, some heather and onions, peaches and soapsuds, together with a dash of sea air and a corpse, and mixed them up together. You cannot define any particular odour, but you feel they are all there—all the odours that the world has yet discovered. People who live in these houses are fond of this mixture. They do not open the window and lose any of it; they keep it carefully bottled up. If you want any other scent, you can go outside and smell the wood violets and the pines: inside there is the house; and after a while, I am told, you get used to it, so that you miss it, and are unable to go to sleep in any other atmosphere.

We had a long walk before us the next day, and it was our desire, therefore, to get up early, even so early as six o'clock, if that could be managed without disturbing the whole household. We put it to our hostess whether she thought this could be done. She said she thought it could. She might not be about herself at that time; it was her morning for going into the town, some eight miles off, and she rarely got back much before seven; but, possibly, her husband or one of the boys would be returning home to lunch about that hour. Anyhow, somebody should be sent back to wake us and get our breakfast.

As it turned out, we did not need any waking. We got up at four, all by ourselves. We got up at four in order to get away from the noise and the din that was making our heads ache. What time the Black Forest peasant rises in the summer time I am unable to say; to us they appeared to be getting up all night. And the first thing the Black Forester does when he gets up is to put on a pair of stout boots with wooden soles, and take a constitutional round the house. Until he has been three times up and down the stairs, he does not feel he is up. Once fully awake himself, the next thing he does is to go upstairs to the stables, and wake up a horse. (The Black Forest house being built generally on the side of a steep hill, the ground floor is at the top, and the hay-loft at the bottom.) Then the horse, it would seem, must also have its constitutional round the house; and this seen to, the man goes downstairs into the kitchen and begins to chop wood, and when he has chopped sufficient wood he feels pleased with himself and begins to sing. All things considered, we came to the conclusion we could not do better than follow the excellent example set us. Even George was quite eager to get up that morning.

We had a frugal breakfast at half-past four, and started away at five. Our road lay over a mountain, and from enquiries made in the village it appeared to be one of those roads you cannot possibly miss. I suppose everybody knows this sort of road. Generally, it leads you back to where you started from; and when it doesn't, you wish it did, so that at all events you might know where you were. I foresaw evil from the very first, and before we had accomplished a couple of miles we came up with it. The road divided into three. A worm-eaten signpost indicated that the path to the left led to a place that we had never heard of—that was on no map. Its other arm, pointing out the direction of the middle road, had disappeared. The road to the right, so we all agreed, clearly led back again to the village.

'The old man said distinctly,' so Harris reminded us, 'keep straight on round the hill.'

'Which hill?' George asked, pertinently.

We were confronted by half a dozen, some of them big, some of them little.

'He told us,' continued Harris, 'that we should come to a wood.'

'I see no reason to doubt him,' commented George, 'whichever road we take.'

As a matter of fact, a dense wood covered every hill.

'And he said,' murmured Harris, 'that we should reach the top in about an hour and a half.'

'There it is,' said George, 'that I begin to disbelieve him.'

'Well, what shall we do?' said Harris.

Now I happen to possess the bump of locality. It is not a virtue; I make no boast of it. It is merely an animal instinct that I cannot help. That things occasionally get in my way—mountains, precipices, rivers, and such like obstructions—is no fault of mine. My instinct is correct enough; it is the earth that is wrong. I led them by the middle road. That the middle road had not character enough to continue for any quarter of a mile in the same direction; that after three miles up and down hill it ended abruptly in a wasps' nest, was not a thing that should have been laid to my door. If the middle road had gone in the direction it ought to have done, it would have taken us to where we wanted to go, of that I am convinced.

Even as it was, I would have continued to use this gift of mine to discover a fresh way had a proper spirit been displayed towards me. But I am not an angel—I admit this frankly,—and I decline to exert myself for the ungrateful and the ribald. Besides, I doubt if George and Harris would have followed me further in any event. Therefore it was that I washed my hands of the whole affair, and that Harris entered upon the vacancy.

'Well,' said Harris, 'I suppose you are satisfied with what you have done?'

'I am quite satisfied,' I replied from the heap of stones where I was sitting. 'So far, I have brought you with safety. I would continue to lead you further, but no artist can work without encouragement. You appear dissatisfied with me because you do not know where you are. For all you know, you may be just where you want to be. But I say nothing as to that; I expect no thanks. Go your own way; I have done with you both.'

I spoke, perhaps, with bitterness, but I could not help it. Not a word of kindness had I had all the weary way.

'Do not misunderstand us,' said Harris; 'both George and myself feel that without your assistance we should never be where we now are. For that we give you every credit. But instinct is liable to error. What I propose to do is to substitute for it Science, which is exact. Now, where's the sun?'

'Don't you think,' said George, 'that if we made our way back to the village, and hired a boy for a mark to guide us, it would save time in the end?'

'It would be wasting hours,' said Harris, with decision. 'You leave this to me. I have been reading about this thing, and it has interested me.' He took out his watch, and began turning himself round and round.

'It's as simple as A B C,' he continued. 'You point the short hand at the sun, then you bisect the segment between the short hand and the twelve, and thus you get the north.'

He worried up and down for a while, then he fixed it.

'Now I've got it,' he said; 'that's the north, where that wasps' nest is. Now give me the map.'

We handed it to him, and seating himself facing the wasps, he examined it.

'Todtmoos from here,' he said, 'is south by south-west.'

'How do you mean, from here?' asked George.

'Why, from here, where we are,' returned Harris.

'But where are we?' said George.

This worried Harris for a time, but at length he cheered up.

'It doesn't matter where we are,' he said. 'Wherever we are, Todtmoos is south by south-west. Come on, we are only wasting time.'

'I don't quite see how you make it out,' said George, as he rose and shouldered his knapsack; 'but I suppose it doesn't matter. We are out for our health, and it's all pretty!'

'We shall be all right,' said Harris, with cheery confidence. 'We shall be in at Todtmoos before ten, don't you worry. And at Todtmoos we will have something to eat.'

He said that he, himself, fancied a beefsteak, followed by an omelette. George said that, personally, he intended to keep his mind off the subject until he saw Todtmoos.

We walked for half an hour, then emerging upon an opening, we saw below us, about two miles away, the village through which we had passed that morning. It had a quaint church with an outside staircase, a somewhat unusual arrangement.

The sight of it made me sad. We had been walking hard for three hours and a half, and had accomplished, apparently, about four miles. But Harris was delighted.

'Now, at last,' said Harris, 'we know where we are.'

'I thought you said it didn't matter,' George reminded him.

'No more it does, practically,' replied Harris, 'but it is just as well to be certain. Now I feel more confidence in myself.'

'I'm not so sure about that being an advantage,' muttered George. But I do not think Harris heard him.

'We are now,' continued Harris, 'east of the sun, and Todtmoos is south-west of where we are. So that if——'

He broke off. 'By-the-by,' he said, 'do you remember whether I said the bisecting line of that segment pointed to the north or to the south?'

'You said it pointed to the north,' replied George.

'Are you positive?' persisted Harris.

'Positive,' answered George; 'but don't let that influence your calculations. In all probability you were wrong.'

Harris thought for a while; then his brow cleared.

'That's all right,' he said; 'of course, it's the north. It must be the north. How could it be the south? Now we must make for the west. Come on.'

'I am quite willing to make for the west,' said George; 'any point of the compass is the same to me. I only wish to remark that, at the present moment, we are going dead east.'

'No we are not,' returned Harris; 'we are going west.'

'We are going east, I tell you,' said George.

'I wish you wouldn't keep saying that,' said Harris; 'you confuse me.'

'I don't mind if I do,' returned George; 'I would rather do that than go wrong. I tell you we are going dead east.'

'What nonsense!' retorted Harris; 'there's the sun.'

'I can see the sun,' answered George, 'quite distinctly. It may be where it ought to be, according to you and Science, or it may not. All I know is, that when we were down in the village, that particular hill with that particular lump of rock upon it was due north of us. At the present moment we are facing due east.'

'You are quite right,' said Harris; 'I forgot for the moment that we had turned round.'

'I should get into the habit of making a note of it, if I were you,' grumbled George; 'it's a manœuvre that will probably occur again more than once.'

We faced about, and walked in the other direction. At the end of forty minutes' climbing we again emerged upon an opening, and again the village lay just under our feet. On this occasion it was south of us.

'This is very extraordinary,' said Harris.

'I see nothing remarkable about it,' said George. 'If you walk steadily round a village it is only natural that now and then you get a glimpse of it. Myself, I am glad to see it. It proves to me that we are not utterly lost.'

'It ought to be the other side of us,' said Harris.

'It will be in another hour or so,' said George, 'if we keep on.'

I said little myself; I was vexed with both of them; but I was glad to notice George evidently growing cross with Harris. It was absurd of Harris to fancy he could find the way by the sun.

'I wish I knew,' said Harris, thoughtfully, 'for certain whether that bisecting line points to the north or to the south.'

'I should make up my mind about it,' said George; 'it's an important point.'

'It's impossible it can be the north,' said Harris, 'and I'll tell you why.'

'You needn't trouble,' said George; 'I am quite prepared to believe it isn't.'

'You said just now it was,' said Harris, reproachfully.

'I said nothing of the sort,' retorted George. 'I said you said it was—a very different thing. If you think it isn't, let's go the other way. It'll be a change, at all events.'

So Harris worked things out according to the contrary calculation, and again we plunged into the wood; and again after half an hour's stiff climbing we came in view of that same village. True, we were a little higher, and this time it lay between us and the sun.

'I think,' said George, as he stood looking down at it, 'this is the best view we've had of it, as yet. There is only one other point from which we can see it. After that, I propose we go down into it and get some rest.'

'I don't believe it's the same village,' said Harris; 'it can't be.'

'There's no mistaking that church,' said George. 'But maybe it is a case on all fours with that Prague statue. Possibly, the authorities hereabout have had made some life-sized models of that village, and have stuck them about the Forest to see where the thing would look best. Anyhow, which way do we go now?'

'I don't know,' said Harris, 'and I don't care. I have done my best; you've done nothing but grumble, and confuse me.'

'I may have been critical,' admitted George; 'but look at the thing from my point of view. One of you says he's got an instinct, and leads me to a wasps' nest in the middle of a wood.'

'I can't help wasps building in a wood,' I replied.

'I don't say you can,' answered George. 'I am not arguing; I am merely stating incontrovertible facts. The other one, who leads me up and down hill for hours on scientific principles, doesn't know the north from the south, and is never quite sure whether he's turned round or whether he hasn't. Personally, I profess to no instincts beyond the ordinary, nor am I a scientist. But two fields off I can see a man. I am going to offer him the worth of the hay he is cutting, which I estimate at one mark fifty pfennig, to leave his work, and lead me to within sight of Todtmoos. If you two fellows like to follow, you can. If not, you can start another system and work it out by yourselves.'

George's plan lacked both originality and aplomb, but at the moment it appealed to us. Fortunately, we had worked round to a very short distance away from the spot where we had originally gone wrong; with the result that, aided by the gentleman of the scythe, we recovered the road, and reached Todtmoos four hours later than we had calculated to reach it, with an appetite that took forty-five minutes' steady work in silence to abate.

From Todtmoos we had intended to walk down to the Rhine; but having regard to our extra exertions of the morning, we decided to promenade in a carriage, as the French would say; and for this purpose hired a picturesque-looking vehicle, drawn by a horse that I should have called barrel-bodied but for contrast with his driver, in comparison with whom he was angular. In Germany every vehicle is arranged for a pair of horses, but drawn generally by one. This gives to the equipage a lop-sided appearance, according to our notions, but it is held here to indicate style. The idea to be conveyed is that you usually drive a pair of horses, but that for the moment you have mislaid the other one. The German driver is not what we should call a first-class whip. He is at his best when he is asleep. Then, at all events, he is harmless; and the horse being, generally speaking, intelligent and experienced, progress under these conditions is comparatively safe. If in Germany they could only train the horse to collect the money at the end of the journey, there would be no need for a coachman at all. This would be a distinct relief to the passenger, for when the German coachman is awake and not cracking his whip he is generally occupied in getting himself into trouble or out of it. He is better at the former. Once I recollect driving down a steep Black Forest hill with a couple of ladies. It was one of those roads winding corkscrew-wise down the slope. The hill rose at an angle of seventy-five on the off-side, and fell away at an angle of seventy-five on the near-side. We were proceeding very comfortably, the driver, we were happy to notice, with his eyes shut, when suddenly something, a bad dream or indigestion, awoke him. He seized the reins, and, by an adroit movement, pulled the near-side horse over the edge, where it clung, half supported by the traces. Our driver did not appear in the least annoyed or surprised; both horses, I also noticed, seemed equally used to the situation. We got out, and he got down. He took from under the seat a huge clasp-knife, evidently kept there for the purpose, and deftly cut the traces. The horse, thus released, rolled over and over until he struck the road again some fifty feet below us. There he regained his feet and stood waiting for us. We re-entered the carriage and descended with the single horse until we came to him. There, with the help of some bits of string, our driver harnessed him again, and we continued on our way. What impressed me was the evident accustomedness of both driver and horses to this method of working down a hill.

Evidently to them it appeared a short and convenient cut. I should not have been surprised had the man suggested our strapping ourselves in, and then rolling over and over, carriage and all, to the bottom.

Another peculiarity of the German coachman is that he never attempts to pull in or to pull up. He regulates his rate of speed, not by the pace of the horse, but by manipulation of the brake. For eight miles an hour he puts it on slightly, so that it only scrapes the wheel, producing a continuous sound as of the sharpening of a saw; for four miles an hour he screws it down harder, and you travel to an accompaniment of groans and shrieks, suggestive of a symphony of dying pigs. When he desires to come to a full stop, he puts it on to its full. If his brake be a good one, he calculates he can stop his carriage, unless the horse be an extra powerful animal, in less than twice its own length. Neither the German driver nor the German horse knows, apparently, that you can stop a carriage by any other method. The German horse continues to pull with his full strength until he finds it impossible to move the vehicle another inch; then he rests. Horses of other countries are quite willing to stop when the idea is suggested to them. I have known horses content to go even quite slowly. But your German horse, seemingly, is built for one particular speed, and is unable to depart from it. I am stating nothing but the literal, unadorned truth, when I say I have seen a German coachman, with the reins lying loose over the splash-board, working his brake with both hands, in terror lest he would not be in time to avoid a collision.

At Waldshut, one of those little sixteenth-century towns through which the Rhine flows during its earlier course, we came across that exceedingly common object of the Continent: the travelling Briton grieved and surprised at the unacquaintance of the foreigner with the subtleties of the English language. When we entered the station he was, in very fair English, though with a slight Somersetshire accent, explaining to a porter for the tenth time, as he informed us, the simple fact that though he himself had a ticket for Donaueschingen, and wanted to go to Donaueschingen, to see the source of the

Danube, which is not there, though they tell you it is, he wished his bicycle to be sent on to Engen and his bag to Constance, there to await his arrival. He was hot and angry with the effort of the thing. The porter was a young man in years, but at the moment looked old and miserable. I offered my services. I wish now I had not—though not so fervently, I expect, as he, the speechless one, came subsequently to wish this. All three routes, so the porter explained to us, were complicated, necessitating changing and re-changing. There was not much time for calm elucidation, as our own train was starting in a few minutes. The man himself was voluble—always a mistake when anything entangled has to be made clear; while the porter was only too eager to get the job done with and so breathe again. It dawned upon me ten minutes later, when thinking the matter over in the train, that though I had agreed with the porter that it would be best for the bicycle to go by way of Immendingen, and had agreed to his booking it to Immendingen, I had neglected to give instructions for its departure from Immendingen. Were I of a despondent temperament I should be worrying myself at the present moment with the reflection that in all probability that bicycle is still at Immendingen to this day. But I regard it as good philosophy to endeavour always to see the brighter side of things. Possibly the porter corrected my omission on his own account, or some simple miracle may have happened to restore that bicycle to its owner some time before the end of his tour. The bag we sent to Radolfzell: but here I console myself with the recollection that it was labelled Constance; and no doubt after a while the railway authorities, finding it unclaimed at Radolfzell, forwarded it on to Constance.

But all this is apart from the moral I wished to draw from the incident. The true inwardness of the situation lay in the indignation of this Britisher at finding a German railway porter unable to comprehend English. The moment we spoke to him he expressed this indignation in no measured terms.

'Thank you very much indeed,' he said; 'it's simple enough. I want to go to Donaueschingen myself by train; from Donaueschingen I am going to walk to Geisengen; from Geisengen I am going to take the train to Engen, and from Engen I am going to bicycle to Constance. But I don't want to take my bag with me; I want to find it at Constance when I get there. I have been trying to explain the thing to this fool for the last ten minutes; but I can't get it into him.'

'It is very disgraceful,' I agreed. 'Some of these German workmen know hardly any other language than their own.'

'I have gone over it with him,' continued the man, 'on the time table, and explained it by pantomime. Even then I could not knock it into him.'

'I can hardly believe you,' I again remarked; 'you would think the thing explained itself.'

Harris was angry with the man; he wished to reprove him for his folly in journeying through the outlying portions of a foreign clime, and seeking in such to accomplish complicated railway tricks without knowing a word of the language of the country. But I checked the impulsiveness of Harris, and pointed out to him the great and good work at which the man was unconsciously assisting.

Shakespeare and Milton may have done their little best to spread acquaintance with the English tongue among the less favoured inhabitants of Europe. Newton and Darwin may have rendered their language a necessity among educated and thoughtful foreigners. Dickens and Ouida (for your folk who imagine that the literary world is bounded by the prejudices of New Grub Street,* would be surprised and grieved at the position occupied abroad by this at-home-sneered-at lady) may have helped still further to popularise it. But the man who has spread the knowledge of English from Cape St Vincent to the Ural Mountains is the Englishman who, unable or unwilling to learn a single word of any language but his own, travels purse in hand into every corner of the Continent. One may be shocked at his ignorance, annoyed at his stupidity, angry at his presumption. But the practical fact remains; he it is that is anglicising Europe. For him the Swiss peasant tramps through the snow on winter evenings to attend the English class open in every village. For him the coachman and the guard, the chambermaid and the laundress, pore over their English grammars and colloquial phrase books. For him the foreign shopkeeper and merchant send their sons and daughters in their thousands to study in every English town. For him it is that every foreign hotel- and restaurant-keeper adds to his advertisement: 'Only those with fair knowledge of English need apply.'

Did the English-speaking races make it their rule to speak any-thing else than English, the marvellous progress of the English tongue throughout the world would stop. The English-speaking man stands amid the strangers and jingles his gold.

'Here,' he cries, 'is payment for all such as can speak English.'

He it is who is the great educator. Theoretically we may scold him; practically we should take our hats off to him. He is the missionary of the English tongue.

CHAPTER XII

We are grieved at the earthly instincts of the German—A superb view, but no restaurant—Continental opinion of the Englishman—That he does not know enough to come in out of the rain—There comes a weary traveller with a brick—The hunting of the dog—An undesirable family residence—A fruitful region—A merry old soul comes up the hill —George, alarmed at the lateness of the hour, hastens down the other side—Harris follows him, to show him the way—I hate being alone, and follow Harris—Pronunciation specially designed for use of foreigners.

A THING that vexes much the high-class Anglo-Saxon soul is the earthly instinct prompting the German to fix a restaurant at the goal of every excursion. On mountain summit, in fairy glen, on lonely pass, by waterfall or winding stream, stands ever the busy Wirtschaft. How can one rhapsodise over a view when surrounded by beer-stained tables? How lose one's self in historical reverie amid the odour of roast veal and spinach?

One day, on elevating thoughts intent, we climbed through tangled woods.

'And at the top,' said Harris, bitterly, as we paused to breathe a space and pull our belts a hole tighter, 'there will be a gaudy restaurant, where people will be guzzling beefsteaks and plum tarts and drinking white wine.'

'Do you think so?' said George.

'Sure to be,' answered Harris; 'you know their way. Not one grove will they consent to dedicate to solitude and contemplation; not one height will they leave to the lover of nature unpolluted by the gross and the material.'

'I calculate,' I remarked, 'that we shall be there a little before one o'clock, provided we don't dawdle.'

'The "Mittagstisch"* will be just ready,' groaned Harris, 'with possibly some of those little blue trout they catch about here. In

Germany one never seems able to get away from food and drink. It is maddening!'

We pushed on, and in the beauty of the walk forgot our indignation. My estimate proved to be correct.

At a quarter to one, said Harris, who was leading:

'Here we are; I can see the summit.'

'Any sign of that restaurant?' said George.

'I don't notice it,' replied Harris; 'but it's there, you may be sure; confound it!'

Five minutes later we stood upon the top. We looked north, south, east and west; then we looked at one another.

'Grand view, isn't it?' said Harris.

'Magnificent,' I agreed.

'Superb,' remarked George.

'They have had the good sense for once,' said Harris, 'to put that restaurant out of sight.'

'They do seem to have hidden it,' said George.

'One doesn't mind the thing so much when it is not forced under one's nose,' said Harris.

'Of course, in its place,' I observed, 'a restaurant is right enough.'

'I should like to know where they have put it,' said George.

'Suppose we look for it?' said Harris, with inspiration.

It seemed a good idea. I felt curious myself. We agreed to explore in different directions, returning to the summit to report progress. In half an hour we stood together once again. There was no need for words. The face of one and all of us announced plainly that at last we had discovered a recess of German nature untarnished by the sordid suggestion of food or drink.

'I should never have believed it possible,' said Harris; 'would you?'

'I should say,' I replied, 'that this is the only square quarter of a mile in the entire Fatherland unprovided with one.'

'And we three strangers have struck it,' said George, 'without an effort.'

'True,' I observed. 'By pure good fortune we are now enabled to feast our finer senses undisturbed by appeal to our lower nature. Observe the light upon those distant peaks; is it not ravishing?'

'Talking of nature,' said George, 'which should you say was the nearest way down?'

'The road to the left,' I replied, after consulting the guide book, 'takes us to Sonnensteig—where, by-the-by, I observe the "Goldener Adler" is well spoken of—in about two hours. The road to the right, though somewhat longer, commands more extensive prospects.'

'One prospect,' said Harris, 'is very much like another prospect; don't you think so?'

'Personally,' said George, 'I am going by the left-hand road.' And Harris and I went after him.

But we were not to get down so soon as we had anticipated. Storms come quickly in these regions, and before we had walked for quarter of an hour it became a question of seeking shelter or living for the rest of the day in soaked clothes. We decided on the former alternative, and selected a tree that, under ordinary circumstances, should have been ample protection. But a Black Forest thunderstorm is not an ordinary circumstance. We consoled ourselves at first by telling each other that at such a rate it could not last long. Next, we endeavoured to comfort ourselves with the reflection that if it did we should soon be too wet to fear getting wetter.

'As it turned out,' said Harris, 'I should have been almost glad if there had been a restaurant up here.'

'I see no advantage in being both wet *and* hungry,' said George. 'I shall give it another five minutes, then I am going on.'

'These mountain solitudes,' I remarked, 'are very attractive in fine weather. On a rainy day, especially if you happen to be past the age when——'

At this point there hailed us a voice, proceeding from a stout gentleman, who stood some fifty feet away from us under a big umbrella.

'Won't you come inside?' asked the stout gentleman.

'Inside where?' I called back. I thought at first he was one of those fools that will try to be funny when there is nothing to be funny about.

'Inside the restaurant,' he answered.

We left the shelter and made for him. We wished for further information about this thing.

'I did call to you from the window,' said the stout gentleman, as we drew near to him, 'but I suppose you did not hear me. This storm may last for another hour; you will get *so* wet.'

He was a kindly old gentleman; he seemed quite anxious about us.

I said: 'It is very kind of you to have come out. We are not lunatics. We have not been standing under that tree for the last half-hour knowing all the time there was a restaurant, hidden by the trees, within twenty yards of us. We had no idea we were anywhere near a restaurant.'

'I thought maybe you hadn't,' said the old gentleman; 'that is why I came.'

It appeared that all the people in the inn had been watching us from the windows also, wondering why we stood there looking miserable. If it had not been for this nice old gentleman the fools would have remained watching us, I suppose, for the rest of the afternoon. The landlord excused himself by saying he thought we looked like English. It is no figure of speech. On the Continent they do sincerely believe that every Englishman is mad. They are as convinced of it as is every English peasant that Frenchmen live on frogs. Even when one makes a direct personal effort to disabuse them of the impression one is not always successful.

It was a comfortable little restaurant, where they cooked well, while the Tischwein* was really most passable. We stopped there for a couple of hours, and dried ourselves and fed ourselves, and talked about the view; and just before we left an incident occurred that shows how much more stirring in this world are the influences of evil compared with those of good.

A traveller entered. He seemed a careworn man. He carried a brick in his hand, tied to a piece of rope. He entered nervously and hurriedly, closed the door carefully behind him, saw to it that it was fastened, peered out of the window long and earnestly, and then, with a sigh of relief, laid his brick upon the bench beside him and called for food and drink.

There was something mysterious about the whole affair. One wondered what he was going to do with the brick, why he had closed the door so carefully, why he had looked so anxiously from the window; but his aspect was too wretched to invite conversation, and we forbore, therefore, to ask him questions. As he ate and drank he grew more cheerful, sighed less often. Later he stretched his legs, lit an evil-smelling cigar, and puffed in calm contentment.

Then it happened. It happened too suddenly for any detailed explanation of the thing to be possible. I recollect a Fräulein entering the room from the kitchen with a pan in her hand. I saw her cross to the outer door. The next moment the whole room was in an uproar. One was reminded of those pantomime transformation scenes where, from among floating clouds, slow music, waving flowers, and reclining fairies, one is suddenly transported into the midst of shouting policemen tumbling over yelling babies, swells fighting pantaloons, sausages and harlequins, buttered slides and clowns. As the Fräulein of the pan touched the door it flew open, as though all the spirits of sin had been pressed against it, waiting. Two pigs and a chicken rushed into the room; a cat that had been sleeping on a beer-barrel spluttered into fiery life. The Fräulein threw her pan into the air and lay down on the floor. The gentleman with the brick sprang to his feet, upsetting the table before him with everything upon it.

One looked to see the cause of this disaster: one discovered it at once in the person of a mongrel terrier with pointed ears and a squirrel's tail. The landlord rushed out from another door, and attempted to kick him out of the room. Instead, he kicked one of the pigs, the fatter of the two. It was a vigorous, well-planted kick, and the pig got the whole of it; none of it was wasted. One felt sorry for the poor animal; but no amount of sorrow anyone else might feel for him could compare with the sorrow he felt for himself. He stopped running about; he sat down in the middle of the room, and appealed to the solar system, generally to observe this unjust thing that had come upon him. They must have heard his complaint in the valleys round about, and have wondered what upheaval of nature was taking place among the hills.

As for the hen it scuttled, screaming, every way at once. It was a marvellous bird: it seemed to be able to run up a straight wall quite easily; and it and the cat between them fetched down mostly everything that was not already on the floor. In less than forty seconds there were nine people in that room, all trying to kick one dog. Possibly, now and again, one or another may have succeeded, for occasionally the dog would stop barking in order to howl. But it did not discourage him. Everything has to be paid for, he evidently argued, even a pig and chicken hunt; and, on the whole, the game was worth it.

Besides, he had the satisfaction of observing that, for every kick he received, most other living things in the room got two. As for the unfortunate pig—the stationary one, the one that still sat lamenting in the centre of the room—he must have averaged a steady four.

Trying to kick this dog was like playing football with a ball that was never there—not when you went to kick it, but after you had started to kick it, and had gone too far to stop yourself, so that the kick had to go on in any case, your only hope being that your foot would find something or another solid to stop it, and so save you from sitting down on the floor noisily and completely. When anybody did kick the dog it was by pure accident, when they were not expecting to kick him; and, generally speaking, this took them so unawares that, after kicking him, they fell over him. And everybody, every half-minute, would be certain to fall over the pig—the sitting pig, the one incapable of getting out of anybody's way.

How long the scrimmage might have lasted it is impossible to say. It was ended by the judgment of George. For a while he had been seeking to catch, not the dog but the remaining pig, the one still capable of activity. Cornering it at last, he persuaded it to cease running round and round the room, and instead to take a spin outside. It shot through the door with one long wail.

We always desire the thing we have not. One pig, a chicken, nine people, and a cat, were as nothing in that dog's opinion compared with the quarry that was disappearing. Unwisely, he darted after it, and George closed the door upon him and shot the bolt.

Then the landlord stood up, and surveyed all the things that were lying on the floor.

'That's a playful dog of yours,' said he to the man who had come in with the brick.

'He is not my dog,' replied the man, sullenly.

'Whose dog is it then?' said the landlord.

'I don't know whose dog it is,' answered the man.

'That won't do for me, you know,' said the landlord, picking up a picture of the German Emperor, and wiping beer from it with his sleeve.

'I know it won't,' replied the man; 'I never expected it would. I'm tired of telling people it isn't my dog. They none of them believe me.'

'What do you want to go about with him for, if he's not your dog?' said the landlord. 'What's the attraction about him?'

'I don't go about with him,' replied the man; 'he goes about with me. He picked me up this morning at ten o'clock, and he won't leave me. I thought I had got rid of him when I came in here. I left him busy killing a duck more than a quarter of an hour away. I'll have to pay for that, I expect, on my way back.'

'Have you tried throwing stones at him?' asked Harris.

'Have I tried throwing stones at him!' replied the man, contemptuously. 'I've been throwing stones at him till my arm aches with throwing stones; and he thinks it's a game, and brings them back to me. I've been carrying this beastly brick about with me for over an hour, in the hope of being able to drown him, but he never comes near enough for me to get hold of him. He just sits six inches out of reach with his mouth open, and looks at me.'

'It's the funniest story I've heard for a long while,' said the landlord.

'Glad it amuses somebody,' said the man.

We left him helping the landlord to pick up the broken things, and went our way. A dozen yards outside the door the faithful animal was waiting for his friend. He looked tired, but contented. He was evidently a dog of strange and sudden fancies, and we feared for the moment lest he might take a liking to us. But he let us pass with indifference. His loyalty to this unresponsive man was touching; and we made no attempt to undermine it.

Having completed to our satisfaction the Black Forest, we journeyed on our wheels through Alt Breisach and Colmar to Münster; whence we started a short exploration of the Vosges range, where, according to the present German Emperor, humanity stops. Of old, Alt Breisach, a rocky fortress with the river now on one side of it and now on the other—for in its inexperienced youth the Rhine never seems to have been quite sure of its way,—must, as a place of residence, have appealed exclusively to the lover of change and excitement. Whoever the war was between, and whatever it was about, Alt Breisach was bound to be in it. Everybody besieged it, most people captured it; the majority of them lost it again; nobody seemed able to keep it. Whom he belonged to, and what he was, the dweller in Alt Breisach could never have been quite sure. One day he would be a Frenchman, and then before he could learn enough French to pay his taxes he would be an Austrian. While trying to discover what you did in order to be a good Austrian, he would find he was no longer an Austrian, but a German, though what particular German out of the dozen must always have been doubtful to him. One day he would discover that he was a Catholic, the next an ardent

Protestant. The only thing that could have given any stability to his existence must have been the monotonous necessity of paying heavily for the privilege of being whatever for the moment he was. But when one begins to think of these things one finds oneself wondering why anybody in the Middle Ages, except kings and tax collectors, ever took the trouble to live at all.

For variety and beauty, the Vosges will not compare with the hills of the Schwarzwald. The advantage about them from the tourist's point of view is their superior poverty. The Vosges peasant has not the unromantic air of contented prosperity that spoils his *vis-à-vis* across the Rhine. The villages and farms possess more the charm of decay. Another point wherein the Vosges district excels is its ruins. Many of its numerous castles are perched where you might think only eagles would care to build. In others, commenced by the Romans and finished by the Troubadours, covering acres with the maze of their still standing walls, one may wander for hours.

The fruiterer and greengrocer is a person unknown in the Vosges. Most things of that kind grow wild, and are to be had for the picking. It is difficult to keep to any programme when walking through the Vosges, the temptation on a hot day to stop and eat fruit generally being too strong for resistance. Raspberries, the most delicious I have ever tasted, wild strawberries, currants, and gooseberries, grow upon the hill-sides as blackberries by English lanes. The Vosges small boy is not called upon to rob an orchard; he can make himself ill without sin. Orchards exist in the Vosges mountains in plenty; but to trespass into one for the purpose of stealing fruit would be as foolish as for a fish to try and get into a swimming bath without paying. Still, of course, mistakes do occur.

One afternoon in the course of a climb we emerged upon a plateau, where we lingered perhaps too long, eating more fruit than may have been good for us; it was so plentiful around us, so varied. We commenced with a few late strawberries, and from those we passed to raspberries. Then Harris found a greengage-tree with some early fruit upon it, just perfect.

'This is about the best thing we have struck,' said George; 'we had better make the most of this.' Which was good advice, on the face of it.

'It is a pity,' said Harris, 'that the pears are still so hard.'

He grieved about this for a while, but later on I came across some remarkably fine yellow plums, and these consoled him somewhat.

'I suppose we are still a bit too far north for pineapples,' said George. 'I feel I could just enjoy a fresh pineapple. This commonplace fruit palls upon one after a while.'

'Too much bush fruit and not enough tree, is the fault I find,' said Harris. 'Myself, I should have liked a few more greengages.'

'Here is a man coming up the hill,' I observed, 'who looks like a native. Maybe, he will know where we can fine some more greengages.'

'He walks well for an old chap,' remarked Harris.

He certainly was climbing the hill at a remarkable pace. Also, so far as we were able to judge at that distance, he appeared to be in a remarkably cheerful mood, singing and shouting at the top of his voice, gesticulating, and waving his arms.

'What a merry old soul it is,' said Harris; 'it does one good to watch him. But why does his carry his stick over his shoulder? Why doesn't he use it to help him up the hill?'

'Do you know, I don't think it is a stick,' said George.

'What can it be, then?' asked Harris.

'Well, it looks to me,' said George, 'more like a gun.'

'You don't think we can have made a mistake?' suggested Harris. 'You don't think this can be anything in the nature of a private orchard?'

I said: 'Do you remember the sad thing that happened in the South of France some two years ago? A soldier picked some cherries as he passed a house, and the French peasant to whom the cherries belonged came out, and without a word of warning shot him dead.'

'But surely you are not allowed to shoot a man dead for picking fruit, even in France?' said George.

'Of course not,' I answered. 'It was quite illegal. The only excuse offered by his counsel was that he was of a highly excitable disposition, and especially keen about these particular cherries.'

'I recollect something about the case,' said Harris, 'now you mention it. I believe the district in which it happened—the "Commune", as I think it is called—had to pay heavy compensation to the relatives of the deceased soldier; which was only fair.'

George said: 'I am tired of this place. Besides, it's getting late.'

Harris said: 'If he goes at that rate he will fall and hurt himself. Besides, I don't believe he knows the way.'

I felt lonesome up there all by myself, with nobody to speak to.

Besides, not since I was a boy, I reflected, had I enjoyed a run down a really steep hill. I thought I would see if I could revive the sensation. It is a jerky exercise, but good, I should say, for the liver.

We slept that night at Barr, a pleasant little town on the way to St Ottilienberg, an interesting old convent among the mountains, where you are waited upon by real nuns, and your bill made out by a priest. At Barr, just before supper a tourist entered. He looked English, but spoke a language the like of which I have never heard before. Yet it was an elegant and fine-sounding language. The landlord stared at him blankly; the landlady shook her head. He sighed, and tried another, which somehow recalled to me forgotten memories, though, at the time, I could not fix it. But again nobody understood him.

'This is damnable,' he said aloud to himself.

'Ah, you are English!' exclaimed the landlord, brightening up.

'And Monsieur looks tired,' added the bright little landlady. 'Monsieur will have supper.'

They both spoke English excellently, nearly as well as they spoke French and German; and they bustled about and made him comfortable. At supper he sat next to me, and I talked to him.

'Tell me,' I said—I was curious on the subject—'what language was it you spoke when you first came in?'

'German,' he explained.

'Oh,' I replied, 'I beg your pardon.'

'You did not understand it?' he continued.

'It must have been my fault,' I answered; 'my knowledge is extremely limited. One picks up a little here and there as one goes about, but of course that is a different thing.'

'But *they* did not understand it,' he replied, 'the landlord and his wife; and it is their own language.'

'I do not think so,' I said. 'The children hereabout speak German, it is true, and our landlord and landlady know German to a certain point. But throughout Alsace and Lorraine the old people still talk French.'

'And I spoke to them in French also,' he added, 'and they understood that no better.'

'It is certainly very curious,' I agreed.

'It is more than curious,' he replied; 'in my case it is incomprehensible. I possess a diploma for modern languages. I won my scholarship purely on the strength of my French and German. The correctness of my construction, the purity of my pronunciation, was considered at my college to be quite remarkable. Yet, when I come abroad hardly anybody understands a word I say. Can you explain it?'

'I think I can,' I replied. 'Your pronunciation is too faultless. You remember what the Scotsman said when for the first time in his life he tasted real whisky: "It may be puir, but I canna drink it"; so it is with your German. It strikes one less as a language than as an exhibition. If I might offer advice, I should say: Mispronounce as much as possible, and throw in as many mistakes as you can think of.'

It is the same everywhere. Each country keeps a special pronunciation exclusively for the use of foreigners—a pronunciation they never dream of using themselves, that they cannot understand when it is used. I once heard an English lady explaining to a Frenchman how to pronounce the word Have.

'You will pronounce it,' said the lady reproachfully, 'as if it were spelt H-a-v. It isn't. There is an "e" at the end.'

'But I thought,' said the pupil, 'that you did not sound the "e" at the end of h-a-v-e.'

'No more you do,' explained his teacher. 'It is what we call a mute "e"; but it exercises a modifying influence on the preceding vowel.'

Before that, he used to say 'have' quite intelligently. Afterwards, when he came to the word he would stop dead, collect his thoughts, and give expression to a sound that only the context could explain.

Putting aside the sufferings of the early martyrs, few men, I suppose, have gone through more than I myself went through in trying to attain the correct pronunciation of the German word for church—'Kirche.' Long before I had done with it I had determined never to go to church in Germany, rather than be bothered with it.

'No, no,' my teacher would explain—he was a painstaking gentleman; 'you say it as if it were spelt K-i-r-c-h-k-e. There is no k. It is——.' And he would illustrate to me again, for the twentieth time that morning, how it should be pronounced; the sad thing being that I could never for the life of me detect any difference between the way he said it and the way I said it. So he would try a new method.

'You say it from your throat,' he would explain. He was quite right; I did. 'I want you to say it from down here,' and with a fat forefinger he would indicate the region from where I was to start. After painful efforts, resulting in sounds suggestive of anything rather than a place of worship, I would excuse myself.

'I really fear it is impossible,' I would say. 'You see, for years I have always talked with my mouth, as it were; I never knew a man could talk with his stomach. I doubt if it is not too late now for me to learn.'

By spending hours in dark corners, and practising in silent streets, to the terror of chance passers-by, I came at last to pronounce this word correctly. My teacher was delighted with me, and until I came to Germany I was pleased with myself. In Germany I found that nobody understood what I meant by it. I never got near a church with it. I had to drop the correct pronunciation, and painstakingly go back to my first wrong pronunciation. Then they would brighten up, and tell me it was round the corner, or down the next street, as the case might be.

I also think pronunciation of a foreign tongue could be better taught than by demanding from the pupil those internal acrobatic feats that are generally impossible and always useless. This is the sort of instruction one receives:

'Press your tonsils against the underside of your larynx. Then with the convex part of the septum curved upwards so as almost—but not quite—to touch the uvula, try with the tip of your tongue to reach your thyroid. Take a deep breath, and compress your glottis. Now, without opening your lips, say "Garoo."'

And when you have done it they are not satisfied.

CHAPTER XIII

An examination into the character and behaviour of the German student —The German Mensur—Uses and abuses of use—Views of an impressionist—The humour of the thing—Recipe for making savages—The Jungfrau: her peculiar taste in faces—The Kneipe—How to rub a Salamander—Advice to the stranger—A story that might have ended sadly—Of two men and two wives—Together with a bachelor.

ON our way home we included a German University town, being wishful to obtain an insight into the ways of student life, a curiosity that the courtesy of German friends enabled us to gratify.

The English boy plays till he is fifteen, and works thence till twenty. In Germany it is the child that works; the young man that plays. The German boy goes to school at seven o'clock in the summer, at eight in the winter, and at school he studies. The result is that at sixteen he has a thorough knowledge of the classics and mathematics, knows as much history as any man compelled to belong to a political party is wise in knowing, together with a thorough grounding in modern languages. Therefore his eight College Semesters, extending over four years, are, except for the young man aiming at a professorship, unnecessarily ample. He is not a sportsman, which is a pity, for he should make a good one. He plays football a little, bicycles still less; plays French billiards in stuffy cafés more. But generally speaking he, or the majority of him, lays out his time bummeling, beer drinking, and fighting. If he be the son of a wealthy father he joins a Korps*—to belong to a crack Korps costs about four hundred pounds a year. If he be a middle-class young man, he enrols himself in a Burschenschaft, or a Landsmannschaft,* which is still a little cheaper. These companies are again broken into smaller circles, in which attempt is made to keep to nationality. There are the Swabians, from Swabia; the Frankonians, descendants of the Franks; the Thuringians, and so forth. In practice, of course, this results as all such attempts do result—I believe half our Gordon Highlanders are Cockneys—but the picturesque object is obtained of dividing each University into some dozen or so separate companies of students, each one with its distinctive cap and colours, and, quite as important, its own particular beer hall, into which no other student wearing his colours may come.

The chief work of these student companies is to fight among themselves, or with some rival Korps or Schaft, the celebrated German Mensur.*

The Mensur has been described so often and so thoroughly that I do not intend to bore my readers with any detailed account of it. I merely come forward as an impressionist, and I write purposely the impression of my first Mensur, because I believe the first impressions are more true and useful than opinions blunted by intercourse, or shaped by influence.

A Frenchman or a Spaniard will seek to persuade you that the bull-ring is an institution got up chiefly for the benefit of the bull. The horse which you imagined to be screaming with pain was only laughing at the comical appearance presented by its own inside. Your French or Spanish friend contrasts its glorious and exciting death in the ring with the cold-blooded brutality of the knacker's yard. If you do not keep a tight hold of your head, you come away with the desire to start an agitation for the inception of the bull-ring in England as an aid to chivalry. No doubt Torquemada* was convinced of the humanity of the Inquisition. To a stout gentleman, suffering, perhaps, from cramp or rheumatism, an hour or so on the rack was really a physical benefit. He would rise feeling more free in his joints —more elastic, as one might say, than he had felt for years. English huntsmen regard the fox as an animal to be envied. A day's excellent sport is provided for him free of charge, during which he is the centre of attraction.

Use blinds one to everything one does not wish to see. Every third German gentleman you meet in the street still bears, and will bear to his grave, marks of the twenty to a hundred duels he has fought in his student days. The German children play at the Mensur in the nursery, rehearse it in the gymnasium. The Germans have come to persuade themselves there is no brutality in it—nothing offensive, nothing degrading. Their argument is that it schools the German youth to coolness and courage. If this could be proved, the argument, particularly in a country where every man is a soldier, would be sufficiently one-sided. But is the virtue of the prize-fighter the virtue of the soldier? One doubts it. Nerve and dash are surely of more service in the field than a temperament of unreasoning indifference as to what is happening to one. As a matter of fact, the German student would have to be possessed of much more courage not to fight. He fights not to please himself, but to satisfy a public opinion that is two hundred years behind the times.

All the Mensur does is to brutalise him. There may be skill displayed—I am told there is,—but it is not apparent. The mere fighting is like nothing so much as a broadsword combat at a Richardson's show;* the display as a whole a successful attempt to combine the ludicrous with the unpleasant. In aristocratic Bonn, where style is considered, and in Heidelberg, where visitors from other nations are more common, the affair is perhaps more formal. I am told that there the contests take place in handsome rooms; that grey-haired doctors wait upon the wounded, and liveried servants upon the hungry, and that the affair is conducted throughout with a certain amount of picturesque ceremony. In the more essentially German Universities, where strangers are rare and not much encouraged, the simple essentials are the only things kept in view, and these are not of an inviting nature.

Indeed, so distinctly uninviting are they, that I strongly advise the sensitive reader to avoid even this description of them. The subject cannot be made pretty, and I do not intend to try.

The room is bare and sordid; its walls splashed with mixed stains of beer, blood, and candle-grease; its ceiling, smoky; its floor, sawdust covered. A crowd of students, laughing, smoking, talking, some sitting on the floor, others perched upon chairs and benches, form the framework.

In the centre, facing one another, stand the combatants, resembling Japanese warriors, as made familiar to us by the Japanese tea-tray. Quaint and rigid, with their goggle-covered eyes, their necks tied up in comforters, their bodies smothered in what looks like dirty bed quilts, their padded arms stretched straight above their heads, they might be a pair of ungainly clockwork figures. The seconds, also more or less padded—their heads and faces protected by huge leather-peaked caps,—drag them out into their proper position. One almost listens to hear the sound of the castors. The umpire takes his place, the word is given, and immediately there follow five rapid clashes of the long straight swords. There is no interest in watching the fight: there is no movement, no skill, no grace. (I am speaking of my own impressions.) The strongest man wins; the man who, with his heavily-padded arm, always in an unnatural position, can hold his huge clumsy sword longest without growing too weak to be able either to guard or to strike.

The whole interest is centred in watching the wounds. They come always in one of two places—on the top of the head or the left side of the face. Sometimes a portion of hairy scalp or section of cheek flies up into the air, to be carefully preserved in an envelope by its proud possessor, or, strictly speaking, its proud former possessor, and shown round on convivial evenings; and from every wound, of course, flows a plentiful stream of blood. It splashes doctors, seconds, and spectators; it sprinkles ceiling and walls; it saturates the fighters, and makes pools for itself in the sawdust. At the end of each round the doctors rush up, and with hands already dripping with blood press together the gaping wounds, dabbing them with little balls of wet cotton wool, which an attendant carries ready on a plate. Naturally, the moment the men stand up again and commence work, the blood gushes out again, half blinding them, and rendering the ground beneath them slippery. Now and then you see a man's teeth laid bare almost to the ear, so that for the rest of the duel he appears to be grinning at one half of the spectators, his other side remaining serious; and sometimes a man's nose gets slit, which gives to him as he fights a singularly supercilious air.

As the object of each student is to go away from the University bearing as many scars as possible, I doubt if any particular pains are taken to guard, even to the small extent such method of fighting can allow. The real victor is he who comes out with the greatest number of wounds; he who then, stitched and patched almost to unrecognition as a human being, can promenade for the next month, the envy of the German youth, the admiration of the German maiden. He who obtains only a few unimportant wounds retires sulky and disappointed.

But the actual fighting is only the beginning of the fun. The second act of the spectacle takes place in the dressing-room. The doctors are generally mere medical students—young fellows who, having taken their degree, are anxious for practice. Truth compels me to say that those with whom I came in contact were coarse-looking men who seemed rather to relish their work. Perhaps they are not to be blamed for this. It is part of the system that as much further punishment as possible must be inflicted by the doctor, and the ideal medical man might hardly care for such job. How the student bears the dressing of his wounds is as important as how he receives them. Every operation has to be performed as brutally as may be, and his companions carefully watch him during the process to see that he goes through it with an appearance of peace and enjoyment. A clean-cut wound that gapes wide is most desired by all parties. On purpose it is sewn up clumsily, with the hope that by this means the scar will last a lifetime. Such a wound, judiciously mauled and interfered with during the week afterwards, can generally be reckoned on to secure its fortunate possessor a wife with a dowry of five figures at the least.

These are the general bi-weekly Mensurs, of which the average student fights some dozen a year. There are others to which visitors are not admitted. When a student is considered to have disgraced himself by some slight involuntary movement of the head or body while fighting, then he can only regain his position by standing up to the best swordsman in his Korps. He demands and is accorded, not a contest, but a punishment. His opponent then proceeds to inflict as many and as bloody wounds as can be taken. The object of the victim is to show his comrades that he can stand still while his head is half sliced from his skull.

Whether anything can properly be said in favour of the German Mensur I am doubtful; but if so it concerns only the two combatants. Upon the spectators it can and does, I am convinced, exercise nothing but evil. I know myself sufficiently well to be sure I am not of an unusually bloodthirsty disposition. The effect it had upon me can only be the usual effect. At first, before the actual work commenced, my sensation was curiosity mingled with anxiety as to how the sight would trouble me, though some slight acquaintance with dissecting-rooms and operating tables left me less doubt on that point than I might otherwise have felt. As the blood began to flow, and nerves and muscles to be laid bare, I experienced a mingling of disgust and pity. But with the second duel, I must confess, my finer feelings began to disappear; and by the time the third was well upon its way, and the room heavy with the curious hot odour of blood, I began, as the American expression is, to see things red.

I wanted more. I looked from face to face surrounding me, and in most of them I found reflected undoubtedly my own sensations. If it be a good thing to excite this blood thirst in the modern man, then the Mensur is a useful institution. But is it a good thing? We prate about our civilisation and humanity, but those of us who do not carry hypocrisy to the length of self-deception know that underneath our starched shirts there lurks the savage, with all his savage instincts untouched. Occasionally he may be wanted, but we never need fear his dying out. On the other hand, it seems unwise to over-nourish him.

In favour of the duel, seriously considered, there are many points to be urged. But the Mensur serves no good purpose whatever. It is childishness, and the fact of its being a cruel and brutal game makes it none the less childish. Wounds have no intrinsic value of their own; it is the cause that dignifies them, not their size. William Tell is rightly one of the heroes of the world; but what should we think of the members of a club of fathers, formed with the object of meeting twice a week to shoot apples from their sons' heads with cross-bows? These young German gentlemen could obtain all the results of which they are so proud by teasing a wild cat! To join a society for the mere purpose of getting yourself hacked about reduces a man to the intellectual level of a dancing Dervish. Travellers tell us of savages in

Central Africa who express their feelings on festive occasions by jumping about and slashing themselves. But there is no need for Europe to imitate them. The Mensur is, in fact, the *reductio ad absurdum* of the duel; and if the Germans themselves cannot see that it is funny, one can only regret their lack of humour.

But though one may be unable to agree with the public opinion that supports and commands the Mensur, it at least is possible to understand. The University code that, if it does not encourage it, at least condones drunkenness, is more difficult to treat argumenta- tively. All German students do not get drunk; in fact, the majority are sober, if not industrious. But the minority, whose claim to be representative is freely admitted, are only saved from perpetual inebriety by ability, acquired at some cost, to swill half the day and all the night, while retaining to some extent their five senses. It does not affect all alike, but it is common in any University town to see a young man not yet twenty with the figure of a Falstaff and the complexion of a Rubens Bacchus. That the German maiden can be fascinated with a face, cut and gashed till it suggests having been made out of odd materials that never could have fitted, is a proved fact. But surely there can be no attraction about a blotched and bloated skin and a 'bay window' thrown out to an extent threatening to overbalance the whole structure. Yet what else can be expected, when the youngster starts his beer-drinking with a 'Frühschoppen'* at 10 a.m., and closes it with a 'Kneipe' at four in the morning?

The Kneipe is what we should call a stag party, and can be very harmless or very rowdy, according to its composition. One man invites his fellow-students, a dozen or a hundred, to a café, and provides them with as much beer and as many cheap cigars as their own sense of health and comfort may dictate, or the host may be the Korps itself. Here, as everywhere, you observe the German sense of discipline and order. As each new comer enters all those sitting round the table rise, and with heels close together salute. When the table is complete, a chairman is chosen, whose duty it is to give out the number of the songs. Printed books of these songs, one to each two men, lie round the table. The chairman gives out number twenty-nine. 'First verse,' he cries, and away all go, each two men holding a book between them exactly as two people might hold a hymn-book in church. There is a pause at the end of each verse until the chairman starts the company on the next. As every

German is a trained singer, and as most of them have fair voices, the general effect is striking.

Although the manner may be suggestive of the singing of hymns in church, the words of the songs are occasionally such as to correct this impression. But whether it be a patriotic song, a sentimental ballad, or a ditty of a nature that would shock the average young Englishman, all are sung through with a stern earnestness, without a laugh, without a false note. At the end, the chairman calls 'Prosit!'* Everyone answers 'Prosit!' and the next moment every glass is empty. The pianist rises and bows, and is bowed to in return; and then the Fräulein enters to refill the glasses.

Between the songs, toasts are proposed and responded to; but there is little cheering, and less laughter. Smiles and grave nods of approval are considered as more seeming among German students.

A particular toast, called a Salamander, accorded to some guest as a special distinction, is drunk with exceptional solemnity.

'We will now,' says the chairman, 'a Salamander rub' ('Einen Salamander reiben'). We all rise, and stand like a regiment at attention.

'Is the stuff prepared?' ('Sind die Stoffe parat?') demands the chairman.

'Sunt,' we answer, with one voice.

'Ad exercitium Salanandri,' says the chairman, and we are ready.

'Eins!' We rub our glasses with a circular motion on the table.

'Zwei!' Again the glasses growl; also at 'Drei!'

'Drink!' ('Bibite!').

And with mechanical unison every glass is emptied and held on high.

'Eins!' says the chairman. The foot of every empty glass twirls upon the table, producing a sound as of the dragging back of a stony beach by a receding wave.

'Zwei!' The roll swells and sinks again.

'Drei!' The glasses strike the table with a single crash, and we are in our seats again.

The sport at the Kneipe is for two students to insult each other (in play, of course), and to then challenge each other to a drinking duel. An umpire is appointed, two huge glasses are filled, and the men sit opposite each other with their hands upon the handles, all eyes fixed upon them. The umpire gives the word to go, and in an instant the beer is gurgling down their throats. The man who bangs his perfectly finished glass upon the table first is victor.

Strangers who are going through a Kneipe, and who wish to do the thing in German style, will do well, before commencing proceedings, to pin their name and address upon their coats. The German student is courtesy itself, and whatever his own state may be, he will see to it that, by some means or another, his guest gets home safely before the morning. But, of course, he cannot be expected to remember addresses.

A story was told me of three guests to a Berlin Kneipe which might have had tragic results. The strangers determined to do the thing thoroughly. They explained their intention, and were applauded, and each proceeded to write his address upon his card, and pin it to the tablecloth in front of him. That was the mistake they made. They should, as I have advised, have pinned it carefully to their coats. A man may change his place at a table, quite unconsciously he may come out the other side of it; but wherever he goes he takes his coat with him.

Some time in the small hours, the chairman suggested that to make things more comfortable for those still upright, all the gentlemen unable to keep their heads off the table should be sent home. Among those to whom the proceedings had become uninteresting were the three Englishmen. It was decided to put them into a cab in charge of a comparatively speaking sober student, and return them. Had they retained their original seats throughout the evening all would have been well; but, unfortunately, they had gone walking about, and which gentleman belonged to which card nobody knew—least of all the guests themselves. In the then state of general cheerfulness, this did not to anybody appear to much matter. There were three gentlemen and three addresses. I suppose the idea was that even if a mistake were made, the parties could be sorted out in the morning. Anyhow, the three gentlemen were put into a cab, the comparatively speaking sober student took the three cards in his hand, and the party started amid the cheers and good wishes of the company.

There is this advantage about German beer: it does not make a man drunk as the word drunk is understood in England. There is nothing objectionable about him; he is simply tired. He does not want to talk; he wants to be let alone, to go to sleep; it does not matter where—anywhere.

The conductor of the party stopped his cab at the nearest address. He took out his worst case; it was a natural instinct to get rid of that first. He and the cabman carried it upstairs, and rang the bell of the Pension. A sleepy porter answered it. They carried their burden in, and looked for a place to drop it. A bedroom door happened to be open; the room was empty; could anything be better?—they took it in there. They relieved it of such things as came off easily, and laid it in the bed. This done, both men, pleased with themselves, returned to the cab.

At the next address they stopped again. This time, in answer to their summons, a lady appeared, dressed in a teagown, with a book in her hand. The German student looked at the top one of the two cards remaining in his hand, and enquired if he had the pleasure of addressing Frau Y. It happened that he had, though so far as any pleasure was concerned that appeared to be entirely on his side. He explained to Frau Y. that the gentleman at the moment asleep against the wall was her husband. The reunion moved her to no enthusiasm; she simply opened the bedroom door, and then walked away. The cabman and the student took him in, and laid him on the bed. They did not trouble to undress him; they were feeling tired! They did not see the lady of the house again, and retired therefore without adieus.

The last card was that of a bachelor stopping at an hotel. They took their last man, therefore, to that hotel, passed him over to the night porter, and left him.

To return to the address at which the first delivery was made, what had happened there was this. Some eight hours previously had said Mr X. to Mrs X.: 'I think I told you, my dear, that I had an invitation for this evening to what, I believe, is called a Kneipe?'

'You did mention something of the sort,' replied Mrs X. 'What is a Kneipe?'

'Well, it's a sort of bachelor party, my dear, where the students meet to sing and talk and—and smoke, and all that sort of thing, you know.'

'Oh, well, I hope you will enjoy yourself!' said Mrs X., who was a nice woman and sensible.

'It will be interesting,' observed Mr X. 'I have often had a curiosity to see one. I may,' continued Mr X.,—'I mean it is possible, that I may be home a little late.'

'What do you call late?' asked Mrs X.

'It is somewhat difficult to say,' returned Mr X. 'You see these students, they are a wild lot, and when they get together—— And then, I believe, a good many toasts are drunk. I don't know how it will affect me. If I can see an opportunity I shall come away early, that is if I can do so without giving offence; but if not——'

Said Mrs X., who, as I remarked before, was a sensible woman: 'You had better get the people here to lend you a latchkey. I shall sleep with Dolly, and then you won't disturb me whatever time it may be.'

'I think that an excellent idea of yours,' agreed Mr X. 'I should hate disturbing you. I shall just come in quietly, and slip into bed.'

Some time in the middle of the night, or maybe towards the early morning, Dolly, who was Mrs X.'s sister, sat up in bed and listened.

'Jenny,' said Dolly, 'are you awake?'

'Yes, dear,' answered Mrs X. 'It's all right. You go to sleep again.'

'But whatever is it?' asked Dolly. 'Do you think it's fire?'

'I expect,' replied Mrs X., 'that it's Percy. Very possibly he has stumbled over something in the dark. Don't you worry, dear; you go to sleep.'

But so soon as Dolly had dozed off again, Mrs X., who was a good wife, thought she would steal off softly and see to it that Percy was all right. So, putting on a dressing-gown and slippers, she crept along the passage and into her own room. To awake the gentleman on the bed would have required an earthquake. She lit a candle and stole over to the bedside.

It was not Percy; it was not anyone like Percy. She felt it was not the man that ever could have been her husband, under any circumstances. In his present condition her sentiment towards him was that of positive dislike. Her only desire was to get rid of him.

But something there was about him which seemed familiar to her. She went nearer, and took a closer view. Then she remembered. Surely it was Mr Y., a gentleman at whose flat she and Percy had dined the day they first arrived in Berlin.

But what was he doing here? She put the candle on the table, and taking her head between her hands sat down to think. The explanation of the thing came to her with a rush. It was with this Mr Y. that Percy had gone to the Kneipe. A mistake had been made. Mr Y. had been brought back to Percy's address. Percy at this very moment——

The terrible possibilities of the situation swam before her. Returning to Dolly's room, she dressed herself hastily, and silently crept downstairs. Finding, fortunately, a passing night-cab, she drove to the address of Mrs Y. Telling the man to wait, she flew upstairs and rang persistently at the bell. It was opened as before by Mrs Y., still in her tea-gown, and with her book still in her hand.

'Mrs X.!' exclaimed Mrs Y. 'Whatever brings you here?'

'My husband!' was all poor Mrs X. could think to say at the moment, 'is he here?'

'Mrs X.,' returned Mrs Y., drawing herself up to her full height, 'how dare you!'

'Oh, please don't misunderstand me!' pleaded Mrs X. 'It's all a terrible mistake. They must have brought poor Percy here instead of to our place, I'm sure they must. Do please look and see.'

'My dear,' said Mrs Y., who was a much older woman, and more motherly, 'don't excite yourself. They brought him here about half an hour ago, and, to tell you the truth, I never looked at him. He is in here. I don't think they troubled to take off even his boots. If you keep cool, we will get him downstairs and home without a soul beyond ourselves being any the wiser.'

Indeed, Mrs Y. seemed quite eager to help Mrs. X.

She pushed open the door, and Mrs X. went in. The next moment she came out with a white, scared face.

'It isn't Percy,' she said. 'Whatever am I to do?'

'I wish you wouldn't make these mistakes,' said Mrs Y., moving to enter the room herself.

Mrs X. stopped her. 'And it isn't your husband either.'

'Nonsense,' said Mrs Y.

'It isn't really,' persisted Mrs X. 'I know, because I have just left him, asleep on Percy's bed.'

'What's he doing there?' thundered Mrs Y.

'They brought him there, and put him there,' explained Mrs X., beginning to cry. 'That's what made me think Percy must be here.'

The two women stood and looked at one another; and there was silence for awhile, broken only by the snoring of the gentleman on the other side of the half-open door.

'Then who is that, in there?' demanded Mrs Y., who was the first to recover herself.

'I don't know,' answered Mrs X., 'I have never seen him before. Do you think it is anybody you know?'

But Mrs Y. only banged to the door.

'What are we to do?' said Mrs X.

'I know what *I* am going to do,' said Mrs Y. 'I'm coming back with you to fetch my husband.'

'He's very sleepy,' explained Mrs X.

'I've known him to be that before,' replied Mrs Y., as she fastened on her cloak.

'But where's Percy?' sobbed poor little Mrs X., as they descended the stairs together.

'That, my dear,' said Mrs Y., 'will be a question for you to ask *him.*'

'If they go about making mistakes like this,' said Mrs X., 'it is impossible to say what they may not have done with him.'

'We will make enquiries in the morning, my dear,' said Mrs Y., consolingly.

'I think these Kneipes are disgraceful affairs,' said Mrs X. 'I shall never let Percy go to another, never—so long as I live.'

'My dear,' remarked Mrs Y., 'if you know your duty, he will never want to.' And rumour has it that he never did.

But, as I have said, the mistake was in pinning the card to the tablecloth instead of to the coat. And error in this world is always severely punished.

CHAPTER XIV

Which is serious: as becomes a parting chapter—The German from the Anglo-Saxon's point of view—Providence in buttons and a helmet —Paradise of the helpless idiot—German conscience: its aggressiveness —How they hang in Germany, very possibly—What happens to good Germans when they die?—The military instinct: is it all-sufficient?—The German as a shopkeeper—How he supports life—The New Woman, here as everywhere—What can be said against the Germans, as a people—The Bummel is over and done.

'ANYBODY could rule this country,' said George; '*I* could rule it.'

We were seated in the garden of the Kaiser Hof at Bonn, looking down upon the Rhine. It was the last evening of our Bummel; the early morning train would be the beginning of the end.

'I should write down all I wanted the people to do on a piece of paper,' continued George; 'get a good firm to print off so many copies, have them posted about the towns and villages; and the thing would be done.'

In the placid, docile German of to-day, whose only ambition appears to be to pay his taxes, and do what he is told by those whom it has pleased Providence to place in authority over him, it is difficult, one must confess, to detect any trace of his wild ancestor, to whom individual liberty was as the breath of his nostrils; who appointed his magistrates to advise, but retained the right of execution for the tribe; who followed his chief, but would have scorned to obey him. In Germany to-day one hears a good deal concerning Socialism, but it is a Socialism that would only be despotism under another name. Individualism makes no appeal to the German voter. He is willing, nay, anxious to be controlled and regulated in all things. He disputes, not government, but the form of it. The policeman is to him a religion, and, one feels, will always remain so. In England we regard our man in blue as a harmless necessity. By the average citizen he is employed chiefly as a signpost, though in busy quarters of the town he is considered useful for taking old ladies across the road. Beyond feeling thankful to him for these services, I doubt if we take much thought of him. In Germany, on the other hand, he is worshipped as a little god and loved as a guardian angel. To the German child he is a combination of Santa Claus and the Bogie Man. All good things come from him: Spielplätze to play in, furnished with swings and giant-strides, sand heaps to fight around, swimming baths, and fairs. All misbehaviour is punished by him. It is the hope of every well-meaning German boy and girl to please the police. To be smiled at by a policeman makes it conceited. A German child that has been patted on the head by a policeman is not fit to live with; its self-importance is unbearable.

The German citizen is a soldier, and the policeman is his officer. The policeman directs him where in the street to walk, and how fast to walk. At the end of each bridge stands a policeman to tell the German how to cross it. Were there no policeman there, he would probably sit down and wait till the river had passed by. At the railway station the policeman locks him up in the waiting-room, where he can do no harm to himself. When the proper time arrives, he fetches him out and hands him over to the guard of the train, who is only a policeman in another uniform. The guard tells him where to sit in the train, and when to get out, and sees that he does get out. In Germany you take no responsibility upon yourself whatever. Everything is done for you, and done well. You are not supposed to look after yourself; you are not blamed for being incapable of looking after yourself; it is the duty of the German policeman to look after you. That you may be a helpless idiot does not excuse him should anything happen to you. Wherever you are and whatever you are doing you are in his charge, and he takes care of you—good care of you; there is no denying this.

If you lose yourself, he finds you; and if you lose anything belonging to you, he recovers it for you. If you don't know what you want, he tells you. If you want anything that is good for you to have, he gets it for you. Private lawyers are not needed in Germany. If you want to buy or sell a house or field, the State makes out the conveyance. If you have been swindled, the State takes up the case for you. The State marries you, insures you, will even gamble with you for a trifle.

'You get yourself born,' says the German Government to the German citizen, 'we do the rest. Indoors and out of doors, in sickness and in health, in pleasure and in work, we will tell you what to do, and we will see to it that you do it. Don't you worry yourself about anything.'

And the German doesn't. Where there is no policeman to be found, he wanders about till he comes to a police notice posted on a wall. This he reads; then he goes and does what it says.

I remember in one German town—I forget which; it is immaterial; the incident could have happened in any—noticing an open gate leading to a garden in which a concert was being given. There was nothing to prevent anyone who chose from walking through that gate, and thus gaining admittance to the concert without paying. In fact, of the two gates quarter of a mile apart it was the more convenient. Yet of the crowds that passed, not one attempted to enter by that gate. They plodded steadily on under a blazing sun to the other gate, at which a man stood to collect the entrance money. I have seen German youngsters stand longingly by the margin of a lonely sheet of ice. They could have skated on that ice for hours, and nobody have been the wiser. The crowd and the police were at the other end, more than half a mile away, and round the corner. Nothing stopped their going on but the knowledge that they ought not. Things such as these make one pause to seriously wonder whether the Teuton be a member of the sinful human family or not. Is it not possible that these placid, gentle folk may in reality be angels, come down to earth for the sake of a glass of beer, which, as they must know, can only in Germany be obtained worth the drinking?

In Germany the country roads are lined with fruit trees. There is no voice to stay man or boy from picking and eating the fruit, except conscience. In England such a state of things would cause public indignation. Children would die of cholera by the hundred. The medical profession would be worked off its legs trying to cope with the natural results of over-indulgence in sour apples and unripe walnuts. Public opinion would demand that these fruit trees should be fenced about, and thus rendered harmless. Fruit growers, to save themselves the expense of walls and palings, would not be allowed in this manner to spread sickness and death throughout the community.

But in Germany a boy will walk for miles down a lonely road, hedged with fruit trees, to buy a pennyworth of pears in the village at the other end. To pass these unprotected fruit trees, drooping under their burden of ripe fruit, strikes the Anglo-Saxon mind as a wicked waste of opportunity, a flouting of the blessed gifts of Providence.

I do not know if it be so, but from what I have observed of the German character I should not be surprised to hear that when a man in Germany is condemned to death he is given a piece of rope, and told to go and hang himself. It would save the State much trouble and expense, and I can see that German criminal taking that piece of rope home with him, reading up carefully the police instructions, and proceeding to carry them out in his own back kitchen.

The Germans are a good people. On the whole, the best people perhaps in the world; an amiable, unselfish, kindly people. I am positive that the vast majority of them go to Heaven. Indeed, comparing them with the other Christian nations of the earth, one is forced to the conclusion that Heaven will be chiefly of German manufacture. But I cannot understand how they get there. That the soul of any single individual German has sufficient initiative to fly up by itself and knock at St Peter's door, I cannot believe. My own opinion is that they are taken there in small companies, and passed in under the charge of a dead policeman.

Carlyle said of the Prussians,* and it is true of the whole German nation, that one of their chief virtues was their power of being drilled. Of the Germans you might say they are a people who will go anywhere, and do anything, they are told. Drill him for the work and send him out to Africa or Asia under charge of somebody in uniform, and he is bound to make an excellent colonist, facing difficulties as he would face the devil himself, if ordered. But it is not easy to conceive of him as a pioneer. Left to run himself, one feels he would soon fade away and die, not from any lack of intelligence, but from sheer want of presumption.

The German has so long been the soldier of Europe, that the military instinct has entered into his blood. The military virtues he possesses in abundance; but he also suffers from the drawbacks of the military training. It was told me of a German servant, lately released from the barracks, that he was instructed by his master to deliver a letter to a certain house, and to wait there for the answer. The hours passed by, and the man did not return. His master, anxious and surprised, followed. He found the man where he had been sent, the answer in his hand. He was waiting for further orders. The story sounds exaggerated, but personally I can credit it.

The curious thing is that the same man, who as an individual is as helpless as a child, becomes, the moment he puts on a uniform, an intelligent being, capable of responsibility and initiative. The German can rule others, and be ruled by others, but he cannot rule himself. The cure would appear to be to train every German for an officer, and then put him under himself. It is certain he would order himself about with discretion and judgment, and see to it that he himself obeyed himself with smartness and precision.

For the direction of German character into these channels, the schools, of course, are chiefly responsible. Their everlasting teaching is duty. It is a fine ideal for any people; but before buckling to it, one would wish to have a clear understanding as to what this 'duty' is. The German idea of it would appear to be: 'blind obedience to everything in buttons.' It is the antithesis of the Anglo-Saxon scheme; but as both the Anglo-Saxon and the Teuton are prospering, there must be good in both methods. Hitherto, the German has had the blessed fortune to be exceptionally well governed; if this continue, it will go well with him. When his troubles will begin will be when by any chance something goes wrong with the governing machine. But maybe his method has the advantage of producing a continuous supply of good governors; it would certainly seem so.

As a trader, I am inclined to think the German will, unless his temperament considerably change, remain always a long way behind his Anglo-Saxon competitor; and this by reason of his virtues. To him life is something more important than a mere race for wealth. A country that closes its banks and post-offices for two hours in the middle of the day, while it goes home and enjoys a comfortable meal in the bosom of its family, with, perhaps, forty winks by way of dessert, cannot hope, and possibly has no wish, to compete with a people that takes its meals standing and sleeps with a telephone over its bed. In Germany there is not, at all events as yet, sufficient distinction between the classes to make the struggle for position the life and death affair it is in England. Beyond the landed aristocracy, whose boundaries are impregnable, grade hardly counts. Frau Professor and Frau Candlestickmaker meet at the weekly Kaffeeklatsch* and exchange scandal on terms of mutual equality. The livery-stable keeper and the Doctor hobnob together at their favourite beer hall. The wealthy master builder, when he prepares his roomy waggon for an excursion into the country, invites his foreman and his tailor to join him with their families. Each brings his share of drink and provisions, and returning home they sing in chorus the same songs. So long as this state of things endures, a man is not induced to sacrifice the best years of his life to win a fortune for his dotage. His tastes, and, more to the point still, his wife's, remain inexpensive. He likes to see his flat or villa furnished with much red plush upholstery and a profusion of gilt and lacquer. But that is his idea; and maybe it is in no worse taste than is a mixture of bastard Elizabethan with imitation Louis XV, the whole lit by electric light, and smothered with photographs. Possibly, he will have his outer walls painted by the local artist: a sanguinary battle, a good deal interfered with by the front door, taking place below, while Bismarck, as an angel, flutters vaguely about the bedroom windows. But for his Old Masters he is quite content to go to the public galleries; and 'the Celebrity at Home' not having as yet taken its place amongst the institutions of the Fatherland, he is not impelled to waste his money turning his house into an old curiosity shop.

The German is a gourmand. There are still English farmers who, while telling you that farming spells starvation, enjoy their seven solid meals a day. Once a year there comes a week's feast throughout Russia, during which many deaths occur from the over-eating of pancakes; but this is a religious festival, and an exception. Taking him all round, the German as a trencherman stands pre-eminent among the nations of the earth. He rises early, and while dressing tosses off a few cups of coffee, together with half a dozen hot buttered rolls. But it is not until ten o'clock that he sits down to anything that can properly be called a meal. At one or half-past takes place his chief dinner. Of this he makes a business, sitting at it for a couple of hours. At four o'clock he goes to the café, and eats cakes and drinks chocolate. The evening he devotes to eating generally—not a set meal, or rarely, but a series of snacks,—a bottle of beer and a Belegte-Semmel or two at seven, say; another bottle of beer and an Aufschnitt* at the theatre between the acts; a small bottle of white wine and a Spiegeleier* before going home; then a piece of cheese or sausage, washed down by more beer, previous to turning in for the night.

But he is no gourmet. French cooks and French prices are not the rule at his restaurant. His beer or his inexpensive native white wine he prefers to the most costly clarets or champagnes. And, indeed, it is well for him he does; for one is inclined to think that every time a French grower sells a bottle of wine to a German hotel- or shop-keeper, Sedan is rankling in his mind. It is a foolish revenge, seeing that it is not the German who as a rule drinks it; the punishment falls upon some innocent travelling Englishman. Maybe, however, the French dealer remembers also Waterloo, and feels that in any event he scores.

In Germany expensive entertainments are neither offered nor expected. Everything throughout the Fatherland is homely and friendly. The German has no costly sports to pay for, no showy establishment to maintain, no purse-proud circle to dress for. His chief pleasure, a seat at the opera or concert, can be had for a few marks; and his wife and daughters walk there in home-made dresses, with shawls over their heads. Indeed, throughout the country the absence of all ostentation is to English eyes quite refreshing. Private carriages are few and far between, and even the Droschke is made use of only when the quicker and cleaner electric car is not available.

By such means the German retains his independence. The shopkeeper in Germany does not fawn upon his customers. I accompanied an English lady once on a shopping excursion in Munich. She had been accustomed to shopping in London and New York, and she grumbled at everything the man showed her. It was not that she was really dissatisfied; this was her method. She explained that she could get most things cheaper and better elsewhere; not that she really thought she could, merely she held it good for the shopkeeper to say this. She told him that his stock lacked taste—she did not mean to be offensive; as I have explained, it was her method;—that there was no variety about it; that it was not up to date; that it was commonplace; that it looked as if it would not wear. He did not argue with her; he did not contradict her. He put the things back into their respective boxes, replaced the boxes on their respective shelves, walked into the little parlour behind the shop, and closed the door.

'Isn't he ever coming back?' asked the lady, after a couple of minutes had elapsed.

Her tone did not imply a question so much as an exclamation of mere impatience.

'I doubt it,' I replied.

'Why not?' she asked, much astonished.

'I expect,' I answered, 'you have bored him. In all probability he is at this moment behind that door smoking a pipe and reading the paper.'

'What an extraordinary shopkeeper!' said my friend, as she gathered her parcels together and indignantly walked out.

'It is their way,' I explained. 'There are the goods; if you want them, you can have them. If you do not want them, they would almost rather that you did not come and talk about them.'

On another occasion I listened in the smoke-room of a German hotel to a small Englishman telling a tale which, had I been in his place, I should have kept to myself.

'It doesn't do,' said the little Englishman, 'to try and beat a German down. They don't seem to understand it. I saw a first edition of *The Robbers** in a shop in the Georg Platz. I went in and asked the price. It was a rum old chap behind the counter. He said: "Twenty-five marks," and went on reading. I told him I had seen a better copy only a few days before for twenty—one talks like that when one is bargaining; it is understood. He asked me "Where?" I told him in a shop at Leipsig. He suggested my returning there and getting it; he did not seem to care whether I bought the book or whether I didn't. I said:

'"What's the least you will take for it?"

'"I have told you once," he answered, "twenty-five marks." He was an irritable old chap.

'I said: "It's not worth it."

'"I never said it was, did I?" he snapped.

'I said: "I'll give you ten marks for it." I thought, maybe, he would end by taking twenty.

'He rose. I took it he was coming round the counter to get the book out. Instead, he came straight up to me. He was a biggish sort of man. He took me by the two shoulders, walked me out into the street, and closed the door behind me with a bang. I was never more surprised in all my life.'

'Maybe the book was worth twenty-five marks,' I suggested.

'Of course it was,' he replied; 'well worth it. But what a notion of business!'

If anything change the German character, it will be the German woman. She herself is changing rapidly—advancing, as we call it. Ten years ago no German woman caring for her reputation, hoping for a husband, would have dared to ride a bicycle: to-day they spin about the country in their thousands. The old folks shake their heads at them; but the young men, I notice, overtake them and ride beside them. Not long ago it was considered unwomanly in Germany for a lady to be able to do the outside edge. Her proper skating attitude was thought to be that of clinging limpness to some male relative. Now she practises eights in a corner by herself, until some young man comes along to help her. She plays tennis, and, from a point of safety, I have even noticed her driving a dog-cart.

Brilliantly educated she always has been. At eighteen she speaks two or three languages, and has forgotten more than the average Englishwoman has ever read. Hitherto, this education has been utterly useless to her. On marriage she has retired into the kitchen, and made haste to clear her brain of everything else, in order to leave room for bad cooking. But suppose it begins to dawn upon her that a woman need not sacrifice her whole existence to household drudgery any more than a man need make himself nothing else than a business machine. Suppose she develop an ambition to take part in the social and national life. Then the influence of such a partner, healthy in body and therefore vigorous in mind, is bound to be both lasting and far-reaching.

For it must be borne in mind that the German man is exceptionally sentimental, and most easily influenced by his women folk. It is said of him, he is the best of lovers, the worst of husbands. This has been the woman's fault. Once married, the German woman has done more than put romance behind her; she has taken a carpet-beater and driven it out of the house. As a girl, she never understood dressing; as a wife, she takes off such clothes even as she had, and proceeds to wrap herself up in any odd articles she may happen to find about the house; at all events, this is the impression she produces. The figure that might often be that of a Juno, the complexion that would sometimes do credit to a healthy angel, she proceeds of malice and intent to spoil. She sells her birth-right of admiration and devotion for a mess of sweets.* Every afternoon you may see her at the café, loading herself with rich cream-covered cakes, washed down by copious draughts of chocolate. In a short time she becomes fat, pasty, placid, and utterly uninteresting.

When the German woman gives up her afternoon coffee and her evening beer, takes sufficient exercise to retain her shape, and continues to read after marriage something else than the cookery book, the German Government will find it has a new and unknown force to deal with. And everywhere throughout Germany one is confronted by unmistakable signs that the old German Frauen are giving place to the newer Damen.

Concerning what will then happen one feels curious. For the German nation is still young, and its maturity is of importance to the world. They are a good people, a lovable people, who should help much to make the world better.

The worst that can be said against them is that they have their failings. They themselves do not know this; they consider themselves perfect, which is foolish of them. They even go so far as to think themselves superior to the Anglo-Saxon: this is incomprehensible. One feels they must be pretending.

'They have their points,' said George; 'but their tobacco is a national sin. I'm going to bed.'

We rose, and leaning over the low stone parapet, watched the dancing lights upon the soft, dark river.

'It has been a pleasant Bummel, on the whole,' said Harris; 'I shall be glad to get back, and yet I am sorry it is over, if you understand me.'

'What is a "Bummel"?' said George. 'How would you translate it?'

'A "Bummel,"' I explained, 'I should describe as a journey, long or short, without an end; the only thing regulating it being the necessity of getting back within a given time to the point from which one started. Sometimes it is through busy streets, and sometimes through the fields and lanes; sometimes we can be spared for a few hours, and sometimes for a few days. But long or short, but here or there, our thoughts are ever on the running of the sand. We nod and smile to many as we pass; with some we stop and talk awhile; and with a few we walk a little way. We have been much interested, and often a little tired. But on the whole we have had a pleasant time, and are sorry when 'tis over.'

COUNDON

EXPLANATORY NOTES

Three Men in a Boat

9 *humpy*: out of humour (a Jeromian coinage).

Referee: a weekly sporting paper, founded in 1877 and published on Sundays at one penny. It covered racing, billiards, rowing, and football and also included the theatre, the weather forecast, and humour. It closed in 1928.

24 *shilling shockers*: short sensational novels, priced at one shilling.

29 *fifteen guineas*: £15. 75.

eight-and-sixpence: 42½p.

30 *Gladstone*: a travelling bag.

35 *slavey*: a maid of all work.

37 *Boots*: the name for a hotel servant who cleans boots.

39 *Great Coram Street murder*: the murder of Harriet Buswell, on Christmas Day 1872, aroused considerable interest in the newspapers. A Dr Hessel was initially charged, but the file records murder by a person or persons unknown. I am indebted for this information to the Librarian of the Metropolitan Police Archives.

40 *Stanley*: Sir Henry Morton Stanley (1841–1904), explorer, author, and journalist; famous for having found the missionary Dr David Livingstone at Ujiji in the region of Lake Tanganyika in 1871.

44 *Sandford and Merton*: *The History of Sandford and Merton* is a didactic children's tale, with the theme that instruction may produce goodness, written by Thomas Day, and published in three volumes between 1783 and 1789. Jerome's Stivvings get his nickname from the characters of the story: the morally upright Harry Sandford, the farmer's son, and the wealthy and unpleasant Tommy Merton, who in due course reforms.

45 *we are but as grass . . . oven*: a partial quotation from Matthew 6: 30 (also in Luke 12: 28), which stresses God's care. However, Jerome chooses to dwell on the transience of life, and typically adds the comically emphatic, 'and baked'.

'old blue': eighteenth-century English porcelain. Factories either painted or printed a large range of utilitarian objects with a blue underglaze.

46 *Sarah Janes*: housemaids.

51 *Margate nigger*: probably an allusion to the minstrel shows which were a popular entertainment at seaside resorts at this time.

60 *Pinafore*: HMS *Pinafore*, a light opera by Sir W. S. Gilbert and Sir Arthur Sullivan, first produced in 1878.

60 *Trial by Jury*: a light opera, also by Gilbert and Sullivan, first produced in 1875.

62 *morceaux*: fragments.

65 *Bradshaw*: George Bradshaw was the author of the Railway Guide, while John Bradshaw was the president of the council that condemned Charles I to death.

76 *Faust*: an opera by Charles François Gounod (1818–93), after the play by Goethe, first produced in Paris in 1850. It is based on the story of the legendary German medieval scholar and magician, who sold his soul to the devil in exchange for knowledge and power.

85 *Angels and ministers of grace defend us!*: *Hamlet*, I. iv. 39.

93 *Runningmede . . . Magna Charta Island*: King John signed Magna Charta in 1215, either at Runnymede on the south bank of the Thames near Egham or on the island in the river, in response to the barons' unrest that resulted from his arbitrary government. The Great Charter defined the limits of royal power, and established fundamental freedoms.

94 *Irish question*: Gladstone's Home Rule Bill had recently been defeated, in 1886.

102 *man was born . . . fly upward*: Job 5: 7.

104 *Poitiers*: a town in west central France, and the site of a battle in 1356 in which the English under the Black Prince defeated the French commanded by John the Good.

The Revolt of Islam: published in 1817, the poem develops Shelley's revolutionary point of view; although he chose to set his master-theme of the epoch, as he called the French Revolution, in Argolis and Byzantium.

105 *Wilkes*: John Wilkes (1725–97), journalist and MP for Aylesbury. Sir Francis Dashwood enrolled him among the community at Medmenham, where on one occasion he created terror during a black mass, by letting loose a baboon, dressed to represent Satan.

106 *Lowther Arcade*: an arcade in the Strand in London, named after Lord Lowther. Built in 1830, initially with small shops selling luxury goods, it gradually gave way to toy-shops and became a delight for Victorian children. It was demolished in 1904 to make way for Coutts Bank.

109 *Henley week*: Henley Regatta, established in 1839, and designated a Royal Regatta in 1851, had become a major social event by the 1880s.

111 *beanfeast*: slang for an employer's annual dinner for his workpeople.

Messrs Cubit's lot . . . Bermondsey Good Templars: workpeople employed by the firm of Cubit, or members of a Bermondsey charitable club, who are taking excursions on the Thames.

114 *Who shall escape calumny?*: *Hamlet*, III. i. 143.

115 *Leslie . . . Hodgson*: both Victorian Professors of Painting at the Royal Academy. Charles Robert Leslie, whose portraits included one of the

Queen, also illustrated Scott's Waverley novels, while John Evan Hodgson painted historical subjects and landscapes.

123 *Seven Sleepers*: seven Christian youths of Ephesus who were said to have hidden in a cave during the persecution by the emperor Decius and to have slept there for several hundred years.

127 *various suburban brickfields*: the brick-making industry used to be localized, and the process of extracting clay for the manufacture of the bricks created large ponds.

134 *rounders and touch*: children's games. Rounders is played by two teams with a bat and ball: The players take turns to strike the ball and run round the course while it is being fielded. In the game of touch, or touch-last, the aim is simply to be the last participant touched by another.

140 *shilling shocker*: see note to p. 24.

146 *Conservancy*: the Thames Conservancy, formed in 1857, had its jurisdiction extended in 1866, from the river below Staines upstream as far as Cricklade.

158 *Alhambra*: built in Moorish style, and named after the palace in Granada, it was formerly the home of circus, music-hall, and ballet, reverting to music-hall in 1884.

Three Men on the Bummel

168 *Limehouse Hole*: a flourishing commercial area based on shipping, situated in London on the bank of the Thames close to the West India Docks.

208 *Mr Turveydrop*: a character in Charles Dickens's *Bleak House* (1853), who lived on his reputation for deportment.

209 *Behalten Sie Ihr Haar auf*: 'Keep your hair on.' Contrary to Jerome's humorous assertion, this is an English idiom translated literally.

212 *kailyard*: kitchen garden.

215 *Glorious Goodwood*: the week-long horse-race meeting, which includes the 'Goodwood Cup' race, held near Goodwood Park, Sussex.

216 *Ben Jonson . . . Rabelais*: a humorous instance of journalistic ignorance and confusion. Dr Samuel Johnson wrote *Rasselas* (1759).

   lean and slippered: see Jaques's speech on the seven ages of man, *As You Like It*, II. vii. 158.

219 *Gibbon*: Edward Gibbon (1737–94), the historian and author of the *History of the Decline and Fall of the Roman Empire*.

   Caesar's Commentaries: Gaius Julius Caesar (102/100–44 BC) wrote *Commentaries on the Gallic Wars*, which used to be standard reading in English schools.

223 *Hebel*: Johann Peter Hebel (1760–1826), whose poetry, produced during the Romantic period, and written in both dialect and educated German, was popular.

233 *Carlyle*: Thomas Carlyle (1795–1881), historian and author of *The History of Friedrich II of Prussia, Called Frederick the Great*.

Droschke: hackney cab.

234 *camelopard*: giraffe.

Gott im Himmel!: good heavens!

235 *Brandenburger Tor*: Brandenburg Gate, a ceremonial gate built in 1789 in the neo-classical style at the western end of the Unter den Linden.

Tiergarten: a park with zoological gardens.

Reichstag House: the building where the legislative assembly of the German Empire met between 1871 and 1918, and of the Weimar Republic from 1919 until 1933, when it was burnt out.

'Properleer' in Athens: the driver is endeavouring to explain that the Gate is an imitation of the Propylaea, the entrance to the Acropolis.

237 *Welsh Harp*: the Welsh Harp Reservoir in North London, created in the 1830s by the Regent's Canal Company. Originally surrounded by water meadows, it was increasingly visited by day-trippers from the suburbs, becoming a park area where boating and fishing were popular amusements.

238 *Belegte-Semmel*: a filled roll.

239 *Southey*: Robert Southey, one of the Lake Poets, and a prolific author. He composed the doggerel poem 'The Cataract of Lodore' for the amusement of his eldest daughter. It was later expanded for the benefit of his youngest child, Cuthbert, in 1822.

240 *August the Strong*: Augustus II (1670–1733), King of Poland, whose invasion of Livonia in 1700 began the Great Northern War.

246 *Dundreary whiskers*: long side-whiskers worn without a beard. Lord Dundreary is a character in Tom Taylor's comedy *Our American Cousin* (1858).

alpenstock: long staff, tipped with iron, first used in climbing in the Alps, but afterwards in general use in mountain-climbing.

Mrs Hemans: Felicia Dorothea Hemans (1793–1835), a poet who popularized Romantic themes.

Baedeker: a guidebook founded by Karl Baedeker which, by his death in 1859, covered most of Europe.

247 *Fashoda incident*: the climax, in 1898, of a series of territorial disputes in Africa involving Britain and France, concluding in the compromise flying of Egyptian, British, and French flags over the fort at Fashoda.

Transvaal question: Germany had an economic stake in the Transvaal State, the core of the South African Republic, and supported its resistance to British domination. Events were complicated by the intervention of the German government on 3 January 1896, when the Kaiser dispatched his famous telegram of support for Transvaal independence.

248 *Rathaus*: city hall.

   Fenstersturz: literally a fall from a window. The Defenestration of Prague took place on 23 May 1618. An assembly of Protestants at Prague found the imperial regents and their secretary guilty of violating their guarantee of religious freedom, and they were thrown from the windows of the council room of Hradčany Castle. This signalled the beginning of the Bohemian revolt against the Habsburg emperor, Ferdinand II.

   John Huss: 1372/3–1415; the fifteenth-century Czech religious reformer, whose work anticipated the Lutheran Reformation.

249 *Taborites*: a group of Bohemian religious reformers, called after the city of Tábor, which they founded south of Prague in 1420 and which became the radical centre of the Hussite movement.

   fought upon its bridges: following rivalry between the Czechs and the Germans, Prague became the centre of the religious reform movement, whose Hussite armies led by Jan Hrabe Žižka crushed the German king, Sigismund, near Prague in 1420. Prague was later the focus of the Thirty Years War (1618–48), when Protestants in Bohemia revolted against the Counter-Reformation policies of the imperial government. Albrecht von Wallenstein, commanding the forces of the Holy Roman Emperor, dispossessed many German Protestants until the intervention of Gustavus Adolphus of Sweden in 1630. Frederick the Great's victory in the Seven Years War (1756–63) confirmed Prussia's military supremacy in Europe.

256 *Ibsen's plays*: Henrik Ibsen (1828–1906), the Norwegian playwright and creator of modern realistic drama.

257 *Stadtgarten*: public park.

260 *Schnellzug ticket*: express train ticket.

   Platz ticket: seat ticket.

261 *eater . . . at the Temple*: law students at the Inns of Court were required to keep their terms and to eat a certain number of dinners within the Inn.

   Criterion: built in 1874, the Criterion Theatre was renowned for its brilliant comedy.

262 *Tom and Jerryism*: Tom and Jerry are roistering young men in Pierce Egan's *Life in London; or, the Day and Night Scenes of Jerry Hawthorn, Esq., and his Elegant Friend Corinthian Tom* (1821).

266 *Hunde verboten*: dogs forbidden.

267 *Ausgang*: exit.

   new women: the phrase 'new woman', attributed to Sarah Grand in 1894 in the *North American Review*, described those who believed in equal rights and opportunities for women.

267 *Nur für Fussgänger*: pedestrians only.

269 *Overture to 'Zampa'*: *Zampa, ou La Fiancée de marbre* (1831), a comic opera by Louis Joseph Ferdinand Hérold.

270 *Blick*: a look, or view.

271 *Resolutions . . . resolutions*: a jocular allusion to Mark 2: 27, 'The sabbath was made for man, and not man for the sabbath.'

The devil can paraphrase Scripture: see *The Merchant of Venice*, I. iii.99: 'The devil can cite Scripture for his purpose.'

290 *Ouida . . . New Grub Street*: Ouida was the pen-name of Marie Louise de la Ramée (1839–1908), a prolific author whose novels, often set in a fashionable world, were ridiculed for their exaggerated portrayal of character. Jerome contrasts her career with that of the aspiring author's struggle for survival in the contemporary literary world in George Gissing's novel *New Grub Street* (1891).

291 *Mittagstisch*: midday meal.

294 *Tischwein*: table wine.

303 *Korps*: students' duelling fraternity.

Burschenschaft, or a Landsmannschaft: student fraternity, or one whose members are drawn from the same area of Germany.

Mensur: a fencing duel between students.

304 *Torquemada*: Tomás de Torquemada (1420–98), the first grand inquisitor in Spain, whose name came to stand for the cruelty of the Inquisition.

Richardson's show: John Richardson, a well-known itinerant showman in the early nineteenth century, one of whose favourite haunts was Bartholomew Fair, the chief cloth fair in England, which had been held at West Smithfield in London since 1133. Over the centuries it had declined as a trading institution although its entertainments were still very lively. It ceased in 1885.

308 *Frühschoppen*: early morning drinks.

309 *Prosit!*: Cheers!

318 *Carlyle said of the Prussians*: see note to p. 233.

319 *Kaffeeklatsch*: a women's afternoon coffee-party.

320 *Aufschnitt*: cold meats.

Spiegeleier: fried eggs.

321 *The Robbers*: *Die Räuber*, a tragedy by Friedrich Schiller, published anonymously in 1781.

323 *sells her birth-right . . . mess of sweets*: a jocular allusion to Genesis 25: 29–34, in which Esau sells his birthright for a mess of pottage.

The Oxford World's Classics Website

www.worldsclassics.co.uk

- Information about new titles
- Explore the full range of Oxford World's Classics
- Links to other literary sites and the main OUP webpage
- Imaginative competitions, with bookish prizes
- Peruse the Oxford World's Classics Magazine
- Articles by editors
- Extracts from Introductions
- A forum for discussion and feedback on the series
- Special information for teachers and lecturers

www.worldsclassics.co.uk

American Literature

British and Irish Literature

Children's Literature

Classics and Ancient Literature

Colonial Literature

Eastern Literature

European Literature

History

Medieval Literature

Oxford English Drama

Poetry

Philosophy

Politics

Religion

The Oxford Shakespeare

A complete list of Oxford Paperbacks, including Oxford World's Classics, Oxford Shakespeare, Oxford Drama, and Oxford Paperback Reference, is available in the UK from the Academic Division Publicity Department, Oxford University Press, Great Clarendon Street, Oxford OX2 6DP.

In the USA, complete lists are available from the Paperbacks Marketing Manager, Oxford University Press, 198 Madison Avenue, New York, NY 10016.

Oxford Paperbacks are available from all good bookshops. In case of difficulty, customers in the UK can order direct from Oxford University Press Bookshop, Freepost, 116 High Street, Oxford OX1 4BR, enclosing full payment. Please add 10 per cent of published price for postage and packing.

JANE AUSTEN	Emma
	Mansfield Park
	Persuasion
	Pride and Prejudice
	Sense and Sensibility
MRS BEETON	Book of Household Management
LADY ELIZABETH BRADDON	Lady Audley's Secret
ANNE BRONTË	The Tenant of Wildfell Hall
CHARLOTTE BRONTË	Jane Eyre
	Shirley
	Villette
EMILY BRONTË	Wuthering Heights
SAMUEL TAYLOR COLERIDGE	The Major Works
WILKIE COLLINS	The Moonstone
	No Name
	The Woman in White
CHARLES DARWIN	The Origin of Species
CHARLES DICKENS	The Adventures of Oliver Twist
	Bleak House
	David Copperfield
	Great Expectations
	Nicholas Nickleby
	The Old Curiosity Shop
	Our Mutual Friend
	The Pickwick Papers
	A Tale of Two Cities
GEORGE DU MAURIER	Trilby
MARIA EDGEWORTH	Castle Rackrent